THE TRIDENT SERIES

DINO

Volume 1 – Book 6

Jaime Lewis

This is a work of fiction. Names, characters, business, events, and incidents are the products of the author's imagination. Any resemblance to actual persons, living or dead, or actual events is purely coincidental.

The Trident Series - Dino

ISBN: 978-1-952734-15-1

TABLE OF CONTENTS

PROLOGUE

Arianna Roland knew something big was going down when a couple of men in suits showed up in the FBI cyber department to speak with her boss. It wasn't exactly an odd thing that agents came to meet with her boss. It was the fact that the meeting took place at five o'clock in the morning when the majority of the staff didn't start until nine. Well, except for her. Being an FBI Forensic Accountant, she worked tirelessly in front of a computer all day to identify criminal activity and uncover hidden assets. Her expertise would assist in tracing transactions to their source. In the six years, she'd been contracting with the FBI, she helped solve crimes from cybersecurity and counterintelligence to organized crime and terrorism. It was a good-paying job, and she got to work independently, meaning she didn't have to interact with actual humans to do her job. Because of that, she could make her own work schedule. As long as she put in a solid eight hours a day as required by her contract, her boss didn't care when she worked. Her preference was to start work in the early morning hours and then get off in the early afternoon giving her time for other activities or just to chill out at home. It also helped her avoid rush hour traffic. That was a nightmare all on its own.

As she scrolled and clicked on the following line of numbers, she tried to ignore the two agents and her boss as they held their little pow-wow. Still, it was difficult not to take a glance every so often, considering they were in the glass-walled conference room directly across from her workstation. Judging from her boss, Sam's, sour expression, it didn't seem to be a good conversation.

A few minutes went by when she heard the click sound the door made when it was opened. She struggled not to look up, but then Sam called her name though it was muffled because she had earbuds in. "Arianna." She looked up and removed her earbuds. "Can you please come in here?" He asked.

She bit her lip. Why would two agents and her boss want to speak with her? She wondered if she had done something wrong. She felt her palms begin to sweat. She had that feeling when she was back in high school and had gotten called in the principal's office.

She got up and walked over to the room. Sam held the door for her. When she walked in, the two agents, both tall, one with dirty blonde hair and the other with dark brown, stood and extended their hands, and she shook them.

The one with dirty blonde hair spoke first. "Hi, Arianna. My name is Special Agent Chris Hurts, and this is Agent Russ Callen." He gestured to the empty seat across from them. "Please have a seat."

She looked at Sam, wondering what was going on. Again, he looked like he was either mad or annoyed. She couldn't tell which, but either way, it gave her a bad vibe that she wasn't going to like what these agents had to say. She took the seat that was offered to her then Sam sat down next to her.

She couldn't take the suspense any longer, and she looked over at Sam. "Sam, what's going on? Am I in some sort of trouble, or did I do something wrong?"

His hardened face softened a smidge. "No, of course not. You're one of the best employees I've got working for me. In fact, I wish you'd take the permanent job that is opening up with George leaving."

She scrunched her eyebrows together. "Is this what this meeting is about? To offer me the permanent full-time job?" She loved what she did and had waited patiently for a regular spot on the team to open up.

"Not exactly," Sam said, expressing his disappointment.

Special Agent Hurts' voice pulled her attention in his direction. "Arianna, we have an assignment that we need help with, and we believe that with your background, you would be a valuable asset to the team."

"What kind of assignment?" She asked, clearly confused at what was happening.

"Undercover."

Her eyes widened, and she looked over at Sam. Again he looked like he was biting the inside of his cheek, but he kept quiet and let the agents talk.

She turned back to Special Agent Hurts. "An undercover assignment? You do realize that I'm not an actual agent, right? I'm just a contractor who looks at numbers all day."

Hurts nodded his head. "We are well aware of your qualifications, as are the directors overseeing this operation. They have given us the green light to recruit you for the agency and have you go through all the necessary training needed to complete the assignment."

Her hands were in her lap, and she twisted her fingers. "What is the assignment exactly? I mean, what would I have to do?"

The other agent spoke. "Because of the nature and confidentiality concerning this assignment, we cannot disclose any details until you fully agree to the assignment in writing."

Well, that was a red flag right there. How could she agree to something when she wasn't even sure what she agreed to?

She again looked to Sam. "Sam?"

He blew out a deep breath and ran his hand down his face. "Look, Arianna, I'll be honest with you. When these guys first told me what they were planning, I was totally against it. I'm still not fully sold on the idea. However, after listening to them plead their case, I have to agree with Special Agent Hurts; you would be a valuable asset."

She looked at all three of them. "How do you expect me to agree to something when I don't even know what it is? I mean, I could be signing my death sentence and not even know it. I could be agreeing to you putting me in a gang or shacking me up with a drug lord or something."

"Arianna, your part in this assignment has minimal danger involved."

She stared at him. "Can you guarantee that I won't die?"

He smirked, and she knew the answer that was coming. Nobody could guarantee anything in life. "No, I can't guarantee that, but I can guarantee that you will have a team of professionals watching your back around the clock."

"Would I be working for the two of you?" She asked the two agents.

"You would be under my direction," Agent Hurts told her, nodding his head. She looked the guy over, and he seemed like a likable guy. Trustworthy? That was too soon to decide, but something inside her told her she could rely on him to have her back.

She was all about setting out on new adventures. This would indeed be considered an adventure for sure, but what could it cost? Her life, maybe? *Ahhh...decisions...decisions...*

"When do you need an answer by?"

Everyone looked at one another, and she rolled her eyes. "Let me guess. You want it now?"

"Because of the urgent need to place someone on the inside, yes, an answer is needed now."

She didn't know what to think or even say. How could she decide on something like this in a matter of minutes? Or judging from Agent Callen's tapping of his finger, maybe seconds. She would normally talk to her dad about this, but she guessed that was out of the question.

"What about my family? What do I tell them?"

"You can tell them that you've accepted a job with the FBI and that you'll be out of contact for an unknown period of time," Sam explained to her.

"Unknown period of time?" She asked.

"Nobody ever knows when an assignment will end when they go undercover."

"I have all the documents right here. All we need is your verbal acceptance and your signature." Agent Callen pushed as he pulled a file out of his bag, opened it up, and slid it across the table to her.

She smirked. "You came prepared. You must've been a Boy Scout." She picked up the pen.

Agent Hurts chuckled. "I like you already. You'll fit in just fine."

"I haven't signed yet," she countered as she flipped through the documents reading and trying to decipher what a lot of the legal garbage meant before she signed it. She had hoped something in the stack of papers would have given her a clue as to what she was getting herself into.

When she signed the last page, she slid the folder over to Agent Callen. Agent Callen flipped through each page. Once he confirmed she had indeed signed in every spot she was supposed to, he nodded to Agent Hurts.

Agent Hurts looked her in the eye. “Welcome to the FBI, soon-to-be Agent Roland. Your training starts in two days. You’ll report to this address at o-seven-hundred.” He wrote it down on a piece of paper and slid it across the table to her. “I’ll meet you there.”

She took the paper, but her gaze never wavered from his. “So, now can you tell me what I’ll be doing?”

“Ever heard of Demitri Barros?”

She had. Demitri Barros was famous in many ways, both legally and illegally. She nodded.

“Great, because your ultimate goal is to infiltrate his business and seek the evidence that we need to charge him with trafficking women.”

Her eyes bugged out of her head. “How am I supposed to do that?”

Agent Hurts smirked. “You are going to be Europe’s newest lingerie model.”

Holy fucking shit! What in the hell have I gotten myself into?

CHAPTER ONE

Two and a half years later

Demitri Barros sat back in his chair and studied the photo he held in his hand. The woman was striking. The press nicknamed her *The Black Swan* because of the sexy black lingerie she wore on her debut runway show, her ebony hair color coupled with the way she glided majestically across the runways of Europe. It was a known fact that when the Black Swan took the stage, any side conversations ceased as all eyes were drawn to her beauty. Her presence held control of the entire room until the curtain would fall behind her. For the past year and a half, he had watched her from afar waiting for an opportune time to make his introduction.

He tapped his index finger against his lips while he contemplated the news he had just been given. "I just don't see it," he said, as he held up the picture and flashed it toward Carmine, his second in command and bodyguard. "Are you positive this is the woman that Pierre claims is an undercover FBI agent?"

Carmine shrugged one shoulder as he, too, studied the picture. Judging from his expression, Demitri felt that Carmine shared his opinion. "That's what Pierre said, though he hasn't provided any substantial evidence that backs up his claim. I'll admit that I'm hesitant to believe him. I've been around many fakes, and in my opinion, she seems as real as you can get. She doesn't fit the part of an agent." In his previous interactions with an agent, they've come across on guard all the time and can be overly pushy. "This beauty here," he pointed to the picture, "seems at the other end of the spectrum. She is described as very innocent—respectful, but shy. If it's true and she is an agent, then she's one hell of an actress."

Demitri looked back down at the photo. This was a major decision he had to make. With Anna Humphreys' contract with Claude set to expire in the coming weeks, Demitri was prepared to make her an offer that she couldn't refuse. She would look fabulous in his new lingerie line coming out for the upcoming season. He also had a few pieces from his private label that he had been saving for someone special, and the Black Swan was the perfect candidate.

Considering his organization had previously come under fire from law enforcement agencies, including undercover agents, he had to be cautious with whom he allowed in his inner circle. Thankfully, none had ever succeeded. He had always been able to dispose of those individuals who dared try to topple his empire. However, he had a close call a few weeks ago when an FBI agent had weaseled his way into his New England operation. Fortunately, he had been outed before any damaging information had been shared with him.

He focused back on the picture, and his eyes grazed over every inch of her body. She was sexy, yet modest when it came to the designs she modeled. She showed enough skin to tease her audience but leave them imagining what she concealed behind the sultry lace and satin fabric.

"I've studied her in videos from all the shows she's taken part in. All the major publications in Europe jockey just to land an interview with her. She can put on any piece of lingerie and make it a showstopper. Whatever piece she displays in photo shoots or runway shows sells out within days. I agree with you. I don't see the agent in her. She's so graceful and classy, yet sexy." He looked up and met Carmine's gaze. "She's perfect."

"You've waited a long time for the perfect one to come along. I've spoken with many top executives in the industry, and they all have nothing but compliments about her. Even the other models worship her, and you know how catty most of them can be."

"What about her activities outside of modeling? What does she do? Where does she go? Who does she associate with? Any men in her life?"

Carmine chuckled. "You haven't even been in the same room with the woman, and you're already so possessive."

Demitri smirked. Carmine wasn't wrong. He had been fascinated with the Black Swan ever since she first graced the runway. He was just sorry it had taken him so long to get a front-row seat to one of her shows. His designs were showcased in some of the same events. However, due to some ongoing business obligations back in the states, he hadn't attended any live shows in Europe.

Ignoring Carmine's slight jab, he asked, "Is there anything in her background that stands out as a red flag?"

Carmine slid the manila folder across the desk, and Demitri opened it and skimmed over a couple of pages.

"I see nothing. Everything checks out. She's twenty-seven years old, from San Bernardino, California. She was discovered by the owner of a small local talent agency during a local beauty pageant. She did a few photo shoots for some calendars, but nothing ever materialized. When she turned twenty-one, she moved to Paris—studied at the American University of Paris. She received her master's degree in Global Communications. While she was in college, she signed a contract with Claude Moreau's firm. Her big break came on this exact date two years ago, during the big Annual Designers Showcase show. Claude's top model had refused to walk the runway because of contract negotiations. Anna happened to be there assisting the show organizers when Claude needed a replacement model."

Demitri looked up, surprised to hear that. "Claude replaced his top model with a never before heard of model?" That was intriguing, considering Claude only flaunted famous faces in his prized designs.

Carmine smiled. "You know Claude. That black lace creation was the industry's most anticipated piece. There was no way he was not going to present his masterpiece. It became the most profitable piece of lingerie that year. That was when Black Swan got her name. She swooned over every reporter after that show. I saw some of her interviews. It was unbelievable and quite impressive. You would've thought she had been walking the runways all her life. She's a natural and would be a significant asset to your brand, amongst other things," he said with a sly grin.

The more Carmine told him, the more Demitri was confident that the beautiful creature wasn't living a double life as an FBI agent. He wasn't naïve and knew he was under the FBI's microscope. He had been ever since his father's untimely death, and the Barros business was handed solely over to him. That had been about fifteen years ago. Since then, he had restructured the family business and built it into one of the most notorious and profitable empires in the organized crime profession. He sold off portions that weren't cost-effective but then acquired a few that were sustainable that he believed could be beneficial to the future of the business. It wasn't all about money, though. There was a lot of strategic planning involved. Someone could have all the money in the world, but it wouldn't do them any justice if they didn't know how to use it wisely.

His operations in the United States were what he considered low-level crimes involving; illegal gambling, extortion, money laundering, and counterfeit goods distribution. Overseas was where he really generated his fortune, especially within the human trafficking realm. He was careful to only run that operation in Europe, where it was easier to navigate the system using aliases. But that hadn't stopped the feds from following him across the Atlantic to try and catch him in the act. He made sure that all of his transactions were buttoned up and concealed.

Trafficking women was a brilliant and profitable scheme. It was one area of business that his father never ventured into. However, it had been on his radar right before he was killed during an FBI raid. Shortly after taking the organization's reins, he traveled to Europe to meet with several business associates who had been close to his father. During one of the meetings, Takashi Chen, one of his father's closest allies, provided him the blueprint that his father was working on. It had taken a lot of work and planning to get the business off the ground, but it had been worth it. In less than six months he had already made his money back for the initial expense.

Even though he ran the business, he often distanced himself from the actual hands-on, operational side. Every so often, he would make an impromptu visit to one of the locations to ensure that things were running smoothly. His focus was on the financial side and making sure buyers were happy with their merchandise. His buyers paid a large sum of money for women with specific characteristics, such as; body type, hair color, eye color, just to name a few. Once an order was received and a down payment was made, he would send the order to a team of exploiters who would scour bars, clubs, and restaurants looking for a match. They preyed upon those who were susceptible for a variety of reasons. It was a somewhat tedious process. To avoid being caught, everyone involved had to make sure all their "i's" were dotted, and their "t's" were crossed. They had to ensure that there was nothing that could be traced back to them. Once a scout had a potential victim in their sights, they would sit back for a little bit and examine their behavior. Some women could be lured in with a promise of money, love, or fame. Some didn't quite cooperate, and the exploiter would use force to incapacitate the victim. Once the merchandise was secured, they would transport them to one of the many holding facilities Demitri had all over Europe until arrangements were made with the buyer for shipment or pickup.

Demitri hid his smile as he stared back at her photo. The Black Swan would never be subjected to his trafficking crimes. At least as long as he had anything to do with it. He wanted her. Not only would she make him a ton of money and look fabulous in his designs—she would look incredible under him in bed. If she was as innocent as she portrayed herself to be, he could only imagine how sensational it would be to be her teacher in the bedroom. Just imagining the many ways she would learn to please him, had his dick hardening beneath his trousers. He was more than ready to meet the beauty that has captured the hearts of Europe.

Demitri tapped his fingers on his desk. "Call her agent and set up the introduction for tonight."

Carmine grinned. "Shall I call ahead and see if I can reserve a room at the castle for the evening?"

"That won't be necessary. I figure I'll make my introduction at the after-party. From there, she and I can grab a drink and find a quiet corner to get to know one another. If I play my cards right, I'll be in my own room tonight with her next to me as we celebrate her becoming my newest money maker, amongst other things," he smirked as he reached for his bottle of water and took a drink.

"Lucky man," Carmine said before he handed over two small, oval, greenish gray pills. Demitri looked surprised, and Carmine shrugged. "Just in case she isn't cooperative. Slip her a pill, and I can guarantee she'll sign anything you want her to."

Demitri grinned, but he preferred not to have to drug her. Especially on the first night. But as Carmine said, he'd do anything to make sure she would work for him.

Carmine stood up from the chair and prepared to leave when his phone rang. He looked at Demitri. "It's Monte."

"See what he wants."

There was only one reason Monte Bertola would be calling—and that was to give Demitri a warning that trouble could be headed his way.

Demitri listened and tried to decipher what was being discussed, but Carmine's short one-sided yes or no replies made it difficult. Moments later, Carmine disconnected the call and faced Demitri. Demitri raised his eyebrows in question.

"It seems that Petro will be at the venue this evening as well."

Now that was news Demitri was not prepared for. Petro Shevchenko and Demitri's differences went way back and stemmed from a business deal that Petro stole from under Demitri and his family, costing them hundreds of thousands of dollars. Demitri found it interesting that of all nights, Petro had decided to attend the same event that he was. Primarily, since it was known that Petro had been laying low while he was being investigated for murder along with a handful of other charges.

Unlike Petro, Demitri knew how to run illegal businesses and not get caught. Petro's main problem was the people who worked for him. They were not loyal and would talk for the right price. Petro was a thorn in Demitri's side. There were some business transactions long ago that Petro had been involved in with Demitri. Demitri wouldn't put it past Petro to sell him out should he be questioned about them.

Demitri held Carmine's gaze. "Do we know what business Petro has at the castle?"

"A business meeting is all we know."

"I want someone on him. I don't trust his sudden appearance."

"Not to worry. I'll have Nico seek him out."

"Let Nico know that Petro likes to create distractions, especially if he thinks he has a tail."

"I'll inform him."

"Do that and also draw up Anna's contract. I want it ready to present to her tonight. Fill it with extras so she can't say no."

"Yes, sir."

Carmine left the room, leaving Demitri to himself. He reached for her photo again. She wasn't skin and bones like most models who walked the runway. Anna Humphreys was built to please a man, and he was hoping for a preview of what could blossom between the two of them. He was prepared to offer her an opportunity that she couldn't pass up. If she balked, she would learn quickly that no one turns down Demitri Barros. Ever.

CHAPTER TWO

Special Agent Chris Hurts stood in a room full of other agents as he spoke with his direct supervisor, Assistant Director Scarborough on the phone. It seemed that there had been a breakdown in communication regarding this evening's run of the show.

Hurts and his team were in an abandoned warehouse approximately seven miles from the castle where Demitri Barros was due to arrive in less than one hour. He and the entire team had been anticipating his arrival in hopes of finally having the opportunity to get an agent on the inside of his European operation. A lot of agents had put their lives on hold for two years for this moment. They knew this night wasn't going to end in an arrest, but it was the big break they had all been working towards. But now, it seemed as if that opportunity was in jeopardy.

"How did this happen?" Hurts asked Scarborough, clearly frustrated with the new developments in the operation.

For some apparent unknown reason, the order came from the top to temporarily halt the Barros operation because of new developments in the case. Special Agent Hurts' team was being pulled back until further notice.

Hurts was beyond frustrated and upset with the lack of reasoning.

"I don't know, but I'm trying to get to the bottom of it," Scarborough replied, not sounding happy about the situation either.

"So what do we do?"

"Another team should be arriving at your location momentarily. They will be conducting a separate operation involving another target that is scheduled to attend this evening's festivities."

"Another target?" Hurts had been over the entire list of attendees three or four times and nobody on the list came to mind who could be more critical than Demitri Barros.

"Petro Shevchenko."

"The Ukrainian?"

"Yep."

"I don't remember seeing his name on the attendee list." He walked over to the table and opened the folder that held the list of attendees. He scanned it again.

"He's not on the list."

"Apparently, he was a late add."

Hurts started to get a suspicious feeling. It was widely known that there was no love lost between Petro and Demitri. Both of them had accused the other of trying to destroy the other. Petro had been under investigation for a few months. Hurts was aware that the agency had been working closely with DEA to build a case on him. But even so, it still didn't make sense to halt a two-year operation in exchange for this scenario, not to mention the amount of money that had been poured into the Barros operation to get to where they were.

"It just doesn't make sense," Hurts said, shaking his head as he ran his hand through his hair. He didn't care that his team saw his frustration. They felt the same. "And Demitri? What happens with him? Does he just get to walk away scot-free once again?"

"Not necessarily. They think that Petro will cooperate with investigators and make a deal to save his own ass."

Hurts had to agree. Petro did have a big mouth and commented in the past to other undercover agents that he had evidence that could bury Demitri. But on the other hand, he had to play devil's advocate.

"If Petro wants to be top dog, why hasn't he already provided it to the Feds?"

"Bribery. He was using it to pull Demitri's strings."

"And how has that worked for him?"

"Demitri is calling his bluff."

"What's your opinion?"

"I think the decision to pull in Petro is a mistake and will be a huge setback in the case against Barros, but as I've said, it wasn't my call."

Hurts sensed that Scarborough was leaving something out.

"What aren't you telling me, Scarborough? We go way back, and I've always respected you because you've always been transparent with me."

He heard Scarborough sigh. "The Special Agent in Charge that's coming in is Travis Gabbert."

Hurts thought he had misunderstood his friend and boss. But when Hurts heard the large bay door near the back of the warehouse open, he turned and watched as two vans pulled inside. Once they were parked, the front passenger side door opened, and no other than Special Agent Travis Gabbert stepped out. That prick was the most hated agent in the bureau.

"Your silence tells me he just arrived," Scarborough stated through the phone.

"You would be correct."

"I'm sorry about this, Chris. If it were up to me, you and your team would move forward with tonight's plan. I have my opinion on the matter, which I plan to take up with the Deputy Director."

"Care to share?"

"We'll get together when you return. In the meantime, have your team pull back and stay clear of Gabbert and his team. I don't trust him as far as I can throw him."

That couldn't have been a more accurate statement. Gabbert had a lousy reputation of screwing people over to climb the ladder. There were rumors that years ago he butted heads with his superiors and was almost fired from the bureau.

"What about my two agents inside? It's too late to pull them back. Agent Roland wasn't wearing her earpiece tonight because of the possible meeting with Demitri and Miles; that's another story. I'll try again, but I doubt she has her phone on."

"I was told that Gabbert's team would be conducting their operation on the second floor of the opposite side of the castle from where the party is taking place. She should be safe."

"What happens if Demitri approaches her?"

"Then it happens. The worst that can happen is that he offers her a contract, and she says she'll have her agent look it over."

"God, this sucks! You know, once we pull her out, she won't be able to go back in, right?"

"I know, Chris. Again, I'm not happy about this."

"All right then. I'll touch base with you when we arrive back stateside."

"Take care, man."

"Yeah."

Hurts disconnected the call and walked over to meet his team. As he explained the new developments, he saw the disappointment and anger in their expressions. He felt the same, but he was the agent in charge, so he had to be the professional face for the team.

Moments later, Gabbert approached.

"I guess Assistant Director Scarborough contacted you."

"Yeah, he did."

"I got the orders right here in case you needed to see them physically," Agent Gabbert stated, waving a file folder in front of him.

Agent Hurts snatched the folder out of the other agent's hand. The bastard was practically beaming. Hurts took a quick glance at Gabbert's team, and he noticed they were keeping their distance from their leader. Some even gave a quick nod as if letting them know they weren't down for whatever was planned.

As he flipped through the pages, his temper rose to a boiling point. Angry couldn't even describe how he felt. What was typed up in the report was complete bullshit. Someone had filed an ethics complaint against Agent Roland over her relationship with Enzo Makis. *What the fuck was that all about?* He wondered if Scarborough knew about that but withheld the information. He threw a folder on the table in front of Gabbert. Judging from the sarcastically condescending smirk on Gabbert's face, he knew what Hurts was upset about.

"Looks like your wonder girl got caught trying to sink her claws into her own personal sugar daddy."

Hurts did everything in his power not to take a swing at the bastard. That complaint was bogus and based on nothing but a bullshit lie. Anyone close to the Barros investigation would even say so. But it also made him wonder who had it out for Arianna. As far as he knew, she didn't have any enemies within the agency, let alone any who knew what she had been up to for the last two years.

Hurts starred down Gabbert. "I don't know what the hell you're up to, Gabbert, but I'm telling you right now that you better not fuck this up and put my agent inside in danger."

Special Agent Gabbert shrugged his shoulders as if he didn't have a care in the world. "She's a big girl. She signed the agreement."

Agent Hurts stood in place staring at Agent Gabbert. He was furious. What his superiors were planning was careless and dangerous on so many levels. He still had two agents inside the venue that could be put into the crosshairs of a hazardous situation without their knowledge.

"Yeah, well, if your team erroneously infiltrates at the wrong time or place, she could be placed in a bad situation."

Agent Gabbert smirked. "If you don't have the confidence in your contractor agent, maybe you should've picked a seasoned agent who actually earned the title."

Agent Gabbert's comment towards Arianna pissed Agent Hurts off. Arianna Roland may have been at one time just a Forensic Accountant who contracted with the bureau. Still, she had since earned the respect of being named an Agent considering what she took on when it was apparent that she wasn't comfortable when she was first approached about going undercover. She went through the training that any "real" agent would endure and more. The only difference was her training was completed in less time than what typical recruits went through because of the assignment's timing. When the FBI had been given the opportunity to lay the groundwork to infiltrate Demitri's organization, no other female agent had fit the part. Arianna not only had the beauty to pull off the disguise, but she had the brains and language skills.

Hurts pointed at him with a fierce expression. "So help me god, if she's drawn into your shitshow of an operation that is all on you."

Agent Gabbert shrugged his shoulders. "As you say and according to the agency's records, she's been trained. Although she should be worried about the questioning that's waiting for her at home."

Hurts didn't miss the second comment that Gabbert had dropped concerning the complaint filed against Arianna. Coincidence, or was he behind it?

Agent Hurts ran his hand through his hair. "I want it on record that I disagree with the strategy change. This has disaster written all over it."

"Duly noted Agent Hurts. Now, if you would kindly step aside, I have a team that needs to be updated."

Hurts stared down the other agent. The guy had a reputation within the agency of being a prick. It was rumored that years ago, Agent Gabbert had been involved in a huge undercover assignment that went south under his leadership. Agent Hurts supposed that he was trying to redeem himself. He wasn't about to let some washed-up agent looking for a big comeback ruin his career or put any of his agents in danger. No fucking way.

He wanted no part of the fiasco. His main concern was Arianna's safety. She was going to be blindsided if he couldn't get word to her.

He pulled out his phone and tried dialing her again, but it went to voicemail. He looked at his watch. If the event stayed on schedule, the afterparty should have started twenty minutes ago. He tried Miles's phone as well, but only got his voicemail, which wasn't a big surprise. But there was one other person who could get a message to her. It was risky, but sometimes dire circumstances call for dangerous measures.

All he could do was pray she made it out alive.

CHAPTER THREE

Arianna or Anna Humphreys, the name she had been answering to for the last two years, looked herself over in the full-length mirror. She rolled her eyes as she reached into the fitted black cocktail dress and adjusted her boobs, so they didn't look lopsided. She would have preferred to wear something more modest, but this was a big night. She needed to dress to impress since the show's main sponsor was throwing the party. This assignment was starting to weigh on her. She hoped tonight would lead to the start of the final stage in the operation. She stepped into her heels and gave herself one last look before she opened the door.

She walked down the dimly lit hallway then took the stairs down to the next level toward the reception room where the afterparty was in full swing. The entire event was held in an old renaissance castle in Rome. It was a gorgeous venue with lush courtyards and five-star accommodations. She had the opportunity to spend a few nights before the show to take it all in. The castle was rich in history, not to mention its secrets beyond the floors and walls. Being the explorer that she was, she spent most of her free time exploring the secret passageways she had heard about. The dark and musty corridors appeared spooky, but it was right up her alley. She loved a good mystery with suspense.

She had met many new faces during her time undercover. Most she would consider just business associates, but there were one or two she would consider being a "real" friend. To this day, she was still dumbfounded how she went from a contracted FBI Forensic Accountant to an undercover agent posing as a lingerie model. Never in a million years would she have seen herself in this position.

As she rounded the bend that led into the open room, she heard the music and laughter. She walked through the large double doors and looked around, ignoring the hungry eyes of the men who would love nothing more than to claim her attention for the evening. She always made sure she mingled with a group of people so she wasn't stranded alone with an unfamiliar guy. There were too many untrustworthy people at these types of events.

As she went to turn in the opposite direction, her eyes met a familiar set of dark eyes across the room. She smiled as Enzo said something to the gentleman next to him before he started walking toward her.

"Anna!" The mob boss greeted her and pulled her into an embrace. His deep voice intermingled with his thick Italian accent. She accepted the hug from him. Yes, an FBI agent shouldn't be mingling with a mob boss, but when your orders were to play the part, then you obeyed. Plus, Enzo never gave her a reason to be frightened of him. She'd heard stories but never witnessed him breaking any laws or showing aggression toward someone.

She and Enzo had formed a bond somewhat early in her impromptu modeling career. He had bailed her out of a few of situations early in her assignment. Her inexperience in the industry had almost been costly the very first afterparty she had attended. She had ordered a drink from the bar but hadn't been aware that an older gentleman with a history of abuse had paid off the bartender to spike her drink. Luckily for her, Enzo had seen the entire little operation unfold and had gotten to her in time before she had taken a drink. From that moment on he had been somewhat of a mentor to her showing her how to navigate the industry. There were never any romantic feelings between them—just a great friendship that she would be sad to leave behind once her assignment was finished.

"Enzo, it is so good to see you."

He stared down at her. "Once again, you were the shining star on the runway this evening. Your beauty and stature captivated the audience."

She blushed as she held his gaze. "Now I know you're just pulling my leg."

He squeezed her waist. "I never lie to a woman about her beauty."

She nodded her head. "Well, thank you for the compliment."

"So, I hear that your contract with Claude is coming to an end."

She gave him a coy smile. "That might be true."

"Well, before you entertain any other offers, I would ask that you give consideration to my representation. You know I'd take care of you."

She smiled. She had no doubt. Out of all of the individuals behind the fashion brand names, she would say that Enzo topped the list. If she had an opportunity to cherry-pick who she modeled for, she would definitely lean toward Enzo's brand. He cared for his employees and treated all the women who worked for him with dignity and respect. Claude, the current designer she was contracted with, wasn't as forgiving as Enzo and expected one hundred fifty percent all the time. It was exhausting and frustrating at times.

If she knew modeling was her actual career, which it wasn't, she would jump at the opportunity to work for Enzo and be represented by him. Even knowing he had a dark side.

"We can definitely talk."

"Yes, I think we can." He held her gaze, and she sensed there was something more he wanted to say. She started to ask him, but they were rudely interrupted by Miles. Miles was her colleague and another undercover agent posing as her agent. Although looking at his disheveled appearance, Arianna got a bad feeling that Miles had started his party a little earlier.

"Anna, there you are," Miles said hurriedly. She didn't miss how dilated his pupils were or how jittery he was. Miles was high on whatever drug was floating around the room. Drugs were one of the big things she definitely wouldn't miss when her assignment was over. She did make a note in her reports if anyone wanted to follow up on it. She even had the names of suppliers. Unfortunately, Miles had gotten sucked into the dark abyss, and she was sure that their handlers were aware. Sadly, it was a norm within the industry—so many girls were taken advantage of because of it.

She narrowed her eyes. "Miles, I'm speaking to Enzo right now; whatever it is can wait."

Miles gave Enzo a disgusted look. It wasn't a secret that Miles didn't care for Enzo. That fractured relationship stemmed from an event a few months ago when Enzo caught Miles trying to enter into a contract on Arianna's behalf without her knowledge.

Arianna went to say something about his rude behavior, but then Mile's eyes grew wide and he learned closer and whispered. "He is here."

She pulled back just slightly and really looked at him. Judging from the slight gleam in his eyes, she knew he wasn't joking. She felt her heart jump start, and she could feel the anxiousness start to build, but she didn't let it show. She knew who "he" was that Miles was referring to. This was the moment everyone on the team had been waiting for. Two years of parading her goods around in lingerie and her payday had come.

"Miles, I don't speak your code. Who are you talking about?" She played dumb, not wanting to look overanxious, especially in front of Enzo.

"Demitri Barros wants an introduction to the Black Swan model."

She really wasn't sure what to say. In her mind, she was saying "finally". She literally had put herself in the public eye for this moment. She had shed many tears in private, but the FBI didn't care as long as the job was completed.

"Anna!" Miles shouted at her, which drew a glare from Enzo. "Did you hear me? Demitri Barros is asking for you. You know what this means, right?"

She looked at Miles. If he wasn't careful, his over excitement was going to jeopardize the operation.

She felt Enzo's hand slide to her back before he lowered his head and whispered in her ear. "Be very careful, Anna."

She looked up, and the warning was clear in Enzo's eyes. "If you need me, I'll be around," he told her and kissed her on the cheek before he disappeared into the crowd.

Miles grabbed her hand and pulled her along. As they made their way through the crowd of people, many tried to stop and talk to her, but Miles kept them moving, telling everyone that she had an important engagement she needed to get to. All the while, she kept thinking about Enzo's warning.

"You're going to be the next cover model for Barros lingerie line," Miles said over his shoulder.

She grabbed his hand and yanked him backward. Her actions caught the eye of few individuals close by, but she played it off well with the fake smile she was accustomed to giving people over the last couple of years.

She turned her eyes back to Miles who was looking at her as if knowing he may have crossed the line with her, which he had. She'd had enough of his overaggressive antics.

She stepped closer to him and spoke in a low voice. "You need to get your shit together before you blow both our covers."

He reared his head back and went to refute her statement, but she raised her eyebrow as if daring him to challenge her. She was done with his carelessness and irresponsibility.

Once she saw his shoulders relax, she started moving again and brushed by him, knocking into his shoulder. She could feel his presence following, and she wanted to smile to herself. That had been the first time she called him out on his behavior. But he was a goddamn federal agent, and he needed to act like one.

As they walked through the dark halls of the castle, she tried to get herself back in character. Of course, Miles started to perk up again. In her contract for this assignment, she was allowed to keep whatever money she made from modeling. Miles' contract stated the same meaning that he got half of what she brought in because he was acting as her agent. Signing with Demitri would bring in a motherload of a payday for both of them, so no wonder Miles was excited. The situation made her laugh sometimes—here, she's the one that exposes herself in skimpy outfits to strangers, but Miles gets half the money.

They came to a stop in front of a door labeled private, and her heart began to hammer in her chest, but she took a couple of quick inconspicuous breaths to settle her nerves. Miles opened the door and ushered her through. They were now in a small corridor, and standing about twenty yards from her, she locked gazes with Demitri Barros. A man standing next to him was speaking to him, but Demitri's gaze never left hers. After a few awkward moments, he started walking toward her. Even his gait gave off an authoritative aura.

Miles, of course, practically dragged her to meet him halfway. Arianna put her hand over her mouth to cover her laugh when Miles went to speak, and Demitri hushed him with just his glare. When Miles didn't get the message, she turned and looked at him.

"Miles, can you give Mr. Barros and me a few minutes?"

He tried to argue, but the guy who was with Demitri agreed with her and escorted Miles back through the door they had just come in from.

When she turned back toward Demitri, he was staring at her. She actually felt embarrassed by Miles behavior.

"Mr. Barros," she greeted him and held her hand out. She wasn't sure what type of greeting to use. She knew that Greeks were generally expressive and friendly. Usually, they were big huggers, but Demitri didn't come across as the hugging type of guy.

He looked her over from head to toe. The intensity of his gaze made her squirm a little. He was an attractive man—a man of much power, not just his physical appearance but also his legacy. His dark blue eyes met hers, and he reached for her hand and brought it to his lips. His lips were warm as he kissed the back of her hand. The gesture created goosebumps along her skin—and it wasn't a good feeling.

"Ms. Humphreys, the pleasure is all mine. And please call me Demitri."

She nodded. "I'm really sorry about Miles. He –"

He squeezed her hand. "Let's not waste any time talking about your agent. I'd much rather get to know you."

She swallowed hard but managed to smile softly. "Ok. I believe there are a few open tables in the room; we could grab one of them and talk."

She went to turn, but he stopped her and stepped closer. She tilted her head back to look up at him. He placed his hands on her waist using enough pressure that she wouldn't back away. He was making it known that he was in control. Her throat became parched, and she licked her lips. Immediately she regretted doing that because he probably took that as her trying to be seductive.

"I was thinking a place a little more intimate. Fewer people and less noise." The darkness in his eyes gave warning, and again, Enzo's words of caution came to mind.

She didn't say a word or try to pull away as he took her hand and led her further down the hall. They passed several rooms until they came to a unique room filled with medieval paraphernalia. She recognized the room from when she was scoping out the venue days earlier. She believed she had heard someone call it the gray room.

He ushered her in, and she jumped when the door behind her slammed shut. When she turned toward the door, the man she was plotting to bring down was blocking the only exit. As long as she could convince him to bring her on board to his team of models, she was optimistic that she could pull off the final step to prove he was behind the trafficking of many young girls and women who had gone missing. All she needed to do was gain access to his computer server, where the information was believed to be stored.

He approached her slowly. The sound of his heavy footsteps against the marble flooring resonated off the walls of the open room. She'd only been in Demitri's presence for ten minutes, and already she felt on edge and a tad bit fearful. She needed to push those feelings to the side and be confident and not appear too timid. She hated it, but it had to be done to gain his trust. She had to play the part of the eager model willing to do anything to secure a contract with Barros Designs. She placed her hands against his chest and began to slide them up toward his shoulders. He grabbed her wrists, stopping her, and he looked down into her eyes.

"Many people talk highly of you."

"Do they?" She asked.

"I've had my eye on you. You have poise and grace like no other model, but I can sense you have a backbone hiding under the innocence you portray to the public."

If he only knew. Or did he? She almost started to panic for a minute but then walked herself back from the ledge. If Demitri knew who she was, he would have never stepped foot inside the castle. He wasn't a dumb man.

"To survive in this industry and not get taken advantage of, a girl has to have some smarts and toughness to her. That side of me only comes out when it's needed."

She gave him a coy smile, and his lips twitched. She was chipping away at the wall around him. She could sense he was letting his guard down slightly.

"If you've been eying me, you must've seen something you liked. So, the question I have for you, Mr. Barros, is, what can I do for you?" She purposely called him by his last name as she popped the top two buttons on his dress shirt and pressed her lips gently against his exposed skin. She was pleased when she heard him take a deep breath. His hand tangled in her hair, and he pulled her away. He put a finger under her chin and tilted her face up toward his. The desire in his eyes told her that she had him hook, line and sinker.

"I like your thinking, but how about a drink first while we talk? Then maybe we could end it with a toast of celebration," he asked although it wasn't really a question because suddenly a man appeared in the doorway behind her with a tray of champagne. He handed a glass over to Demitri, who then passed it to her.

She stared at the stranger for a moment. How had she not heard the door open? Unless he came in through one of the two secret passageways that led to other rooms in the castle. When she explored the castle the other day, she was amazed at the number of passageways, including tunnels that ran beneath the centuries-old structure.

"Anna Humphreys, I'd like you to meet Carmine."

"It is lovely to meet you, Ms. Humphreys. Demitri was pleased that his schedule opened up and that he could attend this evening's festivities."

"Nice to meet you as well, Carmine. I'm glad you both could make it."

She extended her hand, and Carmine took it into his. His touch alone caused a shiver to run up her spine. Demitri must've seen her tremble because he frowned.

"Are you cold?" He asked her. It was chilly, so she covered her mistake.

"A little," she replied.

He surprised her when he removed his suit jacket and helped her put it on. She heard him inhale next to her ear, and it caused another shiver to rack her body. She looked up and over her shoulder and smiled.

"Thank you."

He winked before releasing her and picked up his own glass of champagne. "Carmine handles all contract negotiations for my design firm here in Europe."

Arianna glanced at Carmine and hid her smile. She knew from intel that Carmine was much more than a contract negotiator for Demitri. His name was seen in many other case files, including murder.

Demitri tapped his glass against hers.

"To an enjoyable night."

She was reluctant to take a drink because she was ninety-nine-point nine percent positive that her champagne contained a drug that would incapacitate her. She wasn't ready to become one of Demitri's conquests.

He eyed her over the rim of his glass, waiting for her to take a sip. When she didn't, he asked, "Do you not like champagne?" He appeared a bit insulted.

She set the glass down on a nearby table and stepped closer to him. She was thankful for the warmth of his jacket because she was shaking in her heels. She was taking a gamble. She knew Demitri was a control freak, especially when it came to women. She had heard about his fetish with BDSM. He was into hard-core kink. It was rumored that some of his "play" partners suffered severe injuries by his hand.

She snatched his champagne glass and set it next to hers. Then slowly and seductively, she walked toward him. Once in front of him, she pressed her body against his. She hoped like hell he couldn't feel her body trembling. She was trying her hardest to stay calm and collected. Miles was her backup tonight, and with him flying high up in the clouds, she was on her own.

"It isn't the champagne. I like champagne, but the last few times I've drunk it, I had a bad reaction. The last time I was sick for days. I think we both know what we want."

He stared down into her eyes. His gaze was penetrating as if he was searching deep into her soul. It was frightening. She continued to stare back at him, but she struggled internally and wondered how she could play this to her advantage so she didn't become his next victim.

Breaking the heavy silence between them, he said, "I've waited for over a year to see what you would turn out to be. Most women in this business fizzle out. People get tired of seeing the same face on covers of magazines or being the main attraction on a runway. But you, Anna, are a natural, and a figure that no man can look away from. And you know what?"

"What?" She whispered.

"I'm one of those men. I want you. I want to see you in my designs on covers. I want to see you in my designs on the runways. But meeting you tonight validates that I want you in my bed."

Before she could register the last part of his sentence, he covered her mouth with his lips. His hands gripped her face as he took control of the kiss. With her back to the wall, she felt trapped. It was a bruising kiss, and she started to panic and was ready to stop him when suddenly the door burst open.

When Demitri released her and looked toward the doorway, she was shocked to see Enzo standing there, a fierce expression drawn on his face.

"What in the hell are you doing here?" Demitri shouted angrily to Enzo.

Ignoring Demitri, Enzo stalked toward her and took her hand. "Anna, we need to go."

But before she could ask what was going on, two men entered the room, and Arianna knew they weren't there for pleasantries when they pulled their guns and pointed at them.

A canister-type object was thrown into the room next, and before Arianna realized it was a flash-bang grenade, it detonated. Suddenly her world went bright white, and she lost all sense of direction. The loud sound penetrated deep into her head, causing a concussion-type feeling. She lost her balance and fell into a desk nearby, cutting her head just above her left eye on the corner. She slid down to the floor. Within seconds she started to gain back some of her awareness. As she looked around amidst the smoke that filtered through the room, she tried to find Enzo but saw no sign of him. The room was eerily quiet for a few seconds before gunfire pierced the air.

She screamed and ducked as bullets hit the wood paneling behind her. Tiny fragments of the wood punctured her skin. She peeked around the side of the desk and could see both Demitri and Carmine pinned down behind a chair and sofa returning fire.

She tried to catch her breath as her adrenalin hit at an all-time high. She wished she had her weapon, but with the dress she wore, there was nowhere to hide it.

In between the gunfire, she thought she heard someone shout the name Petro. But then another voice yelled out FBI, and she grew alarmed. The only reason the FBI would raid the place was if they had a warrant. If that was the case, why hadn't they informed her?

Carmine shouted over the gunfire to Demitri. "Grab the girl and get out of here. I'll cover you."

Arianna knew one thing, and that was that she was not going anywhere with Demitri. Not now that they were in the middle of a shootout. She took another chance and peered over the ledge of the desk to see if there was anything she could use as a weapon, but it was bare. A bullet whizzed by, just missing her head, and she ducked back down. She flinched and tried covering her arms as more tiny pieces of wood pierced her skin.

She needed to think and focus on finding a way out before falling victim to the madness unfolding. She half wondered if this was the exact type of situation she heard her dad refer to as a clusterfuck. She peered around the desk again. With the amount of gunfire coming through the door leading to the hall, she knew she wouldn't be going that way. She knew somewhere toward the back of the room was a wooden wine rack built into the wall that also functioned as a door leading to a secret passageway.

She was running out of time as the smoke grew thicker. She kicked her heels off and got onto her hands and knees. Just as she was about to make a run for it, she was lifted off the ground by a set of arms.

"Run!" The deep angry voice behind her shouted. When she looked over her shoulder, she saw it was Enzo. *Where the hell had he come from?*

She didn't hesitate and sprinted toward the wine rack. She searched the side, trying to feel for the small lever that would release the door. She knew it was there, but with the smoke, she couldn't see clearly.

She heard a roar from behind her and looked over her shoulder. She saw Demitri coming towards her. His face was all contorted, and blood covered his white shirt. "Prodotis!" He shouted. Prodotis meant traitor in Greek. At first, she thought he was talking to her, but then she realized he was yelling at Enzo, who stood beside her trying to get the door opened.

She heard the click, and then the door started to move. Her eyes were still focused on Demitri and the gun in his hand. He raised it and aimed it at Enzo, who was trying to push the door open faster. She threw herself in front of Enzo just as Demitri pulled the trigger. The shot was loud, and she felt the hit to her arm and cried out as she fell backward into Enzo's arms. He pulled her through the tight space and slammed the door closed, trapping the two of them in complete darkness. The walls were so thick she couldn't even hear the sound of the gunfire.

She turned and held onto Enzo. She was scared, and her body shook so bad that her teeth started to chatter.

He rubbed her back. "We must hurry. That door only has a five-minute locking mechanism."

Her arm felt numb. "Enzo, I'm bleeding. I was shot."

"Shit!" He pulled his cell phone out and used the light from it to look at her arm. He cursed again. She took a look and felt a little queasy when she saw the amount of blood that covered her arm. She had still been wearing Demitri's jacket. She was thankful for the warmth now. "I need something to tie around your arm to stop the bleeding," he told her.

"My dress. Rip some of the material from the bottom."

Quickly he did as she said and tied it around her bicep, creating a tourniquet. He grabbed her hand. "Are you okay to walk?"

She nodded her head though she was still feeling the effects of the flash grenade. "Let's go," he ordered and led her through the dark corridors. They had walked for a few minutes when she started to feel lightheaded. She slowed down, and Enzo stopped.

"Anna?"

She shook her head. She was so scared. Tears formed in her eyes. "I feel like I'm going to pass out."

He hugged her, and she held onto him. She could feel herself getting weaker and the light slowly leaving her body.

"I'm scared," she said, her voice shaking. For the first time since she started this assignment, she was afraid she wasn't going to make it back home.

"I've got you," she heard him say just as her vision blurred and everything turned black.

CHAPTER FOUR

Agent Hurts stood next to Agent Gabbert as they took in the aftermath of an attack that resulted in a bloodbath. It had occurred just moments before Agent Gabbert gave his team the order to move in to take Petro into custody.

Hurts couldn't believe the scene he was looking at. It looked like a war zone with bodies strewn throughout the hallway. But from what he saw, there were no signs of Arianna or Demitri, which concerned him.

Another agent from Gabbert's team walked up. "Petro has been identified as one of the victims."

Agent Gabbert threw his hands up in the air and cursed. "Fuck!"

"What about Demitri Barros? Any word on his whereabouts?" Hurts asked the other agent.

"No. None of the bodies matched his description."

"Do we know what started this? Any witnesses?" Agent Gabbert interjected.

"We have two witnesses who said they saw Petro and a few of his men hanging around that room over there." The agent pointed to the opened door on the left. There were bodies inside there too. "A few moments later, two of the men entered the room. Demitri was said to be inside. We do have one of Petro's men in custody. He is already singing like a canary to the investigators. He claims that Petro had wanted revenge for Demitri setting him up a few months ago."

"Was Demitri alone?" Hurts asked, wondering if Arianna had been inside when the attack began.

"No. A member of the staff said that he was with one of the models." The agent looked down at his notepad. "The guy said her name was Anna. But we have another witness who said they saw a woman matching the same description exiting the castle with Enzo Makris after the attack took place. So, we aren't sure if she was in the room with Demitri or not. And, nobody can locate her or Enzo Makris."

Agent Gabbert's face turned red as he spun around toward Agent Hurts.

"Your agent has some explaining to do."

Agent Hurts held his hand up to stop the bullshit spewing from Agent Gabbert's mouth.

"We both know that Agent Roland had no idea what your team was planning tonight. And if I remember from our earlier conversation, you said so yourself that Agent Roland was a trained agent and should be able to take care of herself.

"She was seen leaving a crime scene with a known criminal. That won't look good for her when the review board hears about this."

Agent Hurts just stared at him. He knew that under normal circumstances, any agent would be investigated for mingling with a criminal such as Enzo Makris. Still, there was so much more to this case that Agent Gabbert wasn't privy to, and unfortunately, Agent Hurts wasn't in a position to explain it to him, so sitting there trying to defend Arianna would be like beating a dead horse.

"You are entitled to your opinion," Agent Hurts told, Agent Gabbert.

Agent Gabbert laughed sarcastically. "My opinion, huh? Well, we will see how my opinion affects Agent Roland's future role in the agency."

Agent Hurts ignored the threat, knowing that he would have Arianna's back if Gabbert tried to take her down. He turned toward the other agent and asked, "What about Miles? Has anyone seen him?" The agent shook his head, and Agent Hurts had a bad feeling that greed had caught up to the young agent. Miles had been sliding down a slippery slope the past few months. Arianna had voiced her concerns regarding his behavior, but they were too far into the assignment to pull him out. It would leave too many questions to answer.

He'd worry about Miles later; right now, he needed to find Arianna before Agent Gabbert got hold of her.

He felt his phone vibrate, and he answered. "Hurts."

"The *swan* is asleep in the country. The feathers are a little ruffled, but it's safe," the voice on the other end said before the line went dead. Agent Hurts took a deep breath and exhaled. Hearing firsthand that Arianna was secure took a little of the weight off his shoulders.

CHAPTER FIVE

Enzo slipped his phone into his pocket. He knew that Agent Hurts would be worried about Arianna, so he wanted to make sure he called as soon as they were far enough from the castle, so he knew she was safe and what her location was. He picked up the bandage and prepared to wrap her arm. He and Ambrose had already cleaned up many of the tiny cuts she sustained, along with a butterfly bandage over her eye.

"Will she be alright?" Ambrose asked Enzo as he helped wrap Arianna's injured arm. Enzo had been alarmed when Arianna passed out in his arms once they were safe inside the tunnels. Luckily, he had Ambrose, his most trusted confidant who had been outside and was able to quickly pull the car up to where the tunnel exited on the side of the structure.

"Her pulse is steady, and Maxwell said she seemed to be okay besides the arm." However, Enzo did frown as he looked at the gunshot wound she sustained on her arm. It had only been a graze, but it still required stitches which angered Enzo. Thankfully, Maxwell, another associate of his who was also a medic, had met them at Enzo's villa in the country to assess Arianna's injuries and patch her up.

Enzo sat next to Arianna on the bed in one of the guest bedrooms. His mind kept reflecting on the events at the castle. She should have never been put in the situation she was in, to begin with. Had Hurts known earlier what the bureau had been planning, they would've had time to warn her before she had wandered off with Demitri. For once, he was glad when he ran into Miles, her imbecile of a coworker, and he had pointed him in the direction where she and Demitri had gone.

"I should've never let her meet with Demitri alone. I take some responsibility for what happened to her."

"Enzo, you had no idea that Petro would react the way he did and go after Demitri."

"No, but I know Petro and what he's capable of. Combine that with the FBI changing their approach on the case, and I should've known that events would head south. If only I had received the call a few minutes sooner, I might've gotten her out of there in time."

"She was always special to you. In the fifteen-plus years that I've known you, I've never seen you as protective of someone as you are with her."

Enzo took a deep breath as he ran his knuckles down Arianna's cheek. She didn't deserve what happened to her, especially when it involved putting her life on the line for him. He felt as if he had failed her.

"She sacrificed herself to save my life," he said as he looked up at Ambrose. "For her selfless actions, I will forever be indebted to her."

Ambrose smiled. "She is a remarkable woman. Though I have to admit, if I hadn't known about her background, I never would have pictured her as an agent."

Enzo grinned. "That is why Agent Hurts always referred to her as his secret weapon."

"What will happen to her now that the FBI has pulled back on Demitri's case?"

"I don't know for sure, but I would imagine she'll be sent back to the agency in the states. It's a shame because her abilities on the runway and in front of the camera are rare. Some models who have been in this industry for years will never meet the caliber of Arianna's talent. She could make a killing before retiring at a young age."

"The police have tried to keep the events that occurred last night on the down-low. Luckily there weren't many people on that side of the castle."

"Any mention of Arianna in the reports?"

"Not yet, but I am hearing that there were witnesses who saw you carrying a female out of the castle that matches her description. I imagine rumors will spread like wildfire."

He looked at Ambrose. "If we're asked, we know nothing."

Arianna started to stir, and Enzo stroked her hair as he spoke softly to her. "That's it, Arianna. You're safe now."

Arianna started to wake, and right away, she recognized one of the two men talking.

"That's it, Arianna. You're safe now."

Slowly she pried open her eyes, and the first thing she saw was Enzo's dark blue orbs staring at her. He was leaning over, looking down at her. It took a minute or two for the blurriness in her vision to fade, though she felt a little loopy and discombobulated.

"Enzo," she whispered, though it came out a little husky. She was lethargic, and her throat felt raw. She coughed.

"Easy now," he told her as he brushed back her hair from her face. She continued to stare at him and knew right away something wasn't right because of the concerned expression. "How are you feeling?" He asked.

She licked her lips. "Thirsty."

"Let me help you up." With Enzo's assistance, she was able to sit up and used the headboard to lean against. She winced as pain tore through her left arm. She closed her eyes, laid her head against the headboard, and took a few deep breaths until the pain subsided.

"Here you go, doll," Ambrose said, appearing next to the bed with a glass of water and two pain pills.

She took the glass from him, but her hand shook so bad that Enzo helped her raise it to her lips. She took a sip, and the cold water felt refreshing as it traveled down her throat.

"Thank you," she told both of them as Enzo took the glass and set it down on the table next to the bed.

She took a few moments to look around. The bedroom they were in was stunning and quaint—like something out of a home magazine. The lighting in the room blended with the sunny yellow walls, and colorful décor gave it a cheery atmosphere, though her mood was anything but cheerful.

"Where are we?" She asked.

"My country estate." He eyed her over. "Do you remember what happened?"

She scrunched her eyebrows together as she played back the timeline of events from the night. She had started in the room with Demitri, and then he had kissed her when Enzo barged in, ordering her to go with him. But then two armed men entered the room and started shooting. There was a lot of smoke, making it hard to see, but Enzo had gotten to her and led her to the secret door behind the wine rack. That was when…

She looked up at Enzo for confirmation, "Demitri shot me." She glanced at her arm, then back up at Enzo, and he nodded his head. She blew off the part where she threw herself in front of Enzo. "I remember everything up until we were in the tunnels. I remember I felt weak, and there was a lot of blood. I was so scared, and I was leaning on you, but after that, everything just faded to black."

"You were in shock and were bleeding pretty badly. Ambrose was able to meet us at the side exit with the car. I carried you out, and here we are."

"What about Demitri? What happened to him?"

"I honestly don't know." Enzo looked as if he had so much more to say but was struggling. He took her hand in his. "Arianna, I can't begin to tell you how brave you are. The bullet you took was meant to end my life."

She covered his hand. "Enzo, I would've done that—" *Wait…did he just call me Arianna?*

She looked at him, and he stared at her waiting for her to continue.

"What did you just call me?"

"Arianna is a beautiful name," he told her, and instantly she became alarmed and pulled her hand back quickly, ignoring the pain in her arm. How did he know her name? For three years, she had been extra careful to only go by Anna. Had he figured out she was working for the FBI? Or worse, did he think she was investigating him? She felt sick to her stomach. She started to slide out of bed, ignoring the pain, but Enzo stopped her by placing his hand on her thigh.

Enzo hurriedly assured her that everything would be fine. But in her opinion, everything wasn't okay. Nobody was supposed to know her true identity.

"Don't be alarmed. Agent Hurts should be here soon, and when he arrives, he'll explain everything to you."

She didn't want to wait for Agent Hurts to get there. She wanted to know what in the hell was going on now and, most notably, how did Enzo know her real name?

"Tell me now," she demanded, glaring at him. "What in the hell is going on. How do you know my name?"

He pressed his lips tight and looked away from her. She knew the look. It was what he did when he was either angry or annoyed. Finally, after a few tense moments, he turned back to her.

"Your people fucked up. That's what happened."

She stared up at him in shock.

"If it wasn't for a phone call from Agent Hurts, there's no telling what would've happened to you."

She pressed her fingertips to her forehead. This new information was mind-blowing yet confusing.

"I don't understand; why were you in contact with Agent Hurts?"

"I may dabble in some borderline dealings that your government frowns upon, but I'm in a position where I can provide substantial and damaging information on others who your government agencies seek on more high-profile crimes. I'll be completely transparent with you. I've never endangered or did wrong to an innocent person."

She thought about his comments for a moment before responding. "Are you saying that you're an informant? Have you been working with the agency the whole time?"

He looked away.

"Enzo..." She squeezed his hand. "You've never once lied to me. At least I don't think you have."

He turned his head towards her and squeezed her hand back. "Never. I've always respected you. Not once have I ever betrayed you."

They were staring at each other when the doorbell rang, bringing their conversation to a halt.

"That would be Agent Hurts."

Ambrose excused himself to go and answer the door.

Before Hurts made it to the bedroom, Enzo placed his palms against her cheeks and stared into her eyes. "No matter what happens after tonight, know that I will always have your back."

He went to stand up, but she grabbed his arm.

"Does anyone else know my identity?"

"No."

"Will, I ever see you again? At least answer that."

Without saying a word, he pulled her into a hug, and her heart sank because it felt like a goodbye hug. There was never any romantic attraction between the two—only a great friendship and one she would cherish for the rest of her life.

"Eis to Epanidein." *Until we meet again*, he murmured to her, and she smiled as she looked up into his eyes.

"Until we meet again, Enzo."

He stood just as Agent Hurts appeared in the doorway and rushed to her side. But she couldn't tear her eyes away from Enzo. She had friends back home, but for the last two years Enzo had been her only friend that she could trust and wouldn't stab her in the back.

Moments later, she watched as Enzo disappeared into the hallway, and then Ambrose appeared, following behind Agent Hurts.

"Ms. Roland, should you wish to change clothes before your departure, Enzo left some spare clothing in the bathroom."

She gave him a soft smile. "Thank you, Ambrose."

Once Ambrose left the room, she turned her attention to the FBI agent, who had a lot of explaining to do.

"Chris?"

Agent Hurts stood next to the bed. "First things first. Are you okay?"

She glanced down at her bandaged arm but then thought about how she was feeling mentally. The news that Enzo had dropped just minutes ago had her head swimming with all kinds of questions she wanted to ask. Not to mention the trust she had instilled in Agent Hurts for the last two and a half years that left her wondering what else he may have kept from her. She was hurt not only physically, but mentally as well.

"I think I'll live," she snapped, keeping her answer short.

Agent Hurts frowned. "Arianna."

She let out a frustrated sigh and looked at him. "Okay, it hurts like hell," she admitted and pointed to her arm. She was exhausted, frustrated, and sore. She just wanted to go to her apartment alone and decompress.

She saw the remorse and worry in his eyes. She didn't want his pity. She was angry and hurt. Sure, she was taught in her brief but thorough training never to wear your feelings on your sleeve, but deceit stung. She could've been seriously injured, or worse, killed last night, and it could've been prevented. All she needed was a heads up.

"Arianna, we need to talk about last night."

She gave him a funny look with her head tilted. "Ya think?"

He pressed his lips together and gave her a stern look. "How bad is your arm?"

She shrugged her shoulders. "I don't know. I didn't have a look at it. I just woke up a little while ago. It was already bandaged."

"We need to get you a doctor and get it looked at."

She shook her head. She trusted Enzo, and because of that bond, she trusted the person he had brought in to stitch her up.

"Enzo took care of it. In fact, Enzo took care of a lot of things last night, including saving my life." She laughed sarcastically. "You'd think my employer would have the best interests of its employee at heart, but last night proved my instincts wrong."

"Arianna, let me explain."

She held her hand up. She needed to know one answer first. "How long has Enzo known my identity?"

He let out a frustrated sigh. "Enzo has been a trusted informant for certain divisions in the FBI for years. Knowing you were going into this operation with no experience, the agency and myself felt more comfortable knowing someone had your back on the inside."

"But I had Miles," she argued.

He squinted his eyes. "Yeah, and how did that turn out? We don't even know Miles' whereabouts."

That wasn't surprising news, though it was concerning.

"Enzo was brought on for precautionary reasons only. It doesn't mean that we didn't think you weren't capable of taking care of yourself; we all knew how dangerous and aggressive this industry is, and you were going into it blind."

He did have a point. Enzo had saved her ass early on because of her lack of experience.

"Why didn't you tell me?"

"Because everything had to look real."

She nodded her head. "What was the deal with last night?"

Hurts' expression grew angry. "The bureau, for the most part, pulled the plug on Demitri's case." He explained everything that went down with Agent Gabbert except for the part about the complaint being filed against her. "I didn't have any way of contacting you, and Miles wasn't answering. Thankfully Enzo answered. And here we are now."

"Did the agency take Petro into custody? What happens with Demitri? Does the bureau just forget the fact that he's responsible for hundreds of girls who've been trafficked across the world, many of whom probably aren't even alive anymore thanks to the cruel and evil owners who purchased them?"

"I'm just as pissed as you are. As for Petro, he was killed during the ordeal last night by Demitri's men. I'm sure now the bureau will re-focus on Demitri, but I'm pretty sure that Demitri retreated into hiding after last night."

That news pissed her off. Then she wondered what her role going forward was.

"What happens now?"

"We pack up and go home," he said, sounding defeated. "The bureau is already working on a cover for your abrupt disappearance."

"Wow…just like that? We're just dismissed?"

"That's the world we work in."

"So, will I go back to working for Sam?"

"I honestly don't know. I hope so because you're good at what you do. amongst other things. Once you get back, the bureau will schedule a debrief with you. From there, they'll discuss your options."

"Wow. The way you say options makes me believe they'll say, 'see ya. later, and don't let the door hit you in the ass'."

"Well, look on the bright side, if the bureau chooses to shut you out, you get to walk away from all the bullshit with a pretty hefty bank account and with everything you've acquired in the last two years."

"That was really true? I get to keep everything?"

He smiled. "All of it. You deserve it."

"Hmmm…that's good to know, but I'd rather work and put my expertise to good use."

"If I have any say so in the bureau's decision, I have your back, one hundred percent."

She smiled. "Thank you. I appreciate it." But in the back of her mind, she wondered if she even wanted to stay with an organization like the FBI where your colleagues could turn on you. Did she really want that? She had a lot to think about—that was even if the agency agreed to keep her on.

Agent Hurts stood and looked around. "Ambrose mentioned that Enzo left you a change of clothes in the bathroom. Once you're changed, we can head out."

"Back to my apartment?"

He shook his head. "No, the airport. There's a plane waiting for us. A team has been dispatched to clear out your apartment. Everything will be shipped back to the agency, and you'll be able to pick it up there."

"Okay," she mumbled. What else was she supposed to say? This was really happening. Why did it feel like she failed?

Chris helped her off the bed, and she walked to the bathroom. Once the door was shut, she leaned against the vanity and looked at herself in the mirror. She couldn't believe everything that had happened in the last two years. But in the grand scheme of it all, she was glad to be going home. She missed her dad. That would be her first stop after she met with the bureau.

Christmas was just weeks away. Being home would make an excellent present for her dad.

She looked over the pile of clothes that Enzo had left for her on the vanity. She chuckled when she saw the deep purple bra and panty set with a note attached that said in exchange for the lingerie; he wanted a picture of her in it. It was one of Enzo's designs from last year that she had fallen in love with but hadn't been able to convince him to give her one. She knew he wasn't serious, but she may just do it to mess with him. As she picked up the clothes, something fell to the floor. She bent down to pick it up and realized it was her clutch from last night. She had set it down on one of the tables when she was with Demitri. She had forgotten all about it until now. Enzo must've picked it up.

Once she was cleaned up and changed, she met Chris downstairs. Ambrose was there to see them off, but Enzo wasn't to be found. She was overcome with sadness, knowing she wouldn't be seeing him again, but she was grateful for his generosity and hospitality the last two years. She would definitely miss him.

The drive to the airport took about forty-five minutes. When they arrived, they immediately boarded the Gulfstream jet that was waiting for them. Being as it was just the two of them, there was more than enough room to spread out. As soon as they were both seated, the pilots wasted no time closing the door and firing up the engines. She leaned her head back against the headrest and looked out the window as they taxied onto the runway. Before she knew it, the plane was racing down the runway and lifted into the air. As they gained altitude, they banked to the left, giving her a bird's eye view of the place that she had called home for the last two years. It was a gorgeous sight to see. She kept looking until the land was no longer visible. She then closed her eyes and hoped for a peaceful nine-and-a-half-hour plane ride home.

CHAPTER SIX

Demitri closed his eyes and gritted his teeth as Carmine tended to the bullet wound to his side. Thankfully it hadn't hit anything significant internally, but it still hurt like hell and needed to be stitched up.

"Sorry, boss."

He waved him off. It wasn't the first time he'd been shot, and most likely wouldn't be the last. What he was more concerned about was his missing flash drive. That specific drive had critical information stored on it, and if it fell into the wrong hands, it could spell trouble for his organization and him personally - although it would take an expert computer hacker and coder to access the files. If they did, they would see every fucking thing on his human trafficking operation.

"Any word on Anna or the flash drive?" Demitri asked Carmine.

"Nothing yet. All we know is that Enzo exited the building with her. As for the flash drive, I have a couple of men stationed at the castle to search the room once the police presence has cleared."

Demitri cursed and slammed his hand down onto the table.

"Fucking Enzo! That bastard is up to something. He had to have been the one who stirred up shit with Petro. How did Petro even know I'd be here? Any word on Petro's status?"

"Dead," Camine said with a deadpan look.

"I hope to hell one of our men took his ass out."

Carmine shook his head. "The FBI is pointing the finger at you, but there was a witness who said that it was an FBI agent who shot him."

"So the FBI was there?" Demitri started to get that feeling in his gut that he had been betrayed. But with so many options to choose from, he wasn't sure who he should seek out first. But one that they had been warned about earlier stood out—the Black Swan.

Carmine secured a bandage to Demitri's side then stood up. He stared down at him. "I know what you're thinking, and I don't think you should jump to conclusions just yet."

Demitri stared up at him. “You don’t think she was involved?”

“No. For the simple fact, she was seen leaving with Enzo. No agent would be caught with someone with his reputation. They are very close. From what I was told, the FBI was there to arrest Petro.”

Demitri was surprised at that revelation. “Petro, huh?”

“Rumor circulating around town is he double-crossed one of his suppliers, and they turned on him. They planted some evidence incriminating some of Petro’s dealers around the city, and when the police brought them in for questioning, they squealed. Our contacts made sure that criminally you were in the clear by being at the castle.”

His mind kept going back to Anna. How he wished the evening had turned out differently because he was confident that he’d be inside her at this very moment. He wanted to explore every inch of her body.

He glanced at Carmine, who was cleaning up the blood-stained towels. “I need to find her. I’ve had a taste of her, Carmine. She is addicting, and I want her.”

Carmine smirked. “I knew you wouldn’t let her go. I’ve got men looking into her whereabouts. We know she lives in the city, but we can’t find anything registered to Anna Humphreys.”

“She could be using an apartment owned by Claude. He’s known to put his models up in a residence under his name or his company.”

“We’ll find her. The problem we face right now is Enzo and how he fits into all of this.”

Demitri stood up and buttoned up his shirt. “Someone out there knows where she is. What about that Miles guy—her agent?”

Carmine snorted. “That guy was so far off his rocker last night he’s probably lying in a ditch somewhere.”

“I bet you that if you find him, you’ll find her.”

“I still say you should look into Enzo. He’s obviously very protective of her. Look at the way he barged into the room, acting all fatherly and protective of her. His people have been quiet.”

“Do we know whose blood was on the wall?”

"No. But I couldn't tell if Anna jumped in front of Enzo or if Enzo pulled her in front of him. If she played hero, then it appears those feelings are reciprocated. She may have taken a bullet for him."

"I wanted to kill that bastard," Demitri growled out.

"You've felt that way for a long time."

"That's because he was involved in the set-up that killed my father."

"Yet you've never been able to prove that."

"Not yet, but eventually, I will. He walks around like he owns the goddamn industry."

"Yet, you are the one that everyone wants to meet. You have that whole cloak and dagger thing going on. Women and even men find that appealing. Have you ever had a model reject an offer made by you?"

Demitri smirked. "Sometimes I don't give them an option."

Carmine finished cleaning up the surgical trash. "And his day will come, Demitri. I've always told you that. Right now, we need to lay low for a while, until the FBI moves onto something or someone else."

"I'm going to lie down for a while. Wake me if you hear anything."

"Will do."

As Demitri made his way up the stairs to his bedroom, he vowed that he'd find Anna before he left Europe. She couldn't stay hidden forever.

CHAPTER SEVEN

Arianna and Special Agent Hurts had gone over the debriefing process she would face once she arrived back at the bureau. She was well aware that she would be questioned, but the grilling she met from the three directors sitting across the table from her felt more like an interrogation, and she almost wondered if she should have called her attorney.

Without Hurts present to help her defend her actions, she felt like she was on an isolated island and left to fend for herself. She'd been home for four days, and the last two had been spent at the agency being shuffled from room to room, retelling the previous two years of her life to every person at the bureau who was above her pay grade.

She hadn't seen or heard from Special Agent Hurts since he dropped her off at her apartment the night they arrived in Washington DC. The second day she spent retrieving her belongings shipped from Italy to the bureau's offices in Quantico. She hadn't realized she had accumulated so much stuff until the guy at the holding facility opened the container, and she saw how many boxes were there. It would've taken her several trips in her tiny compact Honda Civic. She ended up hiring a couple of guys with a truck to transport everything to her apartment. Her small one-bedroom apartment currently looked like a distribution center with so many boxes strewn about. She wasn't sure what she was going to do with everything.

Getting back to the conversation at hand, she eyed the agents in front of her.

"Ms. Roland, can you please tell us what ensued in private with Demitri Barros?" One of the men asked her. She also didn't miss the title the agent used—or lack of, she should say. He had addressed her as Ms., and not Agent. She wondered if that was a clue that her career was over.

Arianna sighed. She was tired of the same questions. She had hoped the last group who had questioned her had been the last of the torture, but it seemed that hadn't been the case. She had done everything by the book and followed every directive that had been given to her. She was becoming agitated with each question fired off at her.

"Agent Scarborough, I have given not only you but what feels like the entire upper echelon of the FBI, my firsthand account of the last two years of my life six times, including the events that occurred last Saturday evening. Nothing has changed since the last statement I gave," she looked at her watch, "two hours and thirty-five minutes ago."

Scarborough cast a skeptical eye in her direction. She wasn't going to let him break her. Finally, after several tense moments, one of the other men spoke. He had yet to ask her any questions but sat quietly studying the conversation at hand. She'd heard of people who were brought into situations like this because of their capabilities to read body language. Maybe that was what he was doing. And that was fine by her because she had nothing to hide.

"Ms. Roland, what is or was your relationship with Enzo Makis?"

"What?" Now that question had shocked her. Why would they ask her that when Enzo was an informant? Then the thought hit her. Did they not know? Was Enzo working secretly for Hurts?

"Enzo Makis," he repeated. "There was a complaint filed against you citing that you and Mr. Makis have a close relationship—possibly a romantic one. You do know he is a known criminal, correct?"

Of course, she knew that. The guy then slid a few photographs across the table. They all had been taken during various events. From the pictures with his arm around her, kissing her cheek, or whispering something into her ear, it would appear to someone not close or familiar with the situation that she and Enzo were engaged in more than just a business relationship. But that was far from the truth.

"You have it all wrong. These pictures don't prove anything. Enzo was just a contact in the industry. There was nothing between Enzo and me except for a business relationship."

"Pictures don't lie, Ms. Roland," he said, nodding toward the photos.

"No, but people do. Anyone that I've had contact with for the last two years can vouch for me and tell you that my relationship with Enzo Makis is strictly platonic." She was now past being agitated. She was pissed off that someone would try to ruin and discredit her name and career.

"You knew who he was, yet you let yourself become dependent on him and welcomed him into your private life."

"Oh, for crying out loud. That is ridiculous. I never saw Enzo Maki outside of industry events."

"There are pictures of the two of you at restaurants."

"He's been trying to get me to sign with his agency. Of course, he may have taken me out to dinner once or twice. But I'd like to point out that your so-called cameraman neglected to photograph the other people at the dinner party. I know for a fact that in this picture," she held up the photo of her and Enzo at the little coffee shop just down the street from her apartment, "there were three other people at the coffee shop with us."

The agent stared straight-faced at her. He looked like a pompous ass with the way he would smirk and eye over the other agents. It was like they spoke in a silent code with each other, and it was making her uncomfortable.

"During the altercation last Saturday evening, why did you purposely put yourself in front of Enzo? Why risk your life for a known criminal?"

She snapped her mouth and thought about the guy's question. She never looked at it that way. Yes, Enzo was a criminal. However, if she weren't an agent and didn't know his background, she wouldn't have known that. She turned and fixed her eyes on the man who questioned her. "I reacted. As a trained agent, I just reacted. Enzo and I were trying to get the hidden door open when Demitri approached with his weapon drawn, all the while other people were firing their weapons around us. Again, I reacted."

"So, you chose sides?"

Her temper flared at the accusations being thrown at her.

"Have you spoken with Special Agent Hurts?"

"Special Agent Hurts will have his chance to give us his account. But right now, we are asking you the questions."

"Look, I did what I did. Do I regret what I did? Absolutely not. Enzo knew what type of a man Demitri was, and he had come to the room to make sure I wasn't being taken advantage of. Enzo may run rampant in organized crime, but one thing I will credit him with is that he takes care of the people he cares about. He respects them, which is a lot more than I can say of you right now, along with everyone else who I've spoken with over the last two days. I mean, how would it look if word got out that the bureau knowingly left one of their own inside when they knew she could be in danger because of a decision they made?" She looked each man in the eye. "I'll definitely make sure that is in my report before I submit it on record."

"I would suggest you watch your tone Ms. Roland. I can have you dismissed from this bureau with a snap of my fingers."

She sealed her mouth. It already seemed as if her fate had been decided, so why bother to plead her case.

"I think we're finished for now," Assistant Director Scarborough said, giving her an odd look. "Ms. Roland. I appreciate your cooperation. We will be in touch should we have any additional questions. You are free to go."

Go, she thought to herself. What in the hell was that supposed to mean?

"I haven't been told anything since I've been back. Does this mean I go back to forensics with Sam?"

Associate Deputy Director Wilson glanced at the other two men, and judging from the blank expressions on their faces, the answer wasn't going to be good. When his eyes met hers, she saw the coldness.

"Because of the severity of the complaint levied against you, the agency has decided to place you on administrative leave until a full investigation is complete. If we have any questions, we'll be sure to contact you. Thank you, Ms. Roland."

She felt like she'd just been slapped in the face. Just like that, she was one step out of a job. With how the three men treated her, she was sure the investigation would not go in her favor. Two and a half years of alienating her family and friends. For what?

She stood from the chair with her shoulders square. As much as she wanted to lash out, she refused to show defeat or act unprofessionally.

As she walked out the door, she took a good look around, knowing this would be the last time she saw the building's insides.

It looked as if her visit back home could be a permanent move.

∽

Assistant Director Scarborough watched through the third-floor window as Arianna exited the building and walked across the street to the parking lot. Deputy Assistant Director Frye stood next to him. Associate Deputy Director Wilson had already left the room. All three of them had been dreading that conversation and felt horrible about what they had just done. Letting an agent believe they had failed was tough, but then to pile on a bogus ethics complaint was an even harder pill to swallow. He just hoped that once everything blew over she would understand why they did what they did and accept their apology.

"That woman has some fire in her," Frey said. "I'll give her credit. For the most part, she handled herself better than I thought she would."

"I hated every bit of that conversation. It literally made me sick," Scarborough stated with his teeth clenched. "We're all aware that Enzo Makis is a resource for the bureau. So, it was no surprise to hear that Arianna had become close to him."

"I noticed when we mentioned the complaint, she didn't admit to him being a bureau resource."

Scarborough gave Frey a wry grin. "And that's what makes her a good agent. She doesn't have a big mouth. From what I was told, Arianna wasn't even aware that Enzo was an informant until after the incident at the castle."

"This is a huge setback in the Barros investigation. If it wasn't for that damn Gabbert sticking his nose into the situation, we could've had someone on the inside of Demitri's organization right now. How did Gabbert even get the Director to sign off on the orders to let him go in after Petro?"

"I don't know. He somehow pleaded his case, and I guess the way it was presented, the bureau saw it as a win-win situation. They get Petro, who they believed would give up information on Demitri, and in turn, it would lead to Demitri's arrest."

"Now we're back to square one with Barros."

"Pretty much. Unless he does something drastic and irresponsible that leaves him vulnerable, but I don't anticipate that happening. I'm sure he's laying low. We have a couple of minor infractions we can bring against him, but I'd rather hold off and go for the big one."

Frye agreed. "What was Gabbert's motive for all of this, including filing a bullshit ethics complaint against Arianna?"

"Glory and revenge."

"I don't understand."

"There's someone close to Arianna that Agent Gabbert has a beef with, so what better way to get back at a person than through a family member?"

"Family?" Frey asked, clearly confused.

Assistant Director Scarborough turned to face him.

"Her father." Frye's eyebrows rose, and Agent Scarborough continued. "Arianna's father, Paul, is a former Marine—brilliant guy. Too bad the agency couldn't convince him to come on full-time. Anyway, one of Paul's friends from the Marines was recruited by the agency after he retired from the service. He had been assigned to assist Gabbert on a high-profile case. Months went by where the agent kept producing evidence against the target, but for some reason, Gabbert wouldn't take it up with brass. His excuse was that they were petty crimes and that if he were going to bring down this one target, it would be big. The agent finally got fed up and went higher up and complained. Eventually, Gabbert was removed from the team and replaced by the agent. The agent wanted to build his own team and requested to bring someone in from the outside with operative experience on a contract basis to assist."

Frye nodded. "Let me guess—he brought in Arianna's father."

Agent Scarbourgh nodded. "Yep, and within weeks the agent, together with Paul's expertise, had pulled together a pretty cohesive case against the target. They had pulled together an abundance of solid evidence on high-profile crimes the guy had committed, including murder, and the bureau issued a warrant for the suspect. When a team of agents, including Paul, served the warrant, it resulted in a massive shootout. Ultimately, the intended suspect, along with many of his adversaries were killed. Today it is still one of the most talked-about cases in the agency. Of course, it had pissed Gabbert off."

"Are you talking about the Elias Barros case?" Frye asked, staring at him.

"Yes."

Frye whistled low. "Elias was Demitri's father."

"Now you see how it is all fitting into place? Gabbert has been skating on thin ice for a long time, and the incident over in Rome, I think, may have been a breaking point for him, and he knows it and is looking for ways to deflect his own blunders by diverting the attention to others. And unfortunately, Arianna is not only a newer agent, but she clearly has a target on her back because of her dad."

Frey shook his head. "What an asshole. So what's the next step?"

"Now we wait and see how the Director wants to move forward. I do know he's been briefed on the situation and wants it resolved quickly. He also wants the Barros case moved back to the top priority list."

"Will Special Agent Hurts take back the lead for the investigation?"

"Yes. But he's going to have to put together a new team now that Arianna is out and Miles is still AWOL. And, once Hurts returns next week from his trip and finds out that Arianna has been placed on administrative leave, he's going to go ballistic."

"Shit. You didn't warn him?"

"No, because I wasn't sure what direction we were going to go. He knows about the complaint and isn't happy."

"That must be why Sam over in Forensics was pissed off earlier when I saw him."

Scarborough nodded his head. "Yeah. He had been ecstatic when he heard that Arianna was returning. But when I informed him this morning of the circumstances surrounding her leave, I thought he would explode - he was so angry. And rightfully so. Arianna is a great agent and would be a valuable resource to his team."

"Yeah, well, the problem with Hurts is that he could potentially go after Gabbert. Our job is to convince Hurts that he has to let the process run its course."

"And, Gabbert—what happens to him?"

"Associate Deputy Director Wilson should be on his way to meet with Gabbert now."

Frey raised his eyebrows in question.

"After today, Special Agent Gabbert will no longer be employed by the bureau."

"Do you think he could be a threat to Arianna?"

"I hope not, but it's hard to tell. He's a crazy son of a bitch. We just need to hang tight until the complaint levied against Arianna is complete."

"Why even investigate when we all know Gabbert's complaint has no truth to it?"

"Because he could come back after us on a legal front and claim he was fired because he filed a complaint. This way, all of our "i's" are dotted, and "t's" are crossed. Nobody can say a damn thing."

"Once Hurts returns to the office next week and I explain everything to him, I'll have him reach out to Arianna." He smirked. "After all, the bureau has all intentions on bringing her back once this blows over."

Frye gave him an odd look. "You really think she'll accept after what we have put her through the past two days?"

Scarborough shrugged his shoulders. "We can only hope."

Travis Gabbert downed another shot of tequila and slammed the glass down onto the bar.

Shane, the bartender, gave him a dirty look and shook his head.

"Why don't you slow down there, Travis?" Shane told him, and Gabbert sneered at him.

"Why don't you quit acting like my mother and do your damn job and pour me another drink?"

Gabbert took the shot glass and flung it down the bar. It almost hit one of the two guys who were sitting at the other end. Both men threw daggers his way. Gabbert didn't give a shit. He glared right back at them.

"What in the hell are you looking at?" He shouted at the two men. They just shook their heads and turned away from him.

Shane then walked over and set a glass of water in front of him.

“What the fuck is this shit?” Gabbert asked, slurring his words and curling his lip up in disgust. He came to drink, not hydrate.

Shane leaned against the bar and stared at him. Gabbert squinted his eyes.

“I asked you a question.”

Shane didn’t respond verbally. He reached over to the cash register and grabbed a small piece of paper, and placed it next to the glass of water.

When Gabbert looked closer, he realized it was his check. He took another look at Shane, who was still eyeing him.

“It’s time for you to leave, Gabbert,” Shane told him.

“You’re kicking me out?” He shouted, drawing even more attention to his behavior. When Shane didn’t answer, Gabbert pulled a wad of cash out of his pocket and threw it down on the bar. “You’re an asshole, just like everyone else in this world.”

Shane just shrugged his shoulders and walked to the other end of the bar to wait on the other customers.

Gabbert slid off the stool, then before he walked away, he purposely knocked over the whole glass of water, spilling it all over the bar and on the floor. He directed one last glare toward the others before he walked out.

He stumbled out the door and started to walk down the street. He passed by a gas station with a small convenience store attached when he decided he wasn’t done drinking for the day. He went inside and grabbed a case of beer off the shelf, and took it up to the register. There were two people in front of him. As he waited, he saw a small television behind the counter. It was airing one of those network news shows. But that wasn’t what had caught his attention. It was the person on the screen. His body began to shake with anger all over again as he watched the FBI director give an update about a big case that the agency had been involved in.

That entire agency could go fuck themselves for all he cared. After today he vowed to get even with every person who contributed to his firing. When he had been called into his Assistant Director’s office earlier today and was told he was being let go from the bureau, he thought it had been a joke. But when he was presented with exit paperwork all packaged up like a fucking present, he realized that his ousting had been planned. They tried to make it seem like it all stemmed from the incident a few nights ago involving Petro Shevchenko and Demitri Barros, but he wasn't stupid. He had a lot of enemies in the agency who'd love to see him gone. Hell, lately, it was a challenge for him just to get selected for a case as most of the seasoned agents refused to work with him because of his history.

When the bureau decided to put an undercover team together to go after Demitri Barros, he'd been the first agent to express interest in leading the team, citing his knowledge of the organization since he had been assigned years ago to the case involving Demitri's dad. But it hadn't been a huge surprise when he was rejected mainly because of the way that case had ended for him. What did infuriate him was the name of an agent who was offered a lead role in the Demitri operation Arianna Roland. Gabbert would never forget the Roland name, ever.

Ever since Paul Roland, Arianna's father, and that other agent had screwed him over on the Elias Barros case fifteen years ago, he had wanted revenge.

So, when the opportunity presented itself for him to take the lead on Petro Schevchenko's case, he snagged it and ran with it. Knowing the history between Petro and Demitri, Gabbert began to form a plan that would not only take down two criminals on the FBI's list but would redeem his name in the agency while giving the Roland family a little taste of their own medicine.

His plan would have been flawless had it been executed how it was supposed to. However, he hadn't been prepared for Petro to take matters into his own hands and screw up the entire operation. Gabbert had promised his superiors that it was a simple snatch-and-grab that would create no disturbances to the event going on. But that was far from what had transpired. It had turned into the biggest clusterfuck of his career. He tried to draw the attention away from him by filing an ethics complaint against the Roland girl, but it hadn't been enough.

He snarled his lip up in disgust. He wasn't about to let the father daughter duo get away with destroying everything he worked for. He was out for blood, and he vowed to take down anyone who got in his way. He'd show the agency just how good of an agent he really was.

CHAPTER EIGHT

Dino sat back and took a swig of his ice-cold beer. He was dragging ass and would rather be back in his own house with his feet kicked up, but he promised the guys that he'd have a drink with them at their local hangout, Bayside. Besides, it was a standing tradition that whenever the team returned home from training or a mission, they would have a drink together.

Their training for an upcoming mission had taken them out west in the middle of no man's land. It had been grueling and exhausting, but that is what they all lived for. For Dino, there was nothing like the high of an adrenaline rush that he experienced every time his feet hit the ground during a mission.

Growing up, he never had any inclination to enlist in the military. His future had been laid out for him when he was born, thanks in part to his family's business. But that all changed midway through his senior year in high school after a tragic accident left him unable to accept what his family was a part of. Knowing his parents would never approve of him joining the military, he waited until his eighteenth birthday to visit a nearby Navy Recruiters office. After talking with the recruiters there, he was convinced that the Navy was his calling. The recruiter set up an appointment for him to visit a Military Entrance Processing Station. During that visit and after speaking with a service enlistment counselor, his future with the SEALs began. Sure, he didn't automatically become one overnight. It had taken a shitload of sweat, tears, emotions, and even sometimes blood. After attending basic training at the Great Lakes Naval Training Center, he was selected for BUD/s training in Coronado, CA. It was a long sixty-five weeks later when he was awarded the famed SEAL Trident Pin. A priceless piece of metal that he would cherish for the rest of his life.

Dino looked around the table he shared with his teammates. He couldn't have asked to be assigned to a better team of men. Each man in his present company wasn't just a teammate—he was a brother, and together they were a family. Or, as Alex, Ace's fiancé, would say, they were a sometimes-dysfunctional family. But Dino wouldn't change it for the world. This was his home.

Just then, Ace's voice brought Dino out of his head and back to the present. Ace was the team's leader.

"Alex wants a count on how many are coming to the house for Christmas dinner." He looked at Potter, Stitch, and Frost. "She already knows you guys are in." His eyes moved to Irish. "What about you and Bailey?"

"I think my parents are coming to town," Irish said.

"Well, the invite extends to them as well. You know Alex and how she likes to plan a party or holiday."

"Go big or go home," They all muttered in unison, then snickered.

"Okay, then count us in, including my parents," Irish said with a smile.

Ace then looked to the three bachelors left on the team. "What about you three? Are you in?"

Both Skittles and Diego said they would be there. That just left Dino.

"You?" Ace asked, and Dino nodded his head.

"I wouldn't miss it," he replied, knowing he wouldn't be anywhere else, and considering he barely contacted his immediate family.

"Thank god everyone is in," Ace mumbled. "I know you all have a family of your own, but Alex loves you guys. She would understand if you wanted to spend the holiday with your family, but she'd be depressed if you all didn't show up."

"Anybody doing anything exciting this weekend?" Frost asked, changing the subject.

Dino lifted his bottle of Bud and smiled. "Absolutely nothing." He planned to lay low for the next two days until they needed to report back to base. His plans included his recliner, home-cooked food, and TV with a lot of football.

Dino was looking forward to a few days of rest at his place, after Ace's sister, Mia's ordeal with her former boss trying to kill her, and then traveling to the mountains out west for training, rest was just what he needed. There were times he wondered why he even bought the house on the water, considering he wasn't home half the time to enjoy it. In hindsight, he purchased the property for when he retired from the SEALs.

Eight years ago, he had been assigned to his current team in Little Creek, Virginia. Because of the town's appeal, he instantly fell in love with Virginia Beach and knew he would retire there. More so now, since many of his teammates now had families and had made it known that, they planned on establishing roots there.

Not that he was expecting to get married and raise a family because that wasn't in the plans for him. However, he envied Ace, Potter, Frost, Irish, and Stitch. They'd found their one and some even now had kids. But with his family's secret that he kept to himself, there was no guarantee that trouble wouldn't arrive at his doorstep, putting those he loved in danger.

He considered his teammates his family. They might not be his biological family, but they were loyal and acted as a family should to one another.

He and the guys talked for about another hour before they called it a night. Shortly after, Dino pulled down his street and into his driveway. He noticed there was a car parked in front of the house next door. It was about time that the asshole had rented out the property. It had sat empty for almost a year. He wasn't a fan of the guy who owned the property. He complained about everything. There was no gray area when it came to him. Dino had wanted to give the jerk a piece of his mind a little over a year ago. He had been painting the exterior of his house, and right in the middle of the project, the team had been called out. The guy had called the city on him because the place hadn't been completed, and when Dino returned from overseas, he had letters from the city threatening code violations. Once he called the city and explained who he was, what he did for a living, and why the house was only half-painted, the nice lady at city hall had deleted all the violations and even called the guy who turned him in a jerk.

He shook his head as he grabbed his bag from the backseat, and made his way inside. He smiled as he entered the house. It was always a great feeling to walk through the doors of his home. He made his way into the kitchen, and as he passed by the glass doors leading to the backyard, a mysterious light at the end of his dock caught his attention. It reminded him of the small lantern light he left out there under the bench, except it didn't look like it was under the bench. It was solar, so there were no batteries that could die and would explain why it was glowing. Curious, he unlocked the door and started down the path towards the dock.

The freezing temperature outside hadn't stopped Arianna from climbing over the chain-link fence and sneaking into her neighbor's backyard.

She had moved into a rental beach house a little over a week ago, but she had been disappointed when she arrived and saw that the landlord had torn down the existing dock in the backyard. That was the main reason she had selected the house to rent in the first place. She loved being near the water. There was nothing she could do about it now, since she had already signed the lease and paid up for the first six months.

She wondered who her neighbor was next door and assumed the person or persons living there were out of town since it had been a week and nobody had been around. At first, she had thought maybe it was a rental like hers but seeing the furniture and décor on the back patio and front porch; it was evident that someone lived there. The landscaping, even for the winter season, was immaculate. But what had caught her eye was the long wooden dock that jetted off the property. The entire last week, the dock had been teasing and tempting her. She just wanted to sit out there and listen to the water while her mind settled.

Being that it was already in the evening, she assumed the owners wouldn't be home for the night, so she had decided to be a rebel and risk it. If she got caught, she got caught. She was already down in the dumps. It would be her first offense, and she didn't even have a speeding ticket to her name, so she was pretty sure she wouldn't serve any jail time, maybe just a fine. At least she hoped.

She picked up the two oversized fuzzy blankets she had brought along and the chilled six-pack of Smirnoff Ice. Not that she was going to drink all six bottles. Surprisingly in the world, she had lived in for the last two years with drugs and alcohol at her disposal, she was a lightweight when it came to alcohol. She wasn't a big drinker—mainly, she only drank on occasion but never exceeded her limit of one drink when she was out in public. Ever since her mom was hit by a drunk driver and killed, she saw alcohol as a weapon and tended to shy away from it. But again, if the occasion called for it, she drank responsibly. Tonight, she was ready to let loose a little. She planned to spend just an hour or two listening to the sounds that nature offered as she tried to push aside all the negative thoughts in her head.

As she tiptoed through the dew-covered grass, she couldn't help the bubble of laughter that rose from her throat. She quickly slapped her hand over her mouth. She had to look ridiculous. Just because her dad was a former Marine Recon soldier didn't mean she automatically inherited his stealth. In her opinion, she felt she had been a promising agent for the bureau, but she was far from a seasoned soldier. Now, put her in front of a computer with numbers, and she was in her element. But she'd admit she was surprisingly a damn good model if she had to be. Ugh, why did that time in her life have to pop into her mind? She wanted to wash those years from her brain. Two freaking years of letting people tell her what to wear, how to stand, how to walk, how to groom herself, and the list went on.

The wood planks creaked under her feet as she padded down the long dock. From the moonlight reflecting off the ocean, she could see the water was calm, but she could still hear it as it rocked against the pylons below her.

Once she made it to the end, she was surprised at how large the sun deck was. She smiled when her eyes landed on the small section that had a roof built over it. She spread one of the blankets out under the covered area before lowering herself and settling in. She used the other blanket to cover herself. Once she was all settled, she started to lean back against the railing when something below the bench on the other side caught her eye. It was a small lantern. She leaned over and pulled it closer and smiled when she saw it was solar-powered. It looked like an expensive tactical one, something her dad would invest in. With a flick of the button, the darkness surrounding her illuminated into a soft glow.

Smiling, she grabbed one of her ice-cold drinks, twisted the top off, and took a big sip before she laid her head back. It was perfect, she thought, as she closed her eyes and just listened to the sounds of the tranquil water around her.

Dino made sure to keep his footsteps light as he made his way to the dock. It was a trait he was taught courtesy of his SEAL instructors during BUD/s training. As he neared the end of the dock where it opened up to the sun deck, he heard a female voice that sounded like humming. He couldn't make out the song, but he'd say it sounded rather nice.

When he rounded the last pylon, all he could see was a mass of long wavy black hair as her head was turned in the opposite direction. He stood there listening to her hum, which he recognized as *Carrie Underwood's—Jesus Take the Wheel.*

He looked around, noting that it didn't seem like she was doing anything illegal. Well, except for the fact that she was trespassing on private property.

After another minute of her singing, he thought it was time to reveal himself and find out who in hell the chick was and why she was on his dock.

"Can I help you?" He asked in a deep voice, but then wanted to laugh at the reaction he got from her.

The woman shrieked as she turned her head and looked over her shoulder. When his eyes landed on her face, he was instantly taken aback by her beauty. She had gorgeous, almond-shaped eyes, especially when they widened in surprise. He almost laughed out loud when the word "shit" slipped out of her mouth as she tried to scramble to her feet but then got tangled in the big-ass blanket she was wrapped up in like a burrito.

Thank goodness for his quick reflexes as he was able to grab her arm before she face-planted into the wood decking.

She was mumbling something he couldn't make out as he helped her to her feet. Once she was steady, he released her arm then took a step back to get a better look at her.

Again, he had to hide his amusement when she looked up at him, and her cheeks turned a bright shade of red. He looked down and noticed the drinks. One bottle was empty, and another was almost empty.

He looked back at her, and she began to fidget under his stare. It was apparent she had a nice little alcohol buzz going on. His instincts told him she wasn't a threat, although he was still cautious. But he was more curious about why she was outside in the cold and in all places, his dock.

She nibbled on her lip—a classic sign of guilt. Tenley, Potter's wife, did it all the time when she was guilty of something.

"I'm guessing you are the owner of this gorgeous piece of property," she asked in a soft voice. The vapor from her breath was visible in the cold air.

He nodded, and she smiled. She had a gorgeous smile.

"And I'm guessing you're wondering why a total stranger is making themselves at home on your dock."

He nodded again, and she extended her hand. "I'm Anna; you're new neighbor."

That tidbit had completely caught him off guard. His surprised expression showed as he took her hand in his. Her skin was soft and smooth. He tried to get a look at her body, but the bulky sweats she wore presented that as a mystery, leaving his imagination to get the better of him. Her face was flawless, free of make-up, and her skin glowed with an olive complexion. She was stunning.

"It's nice to meet you, Anna. I'm Dino." He didn't release her hand. To his surprise, he liked how it felt in his. It was a weird feeling that hit him. He should be pissed off that someone, a total stranger, came onto his property uninvited, but he wasn't. However, he was curious as to why. "Do you make it a habit of sneaking onto your neighbor's property?" He questioned with some humor in his voice, but again he was curious about her answer.

She pulled her lip between her teeth, and he wanted to laugh. She obviously knew she was guilty and was debating what she was going to say, so he waited. He had all night.

Finally, she let out a frustrated sigh. "I'm sorry. I know it was wrong, but I rented my house mainly because it had a dock." She glanced next door and pointed to wooden pylons sticking out of the water where a dock once stood. "But my landlord decided to tear it down a week before I moved in, and, well, your dock just looked so inviting I couldn't resist. I love the water, needed some fresh air, and it just called to me. It is beautiful out here." She looked down and eyed the one empty bottle of Smirnoff and the other one that didn't have much left and then grinned as she met his gaze. "The alcohol helps with relaxation."

He couldn't hold back his laughter. He couldn't fault her for being honest, and he definitely wasn't going to send her home. Surprisingly he found himself intrigued and wanting to know a little more about his new neighbor.

He wasn't that comfortable inviting her inside, but if he was going to hang out for a little bit, he wasn't going to freeze his ass off. He walked over to the far post and flipped the switch. He liked to spend time out on the dock as well, so he had a heater installed when he bought the house. It was in the ceiling of the overhang on the dock. He smirked when he heard her gasp when the heat started blowing down where she had made her little bed. She closed her eyes and tilted her face up toward the blower.

"Damn, that would've been nice to know. I've been freezing my ta-ta's off for the last hour or so."

He chuckled, then waved his hand for her to have a seat.

"You mean you aren't going to kick me out?" She asked, looking shocked.

"For some strange reason, no."

She lowered herself back onto the blanket and held up a bottle of Smirnoff. "Want one?"

"Sure, why not," he told her then followed her down to the blanket. He twisted the top off the bottle and took a sip. He made a pucker face. Smirnoff wasn't his choice of drink, but since she was being polite and had offered, he wouldn't complain.

She stared at him for a few seconds as if sizing him up before saying, "I am trying to figure out if you are for real and not just some hot figment of my imagination. I mean, I've had two drinks, and normally one is a good stopping point for me."

He barked out a laugh. "I promise, I'm real." He pointed at the three remaining bottles. "Are you going to make me drink by myself?"

"Uh...Let me repeat that; I've had two drinks already, and normally one is a good stopping point for me. I mean, hell, I don't need to be stumbling or rolling off the dock into the water."

Funny and beautiful, he thought. He grabbed a bottle and twisted the top off, and handed it to her.

"I promise I won't let you get swallowed up by the water."

She accepted the full bottle and took a small drink.

"I have to ask, is Dino your real name?" She asked with a small smile.

He grinned. "No. Dino is my nickname. While I was out with some buddies hiking, I stumbled across some dinosaur fossils. They started calling me Dino, and it just stuck."

Her eyes widened. "Really? You found a dinosaur?" She shifted her body so she was facing him. "Where?"

"Honest to god's truth. We were backpacking near Patagonia, Argentina. I tripped over what I thought were some rocks, but my buddies recognized them as dinosaur fossils."

That was a mission he would never forget for as long as he lived, mainly because it had been his first deployment with his current team. They had been sent to rescue a young college kid who thought he knew everything there was about backpacking in a foreign country. Apparently, nobody told him that crime still existed, even in areas that were deemed safer than others. The guy had been spotted by a local gang flashing a wad of money while at a local market. The group had followed him back to his hotel and ended up robbing him of everything in his hotel room, and when they found out he was the son of a wealthy businessman back in the states, they kidnapped him and held him for ransom. Everyone knew that if the guy's family paid the ransom, the gang members weren't going to release the kid. They would just kill him.

When Dino and his team had extricated the hostage, they were trekking through the desert on the Argentine side of Patagonia to meet up with their ride when he tripped on what he thought were rocks. But when they examined the rocks closer, both Stitch and Skittles said they were dinosaur fossils known to that region. It had been a pretty cool find and where his nickname originated from.

"That is really cool," she stated, appearing to really be pulled into his story. Then a slow smile spread across her face. "I'll be honest. When you said Dino, the first thing that popped in my head was Dino from the Flintstones. You know Ya-ba-da-ba-do."

Dino burst out laughing, and she gave him a cheeky grin.

"Nope. But the Flintstones was one of my top five cartoons."

"Mine too. It was up there with the Jetsons, Tom and Jerry, Scooby-Doo, and The Smurfs."

Dino had to give his head a little shake. He was in unfamiliar territory. It wasn't that he hadn't ever had a drink with a woman who he didn't know. It was the woman sitting next to him talking about cartoons from the '80s and '90s that intrigued him.

He couldn't believe what his night had turned into. Since their plane had landed hours ago, he had envisioned going home and crashing in his bed. Never in his wildest dreams had he imagined coming home to find this beauty chilling on his dock. He almost looked around to see if there were cameras hidden somewhere, or if he was being punked. Or had Alex put the woman up to it as she'd been known to pull some really good pranks on the guys?

The part that surprised him the most was how much he was enjoying her company. He finished off his drink and placed the empty bottle back into the holder. He grabbed another one.

"May I?" He asked.

"I think I owe you more than one drink for not being a dick and throwing me off your property."

Anyone else, he probably would've done exactly what she just said. But he wouldn't tell her that.

"I'll find a way for you to make it up to me," he stated and threw a wink her way. He was shocked when her cheeks turned a little pink.

Now that they were engaged in conversation, he didn't want it to end.

"So, Anna, other than sneaking onto other people's docks in the middle of the night, what else do you like to do?"

"You're never going to let me forget this, are you?" She asked, smiling, and he shook his head. She shrugged her shoulders. "Honestly, I'm a pretty boring person. I like to read, not much of a TV person."

"Sorry, but I can't put you and boring in the same sentence. What do you like to read?"

"Mystery, suspense, action, with a little bit of romance thrown in."

"You lost me at the romance part. Do you work?"

"I just got into town last week, so I'm sorta in-between jobs right now."

"Where did you move from?"

"D.C."

"What did you do there? Do you have anything lined up here?" *She had to have some money to afford the rent of a waterfront home,* he thought to himself. Although she could come from a wealthy family like he was.

She played with the label on the bottle. Dino could sense his question made her uncomfortable, but then again, she surprised him, "I dabbled in the fashion industry but got tired of that. I've got a pretty good lead on something here in town."

He cocked his head sideways and grinned. "You're not going to tell me where?"

She smiled and shook her head, making her hair bounce. "I don't want to jinx it."

"Okay, fair enough."

He took another drink. He noticed she was halfway done with hers, and by the glassiness in her eyes, she was buzzed pretty good. Maybe it was a good thing he did come out here, or she really could've gotten hurt or worse.

"What did you do in the fashion industry?"

“Worked with models. What about you? What do you do?”

Interesting that she changed the subject so quickly and turned the questioning around on him, but he’d take the bait and play the game.

“I’m in the military.”

“Really? Let me guess,” she said, giving his body a once-over. “You’re definitely not a Marine, nor are you Army. In my opinion, you’re too clean-cut to be a Marine and too polished for the Army. I don’t see you flying planes, so I’m going to rule out Air Force. You have a house on the water, so I’m going to go with the Navy or Coast Guard, but I’m leaning more toward the Navy.”

Dino was impressed as he nodded.

“I’m in the Navy.”

She threw a smile his way. “My dad was a Marine.”

“Oh! You were a military brat. That explains your criminal activities,” he teased her, and she laughed.

“Oh, will you stop that!”

She bumped her shoulder into his before reaching for her bottle. Suddenly she let out an ear-piercing shriek that the neighbors three streets over probably heard. She flew to her feet and began jumping up and down while flapping her arms in the air. She was shouting for him to get it off of her.

Her abrupt actions caused him to leap to his feet. He tried to see what she was telling him to get off of her, but he couldn’t see anything, especially with her floundering around like a fish.

He grabbed her arms. “Stop!” He commanded in a deep voice, and she froze immediately. It was then when he saw the culprit of her antics. An average-sized dock spider rested just below her shoulder.

He flicked it off, and it hit the ground and crawled away. They were ugly spiders and could get pretty big, but usually, they were harmless to humans.

He turned her in his arms, and she looked up at him. “Is it gone?” She asked in a shaky voice.

“Yeah.”

She leaned against him, and he wrapped his arms around her. He could feel her warm breaths through the material of his shirt.

"Oh my god. I hate spiders. They are right up there with snakes for me," she murmured into his chest.

He held her close as he ran his hand up and down her back. He was tempted to tease her but decided against it when he saw how visibly shaken, she was. Damn, he'd hate to see her reaction to the insects and snakes that he'd had the misfortune of running into during some of his missions.

He felt her start to pull away, and he loosened the hold he had on her but didn't wholly release her. He liked the feel of her body in his arms. She appeared to be physically fit from what he could tell.

As he looked down, she raised her head, and their eyes met. The energy he felt between them was new for him, and he wasn't sure how he felt about it. She flicked her tongue out and wet her lips. Her lips were full and plump. *Fuck!* He wanted nothing more than to kiss her. It had been a while since he'd been with a woman, and he knew he shouldn't be thinking about what else he wanted to do with her. But she was testing his will.

"Dino," she called his name; her hands still rested on his waist, sending a sensational feeling through his body.

The seductive tone of her voice mixed with the raspiness in it made his dick even harder.

She shuffled her feet to step closer when suddenly she stopped and looked down toward the ground. He followed her sight and saw her foot tangled in a line rope he kept on the dock. The rope must've wrapped around her foot when she was jumping around.

"Shoot!" She exclaimed and tried to kick it off the same time he lowered to help her. They both lost their balance and fell to the dock with a hard thud. She landed on her back while he landed comfortably on top of her, nestled between her thighs. *Now, if this wasn't a sign, he didn't know what was.*

He brushed her hair from her face.

"Are you alright?" He asked, a little concerned he may have squished her. He wasn't a light man.

Her eyes held a twinkle in them. The light green color of her eyes glowed under the lighting. That was when he noticed the tiny flecks of brown mixed in. Her eyes were large and gorgeous.

"I'm good," she told him. "I guess that was one way to ruin the moment."

With an amused grin, he said, "I wouldn't necessarily say the moment is entirely ruined."

"No?"

He shook his head. "Not by a long shot."

Going against all the reasons why he shouldn't, he dipped his head to kiss her. When she never stopped him but instead closed her eyes before their mouths met, he felt victorious. He softly brushed his lips against hers, and he felt her body begin to relax under him. Her lips parted slightly, allowing him to slip his tongue inside. She tasted like green apples from her drink. As he continued to kiss her, she ran her small delicate hands over his shoulders, making his body come alive. He wanted so much more. As he slid his hand down her body, grazing the side of her breast, those negative thoughts in the back of his mind came flowing to the front, causing him to pause.

Before they went any further, he pulled back—not all the way but enough to see her eyes. As her eyes fluttered open, he saw the hunger there.

"If we go any further, I don't think I can stop," he told her as he watched for any indication that she didn't want him.

Her mouth twitched, and her hand found his ass and gave it a squeeze. "I never said you had to stop."

He had to be honest with her. This was sex. There was no promise of commitment afterward. That was just how he rolled.

"I don't date," he admitted, then waited, looking for a reaction from her. He knew that could be a deal-breaker, and he was okay with that. It would be hard to walk away from what he had within his grasps. But he just wasn't in the market for a steady relationship, and he probably never would be.

She stared back at him looked him in the eye. "I'm not looking for a boyfriend." She started to slide her hands up his shirt. Her hands felt so good touching his skin. "If we stop, you'd have to send me back next door, and then who is going to help me with the ache I have between my legs?"

For fucks sake. How in the hell was he supposed to walk away from that?

"If we do this, I don't want you to wake up tomorrow morning with regrets."

She placed her hand against his cheek. "Dino. I swear. There will be no regrets. It's obvious we both want this. Just live in the moment."

Before he could get a word in, she took his face between her hands and slowly pulled his head down. She kissed him deeply, setting off a carnal reaction within him. However, when he was with a woman, he liked to control the tempo. He took hold of her wrists, and she released his head. He brought her arms above her head. The move caused her chest to arch and her breasts to press firmer against his chest.

"Don't move," he instructed her then began to move down her body. He pushed her sweatshirt up and over her head and was pleased when he saw she wasn't wearing a bra.

He sat up as he kneeled between her legs then yanked his shirt over his head. The timer on the heater must have shut off because he felt the nip of the cold air as it blew over his skin. He wasn't worried because he planned to make some heat of his own.

Anna sat up and started running her hands all over his body. Her soft and gentle touch alone almost set him off. He was wound tight and ready to spring free. Quickly they both helped one another shed the rest of their clothing. Dino carefully lowered Anna to her back, making sure the blanket was under her. The last thing she needed was a splinter in her backside. However, it could make for a good story someday.

His eyes roamed over every luscious curve of her body. She was fit but healthy. Big tits, nice full round ass, and hips made for a woman. When she lifted her arm, he noticed a rather large bandage wrapped around her bicep.

"What's that?" He asked, and he saw a flicker of something in her eyes but it was gone in a single blink.

"Oh, I just cut myself when I was moving," she said, not nearly concerned with the injury as he was. As much as his curiosity wanted to hear more about it, he was more focused on getting inside her.

"Are you just going to stare, or are you going to do something?" Her question brought him out of the sex-induced fog. He could actually just sit back and stare at her body all day long, although the panties she still wore had to go, even though the baby blue lace design looked sinful on her.

He reached over to his jeans and pulled a condom out of his wallet. Once the condom was in place, he lowered his body, settling between her smooth and silky thighs.

"I'll apologize in advance; this is going to be fast and quick. You're too tempting, sweetheart."

Dino laced his fingers into Anna's hair and held her head in place as he crashed his lips down onto hers and devoured her moans.

He surprised himself. He was expecting it to be a quick booty call, but something about Anna called to him. He didn't want it to be over too quickly. He kissed along her neck and down past her chest, barely grazing her breasts with his tongue. As he made his way down her stomach, he gripped the waistband of her panties. She yelped and stared wide-eyed at him when he tore her panties from her body.

"Those were expensive panties," she scolded him, and he couldn't help the arrogant smirk he threw her way. "They were in the way."

Her look of shock quickly turned into bliss as he buried his face between her legs. Her moans of pleasure nearly made him cum. Before long, her body began to quiver, and he knew she was on the edge of an orgasm. He wrapped his arms around her legs and held her down as he feasted on her cream. Her body continued to tremble, and as soon as her fingers latched onto his hair, he gently bit down on her clit, and she shot off like a bottle rocket.

Arianna was still coming down from her high when she felt Dino's cock nudge against her entrance.

She opened her eyes and locked onto his dark blue orbs that were ablaze with lust and anticipation.

"I need to be inside of you," he told her before he lined up his cock and sank into her in one swift motion. She felt the walls of her channel stretch from his thick girth as he plunged into her depths.

"Oh, my god. You feel so good," she told him, panting for breath.

"Ditto," he gasped out. He pulled out and thrust back in again, and another wave of sensations crashed into her.

He slid his hands under her ass and lifted it just enough that with the new angle, his cock hit her sweet spot, sending a wave of butterfly sensations through her belly. He was relentless as he pounded into her with skill and intensity.

She recognized the all too soon sensation stirring in the pit of her stomach. "Oh shit, I'm almost there. Please don't stop," she begged as the crescendo inside her grew. Just as she was about to go over the edge, he pulled out of her. She wanted to scream and beg for him to get back inside her and finish her off.

He was silent, and she opened her eyes and their gazes locked. A weird feeling began to swirl throughout her. Something was happening, and she couldn't explain it, nor was it the time to dwell on it. He lowered her butt to the blanket before he covered her body with his. He braced himself on his forearms as he hovered over her. His expression was unreadable, but something appeared in his intense eyes. She couldn't make it out because as fast as it materialized, it was gone in a flash. Or maybe it was her imagination, considering she'd had a few drinks.

"Dino," she whispered. He continued to stare into her eyes the vapor of their breath visible in the cold air floated between two of them. She ran her nails lightly up his back, and his muscles reacted—twitching under her fingertips. She wanted to question him but also didn't want to ruin the blissful moment. Thankfully she didn't have to decide as he lowered his head and his lips enclosed hers. He was gentle yet powerful. His arms moved closer to her head, and his fingers threaded through her hair. She felt his hips shift above her, and she readied herself, relaxing her inner thighs. She was lost in the kiss as he pushed into her heat again. He filled her with one powerful thrust that reignited that fire in her. She broke from the kiss as her body arched from the heavenly aura flowing through her. She moaned softly. His strokes were slow and steady, opposite from just moments ago. It felt incredible, and she didn't want it to end. But all too soon, his pace quickened, bringing both of them to the brink once again. He buried his face in the crook of her neck, his lips pressed against her skin, just as she went over the edge, and they both exploded together, their low moans echoing across the water.

"Oh my god, that was incredible," she whispered as he rolled them to the side and pulled out of her. He slipped the condom off and set it by the empty bottles before he flipped the blanket over the both of them. She curled into his body, and he kissed her temple. She felt like a limp noodle but couldn't complain because she had gotten more than she had bargained for when she set out for a night of relaxation.

"Yeah, it was."

"Dino?"

"Yeah."

"I really am sorry for sneaking onto your dock."

"Sweetheart, you are more than welcome on this dock any time you'd like."

She smiled to herself, and that was the last thing she remembered before sleep took over.

CHAPTER NINE

Arianna felt groggy as her alarm clock blared with the most annoying sound. Laying on her stomach, she reached for the table next to the bed and blindly felt around until she found the clock and hit the off button. She stretched her legs out and felt the slight ache in her muscles, coupled with a dull headache. She tried to lick her dry lips, but her tongue felt like it was stuck to the roof of her mouth. Jesus, talk about a major case of cottonmouth. Good grief. How much had she drank last night?

She opened her eyes which felt gooey and crusty from sleep. She turned her head toward the table next to the bed, and the first thing she saw was a bottle of water and a bottle of Tylenol sitting there. That was odd because she didn't remember putting those there. She didn't even remember how she got back to her place, let alone in bed and dressed. Rolling to her back, she groaned again at the ache she felt in her inner thigh muscles, wondering if she had pulled one of them.

As she lay in bed staring at the ceiling, the vivid images of last night's happenings became clearer. She bolted up and grabbed her head as the pain intensified. Cradling her head in her hands she asked herself, "Did I really have sex with a complete total stranger?" If that wasn't bad enough, she remembered the stranger was her next-door neighbor.

What had she done? How embarrassing. How was she supposed to act if she saw him? She could always avoid him. That would be awkward since they'd eventually run into each other sometime or another.

She groaned as she ran her hands down her face. "Way to go, Arianna, what a way to make a first impression." At least she remembered she hadn't told him her real name. She wasn't sure why she decided to introduce herself as Anna. But seeing how things turned out last night, maybe it was for the best. As long as they stayed just neighbors, he didn't need to know her on a personal level. *Considering he stuck his penis in you, how much more personal could you get?* The little devil in her subconscious told her. She wanted to swat that little she-devil right off her shoulder. But she did have a point.

She glanced at the clock and shook her head. She couldn't dwell on something she couldn't erase. Right now, she needed to get her butt out of bed and dressed. She had a lot of running around she needed to do, starting with Christmas shopping for her dad. He was going to be so surprised when she showed up at his house tomorrow for Christmas Eve. He wasn't expecting her until New Year's Eve. Later in the afternoon, she had an appointment to get her stitches removed at a medical clinic where she was lucky enough to snag a last-minute appointment. Thank the lord for that because she was ready to pluck the suckers out herself.

After she pulled herself out of bed, took a shower, and got dressed, she made herself some toast to put something in her stomach. The Tylenol had helped with her headache. She poured some coffee into her to-go cup and grabbed her purse and keys. As she made her way to her car, she glanced over at the house next door. Jesus, she couldn't believe she had actually not only snuck onto her neighbor's dock and got busted, but then had gone ahead to screw the guy. She couldn't stop the slow Cheshire Cat smile that spread across her face. She couldn't lie; it had been some crazy and fantastic sex. Considering it had been over three years since she'd been with a guy, she didn't have much to compare to. He was carved like a Greek statue. She did remember him saying he was in the Navy. Maybe his ship would be coming up on tour, and she wouldn't have to see him. She saw his car wasn't in the driveway, and she blew out a sigh of relief.

"You did what?" Diego asked, looking at Dino as if he'd lost his mind. And maybe he had. He still couldn't believe it this morning when he woke up. Judging from Diego's unreadable reaction, perhaps it had been a bad decision.

Dino grabbed the piece of plywood from the pile and positioned it against the two-by-fours. He felt a twinge of anxiety. He'd had one-night stands before, but this particular one topped the charts. One he wouldn't mind a repeat of, but he needed to tread the water carefully. When he was inside her there at the end with his face buried in her neck and her arms were wrapped around him, an odd sensation had hit him. It was like a jolt of energy had struck his body. It was powerful, and something he hadn't experienced before. She touched parts of him deep inside parts he thought he had closed off forever.

Thoughts of Marianna popped into Dino's head. *No!* He shook his head, trying to erase the images of his first love from his brain. He wasn't going down that path again. There was a reason he vowed never to love again, and he was sticking with that.

"You make it sound like I made a bad decision."

Diego chuckled. "I'm not saying that. Hell, we've all had our fair share of hookups. From how you described her, I might have been tempted. Have you seen her yet?"

Dino shook his head. "No, after I got her back to her place and in bed, I went back to my place, showered, and then got in the car and came over here."

"Dude, you can't avoid her. You are bound to see each other, considering you do live next door to each other."

Dino sighed. "I know."

"Who knows, maybe she could be the one. Maybe you're destined to be the next bachelor to succumb to matrimony," Diego teased, but Dino didn't find the same amusement that Diego had.

"Not me. Plus, she isn't interested in a boyfriend. She told me so. So, there's that."

"Man, whoever hardened that heart of yours all those years ago really did a number on you. But you need to remember that not all people are like whoever it was. Hell, look at the guys on the team. Whoever thought Potter would've found what he was looking for in Tenley? Then take Irish as another example; he was just a horny motherfucker who never dreamed of settling down, but then Bailey came along and knocked him for a loop. What I'm trying to say is that there is somebody out there for everyone. And sometimes you find it instantly, but then sometimes you have to search for it."

Dino dropped his head. Diego was right; not all women were liars and disloyal as Marianna had been. He never spoke about his past with guys on the team, especially the situation with Marianna. There was so much more to the story than her being just a girlfriend who broke his heart.

"What did you say she did before moving here?" Diego asked.

Dino shrugged his shoulders before hoisting another piece of plywood and holding it while Diego shot the nails in with the air gun.

"She said something about fashion. Whatever that means. She seemed like she was seasoned at deflecting questions posed to her. She gave concise answers and would then turn the questioning back to me. She was very smooth in the way she went about it."

"Huh. That doesn't really say much about her. Any family around?"

"Not sure. We didn't get that far into the questioning."

Diego grinned. "I still can't believe you slept with someone who trespassed on your property. Wait until the guys hear about this."

"Oh, come on. You're not going to tell them, are you?"

Diego chuckled. "If you don't, I will. This is classic. Since Irish is married now, there hasn't been anybody to pick on."

Dino shook his head. He was screwed and knew there was no way out of it. He was concerned, though, with how he and Anna would interact, being that they were neighbors. And like Diego said, they were going to have to face each other eventually.

He chuckled to himself. She had definitely been a welcome home surprise.

Arianna knew she was in trouble the moment she exited the medical clinic and saw the sign on the yellow and green building across the street—*Virginia Beach Rescue Shelter.*

She was a sucker for all dogs and had always wanted to adopt a rescue dog, but she wasn't able to with her job in the city. But now that it looked like she'd be staying in town, maybe a little companion by her side was what she needed.

With her other errands completed, she decided to go see the dogs. She crossed the road and entered the building. As soon as she stepped inside, she was greeted by a cute blonde girl at the counter.

"Hi! Welcome to Virginia Beach Rescue Shelter."

Arianna smiled at the young, bubbly woman. "Thank you."

"Can I help you?"

Arianna walked up to the counter. "I'm interested in adopting a dog. Can you tell me what the process entails and the costs associated with it?"

"Absolutely. By the way, my name is Grace." She reached her hand out, and Arianna shook it.

"It's nice to meet you, Grace. My name is Arianna."

"That is a gorgeous name."

"Thank you."

"So, what kind of dog are you looking for? Big, small, certain color, particular breed, age?" Grace fired off questions that Arianna hadn't really thought about.

"I don't know. To start, maybe one that isn't very temperamental?"

"That's a start. How about your living conditions? There are a lot of factors that alone can determine the type of dog that would be right for you."

Grace was really good at her job. Arianna hadn't even considered that. Her lease did allow for her to have a pet. She had a nice sized yard that was fenced, so plenty of secured room for an animal to get plenty of exercise. She had always gravitated toward a larger breed of dog. She repeated to Grace everything she had just thought of, and Grace smiled.

"Perfect! We have several dogs that I think you'd be compatible with. Why don't we go in the back to the kennels, and you can have a look and see if any stand out?"

As they made their way toward the back kennels, Grace explained more about the adoption process and a small administrative fee that didn't bother Arianna. Being that the shelter was a no-kill shelter, Arianna knew they ran off of donations and grants.

Arianna could hear some of the dogs barking as they got closer, and it made her smile. It was as if they knew she was coming, and they were vying for her attention.

She walked down the row of kennels, but none had called to her though they were all cute. When she thought she was out of luck, she spotted a rather large grey dog with a small white patch on his chest in the second to the last kennel on the left. He just sat there watching her. As she walked closer, their eyes met, and instantly, she knew this was the dog she wanted. She turned toward Grace who was fixing a gate that one of the other dogs had tried to push open and had bent the latch.

"What's the story with this big guy?" She asked as she held her hand up to the fence. She smiled when the dog lifted his paw and gave her a high five.

Grace grinned. "This mammoth here is Nigel. He is a total sweetheart. He may be huge, but he's a big softy. A tad bit clumsy, with a little bit of a mischievous streak in him."

"What do you mean by mischievous?"

"He is inquisitive about things and tends to wander." Arianna didn't see anything wrong with that. Most dogs were curious. Grace looked at Arianna and continued as she pointed to a hole in the ceiling. "See that?" Arianna nodded. "About two weeks ago, we had to repair the kennel he was in, so I let him out since we were closed. One of the technicians from the vet clinic next door had left the door to the attic stairs open, and Nigel decided to go exploring upstairs. Part of the space doesn't have finished flooring."

Arianna covered her mouth, knowing what was coming. "He fell through the ceiling?"

"Yep. It scared the living daylight out of me. I was standing right over there when he came crashing through the ceiling. Luckily he wasn't hurt." She snickered. "Well, maybe his ego."

Arianna couldn't help but chuckle. That must've been a sight to see. All she could picture in her head was an episode from Scooby-Doo when Scooby found himself in an awkward position, and he'd say, "Ruh-roh."

"Do you want to meet him? Nobody else is here, so you can spend some time with him outside," Grace asked her.

Arianna smiled and looked at the dog. "What do you say, Nigel? Want to get to know each other?"

When the dog let out a loud bark, both Arianna and Grace laughed. "I guess that means he's up for it," Arianna said.

"Let me grab a leash, and I'll be right back," Grace told her.

While Grace went back to the front of the kennels to get a leash, Arianna knelt next to where the dog still sat, looking at her. She smiled at the pooch. "So, Nigel, huh?" She asked the animal, and he pressed his face up against the fence. Arianna stuck her fingers through the metal and scratched behind his ears. He had shiny, short hair.

"Here we are," Grace said, returning with a long lead.

Once they got him on the leash, Arianna led him out into the yard. She played with him a little with the ball. He loved to play fetch.

"What type of breed is he?" Arianna asked as the dog trotted over and sat down right next to her.

"Dr. Chambers, the clinic and shelter owner next door, believes he is a Great Dane and Lab mix. He's estimated to be about a year and a half old. I won't lie; he has a big appetite."

"I bet he does." That didn't bother Arianna. The gray and white pup was a total sweetheart, and she was already in love. He jumped up onto his hindlegs surprising Arianna. In that position, he was about as tall as her. Another lick to her face had her giggling.

"Nigel seems to be smitten with you," Grace told her.

"How long does the adoption process take? Are there home visits involved?"

"Nope. We can get everything processed today, and Nigel is free to go with you if you're interested."

Arianna bent down and scratched Nigel behind the ears. "You want to come home with me?" She asked him, knowing she probably looked stupid talking to a dog. But she couldn't stop laughing when Nigel started making an odd noise like he was moaning, but it almost sounded like he was trying to talk to her by the different tones. It was hilarious.

She looked up at Grace and smiled. "He is definitely coming home with me."

Grace beamed and clapped her hands together. "Excellent! Give me about fifteen to twenty minutes to get his paperwork all printed out. You guys can stay out here if you'd like."

It hadn't even been fifteen minutes, and Grace returned with a pocket folder and a medium-sized tote bag.

"Here are all of his papers—shot records, check-ups, and adoption papers. He is also microchipped, so if this little rascal gets lost, he'll be registered back here. In the bag are some doggie treats, his heartworm pills, and few other goodies for him."

Arianna thanked Grace, and she and Nigel headed to the car. She opened the back door, and he jumped in. She laughed when he climbed through the opening in the center, took the front passenger seat, and sat down. "Okay, boy, you ready to start this adventure?"

When his tail wagged, and he gave her another lick and made that moaning noise again. She knew this had been a great idea.

CHAPTER TEN

It was late in the evening when Agent Hurts entered his home in a quiet subdivision in Alexandria, Virginia. His day had been a complete shitshow of meetings with directors from various divisions across the agency. All of them linked to the clusterfuck that went down in Rome a week and a half ago.

Usually, after an assignment had been concluded, the merry-go-round of debriefing meetings was conducted immediately within days of arriving back at the agency. However, he had been rerouted the morning after he and Arianna had returned because of an urgent situation in Kansas City that warranted his presence. It had been related to a cold murder case from eight years ago that involved an undercover agent.

He walked into the kitchen, went straight for the refrigerator, and grabbed a cold beer before heading into the living room. He sank into the sofa, propped his feet up on the coffee table, and twisted the cap off the bottle. He took a big swig and sighed.

Damn, that tastes good and is exactly what I needed after a day like today, he mumbled to himself.

He had totally been blindsided when he arrived at bureau headquarters earlier and visited the Forensics division expecting to find Arianna down there working. That was when Sam, her former boss, had filled him in on what had happened. He, too, was upset at the accusations Gabbert had leveled against Arianna.

At least Gabbert's sly tactics had finally caught up to him. Hearing that he had been let go was the only positive news he'd gotten all day.

After hearing what happened with Arianna during her debrief, Hurts was pissed off and concerned that the agency wouldn't get her back when the time came. He wanted to be present during her meetings, but he was unable to because of his impromptu trip.

During his conversation with Scarborough, Frey, and Wilson, he made it clear that while he understood their decision to place Arianna on administrative leave, they needed to accept that she may not want to return to the agency. He had been under the impression that the three higher-level directors were going to explain the entire situation to her and why they did what they had done. But instead, they went and acted like she was guilty, ultimately driving her away.

He also now understood why Gabbert held so much hatred toward Arianna. The guy was a total douchebag. Scarborough had also told him that the bureau was looking into other investigations that Gabbert had been a part of. Once the news of his firing was broadcasted through the bureau, some employees came forward with some complaints and concerns of their own. When they were asked why they hadn't come forward earlier, their response had been that they were fearful of Gabbert because they saw what he had done to others who had crossed him.

He let out a frustrated sigh.

He had tried to call Arianna earlier in the day to check in with her, but her phone went straight to voicemail. He had driven by her apartment on his way home, but after knocking on her door for about five minutes, her neighbor had come out and told him that she moved out about a week ago. When he asked if he knew where she went, the guy just shrugged his shoulders.

He was aware that Arianna lived a relatively private life and wasn't one to talk about her personal life much. After he left her apartment and was driving home, he called Sam to see if he had heard anything from her, but Sam had been surprised to hear she moved as well. He did remember that she mentioned she had family in Virginia, but Virginia was reasonably large. Since Sam had still been in the office, he tried to access Arianna's file, but it had been locked down, which was odd, adding to the mystery surrounding the situation.

Hurts felt that he had let Arianna down. Arianna had been one hell of an agent, and if the bureau hadn't pulled the plug on the assignment, he was confident that she would've succeeded in cracking the Barros case wide open and exposing Demitri for the piece of shit he was.

Now that the investigation into Demitri's trafficking scheme was back on the agency radar, Hurts had to develop another plan of action to bring Demitri down. The previous plan couldn't be used any longer since Gabbert had sabotaged it.

He reached for the burner phone on the coffee table and pulled up Enzo in the contacts. It rang twice before the loud Greek answered.

"I expected to hear from you sooner, Agent Hurts," Enzo stated with a hint of sarcasm in his tone.

Hurts leaned back on the couch. "Yeah, I thought that too, however, duty called, and I just got back in town last night."

"What can I do for you?"

"Got any news for me?"

"I thought your agency had backed off the Demitri case."

Hurts let out a frustrated sigh. "As of today, it's back on the agency's top five case list."

Enzo was quiet for a few moments before he finally spoke. "And Arianna? How is she?"

Hurts explained how Arianna had been railroaded by someone within the agency, though he didn't give names.

"That's complete horseshit," Enzo commented.

"You're preaching to the choir."

"How is she holding up with the accusations against her?" Enzo asked, clearly concerned, and Hurts couldn't blame him as he felt the same.

"I haven't spoken to her. She won't answer her phone, and her apartment is empty."

"Damn."

"I know. I've got a few feelers out there to track down her whereabouts. Since you two were close, she may try to reach out to you."

"If I hear from her, I'll let you know."

"Thanks. Speaking of Arianna, are there any rumors within the industry floating that I need to be concerned about since her abrupt disappearance from the public eye?"

Hurts knew it was only a matter of time before people started to talk, considering Arianna was a prominent face in the industry.

"Enough to keep the gossip mill running," Enzo replied.

"Anything I need to be concerned about?" Hurts asked, though he could only imagine what was being circulated. The industry was so vile and cutthroat. If anyone caught wind of anything scandalous, it would escalate and spread like wildfire. In some cases, it was enough to ruin someone's career. In this case, it could destroy Arianna's life.

Hurts heard Enzo sigh. "Let's see…these are a few I've heard personally; she is pregnant, and in hiding, she had a mental breakdown and was admitted to an undisclosed rehabilitation center seeking help, or my favorite; she was one of the seven people killed during the incident at the castle, and the police are covering it up."

"Jesus Christ, people are sick."

"You don't have to tell me that."

"You mean nobody connected her to you, considering a witness saw you leaving the castle with her?"

"They tried, but I shut that down quickly. Until she surfaces, people will talk. On the positive side, nobody but Demitri and Carmine knew I was in the room, and I'm quite sure those two won't be running their mouths. But then you have Miles, your agency's rogue agent. I did confront him when I was looking for Arianna. He could be an issue should he resurface."

Hurts was still pissed that Miles had broken his oath to the bureau and went rogue. There was a warrant for his arrest on multiple counts, including several drug offenses. The real concern over Miles' vanishing act was the information he knew of. If he was drugged up and started spewing classified information regarding cases, they could have a massive problem on their hands.

"Miles is someone else's problem now, but you're right. He could be an issue. How about Demitri? Any word on what he's been up to?"

"For the most part, he and his people have been laying low since the incident at the castle. The local police questioned him, but of course, he was given preferential treatment due to his team of lawyers."

That news hadn't surprised Hurts, but Enzo's following statement made the hair on the back of his neck stand up.

"Be forewarned—Demitri is hunting for Arianna."

"Does he know her true identity?"

"No, at least I don't believe so. A contact of mine close to the situation said that Demitri has become obsessed with Arianna since that night, and he won't stop looking until he finds her."

"Shit. That's not good."

"No, it isn't. Because Demitri, like myself, has a lot of contacts all over the world—some in high places who owe him favors. If you know what I mean."

Agent Hurts knew exactly what Enzo was suggesting. It was no secret that law enforcement agencies worldwide were infiltrated with traitors working for the enemy, mainly because they were greedy, and the pay is good.

"Well, if you hear anything that you think I should be aware of, give me a shout."

"Will do."

The line went dead and Hurts threw the phone on the table. He was beyond frustrated. *Dammit, Arianna. Where in the hell are you?* He said to himself. There were other ways to locate her, but he preferred not to draw attention to the matter considering the FBI was closely monitoring all those involved in the current situation at hand. He was determined, though, to have her name cleared. But first, he had to find her so he could talk to her.

Hurts' gut feeling told him that something huge was in the works, but he wondered at what cost and how it involved Arianna.

CHAPTER ELEVEN

The following day, Arianna decided to sleep in a little bit longer. It was Christmas Eve, after all, and she didn't have anything too pressing to do, so she hit the snooze button when her alarm went off at seven. She had made sure that Nigel was okay and didn't have to go outside. The loud snores coming from the bottom of the bed told her he was content, so she laid back down and fell back asleep for about another hour.

When the alarm went off the second time, she decided to get out of bed. Nigel also decided to climb out of bed, so she let him out in the backyard to do his business before going back upstairs to get ready for the day. Yesterday on the way home, she had stopped by the grocery store right near the house and picked up a small bag of food for Nigel. Her plans for today were to drive to the large pet store in Norfolk to pick up a larger bag of food for Nigel—something that would last longer than two days. She also wanted to stock up on some treats, pick out a few toys, and grab a few other things for him. There was a closer store in town, but she was trying to lay low until she surprised her dad. Being that she knew many people in town, there was a good possibility that she would run into someone she knew or her dad knew, and it would ruin the surprise.

Nigel, for the most part, had an excellent first night in his new home. The only battle she had with him was getting him to share the bed. Throughout the night, he tended to creep up the bed and sleep right up against her, which was fine at first. But as the night went on, he would start to stretch out his legs and keep kicking her in the back. At one point, he had pushed her so far over that she almost fell off the bed. After that, she moved him to a spot near the bottom of the bed. He seemed to be okay with that because he stayed and slept the rest of the night.

Once she was dressed and ready, she went downstairs and got Nigel leashed up since she was taking him along with her. As she left the house and made her way to the car, she noticed that Dino's car still wasn't in the driveway. It hadn't been there when she went to bed last night either, which led her to believe that he had been shipped out.

She got Nigel into the car. She put him in the backseat, but just like yesterday, he climbed over the center console area and took the passenger seat up front. The look on his face made her chuckle. He acted as if she had committed a crime by putting him in the back seat. She glanced at her watch and saw it was already after nine. It would take about thirty to forty minutes to get there, depending on how bad traffic was. Being that it was Christmas Eve, she knew that many stores closed early, so she needed to get a move on.

Two and a half hours later, and her bank account almost three hundred dollars lighter, she and Nigel pulled into the driveway. She couldn't believe how well-behaved Nigel had been inside the store, even with other dogs around. He stayed by her side the whole time, and never once tried to pull. When she would stop to look at something, he would sit down, or sometimes he lie down. She was already in love with the big beast.

Since she had a truckload of items, she walked Nigel to the front door and let him in while she went back to get the bags from the car. She'd need to find a cart or something to haul the bag of food in. It was too heavy for her to carry.

When she walked around to the back of the car and popped the trunk, she noticed that Dino's garage door was open and a car was parked inside. *Wonderful.* She willfully thought to herself as she grabbed all the bags so she wouldn't have to make a second trip. She still wasn't ready to face him just yet. The sooner she got inside the house, the less of a chance she had of running into him. She felt so stupid for what she had done. She could only imagine what he probably thought of her.

Just as she pulled the last bag out of the trunk, she heard a door slam followed by heavy footsteps against the wood. *Shit!* She knew it was his house since he was the only house within hearing distance with a wooden porch. Everyone else had concrete. She closed her eyes and tried to stay hidden behind the car's open trunk lid. Hopefully, he hadn't seen her and would just get in his car and drive away.

Of course, luck wasn't on her side when he called her name. *Craptastic!* She wondered how she should act. Should she acknowledge what happened between them, or should she pretend that he hadn't given her the best orgasm of her life? *Damn!* She was screwed. She almost giggled. She was definitely screwed—by him. Finally, she took a deep breath, knowing she couldn't avoid him any longer. She poked her head around the open trunk with a smile on her face.

"Hey there!" Okay, that was a little over the top, she thought to herself.

Dino grinned and stood next to her car with his hands shoved in the front pockets of his jeans that fit him like jeans were supposed to fit a man. Snug in the thighs and crotch. At least that was her preference. Realizing she was actually staring at his crotch; she redirected her eyes to the rest of him and almost rolled her eyes. Why did he have to look so good? The light blue long sleeve t-shirt he wore was loose-fitting, but she could still make out the outline of his muscles in certain spots. At least she had dressed more appropriately than she was the other night and had actually done her hair and put a little bit of eyeliner and mascara on.

"Do you need some help?" He asked, nodding toward the bags in her hand.

She shook her head. "I think I got them, but thank you." She reached up and pulled the trunk lid down.

They stood there awkwardly staring at each other. She wasn't sure what to say. Should she thank him for getting her home the other night, or maybe thank him for the round of spontaneous and amazing sex? She almost rolled her eyes at her inner she-devil's thoughts again.

Finally, he broke the awkward silence between them. He seemed a little unsure as well, and he reached behind his head and rubbed the back of his neck. "Look, about the other night."

Her mouth fired before her brain, and she injected her thoughts before he could continue.

"I'm so sorry. I know it was a mistake, and I promise I won't ever step foot on your property."

He dropped his arm to his side and scrunched his eyebrows together. "You thought it was a mistake?" He asked, seeming insulted.

"You don't?" She asked, not answering his question. Did he not think it was a mistake? Even though she felt mortified, she would definitely love to go another round with him.

He shook his head. "No, I don't. We both said that we weren't interested in a relationship, so I don't see what the problem would be."

"So, it doesn't bother you that we had sex and we hardly know each other—not to mention we live next door to one another?"

"No," he told her flatly. "Does it bother you?"

"Well, talking to you now and hearing that you're okay with it, I guess it doesn't bother me either. I've been a nervous wreck ever since I woke up yesterday morning wondering how you'd act. I wasn't sure if I could or even wanted to face you."

"Why?" He asked, stepping a little closer to her.

She shrugged her shoulders. "I guess because I was unsure how you'd think of me. I mean, I've never done something like that before. It wasn't exactly the impression I had intended on giving my new neighbor." Suddenly she felt a burst of sassiness hit her. She looked him in the eye. "But I won't lie, it was fun."

She watched as his lips curled into that sexy half-smirk she remembered from the night before last. He took a few more steps toward her until he stood directly in front of her. She shifted on her feet as her head tilted back so she could look up at him. She considered herself average height for a woman at five feet five, but he still towered over her. Having him that close to her made her insides flutter, and that heated sensation she had the other night re-emerged.

His large hands landed on her waist as their gazes locked. She was jealous because she wanted to touch him back. She wanted to run her hands up his back and feel the ripples of his muscles. But with her hands full of shopping bags, she was out of luck. He lowered his head, and her heart began to race. They were cheek to cheek. The warmth of his breath blew softly against her ear, causing goosebumps to emerge all over her skin. She closed her eyes. The feeling was intense and arousing.

"It was fun for me too." His voice was low and deep as it resonated close to her ear. She felt flush, excited; hell, she was horny. It was erotic—it was hot, and it made her want him again. She clenched her legs together, trying to ward off that all-too-familiar feeling that was building below. Just as she was ready to chuck the bags aside, he dropped his hands and took a step. She almost whimpered, feeling the loss of his touch.

"I'll see ya around," he winked and flashed her his signature smirk, turned around, and marched himself back to his house, leaving her standing there melting in a puddle.

It was Nigel's deep bark that pulled her from the fog in her head. Shaking the sexy images, she had floating around her head, she made her way up to the house. She kept asking herself one question—Would she be down with that considering what the consequences could be? With a smile a mile wide, she walked inside the house. *Absolutely!*

After putting away everything that she had purchased, Arianna sat out on her back porch with Nigel. She was fiddling with a device that one of the sales associates at the pet store talked her into buying. She had noticed earlier in the morning when she let Nigel out that he liked to bark at anything that moved while outside. The last thing she wanted was to be the neighborhood nuisance with the dog who wouldn't stop barking. While at the store, the saleswoman pointed out a device similar to the shock collars used on dogs to discourage them from barking. While she wasn't a fan of the electric zapping bark collars, the saleswoman explained to her that there was another type of collar that, instead of shocking the animal, it would instead spray them with a short burst of citronella. It seemed easy to use and was humane, so she thought, why not try it out. The saleswoman said that if it didn't work or she didn't like it, she could always return it.

Since she still had a couple of hours before she needed to be at her dad's, she figured she'd open the package and see how it worked before she put it on, Nigel. She opened the package, put the battery in, and filled the small cylinder with the citronella mixture just like the instructions said. That was where she should've ended the so-called "test" phase and put the dang collar back in the bag to return.

She stood up on the back porch and started barking at the collar. When nothing happened, she barked again at it. Feeling like an idiot, she glanced around the yard, making sure that neither of her neighbors on each side of her was in their yards.

When she saw the coast was clear, she tried barking at it again. She even tried changing the pitch, but still, nothing happened. She made sure it was turned on, rechecked the fill level, and went through the "getting started" checklist one more time to make sure she hadn't missed a step. Once she was positive everything was a go, she barked. Again, nothing. She wasn't sure what possessed her to do it, but she secured the collar around her neck. It was a little snug, so she went to adjust it but ended up tightening it too much, and she grunted. Well, apparently, the collar only worked if it felt a vibration, because she immediately received a blast of the citronella to her face.

She started coughing, which made the stupid collar pump out more citronella. She tried to inhale some clean air but kept coughing, which kept blasting her with citronella one right after another. Nigel sat there on the deck, looking at her with his head cocked to one side. She swore the animal was actually smiling at her as saying, *"and you were going to put that on me?"*

Between the coughing and cursing, she must've emptied over a dozen blasts of citronella to her face, all while trying to get the damn collar off, but she was in such a panic she couldn't figure it out. She was beginning to think the damn thing had permanently attached to her neck. Her eyes had even started to burn, making it hard to see, which was why she didn't see the damn chair and fell over it, landing hard on her left hip.

Laying on the ground, she continued to fight with the damn contraption until she finally loosened it enough to slide over her head. As soon as she was free, she flung it halfway across the yard. She never wanted to see that thing again. She got herself up and took a seat in one of the patio chairs. She continued to take deep breaths, trying to get as much clean air as she could to get the god-awful scent out of her nose. It was beginning to make her sick.

What on earth had she been thinking? That had not been one of the brightest moments of her life, and a moment she would never forget.

She lifted her shirt and sniffed it. *Jesus!* It was even in her clothing. As she got up to head inside to take a shower, deep laughter from the right side of the yard got her attention. When she turned in that direction, there stood Dino laughing hysterically. He was laughing so hard it looked like he couldn't breathe. Once he finally calmed down and wiped his eyes, he said, "I was gonna come help, but every time I started to climb over the fence, you'd cough and set it off again, and then I would start laughing and I couldn't make it."

Her face felt like it was on fire. She was so embarrassed. Feeling flustered and out of sorts, she didn't know what to say or do, so she just flipped him the bird and stomped into the house to get a shower so she wouldn't smell like a freaking Tiki Torch.

After she shed her clothes, she threw them into a separate pile to be burned because there was no way she would get the smell out of those things. As she stepped into the shower, she thought of some valuable lessons she learned. Number one, don't fill the collar before trying to set it off—not that she would ever be trying that again. And number two, remember your neighbor is not a good source of help in a comedy crisis situation. On the plus side, she probably won't have a mosquito problem for days!

She picked up her loofah and drizzled some of her candy apple body wash on it. After ten minutes of scrubbing, she still smelled the citronella. Or it could just be that the smell was now embedded in her nostrils. She wanted to vomit.

She went to wash the loofah out when it slipped from her hand and fell onto the floor. As she bent over to pick it up, the shower door flew open, and she screamed bloody murder. She had flashbacks of the original *Psycho* movie during the shower scene. Everything was a blur, and she tried to scramble away from *Norman Bates,* who was coming at her with a knife. She didn't make it far because she ended up slipping on the damn loofah, she had been trying to pick up in the first place. She closed her eyes, waiting to feel the impact of the tile below her, but it never came. Seconds later, she realized the rock-solid arms holding her up had saved her from busting her ass a second time in the same day.

After talking with Arianna earlier, Dino couldn't get her off his mind. He thought doing some manual labor around the house might deflect some of the thoughts, so he headed out to the backyard to stack some firewood that had been delivered a few days ago. He was on the last few pieces when movement over in the yard next door caught his eye. He knew it was her the woman who had become the lead role in his dreams at night.

He tried to ignore her presence because he knew that he'd want to talk to her if he saw her. He stacked the last piece of wood before loading up his arms to take a few pieces in the house. When he turned to head inside, he couldn't stop his wandering eyes, and what he saw her do next almost made him drop the load of firewood in his arms. She had a black choker or some type of collar in her hand, and as she placed it around her slender neck, he found himself unable to look away. At first, it turned him on, thinking she was into a bit of kink, but what happened next had him laughing so hard that he actually shed a tear.

Seeing that she was struggling with the gadget around her neck, he set the stack of wood down. Just as he was about to hop over the fence, she coughed again, and the damn spray shot her in the face again, making her cough even more. It must've blinded her as well because then she tripped over the chair next to her and fell square on her ass. After struggling with the device, she finally got it off and tossed it out into the yard. He couldn't hold back his amusement any longer and roared with laughter. He laughed so hard his stomach hurt, and his eyes filled with tears.

When he got himself under control and glanced back at her, she stood there glaring at him.

He couldn't help the amusement he found in her misfortune. "I was gonna come help, but every time I started to climb over the fence, you'd set it off again, and then I'd start laughing and couldn't make it."

When she gave him the one-finger salute and stormed into the house, he almost lost it all over again, but when he saw her put her hand on her hip and rub it, he sobered pretty quickly, realizing that she could have hurt herself.

Amusement set aside, for the time being, he hopped over the fence and climbed the steps to the back porch. When he tried to open the sliding glass door, it wouldn't budge. At least he knew she was careful about her safety. Although sliding glass doors weren't the best type of door to have because all someone had to do was break the glass. Even with the latch in the locked position, the door itself was still penetrable. But in Anna's case, she at least had a blocking bar in place at the bottom of the door.

He knocked on the glass but got no answer. He knocked again, and this time he was greeted by a large blueish-grey dog. When the dog barked, Dino took a step back from the door. The dog stopped barking, then sat down and stared at him with his tongue hanging out and his tail wagging. He didn't know she had a dog. She never said anything about having one, nor had he ever seen it outside. He waited another minute or two, seeing if she would come to the door, especially hearing the dog bark. When she never showed Dino became even more worried that she could be hurt or sick.

He wasn't about to break the glass, so he jogged around to the front of the house. He stopped at his car and pulled his lock, picking tools from his bag. He tried to be as quiet as he could as he made his way up the front steps to the front door. Within seconds he had her piece of shit lock picked and slipped inside. He waited, listening for any sign that the dog had heard him. The house had an open floor plan so he could see into the kitchen where the slider was, and he saw the dog's tail. He chuckled to himself when it was still wagging.

Being careful to avoid being detected by *Cujo,* he cleared the main level. As he started up the stairs, he heard the tap of the nails on the tile floor, indicating that the dog was on the move. He double-timed it up the last few steps. There were four doors to choose from. One directly in front of him, which he could see was a bathroom, two doors to the left that were closed, and then a door to the right at the end of the hallway that was opened. He chose door number four, the opened one, and went to the right. He made it to the doorway and heard the shower running in the adjacent bathroom. He breathed a little sigh of relief, knowing she at least made it there, but then he heard her start coughing again, and then she gagged. Concerned, he walked into the bathroom and found her in the large walk-in shower. The room had already begun to fill with steam, but he could still make out her fully naked body through the glass side of the stall.

It was wrong, but he couldn't help the aroused feeling seeing her curves as the water ran down her body. When she dropped her little purple scrubby puff and bent over and her ass pressed against the glass, he lost all control of his thought process. In two long strides, he was at the shower and yanked open the shower door. He wasn't expecting the blood-curdling scream nor for her to lose her balance. She was headed for the shower floor when he rushed into the shower and snagged her around the waist, hoisting her up before she went all the way down.

She surprised him when she tried to throw a punch in his direction. Fortunately, he had good reflexes and was able to duck under her swing. He grabbed her arms and held them by her sides as he pressed his front against her backside.

"It's just me, Anna," he said as they both stood under the warm spray of water.

Slowly she turned in his arms, and when she tilted her head back, and he saw the fire in her eyes, he knew he was in a heap of trouble.

Arianna was startled yet thankful for her savior's timing. Hitting the tiled floor would have hurt like hell. Her left hip was already sore from her earlier debacle outside. Then the added embarrassment knowing he saw the whole thing and had laughed at her reignited the fire within her.

"What are you doing in here? How did you even get into my house?" She fired the two questions off, ignoring the fact that she was naked as a jaybird.

She'd give him some credit. At least his eyes never wavered from hers. Most guys in his shoes would be looking at anything but her eyes.

He snorted a laugh. "I'll be buying you a new lock for your front door. I had that thing picked in no time."

"That doesn't answer my question. Why are you here?"

His facial expression softened, and his body pressed closer. He moved his hands and placed them against the wall on both sides of her head. She felt like a lioness being caged in.

"I felt awful for laughing at you. After you went inside, I realized you could've been seriously hurt. I came over to check on you, but you didn't answer the door when I knocked, and I got worried."

She stared up into his eyes, trying to determine if he was telling the truth. How could she be mad at him when he came and checked on her because he was worried? She wanted to be angry, but was it for the wrong reason? Could it be because she actually felt something for him, and that was what she didn't want to happen, so she was making excuses?

"Anna?" He said, pulling her out of her head. She still didn't correct him on her name. She looked at him. "Are you okay?" He asked as his hand traveled down her body to her hip that she had fallen on outside. He gently caressed her skin as he waited for her to answer.

His touch was distracting in a good way. Why she felt utterly comfortable standing before him naked confused her; was it because, for the last two years, she was used to having to do wardrobe changes in front of strangers? Or was it because *he* made her feel that way? She never had a one-night stand before. But she had always assumed that with encounters as such, the two people involved didn't have much interaction, if any, afterward. In her opinion, it would seem awkward. But with Dino, she felt anything but awkward or uncomfortable. In fact, she was very comfortable standing in his arms in her birthday suit. And that brought her back to the original question—why?

She shook her head, and he chuckled low. "You don't know if you're, okay?" He asked, his voice laced with amusement.

"I think I'm okay, but I don't know if I can get the smell off of me."

"Let's see what we can do about that." His mischievous eyes held hers. "Do you trust me?" He asked.

For some unknown reason, she knew he was someone she could trust. and she nodded.

"Turn around and close your eyes," he ordered.

She raised one of her eyebrows in question, and he raised one of his in return. Remembering she had told him that she trusted him, she turned slowly and faced the tiled wall. As she took a deep breath, she closed her eyes. It felt like an eternity before she felt his large hands sweep over her shoulders, making her body shudder. He continued down her back, following her spine and then back up, stopping at her shoulder blades. Using his thumbs, he kneaded the tight muscles. She wasn't sure how this would help her get rid of the smell, but she'd take a massage any day of the week. He increased the pressure, and she began to feel the tension leave her body. Feeling more relaxed, she placed her hands against the wall in front of her and let her head drop forward. His masculine hands moved down her body until they reached her calves. He took his time massaging each leg, moving higher until reaching her upper thighs. By then, she was not only relaxed but stimulated. The sexual intensity was building inside her. The moment his firm hands touched her inner thighs, she thought she might detonate. She tried holding her breath, but it was no use. She couldn't take the torture any longer.

"Dino," she said, keeping her eyes closed. He dropped his hands from her legs and she felt the instant loss. Just as she thought the moment was over, she felt his warm breath against her neck.

"What do you want?" He whispered. His voice sounded sexy. It was deep, low, and dominant, and it sent tingles all through her body.

Oh hell! She thought to herself, and she squeezed her thighs together. Her body started to tremble because she was on the brink of exploding.

She didn't answer right away as she tried to ward off the sensations taking hold of her. His hands gripped her shoulders, and he began to turn her around. She kept her eyes closed and her head down. She heard him chuckle softly before he used his finger to lift her chin.

"Look at me, Anna."

Her eyes opened slowly. His dark blue eyes were more pronounced as they bored into hers.

"Tell me what you want," he asked her again.

She lifted her hands to his chest. When she felt the skin and the slight dusting of hair beneath her fingertips, it had surprised her. *When had he removed his clothes?* She took a quick peek and was happy to see he was on the same thought process as her as she admired his unclothed body. He wasn't built like a bodybuilder. His form was more lean, similar to a swimmer's body type.

Her eyes traveled back up his body, which was met with that sexy smirk that drove her nuts. Her traitorous hands went right to his abs. She ran her fingers over the dips and peaks of the muscles up his chest to his shoulders before she cupped his cheeks.

"I want you."

"I want you too," he declared and wrapped his arms around her waist.

She focused on his eyes. During her time undercover, she had learned to read people by their eye movements. The way Dino's eyes held hers told her that he was thinking something else, and that nagged at her.

"What aren't you saying?" She found herself asking.

"Anna, you seem like a really great woman with a lot of great qualities. Qualities that I would most definitely look for if I were in the market for a steady girlfriend. But I'm not looking for that. I don't want to lead you on, and ultimately you get hurt."

She loved his honesty and understood completely what he was saying as she felt the same. She still had the mess back at the agency she had to get through, and until she knew more about the outcome stemming from that, she wasn't even sure what the future held for her.

"It's obvious we're both comfortable with one another, although I find that strange, seeing as we've only known each other for three days. But life can throw curveballs at any given time, so it is what it is. We both want the same thing—company with no strings attached. Why can't we just be friends with benefits? Or in our unique case, neighbors with benefits?"

"Are you sure?" He asked with a serious expression.

"Positive."

"If we agree to this, we both need to promise that we'll be honest with each other if either of our feelings changes in any way?"

She smiled softly and pulled him snugly against her body before she kissed his chin, then his neck, and ending at his ear. "Understood."

Arianna wasn't sure how he managed it, but one second her feet were on the floor, and the next, she was hoisted into the air. She straddled his waist as he pressed her back against the shower wall and swooped in and kissed her deeply. She ran her fingers through his thick, black hair as she kissed him back, trying to ease the hunger within her.

"I need you now," he told her as he dipped his head and licked across her breasts.

"Take me," she pleaded, then she kissed his neck.

He reached between her thighs, and she anticipated his penetration. Before she could take her next breath, he plunged into her, filling her. She closed her eyes and laid her head back against the wall as she let him work his magic on her. She was just along for the ride, and damn, was it a good ride.

"Jesus, you feel amazing," he admitted as he stroked into her, alternating his pace from quick to slow.

Her thighs began to quiver, and her breasts started to tingle as the water splashed between their bodies. She was strung so tight. She felt her climax start to build. She wanted—needed him deeper, and she began to counterthrust.

"Oh, God. Please, Dino. Don't stop," she panted and moaned.

"So, fucking good," he called out before he buried his head in her neck. He increased the speed of his thrusts and penetrated her deeper, making her lose her breath.

She felt him start to tighten up. His moans grew louder, his pace quickened, and she felt that familiar flutter sensation hit her belly and knew she was there. He reached between them and pinched her nipple at the same time he slammed into her, and she flew off the edge like a bird taking flight.

She felt like she was floating. Her eyes closed, and she relished in the aftermath. Dino soon followed, squeezing her tight as he rode out his release.

He kissed her neck and cheeks before moving them both under the water as they calmed their breathing. She clung to him, not wanting the moment to end.

Suddenly she felt him tighten up, and he quickly pulled out of her and lowered her feet to the floor.

"Shit!"

"What?" She asked, looking around, wondering what was wrong.

"I'm sorry," he admitted and gave her a deadpan look.

"Sorry about what?" She asked, now believing that something was indeed wrong.

"No condom."

"Oh!" Her eyes widened.

"Fuck!"

She took hands and held him still. "Dino, look at me." When she looked up into his eyes, she could see the remorse and worry. "It's fine—" she started to say, but he cut her off.

"It's not fine, dammit. That was irresponsible of me."

She gave him a soft smile. "First, it was both of our faults, and second, if you had let me finish, I have an IUD. I'm clean, considering before we had sex the other night, I haven't been with anybody in about three years."

The look he gave her almost made her laugh.

"You're joking. The part about not being with a man in three years." That was all he said, and that time she did snicker.

"No joke. I'm assuming since you're in the military, you're tested often."

He nodded, but she could still see the concern in his expression, and she respected him for that. Like he had told her, Dino himself had many qualities that she looked for in a guy. It really was a shame, but she knew this situation was only temporary. That was what they had both agreed to. Part of her knew this arrangement could come back to bite her in the ass, but taking one look at his roped body, she'd take her chances—her feelings be damned. She would deal with any consequences later.

Dino kept wondering what was going through Anna's mind as she looked his body over. He was in shape. He had to be for the sake of his job. But he also took care of his body. He tried to eat healthy when he could and stayed away from junk food for the most part.

He turned the water off and grabbed a towel off the hook, and handed it to her before grabbing one for himself. As they stepped out of the shower and started to head toward the bedroom, he stopped her and turned her to face him.

Using his thumb, he caressed her lower lip then placed a kiss on her forehead.

Her smile was infectious. "You're pretty good at making a woman feel special."

"Growing up, I was taught to respect a woman."

He bent down and grabbed his wet clothes from the floor. "Can I use your dryer?"

"Sure. I can make us something to eat while they're drying. That is if you don't have any plans."

"That sounds nice. I don't have anywhere to be until later."

After they both dried off and changed, Arianna whipped up some burgers and onion rings. Thankfully he didn't have to sit around in a towel until his clothes dried. Arianna had found one of her dad's old t-shirts and a pair of sweat pants. She hadn't a clue how she had them, but all that mattered was that they fit him. At first, he felt awkward wearing her dad's clothes when his were wet because he had fucked his daughter in the shower.

At least she was happy now that she no longer smelled like a walking mosquito repellent. When she told him the whole story about the collar, he laughed all over again.

They sat at the island that separated the kitchen from the living room. Dino took the last bite of his burger then looked down at the large animal sitting between him and Arianna.

"What is that thing?" He finally asked.

"That 'thing' is Nigel, and he is a mixed breed. They think he's a crossbreed of Great Dane and Lab."

She scratched the pooch behind his large ears while making kissy noises. "Nigel is such a good boy, aren't you, buddy?"

For the first time in his life, he wished he were a dog. Shaking that thought from his brain, he asked, "What made you want a dog?"

"I don't know. The house felt lonely, and I always wanted one."

"Where did you find him?"

"That shelter just across town. There's a vet clinic there as well."

Dino wondered if that was the same clinic and shelter that his buddy Stitch's wife Mia had just purchased.

"What's the name of the place?"

"I can't remember, but I think the vet's name is Dr. Chambers."

"Yeah, okay, I know that place. That's my buddy's wife's place."

"Really?"

"Yeah. She just bought it a few weeks ago."

"Small world. Grace, the manager of the shelter, said that there had been a recent change in ownership."

Dino took her plate and his to the sink and rinsed them off. "Do you have any plans tonight for Christmas Eve?"

"I do. I'm spending it with my dad."

That surprised Dino. "Your dad lives in town?"

"Yeah. It'll be a surprise. He was under the impression I wasn't going to be home until a few more days. What about you? Any plans?"

"Not tonight. Tomorrow I'm hanging out at a friend's house."

"That's cool. At least you won't be alone. I know it's hard for those in the military to make it home for holidays. There were a lot of holidays and birthdays that my dad missed."

"Yeah. It can be tough." Though in Dino's position, he didn't have to worry about if he'd make it home for the holidays since he rarely spoke to his family.

Dino glanced at his watch and noted the time. He had promised Diego, he'd give him a hand hanging some drywall at his house.

She got up and walked around the island and started to clean up pans from cooking.

"Do you need help?" He asked, and she smiled as she looked over her shoulder. "I got it, but thank you. Your clothes should be dry if you want to grab them."

He walked to the laundry room just off the kitchen. His jeans were still a little damp, but that was fine since he was just going next door. He quickly changed then headed back out to the kitchen. Arianna was finishing up washing the rest of the dishes.

"You heading home?" She asked, and he nodded.

"Yeah, I promised a friend I'd help him out today."

She grinned. "Dino, you don't have to explain why you need to leave."

"Right."

He didn't want to just walk out with a wave. He met her by the sink and pulled her into a hug.

"Remember, you need to find that asinine collar thing and throw it in the trash."

She snorted a laugh and rolled her eyes. "I don't even know where it landed when I threw it out into the yard. Remember, we both promised never to mention that again."

He grinned. He did promise her that, but he wasn't sure he could keep it a secret forever. It was too funny of a story not to share, at some point."

He gave her one last squeeze. "If I don't see you around, Merry Christmas," he told her.

"Same to you."

CHAPTER TWELVE

Arianna gave her belly a good pat and smiled as her dad put the last dish into the dishwasher.

Everyone knew Paul served some of the best food in town at the restaurant, but none of the patrons had ever had a home-cooked meal of his. His prime rib was to die for. It was similar to the one he had on the menu at Bayside, but he saved his special spices for special occasions.

Getting to spend Christmas with him after missing the last three was a little emotional. Especially when he had answered the front door and she was standing there. She swore she saw the tears start to build in his eyes before he pulled her in for a hug. And, boy had she needed that hug from her dad. He was and always would be her protector.

She and her dad were always very close, but even more so after her mom died. Even after she graduated high school and went off to college, they still had a strong bond. She had chosen to attend George Mason University in Virginia for her undergraduate degree, where she majored in Accounting. She loved studying numbers, but while at college, she acquired an interest in criminal law. After talking with a few of her professors, they encouraged her to look into the Digital Forensics Master's program at the university. She took their advice and read through the material, and then spoke with some of the professors in that program. Then one weekend, while she was visiting her dad, which was often since it wasn't too far of a drive, she brought up the program to get his opinion. He agreed and said it was a good field to venture into, especially if that was what interested her. Her dad had always been her sounding board when it came to big decisions that could impact her life. And she welcomed his advice whether she liked it or not.

Her dad was brilliant and was involved in a lot of classified stuff during his tenure in the military. There had been a few times after he retired where she questioned if he really was fully retired from the government. He wasn't one to talk about his time in the service or what he and his friends from the government liked to "dabble" in their spare time, and she wasn't one to question him. She had learned years ago that her dad was like a vault when it came to his career. Nobody was getting any information out of him, no matter what. However, she loved to imagine in her mind what he had taken part in. One time, she told her dad that she thought he was a Marine turned Black Ops CIA Agent. The only reply she got back from him was a loud laugh. But that didn't mean she was wrong. It had been and still was a fun little game she liked to play with him. Maybe one day down the road, she could put all her clues together and solve the mystery.

"I expected Victoria to be here," Arianna told her dad.

"Yeah, she decided she wanted to spend the holiday with her sister in Vermont."

Arianna stared at her dad. There was obviously more to the story than Victoria wanted to spend the holiday with her sister.

Victoria Prescott was her dad's girlfriend. She was the only girlfriend her dad had since her mom died. Arianna wasn't a fan of the woman, but if she made her dad happy, she would support him.

It had taken her dad a few years to get over his wife's death. They were soul mates. They had been the perfect example of what Arianna wanted in a relationship when she found the right one—love, loyalty, compassion, and trust.

After the funeral, Arianna saw her dad was struggling even though everyone thought he was handling his wife's death quite well in the public eye. But those outsiders weren't at their home to witness his heartbreak when he cleaned out her side of the closet or saw anything that reminded him of her mom. It had been heart wrenching for Arianna to watch. To see her big badass daddy shed a tear destroyed her.

Arianna knew her dad needed help at the restaurant. She had been able to keep things going administratively, like payroll and inventory, because she had learned all that from her mom. But she was supposed to leave for college in a few months. She had offered to forego George Mason and stay closer to home to help him, but he was adamant that she lived her life and find her future. He promised her that he would figure something out.

Needless to say, he went through many managers over the course of a few years. That was where Victoria came into the picture. To her credit, she had applied for the position every time her dad had posted it. And every time, he had called her in for an interview but never offered her the job. He claimed it was because she didn't have the experience he had been looking for. But surprisingly, on the last interview, he offered her one of the waitress positions that had just opened up. She had accepted, and slowly but surely, she learned the ropes. A little while later, the manager at the time was caught stealing. Her dad had fired him on the spot. Instead of posting the job, he offered Victoria the position on a trial basis, and of course, she had accepted. Both Arianna and Bruno, her dad's friend who helped him out at Bayside, weren't huge fans of her, to begin with. Bruno, to this day, always claimed she seemed suspicious.

Arianna's take on Victoria went south when she had come home one weekend to visit her dad but found Victoria in her dad's office going through some financial papers that didn't pertain to her. When she confronted her on it, she tried to laugh it off, spewing something about it was mixed in with the restaurant's stack of mail. It had been total bullshit. She mentioned it to her dad, but again he brushed it off.

Her dad and Victoria had started dating at the end of Arianna's senior year in college. Her dad surprised her with that detail when she was home for Spring Break. Arianna hadn't thought that the romance would last, but to her surprise, a few months before she had left for her undercover assignment, her dad asked Victoria to move in.

Something had changed in her dad that year, and even Bruno thought so too. But neither of them could put their finger on what it was. But hearing that Victoria didn't want to spend the holidays with him made her suspicions grow.

"Arianna, I know you don't approve of Victoria, but trust me when I say there is a reason that she's still around."

"What does that mean, dad? She treats you like a doormat. I mean, if she really loved you and wanted to be with you, why would she want to spend the holiday with her sister and her family and not you?"

"And you know what? That is fine by me because I get to spend the holiday with you." He grinned and pinched her nose like he used to do when she was a young girl.

Arianna shook her head. "You're up to something." Her dad gave her a blank stare, and she knew that look. It was the look that said to "drop it." And she would. "I just hope you know what you're doing."

Her dad walked to the other side of the kitchen and pulled down two coffee mugs and two small plates. She smiled as she watched her dad busy himself around the kitchen. He kept himself in great shape for being in his late fifties and was as healthy as an ox. He cut two slices of apple pie and brought them over to the table.

"So, are you still planning on making your grand appearance at the New Year's party?" He asked over his shoulder as he went back to the counter and poured their coffee.

"That's the plan," she told him as she forked a big bite of apple pie and put it in her mouth. Mmmm…homemade apple pie was her favorite dessert.

He brought the mugs over to the table and set one in front of her.

"How has it been since being back?" He asked her.

She took a sip of the strong, black coffee. It was the only way her dad drank it, and she picked it up from him. Getting back to her dad's question, she almost laughed when the first thing that popped into her head was Dino. But she didn't think she could explain how being back had been pleasurable. At least not to her dad.

"It's different, but it feels great. I'm glad I decided to give myself a couple of weeks to ease back into things and the town before I visit with friends."

"The girls are excited to see you. As are Stitch and Frost."

She smiled, recalling her friends from high school. She couldn't wait to catch up with them. She had met the group of them in middle school.

"I can't wait to see them. It's been a long time."

"They're still the same people, just grown up now like you. A lot has happened since you left. Alex is engaged. Tenley is married with three kids.

Stitch just got engaged, and Frost has a wife and son, and if I heard correctly, they are expecting as well."

"Wow! I'd say things have changed."

She felt a slight pang on the inside, realizing she didn't even have a significant other.

"Hey, what's the sour puss look for?"

"Just everyone seems to be moving on."

"What happened to that guy you were dating? I thought things were good between you two."

She never told her dad that Vinny was a sleazeball who had been sleeping with her next-door neighbor. After several odd encounters with Noreen, the neighbor, and Vinny, Arianna started to put two and two together. It was subtle actions toward each other, like how they would make eye contact while they were in her presence. She may have just been a Forensics Accountant, but she had learned a lot over eight years working for the FBI. She had several co-workers who had taught her what to look for in expressions and body language. Usually, because of his work schedule, Vinny would stay at her place on Tuesdays and Thursdays. Since she preferred to work early morning hours, she always left before him on Wednesday and Friday mornings. So, one Friday morning she got up and got ready for work like she normally would. Before she left, she woke him up and made sure to say goodbye to him because she was positive after that morning, she would never see him again.

When she left her apartment, instead of heading to the elevator, she went the opposite way down the hallway to the laundry room and waited. Ten minutes later, she heard a door down the hall open. She poked her head out into the hall, and just as she suspected, Vinny walked next door and knocked on Noreen's door. When Noreen opened the door, she had been dressed in a siren red itsy-bitsy see-through nightie. Vinny grinned, and Noreen grabbed him and pulled him into her apartment. Arianna gave them a few minutes and then knocked on the door. The look on Vinny's face when he answered the door in nothing but his boxer shorts had been priceless. Of course, he stuttered and tried to make up some lame excuse. But all she could do was shake her head and walk away.

"He didn't hurt you, did he?" Her dad asked.

"Not physically."

"What the hell does that mean?"

She sighed. "Vinny and I broke up before I took on the assignment. I haven't seen or heard from him in over three years."

"Jesus. I still can't believe it's been that long." Arianna could tell he wanted to ask her about the assignment.

"It has been a long time." She took another sip of her coffee. "In fact, there are times that I feel as if I'm a whole new person."

Her dad eyed her over, and he set his mug down. "So, are you going to tell your old man what's eating at you and why you snuck into town undetected earlier than expected?"

She grinned, "How do you do it?" She joked.

He shrugged his shoulders. "I'm a dad. I can tell when something is on his little girl's mind."

If he only knew.

"Want to talk about it?"

"Not just yet. I need to process some things first. But I promise to come to talk to you when the time is right."

"Fair enough. How long are you planning on staying in town? You know you could've stayed here."

She cocked her head sideways and gave that look of hers, telling him that he was out of his mind.

He chuckled. "Yeah, I thought I would get that reaction from you."

"Seriously?" She asked him though she knew he was just teasing. There was no way she'd stay at his place with Victoria there.

"All joking aside, where are you staying?"

"I rented a beach house. Not too far from Bayside."

"You rented a house?" He questioned. "Are we talking long-term rental?"

She used her pointer finger to trace the rim of her mug. "At least six months. I'm sort of on a break from the bureau."

"A break?"

She took a deep breath. She really wasn't ready to get into all this with him right now. Eventually, she would, but she wanted a little more time to process it all. Before she could tell him that, he said, "Forget it. When you're ready to talk, you know where to find me." He winked, and she smiled.

Changing the subject, Paul shifted in his seat. "Well, since you seem to have some time on your hands, how about helping me manage the bar? I have some business that will take a lot of my time for a few weeks, and I'm looking for someone I can trust not to screw me over. What do you say?"

She smiled. "I'd love to. But what about Victoria? I thought she was handling that."

He curled his lip and snarled. "Things change."

Okay....

"Can I start after New Year's?"

"That works. I'm warning you now some of the newer waitresses are difficult to work with."

"That's a simple problem to fix," she told him.

"How so?"

"I'll just fire them."

"Arianna..."

"What? They don't want to work; they don't have to. Plain and simple."

Her dad just shook his head. "I'll leave you to it. Speaking of New Year's, what time are you arriving? Alex has been hounding me."

She smiled, "I'll give Alex a call. Do you have any special events lined up besides New Year's?"

"No, don't need to. As long as I keep providing great food, it's all that I need to keep the customers coming back."

"What about bringing in a band or some kind of entertainment on certain nights?"

"Stick around, and maybe you can see to it that sort of thing happens." He winked, and she laughed. He would never admit it, but deep down, she knew he'd be thrilled if she ended up staying. The more she thought about it, the more she imagined she'd probably enjoy it too. but what job could she get around here where she could use her forensics skills? She didn't think she could go back into a general accounting job. That wouldn't be challenging enough for her. *Hmmm...maybe that was something to think about.*

She finished her coffee and then helped her dad finish cleaning up the kitchen. By then, it was getting late, and even Nigel was snoring by the front door. The dog had instantly taken a liking to her dad. And judging from all the food and playtime her dad had given Nigel, the feeling was mutual. At least she had a dog sitter.

"I think I'm going to head home," she told him and went into the living room to get her purse and coat. "Are you going to the homeless shelter tomorrow to help serve dinner?" She asked him. Volunteering at the shelter on Christmas had been a tradition that her mom had started.

"Of course. Want to join me?"

"Maybe. Who else is going?"

"Bruno and two other guys I know from the service."

She smiled. "I'd like that. That was a great idea that Mom came up with."

He smiled back at her then looked at the Christmas tree sitting in the corner of the room. It was decorated the same way that her mom would have decorated it. "Your mother was a sweet soul."

Her dad stepped closer and pulled her into a hug. She smiled as she snuggled close. God, she'd missed him.

"Try not to let your job get under your skin. I know it's hard. but things happen for a reason."

"I know. Right now, I'm just taking it one day at a time."

He winked and kissed the top of her head. "That's all you can do. Oh! I almost forgot. I've been collecting mail for you." He walked over to the table by the front door and pulled a stack of envelopes from a bin on the shelf. "I'm sure most of it is junk, but I didn't want to throw anything away just in case."

"Wow! Okay, thanks. I'll go through it eventually," she told him and shoved it all inside her purse.

She shook Nigel's leash, and as if a fire lit under his ass, he jumped up onto all fours with his tail wagging. Her dad walked over and gave him another pat on the head.

"You lucked out with this one," he told her.

Grinning, she said, "I know. He's perfect." And, he was. Though it had only been two days since she brought the pup home, she knew the two of them were meant to be together.

After she got Nigel leashed, she walked to the door, and her dad followed her out. As they walked down the driveway, a tingling sensation moved from her arms up to her neck. It was a strange feeling as if the energy in the air had changed—like a warning signal. She took a quick glance at her dad, and his focus seemed to be somewhere else as he looked up and down the street. When their eyes met, he had a hardened look. Something had changed in the few seconds they walked from the house to the car. She wondered if he had felt what she had. Was someone or something out there watching them?

He gave her another hug before she got into the car.

"Do me a favor and call me when you get home."

She looked up at him, and the intensity burning in his eyes told her not to question or argue with him. She swallowed hard.

"I will."

He kissed her forehead. "Drive safe."

"Love you."

"Love you, too, sweetie."

As she pulled out of her dad's driveway and drove down the street, she kept an eye on her dad through the rear-view mirror. He never took his eyes off of her car until she made the right-hand turn taking her to the main street and out of his sight.

Something was going on, and she needed to find a way to talk to her stubborn dad about it.

ൻ

Paul kept a close eye on Arianna's car as it traveled down the street. looking for any sign that she had a tail on her. The anonymous email sent to Bayside's general email account yesterday had heightened the awareness and safety surrounding his daughter.

"Daddy's little girl can't escape the wrath of hell that is about to be brought down on her."

The violent threat on her life made him wonder what she had possibly landed herself in during her time away. The timing of the sender's communication hadn't sat well with him. Knowing that Arianna had been back in town for over a week made him skeptical that the person who sent the email knew her whereabouts and when she had arrived, meaning a predator shadowed her. But who and why, were the top critical questions that needed to be answered?

Concealed behind the vehicle's dark-tinted glass, he watched through a pair of night vision binoculars as the bastard kissed his daughter goodbye.

Paul Roland was a man of mystery and power within the confined walls of the government. But he was also greatly hated by few men who were thirsty for revenge.

Roland's government files were locked down tight. Still, it was rumored that after his career span in the military, he had been recruited by a secret intelligence division that reported directly to the president.

Roland's alertness as he watched his daughter's car drive away confirmed that he had gotten the message loud and clear.

Both Paul Roland and his daughter, the precious Arianna, a.k.a. Anna Humphreys, needed to be put in their place.

CHAPTER THIRTEEN

Dino popped the sweet icing-covered sugar cookie in his mouth as he walked down the hall from the game room to the kitchen, where everyone was gathered. At least the adults were. He loved spending the holidays with the team and their families.

"Uncle Dino, wait for me." Sienna, Irish and Bailey's little girl, called out as she raced down the hallway after him. Dino slowed his pace so her small strides could catch up with him. For the past hour, he'd been playing hide and seek and foosball with her and some of the other kids.

Biologically, Sienna was Irish's niece. Unfortunately, Irish's older sister had gotten involved with the wrong crowd and ended up pregnant by her drug dealer boyfriend. Neither of the parents wanted the baby, so they took off right after Sienna was born and were never heard from again. Irish's parents had stepped in and raised her until a few months ago. With his parents getting up there in age, it became more difficult for them to raise a small child, though they loved her dearly. So, Irish brought her to live with him. That had been around the same time that Irish had met Bailey. In fact, Bailey had been Sienna's kindergarten teacher. He and Bailey were married a few weeks ago on Thanksgiving and had officially adopted Sienna.

At six years old, she was already a firecracker. But nobody would expect less considering she was related to Irish, his sometimes-crazy teammate. Although Dino thought there were times when Sienna gave Irish a run for his money.

He chuckled as she latched onto his leg. "I got you!" She playfully shouted at him.

He bent down and quickly scooped her up with one arm, then flipped her upside down. She squirmed and squealed as he carried her like that until they got to the dining room where everyone was.

"You sure about that squirt? Because from the looks of it, I got you."

"Uncle Dino. You're not playing fair," she giggled but pretended to pout.

"I'm not?"

"No!"

"What isn't fair?"

"You have big muscles."

"So?"

"I can't pick you up."

Dino grinned as he walked further into the room. As it was late in the evening, everyone else had already headed home, and only the guys from the team were left, along with their wives—well, those who were married. Even though Ace and Alex were yet to get married, Dino still considered them a married couple. After all, it was their budding romance in the desert that brought on all the relationships amongst his teammates.

"Daddy!" Sienna called out to Irish.

Irish glanced over, and a slow smiled formed. "Whatcha got there, Dino?"

"Not sure yet. She flounders like a fish, though."

"I'm not a fish! Fish are stinky. I'm not stinky," the little dynamo responded to Dino. "I want to be a seal, like daddy." She started slapping her hands together as if she had flippers, then started making an awful sound that was a mixture of a bark and a wail, making everyone laugh.

He flipped her right side up and held her in his arms. "Hug me, and I'll let you be a seal." Her smile was infectious, and she wrapped her tiny arms around his neck and gave him a big squeeze. If he couldn't have kids of his own, at least he could love his teammates' kids.

He set Sienna down then took the empty seat between Potter and Frost. Christmas at Ace and Alex's hadn't disappointed. Alex was the master when it came to holiday and party planning. Plus, she could cook.

It was nice to be able to spend the holidays all together with all of the families. And, speaking of families, their little group was growing by the numbers. A year and a half ago, it had been just him and the seven other guys on the team. If they were CONUS in the continental United States, they usually crashed at either Frost's or Stitch's parents' house for Christmas dinner.

The team had been lucky on several fronts to have met Alex during a mission in Afghanistan about a year and a half ago. At the time, she was working for a private firm that ran missions on behalf of the government. She had been assigned as an attachment to their team in capturing a terrorist in the region.

She was the only female he'd met who he'd never go one-on-one with in any combat situation. The woman was totally badass. She also had the respect of every member of the military who knew her. She was damn lucky to still be alive, considering she had been kidnapped, shot, and tortured by the man they had hunted. To this day, her ordeal still haunted Dino and the rest of the team. If it weren't for the video footage that showed her taking the lives of her captors before the team had rescued her, nobody would've believed she had done it. She was truly an amazing woman with a heart of gold.

Dino glanced over at the power couple. There were times he felt a slight sting knowing he'd never have what those two shared—love. *Nope…been there, done that, and got burned.* He still had the mental scars from that time in his life, and it was something he never wanted to relive again.

Sienna jumped onto Irish's lap and stole a cookie off the dessert plate. She was nibbling on it like a little squirrel when Tenley asked her, "Sienna, where are Cody and Alejandra?" Alejandra—Tenley and Potter's oldest daughter was seven years old; they had adopted her from Ecuador after an earthquake had struck her home town and her parents were killed. Tenley, who's a nurse, had gone to Ecuador to assist with the injuries. Like Alex, she too had run into trouble that had threatened not only her and Potter's relationship but her actual life.

Cody was a super cool kid and one of the bravest kids he had ever met. Frost had adopted Cody after he and Autumn had gotten married. Cody's biological dad was a Marine and was killed in action a few years ago. When Autumn had her run-in with danger involving her crazy ex-sister-in-law, it was Cody who had come to her rescue. At eleven years old, he was already becoming a little Alpha, but having Frost as a role model, it was no surprise.

Cody and Alejandra had become attached at the hip ever since they first met. Everyone always joked that they'd marry when they got older. It drove Potter batshit crazy.

Sienna turned her cookie-crumbed face to Tenley.

"Umm…I think they went to play with Cody's balls again. He's got those big squishy ones." She tried to give them a visual as she made a fist and began to pump it. She hadn't done a very good job with her explanation because Frost's face had completely lost every ounce of coloring and Potter choked on his drink before he quickly handed off his newborn twins, Kensi and Kelsey, to Tenley and Alex. Just as both Frost and Potter were scrambling to get out of their seats to go in search of the two love-struck kids, Sienna reached into the pocket of her hoodie and pulled out a large stress ball shaped like a dolphin and held it up. "Cody has one like mine but his is bigger."

Dino couldn't help the snort of laughter that emitted from him at the way Potter and Frost sank back into their chairs with a look of relief. If Potter thought he, had it bad now, he was in for a rude awakening when his three daughters were all grown up.

Sienna then turned her attention to Irish, and what came out of her mouth next made Dino wish he had his camera out to catch the moment on video.

"Guess what, daddy?"

"What, peanut?" Irish responded, wiping away some of the cookie crumbs around her mouth.

"Did you know that I have a pussy?"

At first, Dino wasn't sure if he had heard her correctly, but with the sounds of silverware dropping and a couple of gasps from folks at the table, Dino was pretty sure his ears were working just fine.

Alex had her hand over her mouth, and Dino wasn't sure if it was to keep from laughing or if she was literally shocked. Tenley's eyes were so big they looked like they were going to pop from her head, while Mia and Autumn just stared at each other as if asking one another if they had heard Sienna correctly. Poor sweet Bailey; her cheeks were as red as a ripened tomato ready to be plucked from the vine.

When it came to peculiar comments made by Sienna, Irish appeared utterly at a loss for words. He then confirmed what Dino assumed when he turned to Bailey and gave her a pleading look to help him out.

Bailey took a sip of water before she cleared her throat. "Sienna, honey. Where did you hear that?"

"Oh, all the kids at school were talking about it."

"Oh, for the love of God. You heard that in school?" Irish barked out, then looked at Bailey. "She heard that in school? I don't remember learning about that when I was in Kindergarten—maybe middle school in sex ed—"

Bailey slapped his shoulder to make him shut up. She shook her head at Irish before focusing back on Sienna. "Sienna, when you say all the kids were talking about it, did they specifically single you out?"

The young girl's face took on a confused expression.

"Well, no. We talked about Megan's pussy and Ellie's pussy." Sienna turned her head toward Mia and grinned. "We talked about Aunt Mia's pussies and how soft and furry they were."

Stitch, at that moment, had just taken a swig of his beer and spewed it all over the table while Mia's face turned redder than Bailey's was just a few moments ago.

Out of nowhere and breaking the silence at the table, Potter barked out a loud laugh. Tenley gave him a dirty look and told him that it wasn't funny, but he just smiled and shook his head at his feisty wife. He then looked at Sienna and smiled.

"Sweetie, are you talking about Mr. Whiskers, your kitty cat at home, and all of the *pussy cats* that your Aunt Mia has at her shelter?"

When Sienna grinned and nodded her head, Dino could hear every single person slowly release a large amount of air that they had been holding. Then as if unfazed by the discussion of pussies, Sienna leaped off Irish's lap and darted down the hall toward the game room, yelling to the other kids about all the pussies she knew.

For a few moments, everyone sat there staring at one another as if silently asking if that had really just happened. Irish had his head down, resting in his hands. Finally, he looked up and ran his hand down his face. "I think I'm scarred. I don't ever want to hear the "P" word again."

Potter looked at Irish and grinned. "You are such a pussy." Everyone laughed and started to make jokes. There most definitely is never a dull moment when their crazy group gets together.

Changing subjects, Alex asked, "Is everyone going to Bayside for New Year's?" Of course, everyone said they were. Those with kids had already lined up babysitters for the evening.

"Isn't Arianna supposed to be home?" Tenley asked Alex and Alex smiled.

"Yes. In fact, I saw Paul the other day and confirmed it with him. He said she's supposed to arrive tomorrow or the next day. He gave me her new number. I was going to reach out to her."

"She's been MIA for the past few years?" Stitch asked, looking suspicious.

"Yeah. Anytime I asked Paul about it, he gave me short answers and just said it had something to do with her job. Not sure what she's been up to."

"What does she do?" Skittles asked.

"Last I heard, she was contracting with the FBI in their forensics department."

"That sounds interesting," Dino chimed in.

"Yeah, if I remember correctly, I think it was like cyber forensics or something like that. I know she said she investigated numbers and stuff like that."

"Sounds pretty cool. Maybe a Forensics Accountant," Skittles said. He was probably right since he was into all that computer stuff.

"It'll be nice to see her and catch up," Frost admitted, and the others agreed.

Just then, Zuma, Ace, and Alex's chocolate Lab trotted through the room. Seeing the pooch made Dino think of Nigel. Then he remembered that Anna told him she had gotten him from the clinic and shelter that Mia ran.

"Hey Mia, do you have an employee by the name of Grace?"

Mia set her glass down and smiled. "I do. Why do you ask?"

"My neighbor just got a dog from the shelter, and she was saying how nice and informative Grace was."

Diego tried to cover his laugh with a lame cough, just as did Ace. Dino talked with the guys earlier and told them about the collar incident with his neighbor, minus the shower activity. Diego was the only one who knew about his and Anna's *arrangement*. Dino was surprised Diego hadn't let the cat out of the bag. But there was always time.

"Grace is amazing at what she does. Do you know which dog your neighbor adopted?" Mia asked.

"I don't know what kind it is, but he's gray and huge. His name is Nigel."

"Oh! Nigel, yes. He is a big dog, but so friendly. I was thrilled when Grace told me someone adopted him. I think people were scared of him because of his size." Dino nodded his head in agreement. He could understand that. Hell, Nigel had scared him at first.

The conversation turned to another subject, but Dino's mind remained on—his neighbor, Anna. He blasted himself. Their arrangement was supposed to be just that—a no strings attached type of arrangement. But Anna had become a permanent stakeholder in his mind—the image of her and the sound of her voice were always there in the forefront. That wasn't a good thing. Maybe he needed to take a step back and regroup.

"Dude," Diego said as he nudged his arm.

Dino looked up at his best friend. "What?"

"Did you not hear a word I said?"

And that there was a prime example of why he needed to stay away from the raven-haired beauty.

"Sorry. I was just thinking about something."

Judging from Diego's smirk, he knew not what but who had been on his mind.

"I was saying that I want to finish up the kitchen and living room drywall before New Year's. Are you still available to help after work for the next few days? The others said they were in."

"Yeah, man. Of course." Diego had bought a large fixer-upper house and had been refurbishing it room by room in his spare time. The guys on the team would help out when they could. Usually, it would end with the entire team over along with their families, and they would have a big cookout. Except in the colder months, the cookout was brought indoors.

"Cool. I think it's just you, Skittles, and me. I'll pick up some subs and beer."

"Sounds like a plan." Instead of the three amigos, it would be the three bachelors.

A few hours later and feeling worn out, Dino pulled his Chevy Blazer into the driveway. He grabbed the containers of leftover food that Alex had packed up for him. He had watched her fill the containers she gave him enough to feed an entire family. She packed him a little of everything: prime rib, ham, mashed potatoes, green beans, some sort of rice and beef mixture, and his favorite go-to snack when he was in the mood—sugar cookies.

Just as he was about the shut the door, headlights turning into the driveway next door caught his eye. He shook his head and laughed when he saw Nigel sitting in the front passenger seat, looking like he truly belonged there. When the mutt's eyes met his, he started barking which caused his owner to lean forward in her seat to see what he was barking at. That was the moment Dino knew he should've made a mad dash for his front door.

He shut the door and waited for her to get out. He didn't want to be rude and act like he hadn't seen her. He was greeted by Nigel first, who was more interested in the food Dino had in his hands. He gave the furball a good scratch behind his ears.

Anna then appeared dressed in hip hugger jeans, a red long sleeve t-shirt, and white Converse sneakers.

For casual, she looked hot, and he had to bite his lip.

"Nigel, sit," Anna commanded, and surprisingly the dog sat.

Dino looked at Anna. "Did you just teach him that?"

She grinned. "My dad and his friends did."

"I'm impressed."

“Me too.” She gave Nigel a little pat on the head. “He’s a quick learner.”

“Did you have a nice Christmas?” She asked.

He nodded. “It was nice. A lot of friends and family time.”

“You can’t go wrong with good friends and family.”

He chuckled. “No, you can’t.” He nodded toward her. “And you? Did Santa bring you everything you asked for?”

“Ehh…It was okay. I spent the day with my dad and some of his friends. We volunteered at the shelter in town then went for a drink afterward.”

It was nice to know she cared about the community and its people, even those less fortunate. He would have to remember to mention her name to Alex if she needed any help at her charity organization.

“Would you like to come over for a little bit?” She held up a tin. “I don’t have much food, but I have cookies and can make us some coffee.”

So badly he wanted to say yes, but after the thoughts he had earlier, he decided he would pump the brakes before he got sucked in further. It was in no way anything against her personally. It was all him and the ugly past that haunted him.

“I think I’m going to turn in early, but thank you.”

He felt terrible when her smile faltered a bit, but she recovered quickly. “No worries. Well, don’t let me keep you. Good-night,” she told him and called for Nigel to follow her.

Dino stood there and watched her walk up to the porch and let herself inside. *“What in the hell is wrong with me?”* He muttered to himself as he walked the opposite way to his house.

Arianna followed Nigel inside and locked the front door behind her. She felt stupid and embarrassed by Dino’s rejection. The funny thing was she wasn’t even insinuating having sex. She just wanted the company—someone to talk to. Since she had been gone the last two Christmases and had spent them by herself, she hoped to spend more time with her dad, but she understood that he had already made plans since he wasn’t even aware that she’d be home.

She set her things down then went over to the fireplace, threw a couple of logs in, and then lit the fire starter under the grate. It hadn't taken long for the flames to grow and for the warmth to start filtering into the room. When she stood, she looked about the essentially bare room. Except for some basic furniture like her living room and bedroom sets and kitchen table, she hadn't decorated the place. Her plans were still somewhat up in the air, so she had figured why unpack everything until she decided.

Irritated with herself for feeling disappointed, she went into the kitchen and made herself a cup of hot chocolate. She took a sip and almost burned the hell out of her mouth. She set the cup aside and decided to slip into something more comfortable while her drink cooled.

Usually, when she felt down in the dumps, she would change into one of the many sexy lingerie outfits she had acquired during her stint undercover. However, she wasn't in the mood for feeling sexy. She went to the laundry room and rummaged through a basket of clean clothes that she hadn't taken upstairs yet and found a pair of flannel pajama bottoms and a cami top that matched. It was perfect for her frame of mind.

She stopped back in the kitchen and grabbed her mug of hot cocoa, and when she passed by the kitchen table, she saw the large stack of mail that her dad had given her. She grabbed that too and made her way to the couch. Nigel had already made himself comfortable in the corner of the sofa and was already half asleep.

She hit the music app on her phone, and in seconds the joyful sounds of Christmas flooded her living room. She sat down, tucking her feet under her butt, and got comfortable. She went to reach for her fuzzy blanket, but it appeared that Nigel already claimed it.

She took the stack of mail and laid it in her lap. She flipped through the pile, throwing obvious junk mail like advertisement fliers and magazines into a small waste basket next to her on the floor. When she was left with what she would consider being actual mail, she started with the top one and began to open them. One was for her car warranty – that went into the trash since the date had long passed. She opened a couple from George Mason University Alumni and put those to the side to look at later. After a while, she got tired of that and put the rest of the stack on the coffee table in front of her to go through later.

She reached over to the table beside her and turned the lamp off, plummeting the room into darkness except for the glow of the flames coming from the fireplace. When her mom's favorite Christmas song, *The Christmas Shoes*, started to play, Arianna couldn't hold back the tears she'd been trying to keep at bay. She missed her mom so much, but even more so around the holidays. She missed all of the traditions she and her mom had established; baking and decorating cookies, decorating the Christmas tree, shopping, and wrapping presents. But most of all, she missed the presence of her being there to talk to. Her mom had not only been a parent - she had been her best friend.

Just as she wiped away the few tears she had in her eyes, someone knocked on the front door, making her jump. The sound woke up Nigel, and he barked.

Dino was feeling antsy. He felt like an asshole for telling Anna that he was tired, because that was furthest from the truth. Since he entered his house and put away the leftovers, he'd been sitting in his recliner in the dark, staring out the window that faced her house.

The longer he spent thinking about it, the deeper he realized that maybe she was just being friendly and wasn't inviting him over for a quick roll in the hay, but really was offering just coffee and cookies. God, he was an idiot. He just needed to be honest with her that things between them had started to wig him out a little. After all, they both had promised that they'd be open with each other.

Decision made, he stood up and headed out the door. As he walked next door, he casually scanned the area around the houses. It was a perpetual habit no matter where he went. He was trained to always be aware of his surroundings. There were many unfamiliar vehicles parked along the street, but it was expected for neighbors to have friends and family over for the holiday.

He climbed the steps and took a big breath, then knocked on the door. He smiled to himself when he heard Nigel's deep bark. He waited for several moments then knocked a second time. Again, Nigel barked but there was no sign of Anna.

Finally, he saw movement through the sidelight windows next to the door. Moments later, the sound of the lock disengaging echoed in the silent night air.

He readied himself as the door started to open, but the pep talk he had given himself on the way over went out the window when her face came into view. The redness and puffiness in her eyes, along with her strained expression, told him that something was wrong.

"Oh, it's only you," she told him, looking as if she was relieved.

"Were you expecting someone else?" He asked, wondering if she had invited someone else over after he declined her invitation. A sudden feeling of jealousy hit him, but he pushed it aside for the time being.

Ignoring his question, she asked, "Why are you here?"

He grinned. "Well, you did invite me over for coffee and cookies."

"And you declined, stating that you were tired," she raised her manicured eyebrow at him as she threw his words back at him, and boy, had he felt the hit.

"I changed my mind," he said with a shrug of his shoulders.

She huffed a small sigh and turned and walked further into the house, leaving the door open for him to enter. He stepped in, closed the door behind him, and then gave Nigel the attention he was seeking. He loved that dog. Once he got Nigel settled down, he found Anna in the kitchen. She was obviously trying to keep herself busy while trying to avoid him, and he wondered why.

Suddenly, she turned around and faced him. With her arms crossed in front of her chest, appearing defiant, she leveled her gaze with him. "I'm not in the mood for sex," she blurted out.

Her outburst had shocked him, and he became intrigued with her sudden mood shift. Was she pissed and upset at him, or had something or someone else caused the temperament swing?

"Is everything okay?" He asked her as he matched her stance and crossed his arms across his chest.

When she didn't answer immediately, he knew something had happened. Finally, she dropped her arms down to her sides in defeat.

"It's just me feeling sorry for myself," she replied, waving him off. She leaned her hip against the counter, still facing him. "I just wanted to enjoy the night. I wanted to share it with someone—whether you, my dad, just someone. I wanted to sit on the couch and watch Christmas movies while enjoying some hot cocoa and cookies. Is that too much to ask for?"

Now he felt like a real ass knowing she thought that he believed that she had only invited him over for sex. He wouldn't lie, though; sex had crossed his mind.

A sudden possessive feeling ascended over him, and he couldn't stop himself from reaching out. In two long strides, he was in front of her and held her by her shoulders. He could see the emotion swirling in her hazel eyes he thought were beautiful.

He pulled her tightly against him and held her there with his arms wrapped around her, acting as a security blanket. He felt less insecure when she leaned against him. She didn't say a word, and that was okay. He would stand there until she was ready. After a silent minute or two, she finally leaned back and looked up at him. Her eyes were still glistening with leftover tears.

"Better?" He asked, caressing her cheek with his knuckles.

With her head tilted back, staring up at him, she quietly whispered, "I'm sorry."

He tucked a strand of her hair behind her ear and smiled at her. "Why are you sorry?"

"For my behavior just now."

"Anna, you don't have to be sorry. And, just for the record, sex wasn't the reason I came over." She gave him a "don't blow smoke up my ass" look, and he snickered. "Okay…maybe it was part of it, although it was low on the list."

When a smile appeared on her face, he knew things were heading in the right direction.

He leaned forward and pressed his lips against her forehead. God, she fit him perfectly.

"Are you sure you're, okay?"

"I'll be okay. Just thinking about things."

"Do you want to talk about it?"

"Not really. But thank you," she told him and pulled back before she turned and pulled down a box of cocoa from the cabinet above her. That was when he noticed the bright pink, puckered scar on her upper arm just below the shoulder. He remembered the first night she had a bandage wrapped around her upper arm. She had told him that she had cut it somehow while she was moving. Dino hadn't been born yesterday, and especially in his line of work; he knew the difference between a cut from a bullet wound. A bullet most definitely caused her scar.

When she turned around, she must've sensed his scrutiny because her hand immediately went to the area on her arm in question. *Interesting.*

"From the looks of that scar, it must've been a pretty nasty *cut*," he told her, making sure he emphasized the word cut.

With just a nod of her head, he'd let her off the hook, for now. He couldn't promise that the topic wouldn't be revisited. They may just be friends with benefits, but that didn't mean he didn't care about her, and if she were in some sort of trouble, he'd be there to help her.

He could tell his questioning had made her uncomfortable because she started to fidget, and that was the last thing he wanted to do right now. If she wanted non-sexual company for the evening, then that was what he would give her.

He walked into the living room and grabbed her mug from the coffee table, then went back to the kitchen and pulled another mug from the drying rack next to the sink, and began to make hot chocolate.

"What are you doing?" She asked.

"What does it look like? I'm making us some hot chocolate, then we're going to go sit down and watch a movie together."

She scrunched her forehead up and gave him a questionable look. "We are?"

He smiled. "Yep! Now, go sit down and find us a movie. I'll be there in a sec."

A few minutes later, with two piping hot mugs of hot chocolate in his hand and a tin of cookies under his arm, he found Anna on the couch cuddled in one corner while Nigel claimed the other. He set everything down and took the seat in the middle of the two.

Anna looked over at him and grinned. "Thank you," she told him, and he could hear the sincerity in her words.

He softly smiled. "You're welcome. Come here." He put his arm around her shoulders and gently pulled her into his side. Her body immediately relaxed as she laid against him. Moments later, the movie began.

As he sipped his hot chocolate and watched Ralphy from *A Christmas Story* almost shoot his eye out, he wondered to himself if this could be what it would be like all of the time if he could just let the wall down that was guarding his heart.

CHAPTER FOURTEEN

It was New Year's Eve, and Arianna felt a mixture of emotions about the big celebration later that evening at Bayside. On the one hand, she was excited to see all of her friends, but on the other hand, she was nervous if they started to ask questions about her job. Over the last couple of days, she crafted some evasive maneuvers if she was backed into a corner. She knew her friends could be excellent interrogators at times.

To get her mind off the impending event and tone down her anxiousness, she had been excited yet surprised when she got a call from her good friend Alex Hardesty asking if she wanted to get together before the party. Alex had been the one friend who helped Arianna navigate the tough times when she had lost her mom. Alex had lost her dad, a Navy SEAL, when he was killed in action during a mission, so she understood the emotions getting through that time.

Sitting in a frozen yogurt shop just down the street from Alex's charity foundation headquarters, Arianna hadn't realized how much she had missed over the last few years until now as she talked with Alex. For the past two hours or so, they'd been exchanging stories and catching up on what had been going on in their lives. However, Arianna was careful not to divulge too much information.

"Alex, I'm so glad that you called me, and we were able to catch up a little before tonight," Arianna told Alex as she scooped up another spoonful of her favorite—white chocolate with Oreo crumbles on top.

Alex smiled. "I was so happy when your dad said you were coming home for a visit."

"It's nice to be home."

"I bet. I felt the same after I moved back home."

"I still can't believe you left the secret world of operatives," Arianna admitted to Alex.

Alex grinned. "I know. Sometimes I can't believe it myself."

"Do you miss it?"

"Sometimes. I think I miss the adrenaline rush more than the danger I sometimes faced." She glanced at her engagement ring. "But I'm also content here at home with Ace. When he's not deployed, that is."

Arianna chuckled. "You and a Navy SEAL. Who would have thought?"

Alex had always sworn that she'd never date a military guy, let alone marry one.

Alex grinned, and by the sparkle in her eyes, Arianna could see that she was truly in love. She was happy for her.

"I guess you never know where you might find love."

"You got that right," Alex told her.

"How about you?"

"What about me?"

"Is there a special guy in your life? Weren't you dating someone before you disappeared?"

"I was, but it didn't work out. He was involved in some extracurricular activities with my next-door neighbor - if you know what I mean." Alex nodded. "That happened right before I got sucked into the job I was doing up until a few weeks ago." She shrugged her shoulders. "So, no boyfriend for me."

Arianna couldn't help feeling like she was omitting the truth because the first person who popped into her head was Dino. She hadn't talked to him since Christmas when she fell asleep on him while watching Christmas movies. She had seen another side of him that night, and it truly touched her deep inside. He could've been an ass and walked away when she told him he wasn't getting lucky. Instead, he actually listened to what she was saying and spent the evening with her doing what she wanted. He must've been working early mornings and late nights because she never saw or heard him either leaving or coming home the past days. ALSO, she never called her dad when she got home.

She had used the free days to try and organize her garage that's full of boxes. The people that the bureau instructed to pack up her apartment in Italy hadn't known the first thing about packing. They could've packed all her items in half as many boxes as they had. Most of the boxes or containers were only half full. With the consolidating, she had done, she had at least made a path through the garage.

Alex stared at her, and Arianna tried her darndest to avoid eye contact, but Alex was too good of an observer.

"Okay, fess up. Who is he?"

"It's nobody." At least nobody that Alex knew, and it would stay that way.

When she didn't get a response, she had figured that Alex had dropped it, but with one glance toward her friend and the incredulous look she got from her, Arianna knew Alex wasn't going to let it go.

"Fine…he's, my neighbor."

Alex's eyes widened in surprise and a slow, sly smile formed. "You slept with your neighbor?"

Arianna didn't even respond verbally. She instead just nodded her head waiting to see what Alex's reaction would be.

"Are you dating?"

"No!" She shot that down quickly.

"So, was it a one-night stand kind of thing?"

"Not exactly," she answered, and Alex quirked her eyebrow. "More like neighbors with benefits."

Alex covered her mouth, trying to suppress her laugh.

"Neighbors with benefits. That's a new one for me. So, you're not dating?"

"It's complicated."

"How so?"

"Neither one of us had wanted anything permanent."

Alex was quiet for a moment, and Arianna started to believe that maybe Alex disapproved. Not that it mattered, because it was her decision and not Alex's.

"You said neither of you *had* wanted anything. As in past tense. Have your feelings changed since you two made that agreement?"

Oh hell! It shouldn't have surprised Arianna that Alex would take her words and analyze them. But Alex had a point. Her feelings had shifted slightly. Even though she had kept herself busy the last few days, she still found herself thinking about Dino.

"Judging from your silence, I'm going to say they have," Alex said.

Arianna played with her napkin. "So, do you think it was a bad idea?"

Alex grinned. "Girl, obviously you enjoy what he has to offer if you keep going back. I wouldn't say that's bad. As long as that's what you both want."

Arianna shook her head, though she knew Alex was right. Now that she had taken a ride on the Italian Stallion, she wasn't sure if she could walk away—her feelings be damned.

Dino couldn't put his mind to rest. Ever since Christmas night, which he'd admit, he enjoyed, he knew his feelings had changed significantly towards Anna. The last few nights, he had battled with himself and these new feelings he was developing. Thankfully, since there'd been an uptick in activity at work, it hadn't left a lot of time to occupy his mind.

He wondered where she had gone off to for the night. He had seen her leave her house about an hour ago. Had she been on a date with another guy? *Ugh!* Why did he even care? It made him grumpy, and grumpy wasn't how he wanted to start the new year.

Irish took a seat at the table and eyed Dino. "What has you looking down in the dumps? Tonight, should be a celebration. We made it through another year."

"He found a lady friend and isn't sure what to think of it." Diego teased.

"Cool it," Dino glared at Diego, and Diego chuckled.

Irish's lips started to curl at the corners, and Dino knew he was in for it. He'd teased the others in the past when they were courting their women. But that was okay because he was a grown-ass man and could take the payback, though he never expected for it to happen.

"Who is she?" Irish asked, lifting his beer to his lips.

"Who's who?" Ace asked as he, Potter, and Stitch all took the other empty chairs.

Ignoring Ace, Dino gave both Diego and Irish the evil eye, but all it did was cause them to snicker, knowing they had hit a nerve.

Thankfully, Alex appeared looking like she was filled with excitement as she bounced in place, and Dino could only wonder what the feisty former operative had up her sleeve. Alex was known to pull some pretty good pranks on the guys just because she could, and there had been some doozies.

"Oh, good. Everyone is here. Arianna should be here any minute."

Then her smile became bigger. "There she is now." And she took off towards the front door.

Moments later, hearing some chatter behind him, Dino turned around, prepared to meet the woman everyone had been talking about for the last few days. As soon as his eyes locked onto the black-haired beauty walking towards him, he felt his chest tighten, and his eyes went wide. And he wasn't the only one appearing shell shocked as Anna, who he knew her by, stopped mid-stride and stared at him like a deer caught in the headlights.

Alex and Tenley both got up along with Stitch and Frost and met Arianna with hugs but her eyes never abandoned his.

Diego nudged Dino's elbow. "Do you two know each other?"

"Sort of," Dino replied, his eyes still fixed on the woman he'd been slowly falling for.

"Sort of?" Diego questioned.

"Oh shit, Arianna is the neighbor you've been shacking up with, isn't she?" Irish chuckled. "Can't wait until Paul finds out about that."

Dino tore his eyes away from Arianna to look at Irish.

"Paul? What does he have to do with her?"

"There's my girl!" As if on cue, Paul shouted from across the room where he stood by the bar.

"Daddy!" Arianna shouted as she started across the room, and Irish nodded for Dino to follow. When Paul came around the bar and scooped her up into his arms, Dino remembered Alex had mentioned that Arianna was Paul's daughter.

"Damn, she is gorgeous. Now I understand why you did what you did," Diego stated. Dino wasn't sure why Diego's comment bothered him. *Of course, you do. Just admit you have feelings for her,* his subconscious told him. But Dino then thought about it. If she lied about her name, what else had she lied about to him? Then he remembered what she told him about her job before moving here—fashion? Had she fed him a line of bullshit about that as well? And, just like that, the imaginary wall he had started to knock down started to rebuild itself.

He watched as Paul led her over to the table. Irish was still making sarcastic comments under his breath which was now beginning to piss Dino off.

"Let me introduce you to my favorite gang," Paul said, stopping at their table with Arianna by his side.

Dino watched her, knowing his presence and his stare made her uncomfortable. He'd give her some credit; she hadn't caved completely, but she was squirming.

"Of course, you know Stitch, Frost, Alex, and Tenley. There at the end, next to Alex, is Ace, her fiancé. The big scary guy next to Tenley is Potter, her husband. Red down there with Frost is Autumn. Next to them are Irish and his wife, Bailey. Then you got the bachelors at this end. There's Diego, Skittles, and Dino."

She smiled. "It's nice to meet everyone. Although I'll be honest, I am horrible at remembering names—faces I can recognize, though. Her eyes met Dino's.

"Hi, Dino," she said, surprising Dino.

"How…" Paul started to ask, but Arianna interrupted him.

"We're neighbors. We met about a week or so ago."

Paul gave Dino a look as if he knew what he and she had been doing. That made Dino a little uncomfortable.

"Interesting…Well, I'll let you spend tonight with your friends. Go on and have fun, and we'll catch up over breakfast tomorrow to discuss your schedule. Meet me at the old diner at nine sharp."

"Yes, Sir." She saluted her dad, making Paul laugh. He gave her one last hug before he went back over to join his friends near the bar.

"Well, take a seat, and welcome to our little dysfunctional family," Alex told her with a twinkle in her eyes.

Arianna wanted to run and hide under the nearest table the moment her eyes had locked with Dino's. What were the odds that her neighbor was friends with her friends? This arrangement of theirs was going to blow up in her face.

Arianna took the lone seat at the table, which happened to be next to Dino. Before she could say anything, he leaned over and whispered, "You could've warned me."

When she turned her head and met his gaze, she could see the hurt along with reservations in the piercing glare he gave her.

"How was I supposed to know you were friends with Alex, Tenley, Stitch, and Frost? And you even know my dad. It's not like we exchanged our life history."

He draped his arm over the back of her chair; his fingers brushed against her neck, sending tingles through her body. He was doing it on purpose to get her worked up. Though it should've pissed her off, his scheme was working. Anytime his hands touched her, it set off a sensation inside her body that only he could generate.

"Why did you lie about your name?" He flat out asked her.

"Technically, I didn't lie. Anna is part of my name. My mom sometimes would call me Anna." That wasn't a lie. It had also been why the bureau had decided to give her that name for her undercover assignment. It was close to her name, and a name she wouldn't have a hard time getting used to.

"And your job? Forensic Accountant or fashion industry? Which is it?"

His gaze literally made her squirm as he looked deep into her eyes. The intensity almost made her look away, but she didn't. She swallowed hard.

"Both. Please don't be upset with me."

Before he could reply, Stitch shouted down to them. "What are you two whispering about over there?" It was meant to be funny, but both Arianna and Dino just stared at Stitch because neither knew what to say.

"Arianna, you said that you and Dino had met. Where was that?" Tenley asked.

"We live in the same neighborhood."

"Wait, are you the neighbor with the dog?" Ace asked with a slight grin and gleam in his eye.

She felt the heat hit her face, and she turned toward Dino. "Oh my god! You told them about that?" She scolded him, and then she felt her face get even hotter. Had he told them about what happened afterward?

"Oh, come on. Even you thought it was funny as hell after the fact," Dino told her and squeezed her thigh under the table.

It seemed as if only the guys knew about her unfortunate experience with Nigel's bark collar, So Dino proceeded to retell the most embarrassing moment of her life to everyone else at the table. After he finished and everyone laughed at her expense, though she took it in stride, Dino leaned in close and whispered in her ear. "I only told them about the collar. I don't kiss and tell." He gently nipped her ear, and between that and his warm breath moving across the shell of her ear, it nearly made her insides turn to goo.

She grabbed the glass of water in front of her and guzzled half of the glass.

"Well, I think it's great that you have someone like Dino who can watch your six," Alex stated, looking directly at her and winked, before she took a sip of her drink. Arianna wasn't sure if Alex had put two and two together and linked the *arrangement* she had with her neighbor, who she had told her about earlier in the day, to the man who was sitting next to her.

When she looked around the table, she caught Diego's gaze and saw his subtle wink as if knowing what she was thinking. *"Just fucking dandy!"*

A little while later, Arianna, Tenley, and Alex all walked outside to the patio deck. With a large crowd expected, he had set up portable gas heaters out there so folks would have plenty of room. They took one of the tables and sat down.

"So, what exactly has been going on between you and Dino?" Alex asked.

"What do you mean?" She said with a slight tilt of her head.

Tenley jumped to comment first. "Oh, don't give us that look. First, you both looked shell-shocked the moment you saw one another. And, don't think we didn't see you guys down at the other end of the table whispering in each other's ear.

Damn, Tenley had gained some investigative skills, and Arianna felt the heat to her cheeks for the second time this evening, and she picked up her pineapple and rum drink and took a big gulp. When she set it down, she looked at her two friends across the table.

"We were just surprised to see each other, that's all. As he said, we live in the same neighborhood."

She looked away, hoping her friends would drop the third degree, but that was wishful thinking.

Then as if she had an epiphany, Alex blurts out, "Oh Jesus, he's the neighbor you slept with?"

"What?" Tenley asked, looking between Alex and Arianna.

"For Christ's sake, Alex, keep your damn voice down." Arianna whispered, then glanced around the patio, making sure nobody had overheard her friend's loud mouth.

Alex started laughing, and then Tenley chimed in. "Damn, chica, you're home for a week, and you already got yourself a man. And, not any ordinary man. You nabbed yourself a SEAL."

"It's not like that, Tenley." She shook her head as Tenley's words just registered. "Wait, what do you mean I nabbed a SEAL?"

A huge grin spread across Alex's face. "Dino is part of Ace and Potter's team—SEAL Team."

"Oh shit."

"Spill it. What have you and the Italian Stallion been up to the last week or so? Wait? How long have you been home?"

She gave them a well-edited version of the reason she was not with the bureau. They thought her contract wasn't renewed after the *project* she had been assisting on had been completed.

Then she told them all about sneaking onto Dino's dock and how their arrangement came about.

"We both had a little too much to drink, and one thing led to another. And, then another." She covered her face. "I'm so screwed."

"From the sounds of it, you were literally screwed seven ways to Sunday." Tenley couldn't stop laughing.

"So, again, you guys aren't dating?" Alex asked for the third time today.

"No." Arianna wondered if Alex had any insight on his background. It was apparent that she was close to all of the guys on the team.

"What's his story?" She asked Alex as she took in the sight of Dino as he interacted with everyone. He seemed to be enjoying himself around his friends.

"I don't know a lot. Out of all of the guys on the team, he is the quietest and doesn't share too much personal information."

"You've never asked Ace?"

"Nope. Not my business. I don't ask questions where it's related to the guys unless it warrants it. Anyways, most of them end up confiding in me, so I don't really have to ask. But I do sense that there's something from his past that he keeps close to himself."

That was fair. She half wondered why she even asked Alex. Dino's personal life didn't concern her. If he wanted her to know about it, he would tell her.

"So, what are your plans now that you're back? Do you think the bureau will renew your contract?"

Arianna traced the rim of her glass with her finger. How could she honestly answer Alex's questions when she didn't even know the answer? "I don't know, and even if they do, I'm not sure if I want to return. For now, I told my dad I'd help around here with some of the managerial things."

Alex scrunched her forehead up. "I thought Victoria handled that type of stuff for your dad."

"Ehh…I sense there's trouble in paradise between those two."

"Well, whatever you decide, we support you. Although we'd love to have you around here," Alex told her.

Tenley raised her glass in the air. "Well, ladies, I say we toast to a healthy, prosperous - less drama in our lives - New Year."

Alex raised her drink and clicked it against Tenley's. "I second that especially the drama."

They looked at Arianna. She smiled and lifted her glass to theirs. "Happy New Year!"

After they finished their drinks off, they all headed back inside as it was getting close to midnight. Arianna let her friends go in before her, and she watched as both Alex and Tenley met their men in the middle of the room to watch on the large projector screen the last seconds of the year tick down.

She stood back and glanced around. They were in the home stretch twenty seconds to go, and now everyone had congregated into the middle of the room with their drinks and noisemakers in hand, ready for the celebration. Her eyes moved around the open space witnessing the many couples who were hugging each other in anticipation of sharing that first kiss of the new year. She sought out the one person she'd been looking for and was hit with a jolt of jealousy as she saw Dino cuddled with another woman, his arm draped over her shoulders as he held her close. No matter how many times she said to herself that she shouldn't care, it still stung a little.

They were just fuck-buddies. She cringed; just repeating that phrase in her head. Was that what she really wanted to be—just a booty call?"

She searched for her dad and found him near the bar in his usual spot. It made Arianna happy to see him laughing and enjoying the night with his friends. A sudden feeling of loneliness washed over her causing her to take a step backward. Taking in the atmosphere surrounding her, Arianna began to feel as if she was a stranger. Had living the life of an undercover agent with no contact with her friends and family for the last two years set her back personally?

As the clock struck midnight and the crowd erupted into cheers and singing as they welcomed in the New Year, Arianna silently slipped out the back door.

Even though it was blustery she slipped her boots and socks off then walked in the sand down towards the water. Feeling the sand squish between her toes brought a smile to her face as she remembered all of the wonderful memories she had at this beach. Once she was far enough from the light coming from the deck at the restaurant, she took a seat and closed her eyes, listening to the waves wash ashore.

Her mind was riddled with questions that only she had the answers to. But it was complicated. Being that it was New Year's and every year, she would set goals for herself to attain by the end of the year. She wasn't into making resolutions. Anyone could say they would start exercising, but why were they exercising? Was it to lose weight, to feel healthy? Without goals, most resolutions end up in failure.

Arianna had always been goal-oriented. She liked creating a plan of action and working through the steps to sustain her goals. Sometimes she may not complete one by the end of the year, but she was still progressing toward it and would carry it into the following year. She wasn't a quitter.

But how could she create goals for this year when she didn't even know what the future held for her. Her career path was up in the air, and she didn't even want to touch the subject of relationship goals. She honestly couldn't say where she'd even be living.

She tilted her face upward and took in the beauty of what the heavens offered for the night—not a cloud in the black velvet sky and a waning crescent moon shining down on the earth below.

At the stroke of midnight, Dino leaned down and kissed Jess on the cheek. Jess was the wife of a friend of his who was assigned to another SEAL team. Her husband was currently deployed, and she was out celebrating the new year with some of the other wives from the team. He had promised her that he would watch the count-down with her.

Jess hugged him and thanked him for keeping his promise before leaving to find her friends. Stuck in the middle of the floor with partiers surrounding him, acting wild, Dino looked for the one person with who he had wanted to share the first kiss of the new year with but she wasn't to be found. He had seen her come back inside with Alex and Tenley and had been standing by the back hallway that led to the restrooms. He caught Bruno's eye, and as if knowing who Dino was searching for, Bruno nodded toward the patio doors.

He walked out onto the empty deck as everyone had gone inside to watch the countdown. The sound of the ocean waves hitting the shoreline drew him toward the railing overlooking the section of the beach directly in front of the restaurant. For the most part, it was scarce, just a few people he had seen inside earlier who probably lived nearby and were walking home.

Arianna couldn't have gone far. He knew she had driven her car to the restaurant and her house was too far to walk to, so she had to have been out there somewhere. He scanned up and down the beach. Finally, his eyes caught some movement down by the waterline. Once he focused on the object, he realized it was someone sitting out there. His instincts told him it was her.

He took the stairs down to the beach. He was still skeptical about Arianna and had a lot of questions he wanted answers to. But something inside him told him she had valid reasons for hiding her true identity from him. Nonetheless, it also made him wonder if and when she would've told him the truth.

As he walked closer, he got a better view of her as she sat in the sand with her knees propped up, leaning back as her arms braced her frame. She was focused on something out in the water, and he followed her line of sight and saw a ship out in the distance. He wasn't sure which ship it was, as there were several in port at the base in Norfolk, but he knew it was definitely a Navy vessel.

He took the last few steps and sat down next to her. His company must've startled her because she gasped and quickly leaned away from him until she realized it was him.

He smiled at her. "Hi."

With her hand still over her heart, she took a deep breath. "You scared the crap out of me."

He snickered to himself. "Sorry. You must've seen something out there that caught your eye."

"It's beautiful," she told him sitting back up, then nodding her head toward the water.

His eyes traveled back out, over the rippling sea in the direction she was looking. She had been talking about the ship sitting out there with all of its lights on. Even on board, the men and women were most likely welcoming in the new year Navy ship style.

He scooted closer to her.

"I was looking for you."

She stayed staring at the water. "When?"

"At midnight."

"Didn't look that way to me," she told him flatly, and he knew then that she must've seen him with Jess.

Did he hear a tinge of jealousy in her tone?

"Why'd you disappear?"

"I can't really explain why," she admitted, then abruptly jumped to her feet and wiped the sand from her pants. He stood up next to her and studied her. Her face was pinched, and her eyes weren't as bright as they were earlier. He sensed something more besides the Jess thing was bothering her. He wrapped his arm around her waist and pulled her close to his body.

She tilted her head back to look up at him, and he searched her eyes, trying to see through all the emotion filtering through them. Was she calling out to him for help?

The engine of a fighter jet roared in the distance and an idea popped into Dino's head.

"Do you want to get out of here?"

She lifted her hand and looked at her watch. "And do what? I don't think there's much open, considering it's a holiday and a quarter after midnight."

"What I have in mind is open twenty-four, seven."

She looked unsure, but he just smiled as he slipped the palm of his other hand under her hair and cupped the back of her head, holding her in place to ensure she couldn't look away from him. He lowered his head and touched his forehead against hers. They were eye-to-eye and nose-to-nose. Each time she blinked, he felt the brush of her long eye lashes against his, while the steady beat of her heart was felt against his chest.

"Trust me?"

Although her whispered answer was almost drowned out from the sounds of the breakers, her response was heard loud and clear by him.

"Yes."

When her body began to relax under his hold, he lifted his head and kissed her forehead as she leaned into him, showing acceptance of his gesture.

Fifteen minutes later, and a tour of Virginia Beach's back roads at night, they pulled into a grass lot, and Dino backed into a space along the fence. They both exited the vehicle, and he popped the back hatch and motioned for Arianna to have a seat.

During the car ride, Dino had explained how Jess, the woman she saw with Dino, was just a friend and the promise he had made to her. It actually made Arianna feel better, and not because Jess was just a friend, but because it showed her another side of Dino—his compassion and someone who keeps their word.

The butterfly kiss that Dino gave her on the beach was still on her mind. She had remembered an article she had read not too long ago on the real meaning of a kiss and that a butterfly kiss indicated tenderness, trust, and close emotional and physical intimacy.

Whether Dino was aware of that or not, it was still becoming obvious that they were more connected to one another than just through sexual chemistry.

She looked around, and Dino knew she wasn't sure where they were. Seconds later, as the first F/A-18 Hornet fighter jet growled in the air above them, Dino saw her face light up. She glanced at him.

"The Air Station?"

"Yeah."

"I haven't been to this location. My dad always took me to the other side to watch."

"Not many people know about this spot." He wasn't lying. You had to travel down an isolated dirt road and then make a couple of turns before you found the spot. Most people gave up trying to find it. Dino loved to come out here.

They sat there watching jets take off and land.

She turned her body to face him.

"I'm sorry about not being forthcoming about who I really was."

"Apology accepted."

She exhaled. "What would you like to know about me?"

"You can start with telling me how you sustained that gunshot wound to your arm."

At first, he thought she would deny it, but then her facial expression said it all.

"Arianna?"

"I can't talk about it." She looked away from him.

He reached over and placed his finger under her chin and forced her to turn back.

"Can't or won't?"

She leveled her gaze at him. "Can't."

"Does it have to do with your job in the FBI or the fashion business?"

"Dino," she said with a sigh. She sat there for a few moments staring into the darkness. Finally, she asked, "You know how you guys have your secrets?"

He nodded but also wondered where she was going with this.

"Well, I have mine. I'm sorry, but I can't discuss it."

"Because of your job with the FBI?" He wanted her to at least confirm what he was thinking.

When she nodded her head, he said, "Okay. That's fair. But answer me this one question."

"What's that?"

"Are you in danger?"

She blinked her eyelids in rapid succession then swallowed hard. Another jet took off, catching her attention. She was silent as she followed the jet's tail watching the afterburners glow in the night sky. When she turned back to him, her face showed no emotion, and he couldn't gauge what her response was going to be.

"I honestly don't know."

He reached over and laid his hand on hers while it was resting on her leg.

"Promise me that if you are ever in any type of danger, you come to me."

"Dino, what's happening between us?"

He released her hand and ran it down his face. "I don't know, Arianna. I'll be honest, the feelings I'm experiencing are ones I haven't encountered in many, many years, and I'm not sure if I'm comfortable with it."

He turned his head and looked at her. "Does that even make sense?"

She gave him a soft smile and reached for his hand. "Someone hurt you, and you haven't been able to recover from it." She gently caressed the top of his hand, meant as a gesture to show compassion.

He lifted her hand to his lips and kissed her knuckles.

"It didn't just involve one person, and many people were impacted by what occurred."

"It sounds like you've never recovered from the aftermath of what happened." She had hit the nail on the head. Losing both the woman he thought had loved him, and then his best friend who had blown a hole in his heart that he never thought he'd be able to repair.

He hung his head. He wasn't sure how to respond without opening up pandora's box and telling her everything that he had never told another single person outside of his family.

As if sensing his unease, she scooted closer and placed her head against his shoulder.

"I really like you, Arianna," he said in a low voice, and he knew she heard him because she hugged his arm.

"I like you too."

They sat like that together for the next hour. Every once in a while, one or the other would ask a generic question like what their favorite color was or what their favorite food was. They spent the time just getting to know one another.

൭

It was close to two o'clock in the morning when they decided to call it a night. Arianna felt like she and Dino had made a little progress. It was what they both needed. She was curious about the incident he talked about vaguely that involved his past. Eventually, she would get him to open up to her.

As Dino was closing the back to the SUV, Arianna spotted someone on a bicycle riding through the grass towards the fence line. Arianna thought it was odd to see someone riding a bike out in the woods near the base at this time of the night.

When the bicyclist stopped about fifteen yards from their spot, Arianna recognized the woman.

She grabbed Dino's arm. "That's Grace from the shelter where I got Nigel."

"Seriously?" He asked, looking concerned. "What is she doing out here by herself and on a bike?" He looked over at Arianna. "This isn't the safest area, especially at night."

"Should we go find out?"

"It couldn't hurt."

As Arianna and Dino approached, another fighter jet took off above them, and Grace looked straight above her head as it flew over. She had her back to them.

"Grace?"

When Grace spun around and screamed, Arianna felt awful for frightening her, but maybe this could be a lesson learned that she shouldn't be out here alone.

Once Grace found her footing, she looked closer, and her eyes widened. "Arianna, right?"

Dino squeezed Arianna's waist and leaned in toward her ear. "She knew your real name?" He teased.

Arianna smiled. "Yes, hi. We were getting ready to leave and noticed you over here." Arianna gestured to Dino. "This is Dino. A friend of mine."

Dino reached his hand out and Arianna noticed Grace's hesitation as she looked at his hand like it was going to jump up and bite her. But she finally extended her hand and shook his hand.

"Nice to meet you," she greeted Dino.

Dino nodded his head. "Likewise."

"Are you here alone?" Arianna asked as she looked around, hoping maybe there was someone else, but it seemed that she was alone.

"Yes. I come down here several times a week."

"You like planes?"

She shrugged her shoulders and appeared to be uncomfortable with Arianna's questioning. Just then, another plane catapulted down the runway and shot upward, and Grace watched in fascination.

Once the aircraft was long gone, she turned back toward Arianna. "They just remind me of my past."

Arianna could see in Grace's expression and body language that she was on edge. For some strange reason, Arianna wanted to befriend this young girl. Call it instincts, call it whatever you wanted, but Arianna knew this girl needed a friend.

"Hey, my friends and I are going to get together next week at my dad's restaurant. Have you heard of Bayside?"

"I've heard of it, but I've never been."

Arianna smiled. "Well, you should come and hang out with us. It'll be a lot of fun."

Grace looked down towards the ground. "I don't know. I'm not a very social person."

"What are you talking about? I've seen you at the shelter. You are great with people," Arianna pushed.

"That's different. It's my job."

"Well, Mia will be there and of course me, and now you know Dino. So that makes three people that you'd know."

"I'll have to see."

Arianna wasn't counting on her showing up, but at least she had extended an olive branch.

"Okay."

"Well, I better get going."

"Do you need a ride?" Dino offered, and Arianna hoped that Grace would say yes, because she would be worried if she didn't know that she got home okay.

"No, thank you."

Dino raised his eyebrow, and Arianna could tell that he wanted to push the issue, as did she, but she didn't want to scare Grace off for good. She would make sure that she followed up with Mia about it."

"Okay. Well, if you ever want to hang out, talk, or anything, Mia knows where to find me."

"Thank you," she said before glancing at Dino. "It was nice meeting you."

He smiled. "You too, honey. And as Arianna said, we hope to see you around."

Arianna watched Grace as she pedaled across the grass lot to get to the road before she disappeared into the woods. Her gut clenched as the darkness swallowed her up.

Dino whistled low. "Damn, that girl definitely has a story to tell."

Arianna squeezed his hand and looked up at him. "Just like someone else I know." He squinted his eyes, and she laughed then winked at him. "Come on. You need to drop me off so I can pick up my car."

CHAPTER FIFTEEN

Demitri listened as his friend and client of many years, Niran Chaiwong, rattled off the specifics he was looking for in his next custom order. Niran, a former judge for the Thailand judiciary courts, was in the market for a new toy since his previous one didn't cut it and was disposed of. Demitri didn't ask how. The less he knew, the better off he was. Once the merchandise left his possession and he was paid, he didn't care.

"Do you think you can locate what I'm seeking, my friend?" Niran asked him with a heavy Thai accent.

Demitri looked over the notes he had been taking—college age young twenties, introvert, natural blonde hair, bold green eyes, athletic build, preferably European, and ability to speak Thai. His friend was asking for a lot, but Demitri had never let him down before, and he wouldn't be starting now.

"It may take a little longer to locate an exact match, but I think we can accommodate you."

"Excellent. I will wire half of the funds into the usual account."

"Actually, I'll send you instructions for a new account."

As soon as it was apparent that the flash drive was missing, Demitri closed out the old account and opened a new one with another bank in the United Kingdom under a shell corporation name.

"Do I detect trouble?"

Demitri had to be cautious in answering Narin's question because he didn't want to sound any alarms, that would get back to his many clients. A great number of his clients included high-profile individuals business executives, politicians, and other government officials.

"No trouble. I tend to move accounts every so often for precautionary reasons."

"I see. Well then. Send me the account information I'll get the funds wired, and then wait to hear from you."

"Nice talking to you, Niran."

"You as well, my friend."

Demitri disconnected and set the phone on the desk. The leather from his chair creaked as he leaned back. As soon as he was questioned by the police the day of the show in Rome, he fled to his secluded villa on the Island of Crete. The waterfront property was the only residence that he had deeded in a company name not affiliated with him. That way, it wouldn't be traced back to him. He feared more backlash could evolve from the incident, and he wanted to stay hidden for the time being.

He'd been able to keep himself busy with all of his business dealings. But at night, as he laid in his bed, his thoughts always wandered to the woman who got away.

People were starting to question the whereabouts of the Black Swan. Calls were going unreturned from her agent, and nobody knew where to go for answers. Her contract with Claude had ended a few days after the event in Rome, so even he was no help. In Claude's mind, Anna Humphreys was a name of the past; he had already moved on to his next upcoming star.

There was a knock on his door.

"Come in."

Carmine walked in with another guy who worked for Demitri.

"Any news?" Demitri asked.

Carmine shook his head. "No. Both the room and the tunnel were swept. The drive wasn't there."

Demitri tapped his finger against the desk. "I've double-checked the activity, and nobody has tried to access the file."

Demitri had embedded a code in the flash drive that, after three failed login attempts to the file, the program would self-destruct and delete every file saved on the drive. It was an added insurance policy in case it ever fell into the wrong hands.

"It's quite possible that the drive is in the trash by now. You said you placed it in the inside pocket. Remember she was shot? Therefore, I'm sure wherever she ended up, she probably threw the jacket away. I highly doubt that she searched it."

"What about Anna?"

"Nothing. It's confounding. Nobody has seen or heard a peep from her or her agent. It's like they both just fell off the face of the earth."

"Somebody out there knows something."

"You aren't going to stop looking, are you?" Carmine said, giving Demitri an amused half-smirk.

Demitri turned toward the large window to the left of his desk. He had a picture-perfect view of the Sea of Crete and its strikingly clear, turquoise water. He hadn't told Carmine yet, but he had already decided that he would not be returning to the United States. He was working on plans to move all of his operations to Europe. He had many homes throughout Europe and even Asia, but his favorite, and the one he would soon call home, was the Villa he was currently staying in. It had a private beach and many amenities that one could wish for. All that it was missing was his *swan*.

Demitri faced Carmine. "I'll never stop searching until she's found. Trust me. She's out there."

CHAPTER SIXTEEN

Arianna busied herself behind the bar while getting familiar with where everything was. It looked as if she'd be pulling double shifts between the administrative work and bartending until she could find a replacement for the guy she had to fire yesterday.

The guy hadn't been there to work; he was there to pick up women. A few longtime patrons had complained that the guy ignored the customers—unless they were a "cute" girl. She had talked with her dad yesterday morning about it, and he told her that she was in charge of that now and to do what she thought was best for the restaurant and bar.

Her dad always closed the restaurant on New Year's Day, so her first day had been the day after. She got right to work, starting with administrative tasks; making sure the employees' paperwork were up to date, payroll needed to be done, inventory logs, and the list went on. That was a week ago, and she was still buried in paperwork while getting things organized her way. Now she had to add hiring a bartender to her list.

Somewhere she had found a few minutes and decided to call Chris, her former supervisor at the bureau, to check in and see if anything had come to light regarding the complaint filed against her. She had been surprised when he answered the phone. He sounded both excited and relieved to hear from her. He had apologized for throwing her to the wolves during the debriefing process. He explained how he had been called out of town, and she understood. He still hadn't heard any developments on the status of the complaint, but he did tell her that things were progressing, whatever that meant. She was a tad bit suspicious that Chris knew more than what he was letting on. Actions like that just made her take another step away from the bureau.

Before they ended the call, she had flat out asked him who had filed the complaint. At first, he hesitated. Again, another red flag. But then he told her he didn't know. She didn't believe him, but she wasn't going to push the issue. His last words to her had made the hairs on the back of her neck stand up. He told her that she needed to be vigilant until things blew over. When she asked him if he could elaborate more on that comment, he told her to just be careful, aware of her surroundings, and try not to draw attention to herself. Immediately her mind went to Demitri, and a knot formed in her stomach.

She ran to the walk-in cooler to get a case of Miller Lite to restock the small cooler at the bar. When she returned, she smiled when she saw two new customers sitting at the bar. She placed the case on the floor and walked over to Dino and Skittles.

She hadn't really talked to Dino since New Year's Eve. With the hours she had been working, she was never home. She saw him the other morning when he was leaving for work and said hello. But other than that, it had been quiet between the two of them. She missed him.

"Hey, guys!" She greeted them and set down two drink napkins in front of them.

"Hi," Skittles said.

She looked at Dino, and he showed her his signature smirk again. He winked and then said hi to her.

"What can I get you guys?"

"Are you working the bar now too?" Dino asked, looking a bit confused, and she shrugged.

"Yeah. The previous bartender wasn't working out, so I had to let him go."

Skittles shook his head. "That guy was trouble anyway."

Arianna wondered what he meant by that. "Why do you say that?"

Skittles gave Dino a strange look. Dino cleared his throat. "We've heard that the guy would take women to the stock room or basement." Dino raised his eyebrow as if asking her if she understood what he was saying.

Her eyes widened and then narrowed. "That is disgusting, not to mention that we could've been liable if anything had happened."

She was fuming and even more glad that she had made the right decision in firing him. She went to ask Dino how he'd been when a customer shouted at her.

“Hey, sweetheart. How about another drink down here?” a guy called out.

Arianna hadn’t recognized him as one of the regulars. She excused herself and went to pour another beer for the guy. When she set it down in front of him, he winked, but it wasn’t a flirtatious wink; it was a creepy wink.

“Where’s your old man?” he asked, catching her off guard.

“Are you talking about Paul?” she asked.

“What? That is *your* old man, right?”

The guy provided her a predatory grin, and she promptly became uncomfortable. There were many people who she didn’t personally know who knew Paul was her dad, but something in her gut told her this guy was on a fishing expedition to gain information. She gave him another once over, looking for any familiarity but there was nothing about the guy she could connect to.

She didn’t answer his question directly but politely told him that Paul wasn’t around. She didn’t know how to operate the security cameras yet, but she would make sure she left a note for Bruno to tag this guy and show it to her dad.

Well, that had been a total lie considering she knew her dad was home with Victoria.

Her dad had been at the restaurant earlier but left a few hours ago because he hadn’t been feeling well. Earlier, she had found him leaning against the wall in the hallway back by his office. When she asked him if he was okay, he said that he had a dizzy spell. She pushed for him to go home, telling him that she would close up. At first, he just grunted, which meant he was being stubborn and wasn’t going to take her advice. But a little while later, he started to get a pain in his stomach. Again, he tried to blow it off, but thankfully Bruno stepped in and told him he needed to go home and rest. Arianna knew that her dad really wasn’t feeling well when he told her that he had to call Victoria to come and pick him up. Yeah, the wicked witch of the west had flown in on her broom a few days ago. Thank god, she had stayed away from the restaurant and away from her.

Arianna looked back at the guy, and he was staring at her with the same creepy grin.

"Do you know Paul?" Arianna asked, eyeing the guy skeptically. She neither confirmed nor denied that Paul was her dad.

"He and I go way back."

Arianna figured it could be someone her dad had served with in the military.

"What's your name? I can tell him you stopped by."

The guy picked up his beer and chugged in until there was just a small amount left in the bottom. He set the mug down then threw some cash onto the bar.

"Don't bother. I'll catch up with him later," he said as he stood up, put his coat on, and left.

Arianna picked up the cash and walked back down to the cash register. *What an odd encounter*, she thought to herself as she closed out the transaction on the register.

She looked at Dino and Skittles and realized they were still waiting on her to get their drinks.

"Sorry about that," she told them. "What can I get you?"

They waved her off as if it was no problem.

"Yuengling Lager for me," Skittles told her.

"I'll take a Bud," Dino said.

As she started to walk away, Dino caught her hand that was lying on the bar top.

"You okay?"

"Yeah, why?"

"It seemed like that guy was giving you a hard time."

She glanced at the empty seat that the guy had vacated and debated if she wanted to involve Dino in her opinion of the guy. It couldn't hurt for someone else to know about him in case he ever returned.

"He wasn't giving me a hard time. He was asking about my dad."

Dino scrunched his forehead up. "What's wrong with that? Your dad knows a lot of people."

"True. But it was his body language and the way he asked '*if my old man was around.*' I have no idea who the guy is, and when I asked for his name, so I could let my dad know he had stopped by, he clammed up and left saying that he'd catch him later."

"His behavior sounds a little strange. Just keep an eye out and see if he returns. But I'd let your dad know."

"I planned on that," she also told him about having Bruno pull the video footage behind the bar so he could show it to her dad.

Dino still held her, and she looked down at their conjoined hands, then back up at him. He was focused on her and her only, and his intense gaze made her fidget.

"I need to get your drinks."

He grinned. Before he released her hand he lifted it to his lips. His lips felt warm as he softly kissed the top of her hand. She stood there for a beat, shocked that he was showing her affection in public considering he wasn't sure what he wanted.

When he released her hand, she turned on wobbly legs and walked to the cooler. She pulled the bottles out, popped the tops off, and set them down in front of them. They both pulled cash out, but she waved them off.

"This round is on me."

They both thanked her. Her next thought was to head to the walk-in cooler and take a few minutes to lower her body temperature because that man made her hot.

Dino watched Arianna as she ran up and down the bar waiting on customers. Coming to the bar had been a spontaneous decision, just as he and the others were leaving work. Skittles had been the only one who didn't have plans, so he tagged along though he brought his laptop to do some research.

He wasn't there because of the food or drinks. He was there because of her. He missed her. Other than seeing her the other morning when he left for work, he hadn't seen her. He was disappointed that the bar was busy, meaning he wouldn't be able to talk with her much, but at least he could see her.

He had done quite a bit of thinking since their talk on New Year's while watching the Jets. He hadn't lied to her when he admitted that he really liked her. What wasn't to like? She was appealing in so many ways. She was smart, funny, and kind. The only hang-up he still had was the area of trust. She hadn't been forthcoming with him when they first met, and he still somewhat held that against her. When she explained why she did it, he could understand it to a point, but it was still something he would have to overlook. And the only way to do that was to spend time with her and get to know her on a personal level.

He had demons from his past. He had shocked himself that he even mentioned a sliver of what happened to him years ago. But he knew that if he wanted a future with Arianna, he would have to man up and tell her the truth. She would have to know what happened. Just then, she bent over to get a piece of paper she dropped on the floor, and he couldn't help but stare at her ass. He missed that body of hers. He shifted his body on the stool to give his dick a little more room. He picked up his bottle and took a drink, then glanced over at Skittles. He needed something to occupy his mind for a bit.

"What are you doing?"

Skittles shrugged his shoulders, never looking away from the laptop. "Just looking over some information."

Dino leaned in to get a closer look at what had Skittles' interest. It was a newspaper article about a missing girl. Then it clicked.

"Is that information on that girl from your past? The missing one?"

"Yeah, I keep hitting a wall. Things just aren't adding up."

"How so?"

"Her parents were murdered, and she just disappeared out of thin air."

"Her parents were murdered?" Dino repeated, and Skittles face turned grim. She must mean something to him.

"Don't get pissed at me because I'm going to play devil's advocate. Obviously, this chick means something to you, but did you ever consider that maybe she could've been involved?"

"Of course she was involved. Nobody can find her."

"My point exactly. You know what I mean."

"No, I don't," Skittles stated, appearing agitated.

"Is it possible that she killed her parents?"

"She didn't," Skittles said very seriously.

"I'm just saying…"

"And, I'm telling you that she didn't kill her parents," Skittles said, his voice firmer.

Damn, this girl, whoever she was, had the kid twisted up. They all knew that a girl from his past had disappeared, but they didn't really know any of the specifics, just that Skittles spent most of his free time actively searching for information.

"According to the medical examiner, her parents were killed sometime between two and three in the afternoon. A.G. wasn't at home in that timeframe."

"So ,she has an alibi. Is it a reputable one?"

Skittles stared at Dino. "Me. She had been with me all day." Dino raised his eyebrow, and Skittles continued. "She and my sister were supposed to hang out, but then Nicole came down with a stomach bug and couldn't go. So, I went with her."

"Sorry, man. It sounds like she really meant something to you."

"Not just me. She was like a part of our family."

"Did you and she ever…"

"No!"

Dino smiled when he saw a slight pink tint on Skittles cheeks. "But you wished you had."

Skittles blew out a breath. "What I wish is that I would have ended the day differently. Instead, I just dropped her off in front of her driveway."

"Do you honestly think she's out there somewhere?"

Skittles leveled his gaze at Dino. "I do. I know it sounds crazy, but something in my gut keeps telling me not to give up."

"What about any other family? You know, grandparents, aunts, or uncles?"

"As far as I know, it was just her mom and dad. I can't even find death certificates or a burial plot for them."

"That's strange. Who oversaw the crime scene and investigation?"

"Local PD, but I'm really starting to question things. When I accessed their system looking for a report, I couldn't find the case."

"What?"

"Exactly."

"Coverup?" Dino questioned.

"Every time I get a piece of information, it looks more like it, but I don't know who to even reach out to."

"Have you thought about that maybe…maybe she received the same fate as her parents?"

"It crosses my mind every day."

God, he hoped the kid got some answers, and soon. Even if it wasn't the news he wanted to hear, at least he would have closure.

"Well, if there is anything I can do, let me know."

"Thanks, man."

It was close to two o'clock in the morning when Arianna locked up the bar and started walking to her car. She was tuckered out from the long day. Her feet were killing her. She didn't care what time it was; she was soaking in a hot bath when she got home. Poor Nigel had been home all by himself. She was able to run back to the house mid-afternoon to check on him and let him outside for a little bit. Her dad had told her that she could bring him to the restaurant as long as he stayed in the back.

As she moved across the quiet parking lot, she had been looking at her phone and deleting some texts she had received and didn't notice that the car parked next to hers was occupied.

The loud honk of the horn scared the living daylights out of her. She half jumped, half stumbled backward, and in the process dropped her phone on the ground.

When she looked through the windshield of the SUV, her heart felt like it was going to beat itself right out of her chest. She was shocked to see Dino sitting there watching her, and he didn't appear happy. He got out of his car and walked around to the front of it, where she was standing. Dino and Skittles had both left hours ago.

Had he been sitting out here the entire time?

"Dino? What are you doing here?" she stuttered looking up at him standing in front of her with his arms crossed over his chest.

"Don't you ever walk to your car without being aware of what or who is around you?" he barked at her. "Do you know how many women fall victim in parking lots, let alone in the dark, because they aren't paying attention?"

She didn't say a word as she stood there staring up at him while he lectured her. Once he finished his tirade on parking lot safety, she wasn't sure what to say. She knew it was a lack of judgment on her part. But for some reason, his dominant and commanding tone aroused her. She felt the desire building within her.

He stepped toward her and positioned his hands on her hips. She could feel his thumbs lightly rub against the fabric covering skin. Her eyes were still fixed on his. The dark blue orbs appeared black in the darkness.

"I'm sorry," she forced the words out of her mouth, trying not to sound breathless.

"I didn't realize that you've been closing at night by yourself."

She tilted her head. "How did you know?"

"I asked Bruno, and he told me."

"So you're stalking me?" She joked, but he didn't crack a smile. Damn, he was so serious.

"No, I care about you."

Well, shit. How was she supposed to respond to that? She didn't have to when Dino took her face between the palms of his hands, dipped his head, and kissed her deeply.

Dino was trying not to act barbaric, but he'd been a little on edge ever since Arianna told him about that guy earlier at the bar. And he completely lost it when he saw how unaware she was as she walked through the dark parking lot to her car. She acted like she was out for a fucking Sunday stroll. He had run home for a little bit but then came back about an hour ago and had been sitting in his car waiting for her to leave. He wasn't comfortable with her walking out alone.

She had driven him crazy earlier at the bar when he had watched her wiggle her ass in her fitted jeans as she ran up and down the bar waiting on her customers. He'd admit that he was even jealous at the way some of the guys she was serving had hit on her. But he kept his cool.

But now, with her in his arms staring up at him, he couldn't resist. It had been too long since he'd tasted those lips. The smell of her perfume combined with her sweet smile made his dick so hard. His body craved contact with her.

He kissed her harder, deeper, wanting to imprint his taste so she would think about him. Her hands reached around his waist, and he pulled her closer against his body as he slid his hands down against her ass. She rubbed her chest along his body, and holy hell did it excite him.

Remembering they were out in the open, he released her lips. The look on her face was unforgettable. Her lips were wet and swollen, and her eyes shimmered.

Knowing he needed to get her to the car before he did something wild, like throw her in the backseat of his Blazer and fuck her senseless, he took her hand and guided her to her car. He stopped and picked her phone up from the ground and handed it to her.

She hit the button to unlock the car, and Dino opened her door. She turned and faced him.

"Thank you."

He quirked his eyebrow.

"For coming back and seeing that I made it to my car." She nibbled on her bottom lip nervously. Then she surprised him. "And for the kiss." She got up on her tiptoes and kissed his cheek before sliding into her car.

He held onto the door and looked down at her.

"When do you work again?"

"Tomorrow. I'm closing again."

He nodded his head. "Call me when it's near closing time, and I'll come up."

She tried to argue with him but then quickly realized she wasn't going to win the argument. He had meant it when he told that he cared about her—especially her safety.

They said bye, and he closed her door then got into his vehicle. She pulled out first, and he followed. He would always have her six.

CHAPTER SEVENTEEN

Chris Hurts stood in his director's office, reading over some information that had just been brought to their attention. It wasn't good news, as it appeared that ex-Special Agent Gabbert had been acquiring his own little arsenal of information on a few of his colleagues—both present and former.

All of the names listed in the report had at one time or another been involved in some type of conflict with Gabbert. Judging from the details typed out next to each name, Gabbert had wanted to exact revenge on each person who he felt had screwed him over during his tenure in the FBI.

Chris went down the list of names reading each one. "Jesus, there's a federal judge's name on here."

Scarborough didn't say anything. Instead, he nodded for Chris to continue reading. He skimmed the remaining names until his eyes landed on a familiar name—Paul Roland. Next to Paul's name were the initials, A.R. Chris could only assume that A.R. stood for Arianna Roland. It was very clear that Gabbert had extreme hatred toward each person listed on the paper.

"What are these red x's next to these two names?"

Scarborough's expression became tight and grim. "I don't know for sure what they signify on that list. However, I can tell you that those two men are dead."

Chris's head snapped up. "They're dead?" He repeated, and Scarborough again nodded his head.

Chris started to get a bad feeling in his gut. "How'd they die?"

"One was carbon monoxide poisoning while the guy was out camping, citing something about the camper's generator. The other guy's death was ruled a suicide by a gunshot to the head."

"Where did you get this information from?" Chris asked, handing the file back over to Scarborough.

Scarborough took the file and laid it on his desk. "When Gabbert didn't return his bureau-issued laptop, we had our IT department remote into it. We weren't concerned about him accessing any of our servers because that access was cut off immediately after he was let go. We were more interested in what he had saved on it."

"You found this on the bureau's laptop?"

"Afraid so."

"I'm reluctant to ask, but I'm going to anyway. Is this some sort of a hit list?"

"I can't be certain, but the investigators want to speak with him."

"This is insane. I mean, how could this have gone undetected for so long? Obviously, the guy has a lot of hatred for people who cross him in any way."

"Well, he can only blame himself. He had piss poor leadership skills along with insufficient ability to follow through on directives," Scarborough said. It was obvious that he, too, was having a hard time with the information.

"I don't understand why the bureau kept him on the payroll for this long. It's absurd."

The other directors and I talked about it, and apparently, Gabbert was buddy-buddy with a few directors who would let his behavior slide with slaps on the wrist. But when those covering for him transitioned out of the bureau and a new regime was present, his faults weren't overlooked anymore, which led us to where we are now."

"What is the bureau going to do?"

"Well, since this list doesn't prove much, we'll have to wait and see what the investigators can get out of him. They are supposed to visit his home tomorrow."

"When you hear something, will you let me know? I don't trust him—especially seeing Arianna's dad's name on this list and her initials next to his name."

"You'll be the first person I call."

Chris went to leave when Scarborough stopped him.

"There was another reason I wanted to see you."

"What's that?"

"Thought you'd be happy to hear that the investigation into the complaint against Arianna has been completed, and she's been cleared of any wrongdoing."

Chris smiled. "That's excellent news. I'm sure Sam will be thrilled when he hears about it. Arianna is a valuable asset to his team."

"She's a valuable agent, period," Scarborough said as serious as he could be.

Arianna finally had a lull in customers and was able to sneak away to take a quick break. She hadn't been scheduled to work until mid-afternoon, but her dad had called her this morning and told her that he was still feeling under the weather and asked if she could cover for him. At first, she thought about calling in one of the other waitresses, but then she remembered that the beer distributor was making a delivery, and either she or her dad needed to be there to accept it. If it weren't for all the caffeine she'd been drinking throughout the day, she'd probably be passed out in the office.

Dino had followed her home the night before, and they had sat out in the driveway talking for a bit. When they were saying good night, Dino had kissed her again. This time neither of them wanted it to end, which then led to him accompanying her back to her house. They had barely made it inside the door before their hands were all over each other. Before she could even comprehend what exactly they were doing, their clothes had been shed, and he had her hoisted up against the front door. It had been wild, carnal, and totally unexpected, but oh, had it been good. Dino was an amazing lover who enjoyed taking charge, and she didn't have a problem with that whatsoever. His dominance was a major turn-on.

Once things had settled down, and they were both coming down from their sex-induced high, there was a brief moment where Arianna thought that things were going to change between them officially. As he held her in the air, with their sweat-covered bodies pressed against each other, he looked deep into her eyes. It was as if he had a moment of reckoning. That maybe he was able to move on from the past that had haunted him. She could only describe it as special, and something shared between them. But the moment was cut short when Nigel pressed his cold nose against Dino's bare butt cheek, causing him to almost drop her. After they had gotten dressed, he didn't stay long since he had to be up soon for work. She, on the other hand, was left lying in bed, staring at the ceiling, wondering if they'd ever take their arrangement to the next level. She cared for him deeply and enjoyed his company. There had to be a way to get him to move on.

She walked over to the table near the back patio doors and slid into the chair next to Dino as he was talking to Ace, Alex, Derek, and Juliette. Ace and Alex were eating dinner with Derek and Juliette when Dino popped in, and they invited him to sit with them.

She shouldn't have been shocked when she saw Dino walk through the front entrance about twenty minutes ago since he had told her that he'd meet her near closing time so she wouldn't have to walk out to her car by herself.

It warmed her to know that he really did care and hadn't just fed her a line of macho bullshit when he scolded her the previous night.

She had enjoyed getting to catch up a little with Derek, Alex's adopted dad, and Tenley's mom, Juliette.

Derek Connors, a SEAL himself, had been a teammate and best friends to Alex's biological dad, Jacob Hardesty. When her father was killed, there hadn't been any other family, so instead of letting the state take control of Alex, Derek and the rest of the team took Alex under their wing and raised her, with Derek gaining guardianship of her. When Arianna was old enough to really understand the full story of how that all worked out, her respect for the SEAL Commander grew ten times.

Juliette was an absolute sweetheart and had been an essential person in Arianna's life when her mom had died. She'd been there for her anytime she needed a mother figure to talk to.

She had almost fainted when Alex told her that Derek and Juliette were dating and that it was serious—like wedding bells serious. She had also learned that Derek was the commander of Dino's SEAL team. Small world.

Alex smiled. "So, how has it been working up here again?"

Arianna shrugged her shoulders. "I was a little rusty at first, but I'm getting back into the groove again." It hadn't hurt that her dad hadn't upgraded to the new technology he'd been talking about doing. It was the same one they'd been using for years.

"Yeah, but she isn't very careful when it comes to her safety when she's leaving at night," Dino said, giving her the stink eye but then grinning, letting her know he was teasing her. However, he hadn't been joking last night.

Alex scrunched her nose up. "Did something happen?"

Dino explained to them her lapse in judgment the previous night, and not surprisingly, he over-exaggerated its severity. That led to Derek giving her his two-minute lecture on parking lot safety.

Arianna looked down at her watch. *Ugh*…she needed to get back to work. It was just her and Georgia, another waitress, tonight. Thankfully it wasn't too crowded that two of them couldn't manage it. Bruno was supposed to stop in, but he got tied up at a veteran's group in Newport News that he volunteered at.

Just as she was about to get up from her chair and head back to the bar, Georgia came over. "Arianna, I'm sorry to interrupt, but your cell phone keeps ringing behind the bar."

"Thanks, Georgia."

She excused herself from the table. When she got to the bar, her phone started to ring again. She picked it up from next to the register where she kept it. Her eyebrows drew in when she read the caller ID -- Virginia Beach General Hospital. As she answered, she walked to the other end of the bar, where it was less crowded, and she could hear.

"Hello?"

"May I please speak with Arianna Roland?" The female voice on the line asked.

"This is she." Something twisted in her gut.

"Ms. Roland, my name is Nessa Blackburn from Virginia Beach General Hospital. Your name was listed as an emergency contact for Paul Roland."

"That's my dad. Is he okay?"

"Your dad was brought into the emergency room. I don't have specifics on his condition now, but I can tell you he collapsed at home. A neighbor found him and called 9-1-1. We found your name and number in his phone that he had in his possession. You should get here right away."

"Yes, of course. I'm on my way. Thank you."

She stood frozen with the phone in her hand. She felt numb; her dad was her life. So many questions began to swim through her head. What caused him to collapse? How bad was he? What if he didn't make it? Tears had started to form when warm hands landed on her shoulders. She glanced up and over her shoulder and met Dino's hard stare. She couldn't speak about anything as she turned in his arms and buried her face in his chest.

Dino watched Arianna as she went back to the bar. He initially had planned to come up about thirty minutes before the bar closed, but he wanted to see her. And it wasn't like he had anything else to do but sit around at home. Even in the gray Bayside V-neck short sleeve shirt, jeans and sneakers, she looked beautiful. With her long hair pulled back into a ponytail and the way she smiled and laughed as a customer said something to her, she looked absolutely stunning. His eyes never left her as she made her way toward the far side of the bar to take the phone call. But when her bright, cheerful smile faded and was replaced with a pained expression, he was up and out of his chair. Georgia, the waitress, gave him a strange look when he walked behind the bar. When he placed his hands on her shoulders, and she turned into his body with tears building in her eyes, he took her into his arms and held her tight.

"Arianna, what's wrong?" He asked. Something big had to have happened, considering how her body trembled in his arms.

She pulled back just slightly; her eyes glistened with unshed tears.

"My...my...dad," she stuttered, and a couple of tears fell from her eyes, giving Dino the impression that the worst had happened. Ace and Alex, along with Derek and Juliette, must've noticed something was wrong and were now there as well. Dino was glad since the four of them knew her better than he did.

"Ari, what's wrong?" Alex asked.

Arianna wiped her eyes and cleared her throat. "That was the hospital. My dad was just brought in. A neighbor found him unresponsive at home. The lady on the phone said it was serious and that I should get there as soon as possible."

She pulled away from Dino, and he felt the loss immediately.

"I need to grab my keys and purse." She turned back to the three of them. "I was supposed to close tonight, and I have Nigel in the office." She was trembling, and Dino took her hand.

"I'll drive you," he told her.

She took a step back and shook her head. "No, you don't have to."

Alex stepped in front of Arianna.

"Sweetie, listen to me. You're too upset to drive. It wouldn't be good for you or other people on the road. Let Dino drive you. Don't worry about this place. Ace and I will take care of it and make sure things get done and closed up. I know where Paul keeps the extra key, and Georgia knows how to close down the registers. We got this. You go and focus on your dad. He needs you, Arianna."

"Honey, listen to Alex. Juliette and I will take Nigel back to our house." Derek told her.

Dino felt the weight lift from his shoulders when Arianna conceded with a nod of her head. Georgia handed him Arianna's purse, and Dino thanked her before wrapping his arm around Arianna's shoulders then leading her to his car. As he passed Ace, Ace gave him a chin lift and squeezed his shoulder.

When they arrived at the hospital, they were directed to a waiting room where they sat and were told that doctors were working vigorously to keep Paul alive.

It was a busy night at the hospital, and people were coming and going, but one person had caught Dino's attention about forty-five minutes after he and Arianna had arrived. He'd been coming back from the restroom when he saw the guy enter through the main sliding doors and walk up to the triage desk. The ball cap he wore was pulled low, obscuring his face, but there was something familiar about him. Dino had waited for the guy to turn around to see if he could get a better look at him. When the guy turned around a few moments later, Dino grew skeptical. It was the same guy that had creeped out Arianna at the bar the other day. He ended up walking back outside, but Dino's inner alarm bells began to sound. Coincidence or not?

It had been hours later when Paul was moved to the ICU on the second floor. Dino sat in the waiting room while Arianna was visiting her dad. The hospital only allowed one visitor at a time and only immediate family. Either Alex or Juliette must have called Tenley because Dino was surprised when she walked into the waiting room while they were still down in the emergency department. Being that Tenley was a nurse in the department, she had been able to access information and provide them updates as much as she could until they were able to get Paul stabilized, though from sounds of it, it had been touch and go and he still wasn't out of the woods.

He was worried, and not just for Paul but for Arianna too. Dino hadn't known Arianna long, but one thing he did know was that she was a tough cookie and hard to rattle. But this had visibly shaken her up, and rightly so. He may be an outsider when it came to her and Paul's relationship, but anyone could see the love between the father and daughter duo. Paul loved Arianna just as much as Arianna loved her dad. It was heartbreaking to witness.

Dino had a hard time sitting around in hospitals. His anxiety levels would grow the longer he sat waiting to hear any update. It took him back to that ill-fated day sixteen years ago. He remembered it like it was yesterday as his family and Marianna's family all gathered, waiting for the doctors to give them an update on Marianna and Dexter's condition. He remembered the moment vividly when the two doctors had walked into the waiting room and delivered the news that the two hadn't survived.

A light knock on the door brought Dino back to the present. When he looked up, he was shocked to see Ace and Alex standing there, hand-in-hand. He glanced at his watch. It was after two in the morning.

He stood up as they walked in.

"Hey, what are you guys doing here?"

"After we closed up, Ace and I decided to come and be here for Arianna," Alex said, looking somber.

Dino had been keeping Ace informed on the situation at the hospital any time they got an update. But knowing Alex's compassion, he wasn't all that surprised to see her standing in front of him. Alex was the backbone of their little family unit here at home.

"Any new updates on Paul's condition?" Ace asked.

"No. Not since I texted you last. Arianna's with him now. All that matters right now is that he's alive."

They all sat down, and Alex sat between the two men.

"How is Arianna holding up?" Alex asked, appearing shaken up as well with the news. Paul was a staple in the community.

"Now that she's gotten over the initial shock, she's upset, worried, and has a lot of questions that the doctors can't answer right now."

"Damn," Ace said, rubbing a hand along his jaw.

"What about Victoria? Is she here too?"

Dino shot a glare towards Alex though the look wasn't directed at her, and she knew it.

"I'll take that as a no," she rolled her eyes.

They were all well aware of Paul's long-time girlfriend, Victoria Malone. It was obvious that the relationship had been on a rocky slope for the last six months or so.

"Arianna hasn't talked to her. She and a friend supposedly went to Richmond this morning to go shopping or something. Arianna said she left a message for her."

Just then, the doors to the private room opened, and Arianna appeared in the doorway. She looked defeated. Her eyes were red and swollen. Dino stood and met her as she walked in.

"How is he?" He asked, and pulled her in for a hug.

She shook her head, "It doesn't look good."

He took her hand and led her to the empty chair next to Alex. She sat down, and Alex handed her a couple of tissues, and she wiped her eyes. Alex pulled her into a hug, and Dino was glad Alex was there to help comfort, Arianna.

"Do the doctors know what happened?" Alex asked.

Arianna pulled back and took a deep breath. "No, not yet. They are still running all kinds of tests. He was in full cardiac arrest when he was brought in. Luckily, Steve, Dad's next-door neighbor, had gone over to the house to return a chainsaw he had borrowed from Dad. When he knocked on the front door, he saw Dad lying on the floor through the big picture window. They used the paddles three times to restart his heart. As the doctor put it, it is a miracle he's still with us. He's in a coma, they said."

Alex hugged her again. "I'm so sorry, sweetie."

"The doctor said I should go home for the night and that they would call if there is any change in his condition."

Suddenly a woman's high-pitched voice pierced the quiet hallways of the floor they were on. It had come from the nearby nurse's station.

"Oh no," Arianna mumbled. "I don't have the patience or energy right now for her." Not understanding what she meant, Dino asked her what was wrong.

"That would be Victoria." She stood up, and so did Dino. He wasn't going to let her go out there by herself.

As soon as Dino and Arianna stepped into the hall they were in Victoria's line of sight, Victoria's hawkish eyes zeroed in on Arianna, and she started to come at her like she was swooping in on her prey. Her high heels clicked fast against the tile floor, making even more noise. Arianna took a step backward, and Dino went into protective mode and moved slightly in front of Arianna. Dino knew from seeing Victoria in action that her mental state could sometimes be unpredictable. One never knew when she'd shoot off like a loose cannon, and judging from her facial expression and body language as she descended on Arianna, things were about to escalate.

"Those people won't tell me anything," she shrieked as she pointed in the direction of the three nurses standing at the desk.

Dino knew the staff most likely had already notified security. In this day and age, you just never knew the mentality of someone and what that person was capable of doing.

Arianna moved past him, but he kept a hand on her lower back just in case he needed to pull her back.

"Victoria, they're just doing their job."

"But, I'm his girlfriend," she shouted, half shrieking, half sobbing. Jesus, she must've stopped for a drink or two on her way back to town because she reeked of alcohol.

"Exactly. You're not immediate family," Arianna tried to tell her. But Dino knew, that comment was going to set Victoria off.

It was like slow motion as Victoria reared back as if Arianna's words had slapped her in the face. But she regained her composure as she righted herself and squared her shoulders. She stuck her pointer finger with her long fake nails in Arianna's face. Her lip curled into a snarl.

"I was the only family he had for the past two and a half years, you little wench. Do you really think that you can just waltz back into his life after being absent for that long and push me out? Well, I've got news for you, little girl."

Before Victoria could utter another vile word, Dino stepped into her space, causing her to take a step back. Ace and Alex were right there, too, ready to intervene if needed. His eyes were burning with fire. He spoke in a low, firm voice.

"Shut your mouth and listen well."

Victoria's eyes widened, and she pressed her lips together in a firm line. That woman was full of piss and vinegar, and he wasn't having any part of it. Whatever the hell her problem was with Arianna, this wasn't the time nor the place to deal with it.

"Obviously, you're upset. We're all upset. But I will not tolerate you attacking Arianna the way you just did. Paul is a very sick man right now, and the doctors don't know why, as they are still running tests and most likely won't have any answers until sometime in the morning. So, here's what's going to happen. You have two choices. You can either turn around and walk out of this hospital and have whoever brought you here take you home." He nodded towards the two cops that had just arrived on the floor but were waiting to see if Dino could de-escalate the situation. "Or those two fine law enforcement officers will kindly escort you out."

She must have thought he was calling her bluff because when she turned and saw the officers, she was shocked, and she turned back around and faced Arianna.

"When will I be able to see him?"

It might have been barbaric, but he was trying to protect Arianna, and he answered for her.

"When the doctors say he can have visitors besides family."

She threw her purse over her shoulder and huffed out a dramatic sigh. Dino was tired of the act and growing impatient.

Alex stepped forward. "Victoria. All of us are shocked and upset about Paul, but coming here and making a fool of yourself isn't helping the situation any. Take Dino's advice and walk out of here with some dignity. Someone will let you know if there is any change in Paul's condition."

Victoria looked to be considering Alex's words and finally turned on her heel and marched toward the elevators with the two cops following behind to make sure she left.

Once the elevator doors closed with Victoria inside, Dino closed his eyes, took a deep breath, and exhaled. He was caught off guard when the small hand touched his forearm, and when he turned and looked down and saw Arianna's hazel eyes staring up at him, he pulled her into his arms.

"Thank you," she whispered against his chest. He was still fuming from Victoria's outburst and couldn't find the words he wanted to say to her. It wasn't just a simple "you're welcome." It was more than that. So instead, he gave her body a good squeeze, letting her know he had heard her.

Arianna peeled her clothes off and slipped into the shower. She leaned forward against the wall, dropping her head and letting the hot water beat against her shoulders and upper back. She was scared—scared of losing the most important man of her life. Tears streamed down her face, mixing with the water droplets. She was silent, but her body shook as she released all of the sadness, anger, and frustration that she had stored within her.

She had so much to think about and to plan. She not only had her dad she had to worry about, but she had the restaurant and bar that needed to stay running. Alex had told her that she had spoken with Bruno and that he would handle the operations side, but he wasn't comfortable with the administrative part. That was fine because at least paperwork and payroll she could process anywhere as long as she had her laptop and a Wifi connection. The first thing she needed to do was make a list of tasks she needed to complete.

She hadn't been to church in quite some time, but she had always been a believer in God. She sent some prayers up to heaven in the hope that the heavens would listen and release her daddy back to her because she knew he had so much more he needed to accomplish on this earth. He was a good man who would go out of his way to help anyone in need. This community needed him; his friends needed him, but most of all, she needed him.

When the water started to run cold, she turned the shower off and dried off. She changed into a pair of fleece pajama pants and a matching long-sleeved t-shirt. Even after the scalding shower, she still felt cold and numb.

She hadn't heard anything, and she wondered if Dino had left. That made her sad because of all nights, tonight she didn't want to be alone. As she walked down the stairs, she heard his voice coming from the living room. It sounded like he was finishing up a call.

When she walked into the room, he was sitting on the couch with his phone to his ear. Nigel, who they picked up on the way home, was out cold next to him with his head stretched across Dino's lap. Acknowledging her presence, Dino looked up and gave her a grin. It wasn't until then that she realized he had a slight dimple in his cheek.

She wondered who he was on the phone with, considering how late it was. When he disconnected, he moved Nigel's head off of him and stood, meeting her across the room. He didn't say anything—he just pulled her into his arms and held her. She melted into him, sliding her arms around his waist, and held on. It was exactly what she needed.

"How are you feeling?" He spoke to her.

She shrugged her shoulders. She couldn't find the words she was looking for because she felt so many emotions—anger, sadness, hurt.

Finally, she managed to blubber out a few words. "I can't lose my dad."

"I know, babe," he agreed as he rubbed his hand up and down her back. "Your dad is one of the strongest guys I know. I'm sure he is fighting like hell to get back to you. You even said that the doctors told you that it was a miracle he was still with us. That should give you hope."

She pulled back just enough to look up at him, and he smiled as he tucked her hair behind her ear.

"You should get some sleep," he told her, and even though she was exhausted, sleep was the last thing on her mind. But he was right. She was going to need all of her energy to be there for her dad.

"Thank you for everything."

He took her face between the palms of his hands and looked into her eyes.

"You don't have to thank me, babe. I'd be here for you no matter what."

"But I do. You don't know how much it meant to have you there with me. You didn't have to sit at the hospital all night, and you sure as hell didn't have to deal with Victoria for me. But you did, and I want you to know that I appreciate it. I appreciate you."

"I will always be there for you. Don't you ever doubt that?"

He took her hand in his and led her toward the stairs. "You look like you're about to fall over. Come on. I'll walk you up to bed."

Once in her bedroom, she crawled under the covers, and Dino sat down next to her on the bed. Nigel joined them and jumped up onto the bed, and took his spot near the bottom.

He watched as she tried to fight the sleep she so desperately needed. She was going to have a few long days, but she wasn't going to have to do everything alone. She had an entire team behind her, and it started with him.

The following day, Dino had already gone next door to his place to shower and change and make it back to Arianna's house before she woke up. He spoke with Derek and Ace, and since they had a light day on base planned, both of them told him he was cleared to come into work whenever he could get there and that unless they got called up and had to bug out, Arianna came first. None of them knew what frame of mind she would be in this morning. Nobody wanted her to have to go through this alone. Tenley, with her contacts in the hospital, kept tabs on Paul through the night and sent periodic updates. His condition hadn't changed since they had left the hospital. Alex had already called and told him, that if he needed a break to call her. And the kindness didn't stop there. Everyone else from the team had reached out, offering to help with anything they could. This was what he loved about being a part of the team.

First and foremost, they were a family. They were a unit that looked after one another and assisted with whatever was needed, no questions asked. He couldn't have asked to serve with a better group of guys.

Arianna had left her cell phone downstairs last night, and this morning Dino heard it ringing. He usually wouldn't have gone into her purse, but under the circumstances, he thought it could've been the hospital calling, so he retrieved it from her bag. When he saw it was Bruno from Bayside, he answered it. They spoke for a few minutes, and Bruno assured him that he'd handle everything at Bayside until Arianna could get back.

Nigel had come downstairs when Dino returned from his place and hadn't left his side, except when he went outside for a few minutes.

It was almost nine in the morning, and Dino knew that as soon as Arianna woke up, she would hit the ground running, so he decided to make breakfast for her. He had bacon sizzling in the pan and scrambled eggs cooking on the next burner. He walked over to the toaster and popped in four slices of bread.

When he turned around to head back to the stove, he was surprised to see Arianna standing next to the island separating the kitchen and living room. Just as he imagined, she was dressed and ready to go. But the main thing was that she looked rested, which was good.

She smiled. "I thought I smelled bacon."

He grinned and turned back to the stove and placed a scoop of eggs and four strips of bacon on her plate. The toast popped in the toaster, and he grabbed two slices and added them to the plate. He took the plate over to the island and set it down.

"Have something to eat, and then we'll head to the hospital."

She looked at him for a moment like she was confused. "Don't you have to go to work?"

"I talked with Derek and Ace. There isn't much going on today, so I'm going in after I drop you off at the hospital."

"Coffee?" He asked, pulling down two mugs from the cabinet.

"Please," she said as she sat down and looked over the plate of food. "Okay, I may have to have you stay over more often. I can get used to a homecooked breakfast."

He smiled as he poured the coffee. "I enjoy cooking when it isn't just me."

He set the coffee cup down next to her and took the other seat on her left. She looked at him.

"I left my phone down here last night. You didn't hear it ring by any chance, did you? I mean, the hospital could've called, and I wouldn't have even known."

"I heard it ringing this morning. I hope you don't mind, but I went through your purse to find it—for the reason you just mentioned. But it was only Bruno. He told me to tell you that he's holding down the fort at the restaurant until you can get back. He said if there are any issues he'll call."

"So nothing from the hospital?"

"Tenley kept checking in with the hospital through the night and let me know. His condition hasn't changed."

Dino could see the disappointment in her expression. "Hey, focus on the positive—he's alive."

She nodded her head and loaded some eggs on her toast, and took a bite. She washed it down with some coffee.

"I know. It was just wishful thinking. When I woke up this morning, I laid there for a few minutes, wondering if it had all just been a bad dream. Then I started thinking about everything that needed to be done."

He sensed her getting ready to go into panic mode and he reached over and squeezed her hand. “Look at me.” She set her fork down and peered over at him. “You don’t have to go through this alone. You’ve got an entire community who is standing by, ready to assist. You just have to ask. You don’t have to run yourself ragged. It won’t do you or your dad any good if you become too exhausted and run down.”

“I know I do. I’m just not used to having to ask for help, that’s all. But I promise I will.”

His lips curled at the corners, and he leaned over and kissed her temple.

“That’s all I ask.”

He changed the subject. “If you’re feeling up to it, my team, along with the members of Bravo and Delta teams, are holding our annual bonfire tonight. If you want to go, you’re more than welcome to come. Everyone will be there, including the families. It’s sort of a celebration of making it another year. We hold it on the first weekend that everyone is in town.”

“I remember seeing something on the calendar in my dad’s office. He closes the restaurant for it, right?”

“Yeah. We have it down on the beach near the approach just past Bayside.”

“Okay.”

CHAPTER EIGHTEEN

Arianna sat in the chair next to her dad's bed listening to the different sounds of machines hooked up to him. There was still no change in his condition.

Dino had dropped her off a few hours ago. He had told her to call him when she was ready, and he'd come pick her up. She tried to get him to take her to Bayside to get her car, but then he had reminded her that Bruno had picked up her keys that she left in the office.

She wasn't sure what she would've done last night without Dino. Usually, she was level-headed and could work through any situation put in front of her. However, that wasn't the case for her dad and the news she was faced with last night. She had been shaken to her core and was scared. She was still scared because the doctors still didn't know what brought all of it on. All of the routine tests showed nothing out of the ordinary. There were still more intensive tests being run, and doctors had told her that those tests could take up to twenty-four hours to get the results back.

She still wasn't sure if she was going to go to the bonfire. From what Dino described, it sounded like it would be a wonderful time to spend with her friends, but she didn't want her presence to sour the mood for everyone. That wasn't fair when it was meant to be a joyous occasion.

She did text Victoria to let her know that there still hadn't been any change. She wasn't surprised not to get a response back. That woman needed to go away, but for some reason, her dad kept her around, which was perplexing because, under normal circumstances, he wouldn't put up with her type of behavior. But that was another battle for another day. The fight right now was making sure that her dad lived.

She watched the machine that measured her dad's vitals. At first, she had no clue what all of the numbers meant, but one of the nurses had given her a quick tutorial on what they stood for and what her dad's numbers should be.

She sat forward in the chair and took his hand in hers, being careful to avoid the IV line sticking out of his hand. His skin felt cool to the touch.

"I wish you'd wake up and tell me what happened to you," she said to him. Both the doctors and nurses said it was good if she spoke with him. They noted that many patients who were in comas could hear what was going on around them. "It's not your time yet. I know deep in my heart that you still have a lot of fight left in you, and I want you to fight like to hell to get through whatever's holding you back."

She dropped her head, and the tears started to build. "You're all I have left," she told him.

She heard voices near the door, and when she looked up, two doctors were standing in the doorway.

"Ms. Roland?" The taller, dark-haired one with glasses asked.

"Yes." She wiped her eyes and stood up when the doctors entered the room.

"I'm Dr. Rowtowski, and this is Dr. Bradford." Both gentlemen shook her hand, and she greeted them.

Dr. Rowtowski spoke first. "When your dad was brought to the hospital last night, the emergency room doctors attended to him. As we advance, I'll be your dad's primary doctor while he's in our care. I've already notified his primary care physician of his condition. Dr. Bradford here is a toxicologist."

Arianna knew what a toxicologist was, and it concerned her why he was there.

"Arianna, as the doctor told you last night, we had sent off additional blood work to be tested for other substances."

She shifted on her feet and had a queasy feeling in her stomach anticipating what Dr. Bradford was going to tell her.

"I'm guessing, since you're here, that you found something."

Dr. Rowtowski motioned to the chairs in the room. "Let's all have a seat."

Arianna sat down, which was good because her legs had started to tremble as the anxiety, she was feeling continued to build. Her nerves were shot. because her nerves were running wild.

"Arianna, has your dad ever had suicidal thoughts?" Dr. Rowtowski asked, and Arianna quickly answered.

Suicide? "No! That's absurd. Never."

Dr. Rowtowski gave her a soft smile. "Okay, that is good to hear." He then glanced over to Dr. Bradford and nodded his head to go ahead with whatever he was going to say.

"Your dad's blood had an extremely high concentration of cyanide—levels that were so high that he shouldn't have survived."

Arianna was stunned for a moment. She blinked a few times, staring at both doctors waiting for them to tell her that they were kidding, although it would've been a really sick joke. She sat up straighter and looked at Dr. Bradford. "I'm sorry. Did you say cyanide? As in the poison?"

"Yes."

She sank back into the chair. Her mind started going a mile a minute. How could her dad have gotten cyanide poisoning?

"I know this probably comes as a shock to you. To be honest, we were shocked when we received the results. Has he acted any differently in the last few days?

"He wasn't feeling well the day before. He complained of dizziness, fatigue. He thought it was one of those twenty-four-hour bugs."

Dr. Rowtowski wrote down notes on his notepad. "Was he taking any medications that you know of?"

"No. He's normally a very healthy man. He exercises regularly, he eats well."

"Well, being physically fit may have helped him."

"Now that you know what it is, is there something that can be done to help him more?" She asked, even though she couldn't stop thinking about where he had gotten cyanide from. Again, her mind started to wander in many different directions.

"Yes, we have a treatment plan that we will get started right away now that we know what we're dealing with. Because of the severity, we are going to administer the antidote hydroxocobalamin along with one hundred percent oxygen. The hydroxocobalamin will detoxify the cyanide. Then the two combined will produce nontoxic vitamin B-12. This will neutralize the cyanide at a slow enough rate to allow the enzyme rhodanese to help boost detoxifying the cyanide in the liver."

Arianna had no clue what all of that meant, but if it helped save her dad, then she was up for it.

"Do whatever you think is necessary."

Dr. Rowtowski nodded. "Okay, we will get started right away. In the meantime, if you have any questions for either one of us, don't hesitate to contact us. Also, Arianna, cyanide isn't a chemical that is easily accessible to just anyone. My suggestion, especially if your dad was not looking to commit suicide, is to contact the police department and talk with them."

"I will. My dad and I have many contacts in law enforcement. I'll be sure to touch base with them today. Once you start the antidote process, is there any sort of time frame that he should wake up?"

"He is stable, and the antidote should help, but now it's on him to wake up from it."

Both doctors stood. "Do you have any other questions for us?"

She couldn't think of any off the top of her head, but she was pretty sure she'd have some later after everything they just told her had a chance to settle in her brain.

"Not right now. Oh, actually, there is one thing. My dad's girlfriend. Would it be okay if she's allowed to visit? Just for short periods of time?"

"As long you are okay with it, we can add her name to the access list."

"Thank you. I'll speak with the nurses before I leave today."

They both said goodbye and left. She walked over to her dad and leaned over him, and kissed his cheek. "You heard them, Dad. It's up to you now. Don't give up."

"Excuse me, Ms. Roland?"

Arianna turned just as a nurse walked in. She recognized her as one of the nurses from last night.

"Hi. And please call me Arianna."

The nurse smiled. "I wanted to come by and introduce myself. My name is Brianna, and I'll be one of the nurses assigned to your father. I'm going to leave my contact information with you. If you have any questions or concerns, please don't hesitate to reach out."

Arianna took the sheet of paper that Brianna handed to her.

"Thank you."

"I saw Dr. Rowtowski and Dr. Bradford leave. They are some of the best doctors here at the hospital."

"That's encouraging to hear, especially right now."

"I know it's tough. The hardest part is waiting. I can assure you that your dad is in good hands."

"Thank you. I appreciate everything everyone here has done already to help my dad."

"If you'd like, you're welcome to bring some items from home—like pictures, a blanket for him, or anything else you'd think he might like."

"Okay. I can swing by his place and grab a few things." And while she was there, she'd have a look around and do a little investigating herself. At least she would if Victoria wasn't around.

The elevator opened to the second floor, and Dino walked off and was greeted by a dark-haired lady who smiled at him.

"Hi there. Can I help you?"

"Hi. I was looking for a patient's daughter. I dropped her off this morning."

"What's the patient's name?"

"Paul Roland."

The nice lady gave him a warm smile.

"Oh! You must be talking about Arianna."

He smiled. "Yes, ma'am."

"She is a sweetheart. She left a little over an hour ago."

He wondered how she left, considering she didn't have her car. But that would explain why she hadn't called him to come and get her.

"Do you know if anyone else came up to see him that she left with?"

"I don't know if she left with anyone, but I can tell you that nobody else was in to see Mr. Roland today."

"Okay, thank you, ma'am."

She chuckled. "There is no need for the ma'am."

He lowered his head slightly. "Sorry. It's a habit."

"Ah…military?"

"Yes, ma'am." They both laughed.

He looked through the glass and could see Paul lying in bed.

"Has there been any change in his condition?" He asked.

"I'm sorry, but I can't give any information out unless the family approves it," she said very apologetically.

"Right. Sorry, I forgot."

She smiled and glanced into Paul's room. "He's still with us so that in itself is positive news," she winked.

And boy was it. "That is true," he replied.

He didn't want to take any more of her time, so he thanked her again and made his way out of the hospital and to his car. As he pulled out of the parking lot, he looked at the time. He had about thirty minutes before he was supposed to meet everyone at the beach.

Arianna had been on his mind all day, and he was worried about her. He hit her number on his phone, and it started to ring. After the third ring, it went to voicemail. He decided to swing by her house and make sure she was okay.

When he stopped at a red light, he sent Ace a text telling him that he might be a few minutes late.

When he arrived at Arianna's house, he got no answer at the door. Not even a bark from Nigel. He waited for about fifteen minutes, thinking she may have taken Nigel for a walk. When the fifteen minutes passed, he got in his car and drove to the beach approach. Since he was in charge of bringing half of the beer, he couldn't be too late.

As he drove past the restaurant, he saw her car was still parked in the same spot as last night. He tried to call her one more time but again got her voicemail.

He parked and got out of the car. He could see the large group gathered down by the water. He grabbed the cooler from the back of the vehicle then started down the path. Then he thought, maybe she was already down there and had gotten a ride from Alex or Tenley. If not, hopefully, someone had spoken with her.

Arianna looked out toward the water. She didn't want to bother Dino since she knew he was at work, so she called Bruno and asked if he could come and get her from the hospital. When he picked her up, she explained what the doctors told her about the cyanide. She didn't think she had ever seen Bruno that pissed off before. When she asked him if he knew of any reason her dad may have come in contact with the chemical, Bruno had told her that the only way her dad would have ever gone near that stuff was if someone deliberately put it in him.

They went by her dad's house first. Since Victoria wasn't home, they let themselves in. While she grabbed a few things to take to the hospital tomorrow, Bruno looked around the house and her dad's work shed in the backyard. He couldn't find anything, which left more questions.

Bruno agreed that she should talk to the police. He was good friends with the Chief of Police, so he gave him a call and explained the situation. The Chief knew her dad and was not happy with the situation. He asked her to come down to the station and file a report and talk to investigators. She spent about an hour there talking to the Chief and a detective who the Chief assigned to work on the case. She signed some papers giving the hospital the authority to release her dad's records. They asked both her and Bruno if there was anybody that they knew of who would want to have Paul killed. Neither one could name one person. The Chief told her to let him look over some things and that either he or the detective would reach out to her. In the meantime, if Paul's condition changed, let him know immediately, especially if he woke up.

It had been a rough, tiring day, and she wasn't sure if she was feeling up to hanging with her friends tonight.

She kept thinking back to her conversation with Dr. Bradford when he returned later in the day to see how her dad was responding to the antidote. He believed with the levels of cyanide in his system, being where he was found in his house, and how the chemical had attacked his body that he had ingested it.

While the doctor was there, she had tried calling Victoria to ask her a few questions, but of course, she got no answer. However, a few minutes later, she did send her a text telling her that she was out with a friend and that she would call her later. That bothered Arianna because Victoria had put on one hell of a show the night the hospital staff wouldn't allow her back to see him. If she were that concerned for him, she'd be sitting by his side, especially now that Arianna had added her name to the visitor list. It also cast a shadow on Victoria and showed the person she indeed was.

She looked to the right, down towards the beach approach, and saw a large fire and big crowd. A tear fell from her eye and rolled down her cheek. Just then a gust of wind blew, sending her long locks of hair blowing in her face. She shivered and felt on edge.

As much as she wanted to be around her friends, it wouldn't be fair to show up in her mood and ruin the fun evening for everyone. With the restaurant closed for the night, she'd take the free time to catch up on some administrative items that Bruno told her about, plus she needed to get the payroll submitted into the system so the checks would be disbursed on time. And she had started to organize the two, four-drawer file cabinets her dad had that were full of papers—many of which could probably be shredded because they were so old.

She glanced down to tell Nigel to go inside, but he wasn't where he had been lying. She looked all around the patio deck, but there was no sign of him. He was lying right next to her; how had she not heard him get up? Had she been that far inside her own head that she hadn't realized he got up?

Feeling a little panicked, she scanned up and down the beach. Just as she was about to go inside to grab a flashlight so she could look on the beach, movement down by the water caught her eye. Once she could focus on the object, she saw it was not one but two dogs. She couldn't make out if one was Nigel, so she started down the steps to the sand.

By the time she made it halfway down, the two dogs had taken off towards where the bonfire party was going on. Judging from how one of the dogs ran, she was almost one hundred percent that it was Nigel. He had a little bounce in his large stride. Trying to get him to stop, she whistled loudly.

As she jogged in the dogs' direction, she saw someone walking towards her with one of the dogs in tow. She slowed her jog to a brisk walk. Damn, she needed to start running again. She had slacked off since she didn't have to fit herself into revealing lingerie.

Her stride came to a complete stop when she got a good look at who the kind Samaritan was that was bringing her dog back.

Dino helped the guys get the fire going and then ventured over to where Alex was sitting with some of the other ladies and the rest of the team. People were spread out all over.

"Has anyone heard from Arianna today?" He asked the group.

"No, we were hoping you had," Alex replied as she handed him a beer.

"I stopped by the hospital on the way home to pick her up, but the nurse said she had left about an hour before I got there."

"Maybe she went home," Autumn chimed in.

"No, I went by there, and she wasn't home. I'm just not sure how she left, considering she didn't have her car."

"Her car is still in the same spot as it was last night," Ace stated.

"Were you able to get any update on Paul while you were at the hospital?" Alex asked.

"The nurse couldn't say anything because of hospital policy, which I get. She did say he was still with us, though, and I did see him through the window to his room."

"Shit," Mia said.

"Yeah, it sucks."

"Poor Arianna. I can't imagine what she's going through," Bailey said.

Alex suddenly got up and started looking around. "What's wrong, babe?" Ace yelled to her.

"Where did Zuma go?"

Ace scanned the beach then he pointed toward the north. "He's up there. It looks like he found a friend to play with."

Alex's eyes widened. He can't get in the water. It's too cold."

"He's a Lab, for crying out loud. They love the water."

Alex gave him her glare, and Dino wanted to laugh.

Dino turned and saw two, four-legged figures running toward them. As they got a bit closer, Dino thought he imagined it, but the other dog looked a lot like Nigel.

Suddenly, a loud whistle pierced the air. Dino swung his head in the direction of the sound. There on the beach, jogging toward him, was the woman he couldn't get off his mind no matter how hard he tried.

He called out to Nigel, and the big oaf trotted over to him, tail wagging and tongue hanging out. Dino gave him a good scratch. He started walking towards her with Nigel bouncing along beside him.

He smiled as he walked closer, and she smiled back. He had missed seeing that beautiful smile of hers, but he understood there wasn't a lot to smile at in the past two days.

"Hi," he greeted her.

"Hi back," she replied and bent down to pet Nigel. "You were a sneaky little boy, wandering off as you did," she said to the dog and kissed him on the nose. When she stood back up, she looked at him. "Thanks for bringing him back."

"No problem. He met a new friend."

"I saw that. Whose dog was that?"

"Ace and Alex's. His name is Zuma."

"Oh. Well, it is nice to see that Nigel interacts with other dogs okay."

He asked the question he'd been wondering.

"How did you get here?"

"Bruno."

"Why didn't you call me? I would've come to get you. I told you that I would."

"I know. And I appreciate the offer, but I didn't want to pull you away from work. It's all good."

Dino could tell something was bothering her. He could see it in her eyes, and in the defensive way, she stood. She was on guard, and he was about to find out why. He stepped closer, taking her hands into his and bringing them to his chest where he held them. He looked down into her eyes.

"What are you not telling me?"

She grinned. "Why do you think I'm not telling you something?"

He quirked his eyebrow. "I'm trained to read people, remember?"

She sighed. "After Bruno picked me up, we went by my dad's place so I could get a few things to take to the hospital tomorrow. After we left there, we stopped at the Police Department to talk to the Chief."

"About what?"

"About my dad and his medical episode." She looked right into his eyes, and he could see her trying to blink away the tears. "My dad's blood work came back. He had high levels of cyanide in his system."

Dino stared at her. He wanted to ask her if she was joking, but from the seriousness in her voice and the expression on her face, he knew she wasn't.

"We believe that someone tried to kill my dad."

"Jesus, Arianna. Do they have any idea who?"

"No. Like I said, Bruno and I met with the Chief and one of his detectives. They're opening up an investigation. Although it would help if my dad were awake to provide some key information."

"How's he doing? Any change?"

She shook her head. "Not yet, but now that the doctors know what they are battling, they started a new treatment plan this afternoon. As they put it—it is all up to him now."

He pulled her into a hug. "I'm so sorry, babe. I don't even know what to say."

She hugged him back. "I know. I felt the same when the doctors first told me."

"Why didn't you come out to the bonfire?" He asked her. "Everyone was expecting you."

She shrugged her shoulders. "Once I left the police station, I had Bruno bring me here to get my car initially. But once I was here, I didn't want to go back to my place. I needed some alone time, and I feel close to my dad here. Plus, I was able to get some things done around the place."

He understood what she was saying. This was her dad's place, and there was that connection. He stepped closer and ran his hands up and down her arms, trying to infuse some warmth into her. When he looked down and saw her bottom lip start to quiver as she stared up at him, he didn't hesitate and wrapped her up tight with his arms.

When he felt her body begin to shake, he knew she had let go, and he just held onto her as she wept. It was gut-wrenching, but he was glad he had been in the right place at the right time for her to lean on. Whatever the future held for them relationship, no relationship, he would always be there for her.

He buried his face in her hair as she burrowed further into his body. Every once in a while, he would hear a slight sniffle.

He couldn't say he was close to his parents, but if something were to ever happen to either his mom or dad, it would still upset him, so he couldn't begin to imagine what Arianna was feeling right now. Anger started to build in Dino. Whoever was the coward responsible for the heinous act had better hope that when they were found—and they would be—that the police find them before the community did. Because if it was the latter of the two, there was no promise that the individual would be alive to even be prosecuted. One thing was true that Arianna probably wasn't aware of—she had the most extensive and baddest arsenal at her disposal in the form of the SEAL community here in town. Paul may not have been a SEAL, but he was a Marine and someone who was respected in the community's eyes.

Once she seemed to be all cried out, Dino gently placed his hands on her shoulders, and she tilted her head back to look upward. Even with red, puffy eyes and a little red nose, she was a keeper in his book. He seriously needed to talk to someone about what he was going through. He couldn't continue like this. But that could wait—not too long, but right now, they had to deal with the new developments concerning Paul. And one thing he hadn't considered—could Arianna be in danger herself?

Arianna looked way up into the eyes of the man she was definitely falling in love with. No man she had ever been with had treated her with the compassion, true affection, and the support Dino had. She just wished he'd snap out of the fog that was blanketing him and realize that she could be all of those things for him as well. He may think that his heart had been damaged beyond repair, but with what she had witnessed in the three weeks of knowing him, he had a heart that was full of love.

He placed his large warm hands on her hips and pulled her closer. He used his thumb to wipe a stray tear from her cheek.

"What do you say we get out of here?"

"Really? You don't want to spend time with your friends?"

He grinned. "I see them all the time."

"Where are we going?"

"To get food because I'm starving," he said with a big grin on his face.

"Then food it is."

Twenty minutes later, and a quick stop by her place to drop Nigel off, they pulled into the small shopping plaza not too far from the base. She knew in an instant where he was taking her, and she couldn't stop smiling.

"The Sub Shoppe?" She turned to look at him.

"I assumed this place was okay since they sort of have a little bit of everything."

She smiled. "I love this place. It is the only pizza I eat. The sauce alone is to die for. It's so—"

"Sweet," Dino finished for her, and Arianna nodded her head.

They made their way into the small restaurant, and he guided her toward the back of the place.

"It's crowded," he whispered close to her ear, and she nodded.

They found a table right next to the back exit, and she went to take the seat where her back would be against the wall, but Dino stopped her.

"Let me take that seat."

She should've known he would want to sit there. Her dad was the same way, along with any other military and law enforcement person she knew.

They never wanted their back exposed. They always wanted to be on guard and see what was in front of them with something solid at their back.

She swallowed hard. The problem now, though, was that for the last two and a half years, she had learned never to let her guard down, and that included always making sure she looked over her shoulder.

He gave her waist a good squeeze and grinned. "I promise, I've got your back."

The waitress came over and took their drink order. When she returned and set their drinks down, she turned toward Arianna.

"You look very familiar. Were you on a magazine cover or something?"

Oh shit! Arianna pushed a strand of hair behind her ear. She never thought to think of a comeback to use if someone thought they had recognized her. Most of the designs she modeled were only available in Europe and advertised in Europe, but that didn't mean her pictures wouldn't make it across the Atlantic Ocean to the states.

She smiled and shook her head, "No, that wasn't me. I'm afraid I'm just a nobody," she joked, but at the same time, she could feel her nerves start to go into overdrive. The bubbly waitress seemed to buy it and went on her merry way to wait on other customers.

When Arianna turned back around, Dino was in a dead stare at her. *Crap.* Could he see through her lie?

"What?" She asked, putting her straw in her soda and taking a drink.

"You're beautiful enough to be on a magazine cover."

She rolled her eyes. "Yeah, right."

"I'm serious."

She picked up the menu though she already knew she was ordering a pizza.

"I'm not camera friendly. I always feel awkward when someone takes a picture of me." That statement wasn't a complete lie. It always did take her a few minutes to warm up when she first got in front of a photographer.

He just shook his head and grinned as if not wanting to argue over it. "Whatever."

"Why are we both looking at the menu when both know we want pizza?" She asked with a laugh.

He laughed too and set the menu down. "Good point. What toppings?"

She shrugged her shoulders. "Meat lovers?"

His big grin told her he agreed. She wasn't going to say to him that she hadn't had pizza in over two years. That would surely lead to questions she wouldn't and couldn't answer.

Proper nutrition had been the most challenging adjustment for her when she was modeling. Before modeling, she was used to eating what she wanted and when. When she was placed into the role of a lingerie model, all that changed quickly. She was given a strict diet and exercise program to follow. Every week she had to be weighed and measured. Models were given a little leeway, but if there were a significant change in either, you would've sworn that the person had committed treason. A few months ago, there had been an incident when she heard one of the executives at the design firm telling a model that her belly looked bloated and to go into the bathroom and make herself throw up. It had been awful to watch the young girl get berated. The sad part was the girl did what the woman ordered her to do and went right into the bathroom and made herself throw up. It had been disgusting to witness.

But tonight, she would enjoy the gooey cheese, sweet sauce, and freshly made dough because she could and didn't have anybody to tell her she couldn't.

CHAPTER NINETEEN

"What were you able to find out for me?" Travis Gabbert questioned his hacker buddy, who he paid a reasonable sum of money to hack into the Virginia Beach General Hospital's database.

"The rumors you heard were true. Paul Roland is listed as a patient at the hospital."

"Were you able to access his patient file?" Gabbert was hoping so but feared it was unlikely. Hospitals have stepped up the firewalls they had in place to prevent people like him from gaining access to sensitive information.

"No. They have a very complex system. If I had more time, maybe I could find an entry point somewhere, but the timeline you're on, I don't think it's possible."

Damn! "I figured so. Thank you, Luis. I've just wired you the final payment for the job. Keep your phone handy because I'll have some other jobs coming your way soon."

"I'll be waiting."

The line went dead, and Gabbert threw the phone onto the table next to the bed. He was holed up inside his hotel room that overlooked the boardwalk in Virginia Beach. His original plan of torturing Paul Roland by targeting his daughter had been altered now that Paul was in the hospital with an undisclosed condition.

He grinned to himself. Those assholes at the bureau thought that just because he no longer worked for them that he was cut off from the world. Newsflash for them; he had connections worldwide that would come in handy for what he had planned.

He pulled his notebook out and flipped it open to the list he had compiled of all the enemies he'd been accumulating over his twenty-four-year tenure at the FBI. He vowed that one day he'd get even with each one for helping to damage his reputation within the bureau. Most were colleagues he'd worked cases with, but there were also judges, former politicians, and others who worked for other law enforcement agencies.

See, during the day, he played by the FBI's rules, but once he was off the clock and nightfall came, he was a vigilante. The people he investigated were people who broke the law, and lawbreakers had to be punished. Many of the investigations he was given the lead on eventually went cold after weeks or months of gathering and examining evidence. But it wasn't for his lack of trying. It was just hard to close out a case when the main suspect just vanished out of thin air. Then depending on the timing of things, the person would surface, but in a body bag. Thirty-two of them, and he knew the names of every single one of them. He knew he was a sick son of a bitch, but why spend thousands and sometimes hundreds of thousands of dollars trying to bring in one criminal? He believed he was saving his government a lot of money and a lot of time. With a dead suspect, nine times out of ten, the case was closed.

But then some had humiliated him over the years. They were the ones who replaced him on cases that he couldn't close or made it difficult for him during court proceedings. Those individuals would pay the price as well. Two of them already had. Next up on his tour around the country was Paul Roland for his part in having him removed from the Elias Barros case. His daughter, unfortunately, was going to pay the price because of her dad. But not knowing what Paul's condition was had put a slight curve in the plan he had devised. He wanted to make Paul watch his daughter suffer. He could still have a little fun until his grand finale. After all, he had all the time in the world now.

CHAPTER TWENTY

As soon as Arianna opened the door to her dad's office, she knew she was in for one hell of a day. Why in the hell was Victoria sitting at her dad's desk rummaging through the desk drawers?

When she looked up surprised to see Arianna in the doorway, Arianna knew Victoria wasn't just there to look for a simple bill.

"What are you doing here?" Victoria snapped and immediately started straightening everything back on the desk. Could she have looked any more suspicious?

Arianna set her bags down on the small sofa and stood in front of the desk.

"I think the question is, what are *you* doing here? You have no business at this place."

She huffed. "Being that I do help Paul from time to time, I think that I am entitled to be here."

Arianna couldn't stand people who thought they were entitled.

"I beg to differ. According to my dad, you haven't been involved in the business in over six months."

"Well, newsflash honey, your daddy ain't here right now."

Arianna stepped into Victoria's space, making her take a step backward towards the door.

"I've had enough of your shit. I don't know what is going on between you and my father, but while he's out, I'm running the show here now, and I don't want you here."

There was a knock at the door, and when Arianna turned, Bruno stood there with a concerned expression.

"Is everything okay in here?" He asked, looking between the two women.

Arianna turned her gaze back to the witch standing across from her.

"Everything is fine. Victoria was just leaving."

Victoria picked up her designer bag then did the typical dramatic flip of her hair with her hand.

"You're making a big mistake, little girl," she snarled at Arianna.

"Is that a threat Victoria? Because if it is, and something happens, I've got a witness." She pointed to Bruno.

With another huff, she walked out the door.

"What was that all about?" Bruno asked, coming in and taking a seat.

"I found her going through my dad's desk."

Bruno raised his eyebrow in question. "What was she hoping to find?"

"I'm not sure," she replied. She bent down to pick up a few papers that Victoria must have pushed off the desk, and when she went to stand, her head became fuzzy, and her stomach felt funny. She got lightheaded, and Bruno must have seen what was happening because he rushed to her side and held her around the waist.

"Whoa. Easy there," he said as he guided her to the chair.

She fell into the chair and closed her eyes, wishing the sensation would go away. But it only made it worse. She felt like she was going to be sick. She bent over in the chair, holding her stomach, willing away the nausea feeling.

Bruno quickly went to the bathroom and returned with a wet cloth.

"Here, put this on your head. I'm going to run out to the bar and grab you something to drink." He was back within seconds and handed her an orange juice.

She took a sip and leaned her head back against the chair.

"Okay?" He asked.

She stared at Bruno. Bruno was a great guy and a really good friend of her dad's. They had served together, and during their last deployment, Bruno suffered a career-ending injury to his leg. He was lucky to be alive, let alone still have a leg.

"I'll be fine." She half shrugged her shoulders. "I have to be. My dad needs me; this place needs me."

"Arianna, I've always admired you, but let me ask you something. If you're so busy taking care of everyone and everything, who's taking care of you?"

"What do you mean? I'm taking care of me."

Well, didn't he hit the nail on the head? After her mom died, she always looked after her dad. Even though he was a brilliant man, mom always teased him that he didn't have common sense. The truth was nobody looked after her—especially in the last three years. Sure, she was usually around many people unless she was sleeping, but she felt it was just her. She wasn't friends with those people. Hell, most of them would stick the knife in your back, and soon as you turned from them. It was a dog-eat-dog world—a place she never wanted to return to.

"Sweetie, you need to slow down and let others around you help you. Don't see asking for help as a sign of weakness."

"I need to be busy. I can't just sit around, or I'll go crazy."

"I understand, but there has to come a time where you need to recharge your body. Getting burned out isn't going to help your dad or this place if you're not around, because you're in the hospital because you got sick."

"I know, but I can't help it. It's who I am."

"How about this. Why don't you take tonight off?"

"But I was off last night," she argued.

"No, you weren't. The place may not have been open, but you were still working, and don't even try to deny it because the video cameras don't lie."

"Fine! You win," she told him as she threw her hands up in the air. "Let me at least get the payroll sent over to the company so they can cut the checks."

"That's fine. But I'm going to sit here and make sure that's all you do," he smiled at her. She hated that he was right. If she didn't slow down, she would run herself into the ground, and it wouldn't be good for either her or her dad.

Okay, so Arianna hadn't been entirely straight with Bruno. After she finished the payroll, she left like she said she would. However, instead of going home to rest, she headed for the hospital.

When she got off the elevator, she noticed a police officer posted at the nurses' station, and she wondered if it was because of the new developments in her dad's case. The officer looked up and smiled at her. He was a very handsome man. The nurses probably loved his company. She introduced herself as she signed into the visitor's log. Her suspicions were right on. He told her that the Chief specifically assigned him to this post. Four officers would rotate. It made her feel a little better knowing he had some protection when she wasn't around.

When she got to her dad's room, she set her bag down and walked over to his bed. She kissed his cheek like she always did and talked with him a little bit. His coloring had looked a little better today, which hopefully was a good sign that the treatment was working.

She went to her bag and pulled out a blanket she brought from his house. His favorite one was with the Marine Corps logo that she had gotten him for his birthday one year. She placed it over him and straightened it out.

She also brought a couple of pairs of his PJ bottoms. When Arianna was talking with Brianna the other day, she told her that if her father knew he was lying around in a hospital gown with his butt hanging out, he would be so mad. Brianna had laughed but then told her that she could bring in loose bottoms if she wanted to, and they could put them on him.

Besides the pj's and blanket, she brought in a picture of her and him taken a week before she left for Europe. He had taken her out to dinner.

"I thought I saw you sneak in here," a female voice said from behind her.

Arianna turned toward the door and saw Brianna standing there holding a caddy full of medical supplies. She smiled. Arianna really liked Brianna. Brianna seemed to have also taken a real liking to her dad as well. A few times, Arianna had to step out and would come back and find Brianna sitting with her dad and talking to him. Even though her dad was asleep, it touched Arianna seeing Brianna's compassion toward him. Now, that was someone whom she would love to see her dad with. She was a real sweetheart—caring, compassionate.

"Hi, Brianna. How's our guy doing today?"

Arianna hid her grin when Brianna's cheeks pinkened at the comment. Arianna had no clue why she said that. Okay, that was a lie. She wanted to see if there was an inkling that the woman was interested in her dad.

Brianna walked to Paul's bedside and gently brushed his hair off his forehead. The sight warmed Arianna's heart.

"His vitals are steady, and he has more coloring today. That's positive to see. The nurses from the night shift said he had a little movement in his fingers."

"Really? That's great news."

Brianna smiled. "It's progress. He's a fighter. I will say that about him."

Arianna smirked. "That he is and stubborn, but he's my world."

Brianna looked at Arianna. "If he is anything like you, I'm sure he is a wonderful man. He raised a good daughter." Now it was Arianna's turn to blush.

Changing the subject, Arianna asked, "Do you know if Victoria has been by to see him yet?"

Brianna's smile faded. "No, I didn't see her name in the visitor's log."

It made Arianna happy to know that he had an angel watching over him.

"Now, there was a gentleman who came by early this morning. I wasn't here, but one of the other nurses said something."

"Hmmm…I'm not sure who it could've been. My dad knows so many people that it's hard to tell who it could've been."

"Courtney said that this particular guy gave off a bad vibe. Of course, since he wasn't on the approved list, she didn't let him go back."

Arianna thought that did seem strange and wondered who it was.

She and Brianna talked for a few minutes until Arianna's phone vibrated. Arianna retrieved it from her purse and saw it was Alex.

Arianna answered, "Hey, you!"

"Hi. How's your dad doing?" Alex said.

Arianna looked at Paul in the bed and smiled. "His coloring is a little better today, and the nurse told me that he moved his finger last night."

"Arianna, that's great news."

"It's a start."

"Yes, it certainly is. Umm...there was another reason I called. Since I heard you got booted from Bayside for the night, I wondered if you wanted to come over for dinner. I'm making pork chops with macaroni and cheese and southern-style green beans."

Arianna's mouth was already watering. That sounded delicious.

"Sure. What time?"

"You can come whenever you want. I'm not working in the office today."

"Okay. Let me finish up here at the hospital, then run home to let Nigel out, and then I'll be over. Can I bring anything?"

"Nope. I've got it all covered."

"Sounds good. I'll see you soon."

"Bye."

Maybe a little normalcy and a night away from Dino was what she needed. Once again, their dinner last night turned into another impromptu sex romp. Not that she was knocking it because it was damn good. It was just the awkwardness when he'd leave to go back to his place.

Maybe she'd stop at the liquor store on the way to Alex's and pick up something that the two of them could share.

"I cannot believe that Paul had traces of Cyanide in him. That is so scary," Alex said to Arianna.

"I know." Arianna had told Alex everything that had happened yesterday.

"So, since you've taken on the role of manager at Bayside, does that mean you're sticking around?"

Arianna looked up from where she was slicing the cheese to make the macaroni and cheese.

"Honestly, I haven't really thought about it." And, that was true. There had been so much going on that it hadn't crossed her mind much. She had just been living one day to the next.

The front door opened and closed, and moments later, Ace walked into the kitchen, and Arianna watched as Alex's face instantly started to glow at seeing her man.

"Hi, honey!" Alex said to Ace. He leaned down and gave her a quick kiss.

Ace set his bag down and glanced at Arianna.

"Hey. Dino told us what happened with Paul."

"I figured he would." And she was okay with that because she knew they wouldn't go blabbing their mouths. The Chief had told her that the fewer people who knew about the poisoning, the easier it would be for them to do their job of finding who was responsible.

"How's he doing today?"

"Better. Slowly, but better." She explained about him moving his finger and his coloring.

"Well, better is good."

He turned back to Alex.

"I hope you don't mind, but I invited the guys over to watch the football game," Arianna remembered that the College National Championship was being aired.

Alex rolled her eyes, and it made Arianna laugh.

"Are the ladies coming over too? Or it is just the guys?"

"Just the guys."

"Great."

"What? You know you love watching football with us."

Alex's eyes suddenly got a sparkle in them, and she turned toward Arianna.

"Arianna, want to stay for the game after dinner?"

"Oh, I don't want to intrude on your bonding time with the guys."

Alex laughed. "Yeah, it's not like when I first met them and could talk about how their day was. Instead of the details I really want to hear about, all I get is good, okay, or it sucked." She waved her hand in the air. "You get my point?"

"I do." And she did. Alex used to work for the NSA, and then after getting screwed over by them and almost dying, she went to work for a private security firm doing all kinds of secret stuff.

"So, will you stay and keep me company? Please?" Alex pouted with her bottom lip sticking out.

Arianna was hesitant to say yes. On the one hand, she'd love to hang out with Alex, but on the other hand, she didn't want Dino to think she was stalking him. They agreed to be friends and only friends. But she couldn't help it if she was friends with his friends.

She looked at Alex. "I guess I can stay. For just a little while."

Alex grinned. "Thank you!"

Dino didn't want to be sitting around the guys when he knew Arianna was just down the hall from him. He'd been surprised to see her when he arrived at Ace and Alex's house. That explained why she wasn't at home. She was like a drug that he couldn't get out of his system.

"Diego, when are you planning on replacing the roof on your house?" Frost asked as everyone sat around the game room waiting for the game to start.

"Actually, I just got a call this morning from the roofer. He thinks he can start on it next week."

"After the roof, what's left for you to do on the outside?"

"That's pretty much it. Then I can start on the inside. I plan on taking the walls down to the bare bones. Corky, one of the MPs on base, his brother is an electrician and is going to come over and do some re-wiring. It's a mess."

Ace was flipping through the channels when Diego told him to stop.

"What is that?"

When Dino looked at the screen, it was a bunch of women parading up and down a runway in barely-there lingerie while the commentators spoke in what sounded like Italian.

Then a graphic popped up—The 14th Annual Designers Showcase, Rome, Italy.

"What in the hell is this?" Ace asked.

"I don't know, but I don't mind," Irish said as his eyes were glued to the TV.

"Hey, you're a married man now," Potter playfully scolded him.

Irish grinned. "I am to the love of my life, and from the looks of the lingerie those women are wearing, I think I may have to do a little shopping for Bailey. Where did they say this was?"

"Rome," Dino told him.

Dino noticed it was a taped show by the date stamp at the bottom corner of the screen. It was from back in early December.

The camera cut away from the announcers and zoomed in on the next model who stormed the stage through the glitter curtain wearing a very sexy, modest, deep purple strappy outfit. The color complemented her olive skin tone. Dino felt his jaw drop when she started her sexy strut down the runway and flipped her hair off her face. Even with all of the make-up, Dino knew that face and that body. Frost sitting next to him, must have seen what Dino saw because his mouth opened, but no words were spoken. But judging from his facial expression, he too was shocked.

It was Stitch who finally spoke, "Holy shit! Is that..." Before he could finish his sentence, they all heard the crashing of glass behind them. When Dino turned, there stood Arianna and Alex. Alex was in a dead stare at the TV, but Arianna's eyes were on him with her hand over her mouth.

Alex and Arianna were finishing cleaning up in the kitchen before heading to the game room to watch the game with the guys.

Alex reached for her phone when she saw Derek was calling.

"Hey, D!"

"Hey, honey. By chance, is Arianna still at your place?"

Alex glanced at Arianna, who was putting the leftovers in the refrigerator. "Yeah, what's up?"

She heard him sigh and knew that wasn't a good sign. "Tell her to go turn on the TV, channel 45."

"Okay. What's on?"

"She'll understand when she sees it."

"Alright. I'll tell her right now."

"Alex?"

"Yeah?"

"Let her know if she needs anything to call me."

Alex's spidey senses started to come to life. Derek was in commander and protective mode.

"Will do."

"Talk to you later."

Alex set the phone down. "That was strange."

"What was?" Arianna asked as she handed Alex her drink.

"That was Derek. He told me to tell you to turn the TV onto channel 45."

"Why?"

"I don't know, but he sounded weird." She shook her head. "I don't know. Come on, and I'll have the guys flip to it before the game starts."

As Arianna made her way down the hall, she tried to rack her brain about what could be so interesting on television that Derek would call out of the blue like that. Did it have something to do with her dad?

She asked Alex, "What channel is 45?"

Alex shrugged her shoulders. "I don't know. I don't watch much television, but I do know it isn't one of the local channels."

As soon as Arianna hit the doorway leading into the game room, she heard the familiar music, and she stopped dead in her tracks. There on the eighty some-inch TV screen was her walking in her last runway show.

She dropped the bottle in her hand, and it shattered when it hit the tile floor. Her throat felt like it was tightening by the second as her hand flew to her mouth. She was too stunned to speak. How had this made it on television here in the states? The better question was, how did someone even have a copy of it? She had been told that all of the copies had been confiscated.

"Arianna, is that you?" Alex whispered from beside her.

She was mortified. *Oh, god! Who else had seen it? What did this mean? Did the bureau do it? What the fuck!*

She began to feel dizzy; she didn't feel good as her stomach started to churn. She didn't feel steady as she felt her body begin to sway.

Alex grabbed her arm. "She's going to pass out," Alex shouted just as everything in Arianna's vision went black.

Dino had gotten to Arianna just before she smacked the side of her head against the tile floor. He hoisted her up into his arms, walked her over to the couch, and gently laid her down.

Ace hit the power button turning the TV off. The room was eerily quiet as everyone gathered around.

Dino knelt next to her head, and Alex ran over with a cold cloth that he took and placed on Arianna's forehead. Stitch checked her pulse just to make sure everything seemed okay.

"I thought she said she worked as a Forensics Accountant," Skittles asked.

"She was," Frost stated.

Dino was trying to process everything when it suddenly hit him. At the New Year's party was when he found out that Arianna had worked for the FBI. But before that, when he knew her as "Anna," she said she worked in the fashion industry with models. Add in the fact that she'd been off somewhere that Paul called a project for over two years. Then he thought about the waitress at the Sub Shoppe who thought she recognized Arianna from a magazine cover. *Son of a bitch!*

Dino ran his hand down his face and exhaled. "She was working undercover," he said out loud and then heard a few "whats" echo in the room. His eyes traveled from her face down to her arm. The arm she said she cut, but he swore was a bullet wound. She had a long-sleeved shirt on at the moment, or he'd show it to the others and see what they thought it was.

He looked up at the guys standing around them. "She was shot within a week or two before she came home."

"What are you talking about? Did she tell you that?" Ace asked.

He shook his head. "The night we first met; her arm was bandaged. I asked her about it, and she downplayed it, saying she cut it while moving. Then a few days later, she had on a short-sleeved shirt, and the bandage was off, showing a fairly new nasty pink scar. Trust me; I know the difference between a cut and a bullet wound."

Alex had her phone out and was looking up the Designers Showcase in Rome. When she found what she was looking for, she said, "Here it is. Anna Humphreys, a.k.a. The Black Swan of Europe's lingerie industry. It goes on about her career. Holy shit! Our Arianna was famous. Oh no!"

"What?" Dino asked, looking over her shoulder so he could try and read whatever she was reading.

"It says here that Anna abruptly walked away from the industry, sparking rumors of her mysterious and sudden disappearance. One source says that after Anna's last runway show in Rome, she was killed after getting caught in the crosshairs of an organized crime attack gone bad."

Dino glanced up at Ace, who raised his eyebrows. "That could be where that bullet wound came from."

Arianna started to stir, and Dino leaned over her.

"Arianna?"

The blackness slowly faded and gave her the drive to open her eyes slowly. When she blinked, everything seemed like a blur, but as her eyes gradually focused, she was looking into a pool of dark blue eyes.

"Dino…" She whispered.

"Can you sit up?" He asked her.

"What happened?" She asked him as he moved to help her sit upright. She still felt a little woozy.

"You passed out," Alex told her as she handed her a glass of water.

Arianna took a sip of the cold water and leaned her head back. *Well*, she thought, *the cat is out of the bag now*.

When she raised her head, Dino was directly in front of her. She couldn't read his expression, though the others seemed concerned.

"Was that the secret that you couldn't tell me?" He asked, referring to the night when he questioned her about her job.

She couldn't lie to him. She respected and loved him too much to lie. Plus, the assignment was over. She was no longer on the bureau's payroll, at least not until they decided to renew her contract.

She licked her lips and cleared her throat. "Yes."

His eyes seemed to darken, and he stood up but then took the seat next to her and covered her hand with his. He looked so serious.

"We all understand if you can't discuss what you were doing."

She shook her head. "This wasn't supposed to happen. Somebody had to have leaked it. The tapes from all of the shows were always confiscated."

"Do you know who may have leaked them?"

"I have no clue. That assignment turned into one huge clusterfuck that night. It was the same night that I went off the grid. The FBI was supposed to handle my exit from modeling."

She saw Dino glance to the arm where she was shot. She felt so bad for lying to him, but at the time, she never thought anyone would find out what she had been doing or what had happened.

She turned towards him and placed her hand against his cheek. "I'm so sorry that I lied to you."

"Arianna, I get it. I really do. You don't have to apologize. We do secret stuff for a living too."

"I know. This is just a total mess right now. I don't even know what to think."

Then for the first time since her ass was literally on TV, Dino cracked a smile. "I can't believe that you were at one time Europe's hottest lingerie model. Now I know where all those sexy sets you wear came from."

She slapped him in the chest as she felt her cheeks start to warm. The guys laughed, and Alex shook her head at Dino.

"Well, since Dino brought it up. Do you have any connections that I can get Bailey some of those sets?" Irish asked, and Alex slapped him upside the head, and he laughed. "Hey, I said they were for Bailey."

"Undercover or not, you were gorgeous up there," Diego told her, making her blush again.

"It wasn't easy, that's for sure."

As if knowing she was still a bit uncomfortable discussing this, Alex announced that the game was getting ready to start, putting an end to the talk of her assignment. For now, that was. She had a feeling that when Dino got her alone, he'd use those interrogation skills that SEALs were known to have.

After things settled down, everyone appeared to enjoy the football game. A couple of the guys made sarcastic remarks during halftime, asking Arianna if she'd be the halftime show. They were just teasing, and she took it in stride.

When the game ended, Dino followed Arianna home. He got out of his car, and she exited hers. They met in the middle.

"I bet you have a million and one questions for me?" She joked, though she was serious, and it was true. He wanted to know everything.

"Everyone has questions, but some questions aren't meant to be answered," he replied which garnered a laugh from her.

"Come on over, I'll make us some coffee, and you ask me whatever you'd like."

She turned to go inside, and he grabbed her arm. She turned back to face him.

"Arianna, you don't have to."

She smiled. "I know I don't have to. Come on." She grabbed his hand and pulled him along.

When they got inside, Nigel had to have all the attention for the first couple of minutes.

While the coffee was brewing, Arianna went into the garage and came back with a large box. She sat it on the island, then walked over and pulled two mugs down and poured each of them a cup of coffee before she joined him at the island.

She slid the box over, pulled out a couple of photo albums, and then handed them to him. He set his coffee down and opened the first one and was utterly stunned by the beauty staring back at him.

He flipped through the first couple of pages of Arianna's portfolio. It was full of professional photos of her. He couldn't believe these were actually her. She was beautiful and all, but the camera made the beauty pop even more.

He glanced over at Arianna next to him. She was watching him.

"These are gorgeous pictures," he told her.

"Thanks."

"If you were ever offered another opportunity to go back to modeling, would you take it?"

"No."

"Why not?"

She shrugged her shoulders. "Several factors, I guess." He raised his eyebrows.

"My age for one."

"Your age? What does that have to do with it? My god Arianna, I don't know much about modeling or the industry, but why does age matter? You were gorgeous and confident on the runway. At least the little bit I saw."

"That's sweet of you to say."

"I didn't intend for it to be sweet."

"Every day, new girls are entering the industry—younger and more naïve. They're willing to do whatever it takes to make it in the business. I'll admit that once I got over the shyness of modeling lingerie, I actually liked it a little. It made me feel sexy. But what I wasn't willing to do was use my body to progress my career, not that I'd continue it after my assignment was over."

"What do you mean?"

"I had a lot of offers from other designers. Many of them sold scanty pieces, and I wasn't down for showing all of my goods. Plus, I was there to do a job. But I can at least say that I left the industry with my dignity intact."

Dino covered her hand with his.

"What happened the night of your last show?"

She sighed. "Let's see. What didn't happen? Everything I worked for during those two and a half years came crashing down." Arianna explained in detail everything that had gone wrong, starting with her own agency pulling the plug on an operation while she was still inside with no apparent cover. It was careless and selfish. It pissed Dino off immensely.

The more he listened to her ordeal, a knot started to form in his, and he knew it wasn't going to end well.

"Our suspect came on to me and kept trying to get me to have a drink, but I knew from intel that was how he got women to loosen up. He'd drug them and then take advantage of them. Unfortunately, some didn't live up to his expectations and were thrown into his prostitution ring. That was the main reason for the whole assignment—to collect evidence on human trafficking. Anyway, as things started to heat up between us, I felt disgusted, but I had to play the part to get the prize."

Dino hated this for her. He could see how passionate she was about her job and doing the right thing, but then to ignore everything you were trained to fight against had to be difficult.

"He started getting pretty handsy with me. He wanted me to sign with his company and become his next star, which was the ultimate goal. I was there. I was moments away from signing that contract, but then Enzo, an acquaintance within the industry, barged into the room."

"Who's Enzo?"

Arianna smiled. "Enzo also runs businesses on the other side of the law, but not to the extreme as Demitri. However, in my defense, in the two years of knowing Enzo, I never once witnessed him breaking any laws." She looked up at Dino, and Dino saw how her eyes became glassy.

"Enzo's interruption probably saved me from being raped." She looked down at her arm that had been injured. "Enzo, I later found out, was working with the FBI, mainly with my supervisor. His job was to keep an eye on me, though I didn't find that out until after the fact. Demitri and Enzo are known enemies. We weren't aware of another enemy of Demitri's in attendance, and he ordered a hit on Demitri while I was in the room with him. Demitri, not knowing it was Petro who started it all, accused Enzo of setting him up. As Enzo and I were looking for the button to open the secret door, Demitri went to shoot Enzo, but my instincts kicked in."

"You put yourself in the line of fire and took the bullet?"

She nodded her head. "I did. Thank god Enzo was there to catch me and get both of us into the tunnel before Demitri could stop us. The door seals and locks for five minutes."

Dino smirked. "How do you know that?"

She smiled. "I went over the castle with a fine-tooth comb days before the event."

"Smart."

"Once we were inside the tunnels, I started to become weak, and eventually, I passed out."

She finished the story about how someone at the bureau filed a complaint against her, which was why she came home. Dino thought that was complete bullshit. He hated when people would play that type of game. In his opinion, that just meant that the accuser was an insecure asshole who was trying to cover up something he or she had done.

Dino also wondered about the Enzo guy and if he had a thing for Arianna.

"You care about Enzo?" He asked.

"I do. Enzo taught me a lot about the industry and protected me many times from the vultures and sharks. Modeling isn't for the weak. Many girls and women are forced or tricked into drugs, alcohol, and sex. I tried to steer clear of those, but sometimes people wouldn't take no for an answer."

"Arianna, are you saying that men forced themselves on you?" Just imagining that had Dino's temper rising.

"Some tried, but they never succeeded."

"Let me guess, Enzo."

She shrugged her shoulders. “Sometimes. Other times I handled it. Remember, I am a trained agent.” She grinned.

They talked until it got pretty late, and Dino could tell that Arianna was ready for bed. He knew she had a full day planned for tomorrow, so he helped her clean up the kitchen, and then he saw himself out. Knowing he was stalling and possibly running out of time to get his shit together, he launched a personal mission on the way back to his place—*"Operation Capture Arianna's Heart.*”

CHAPTER TWENTY-ONE

Arianna felt a migraine coming on. She rarely got them, but when she did, they were excruciating. It probably stemmed from all of the stress she was under in the past few weeks, and her conversation over the phone with Special Agent Chris Hurts wasn't helping the matter.

He had called for two reasons. One was to apologize for the video debacle on television last night. According to Chris, that had come entirely out of left field, and they were still trying to track down the source of it, considering the FBI had confiscated all the tapes from the show organizers. And, the second was to offer her the permanent position that she had wanted in the Forensics department with Sam—which she graciously declined.

"I told Scarborough and Frey that you wouldn't return when the time came. Damn!"

"Yeah. It's too bad because I really enjoyed working with Sam and his team. But with everything happening around here and dealing with my dad's issue, I just don't see myself leaving."

"What's wrong with your dad?"

She explained what happened to him, and after she was finished, he became quiet—so quiet that she thought she got disconnected from him.

"Chris?"

"Yeah, sorry. You said it was cyanide poisoning?"

"That's what the doctors said."

"And the police? You're sure they are investigating, right?"

"They are. I spoke with the detective today, and he said that they've already spoken to a few people but have ruled them out as suspects." One had been Victoria—her alibi already checked out, so she was in the clear. Arianna still suspected that she was up to something. She still hadn't been by to see Paul yet.

"I see," Chris said, but Arianna sensed there was something he wasn't telling her.

"Chris, we've known each other for a good two years. You're someone who I trust and respect. But right now, I get the feeling you aren't being totally honest with me."

He snickered. "Damn, we sure are going to miss your talents around here." He sighed. "There've been some developments around here."

She stopped what she was doing and sat down at the kitchen table. "What kind of developments?"

"Nothing has been confirmed, so what I'm about to tell you is pure speculation at this point. Understood?"

"Got it."

"Remember Travis Gabbert?"

How could she forget that bastard? Even though she never met the man, he managed to put a significant dent in her career single-handedly.

"I do," she answered bitterly.

"As you know, he was let go by the agency. He never returned his laptop that was issued by the bureau and still the bureau's property. When our IT guys remoted in to clear the device, they found some startling things."

"Startling?"

"There was a file that contained a document that had a single list of names on it. Names of individuals who Gabbert had a conflict with some time or another during his time at the bureau."

The hairs on the back of her neck started to rise. "Do you mean like a hit list?"

"That is the part we aren't sure of. We've got investigators poking around and who want to question him, but he seems to have disappeared."

"What do Gabbert and this list have to do with my dad though?"

"Your dad's name was on the list."

"What?!" she asked as her voice rose.

"Gabbert wasn't a fan of your father, especially when Paul was personally brought in the bureau by the Director of the FBI at the time to take over a case."

"Wait! You've lost me. What do you mean my dad was sought after by the Director of the FBI?"

"You didn't know?"

"Know what?" She anxiously said into the phone.

"Arianna, your dad at one time after his time in the military, was a contractor for the FBI."

She was quiet for a moment as she held her head in her hand; her migraine was now off the charts. This news shouldn't come as a surprise to her because she had always suspected him of being involved in some sort of government activities. It's just that the FBI wasn't one of the alphabet agencies that had crossed her mind.

"So, I'm assuming my dad pushed Gabbert off the case."

"Yep. But Arianna, it wasn't just any case. It was Elias Barros."

Her head snapped up; migraine be damned. "Are you talking about—"

"Demitri's dad?

"Yes."

Now it was all starting to make sense why Gabbert wanted to sabotage the Barros case in Rome, along with filing the false complaint. It was all he could do to take out his frustrations with her dad out on her.

"Chris, be honest with me. Do you think Gabbert had anything to do with poisoning my dad?"

"Honestly, I don't know for sure. Without us knowing his whereabouts, it's hard to tell. Can you send me the detective's name and phone number who's working your dad's case? I can talk with them."

"Of course."

Arianna had never met the guy, so she didn't know what he looked like. "Do you have a picture of the guy that you could forward to me? That way, I can keep an eye out."

"Sure. As soon as I hang up, I'll send it. If you think you see someone who even resembles him, you call me. Okay?"

She swallowed hard. "I will."

They said bye, and she disconnected and set the phone down. Jesus, what else could go wrong? She looked at her watch. She still had an hour or two before she usually went to the hospital. Her dad was still in a coma, but when she called earlier, the nurse had said he moved a couple of fingers during the night.

She got up to go to the garage. There were a few more boxes she wanted to go through. Right now, she had enough stuff that she wanted to get rid of that she could host a garage sale when the weather warmed up. She picked up the scissors and was about to slice open another box when the doorbell rang. Nigel started to go crazy and ran to the door. One thing was for sure; he was protective of his home. The only person he never barked at was Dino. That was probably because Dino always had treats with him.

She wondered if it was the mail carrier. She had been expecting a certified letter from the state regarding Bayside's business license renewal.

Once she got Nigel settled, she opened the door and was shocked to find a sheriff's deputy and another man dressed in a suit standing there. Neither one looked like they wanted to be there.

"Hi, can I help you?" She greeted them.

The guy in the suit spoke first. "I'm Henry Crane from Walford Bank. Our institution holds the mortgage on this property."

"I don't understand. What does this have to do with me? I don't know Mr. Avery personally. I'm just renting his house."

"I'm sorry to inform you, Ms. Roland, but Mr. Avery neglected to pay the mortgage on this property, and the home was foreclosed on."

"What does that mean? I paid Mr. Avery six months of rent in advance. I have a signed lease."

The guy looked remorseful. "I'm sorry, but the bank already filed all the paperwork, and they don't want to sit on the property. Notices were sent to Mr. Avery weeks ago about the sale. The house has been in foreclosure for quite some time now."

"So, what? That means I'm out of a place to live?"

"I truly am sorry. The bank has agreed to give you forty-eight hours instead of the usual twenty-four hours to clear the premises. I'll leave this paperwork for you." He handed her a document that was stapled, and she looked at it—an eviction notice.

She looked back up at him, and even the Sherriff standing next to him looked mad that she had gotten the wrong end of the deal.

"You can go down to the police station and file a report because what your landlord did was against the law. He took money from you, knowing he wasn't going to own the house much longer."

She nodded her head. She would definitely be doing that.

"If you have any questions, I left my business card with the documents. Or, if for some reason you need a little more time, give me a call. I'm sure we can work something out since you have been cooperative, and it appears you're a victim as well."

"Thank you. Umm…what about the keys? Should I leave them somewhere?" She started to laugh, and not because it was funny. The situation was just unbelievably messed up. She didn't know what to do.

"Once you leave, the bank will have the locks changed, so you can throw them out, leave them. It doesn't matter."

"Okay. Well, thanks. I guess."

"Again, I'm sorry about this."

"It's not your fault."

She watched the two gentlemen walk down the steps and toward their cars. She closed the door and walked over to the couch and sat down. She pulled her knees up to her chest and rested her head on them. Nigel joined her and laid down next to her.

With everything going on, she wasn't going to be able to find a place to live and move everything in within forty-eight hours. She couldn't go to her dad's because there was no way she was living under the same roof as Victoria. She could move everything to storage and stay in a hotel until she found a place. No, that wasn't going to work either because she had Nigel now, and there was no way in hell she was giving up that dog. *Ugh!*

Dino had seen a County Sherriff's SUV pull into Arianna's driveway, followed by another vehicle. He waited by the front window and watched as both men got out of their vehicles and walked to the front door. He couldn't see Arianna, but he could see the men and knew they were talking to her. The one guy in the suit handed over what looked like papers before they both left. They were there for just a short time. Once they left, he walked over to make sure everything was okay.

He knocked on the door and heard Nigel bark. When Arianna opened the door, he knew from the blank look on her face that something was wrong.

"Hi. I saw the Sherriff's vehicle and wanted to come over and make sure everything was okay," he told her as she opened the door more to let him in.

He walked in, and she closed the door then handed him a packet of papers.

"I just got served this."

He read the top line. *Eviction Notice.*

"What is this?" he asked.

"Exactly what it says. Apparently, Mr. Avery screwed me over." She told him everything, and he had to bite the inside of his cheek so he wouldn't go off. He was pissed.

"So, when do you have to be out?"

"Because I was cooperative, they gave me an extra twenty-four hours, so I have forty-eight hours to be out. I can't go to my dad's because of Victoria. I thought about a hotel just until I can find something, but I have Nigel."

Without even thinking and before she said anything else, he blurted out, "Move into my place."

She stared at him like he just had the most ridiculous idea, and maybe it was, considering the circumstances between them right now. He honestly didn't know what they were. But he was going to be damned if he let her stay in a fucking hotel.

"Your place?" she asked, in a tone that sounded like she didn't believe him.

He shrugged his shoulders. "Why not? I have plenty of room. You'd have the one side of the upstairs to yourself. Plus, I'm dog friendly." He grinned, and she cracked a small smile.

She nibbled on her bottom lip, and he knew she was considering it. "I have a lot of stuff. I can move most of it to storage. I just need basic necessities for a few days."

He raised an eyebrow. "Does that mean yes?" he asked, hoping it was. He knew this could further complicate things—living in the same house with each other, but it was the right thing to do. This wasn't her fault, and she didn't need the extra hassle on top of everything else she was dealing with.

"Okay. For a few days."

He stepped forward and pulled her into a hug. Not only because he wanted to, but because she needed one.

Nine hours later, and feeling like she had been run over by a truck, Arianna plopped down on the couch in Dino's living room with the other ladies. All of the guys were in the kitchen, sitting around the table.

Arianna couldn't believe that every single one of Dino's teammates stopped what they were doing and came to help them. It brought a smile to her face, and she was proud to call them her friends.

"I can't thank y'all enough. I never would've been able to get everything moved today."

Bailey took the seat next to her on the couch. "I can't believe that a-hole rented you the place knowing it was being auctioned off."

Neither could Arianna.

"That is just about as low as someone can go. I'm glad that Deputy from the Sherriff's office explained several options you have to go after the guy."

"Yeah, but it's doubtful I'll get my money back."

"Still, he needs to be punished. He stole from you, amongst other things."

Alex handed Arianna a Coke Zero. "Where are you going to look?"

"I have no idea. Right now, I'm just thankful that Dino was kind enough to offer me a temporary place. I'll start looking around tomorrow and see what's out there."

Tenley smirked as she held one of her beautiful babies, Kelsey. Autumn was holding her twin sister, Kensi. "Are you sure Dino meant the *offer* to be temporary? I mean, it's obvious you guys are great for each other."

Arianna played with the soda can. She wasn't sure how to respond to Tenley, though Tenley was right—they were perfect for each other. "I think Dino has some things he needs to work out before anything serious happens."

"Well, our house is always open, and we, too, have plenty of room," Alex told her, and Arianna appreciated her generosity. She'd play things by ear.

Arianna glanced over and smiled. "Thank you."

"Okay, now that we got your living arrangements taken care of, tell us what it was like to be a lingerie model," Mia said with some excitement in her voice.

"Oooo...yes! Please do tell. And by the way, I googled you after we heard, and I have to say, you are a natural. Would you ever consider doing it again?" Bailey asked as she sipped on her iced tea.

Arianna laughed. "No. My modeling days are done and over with. The fashion world can be a cruel and dangerous place if you don't have the right guidance."

"What about the FBI? Have you thought about going back if they offer you the job?"

Arianna looked at Tenley. "They did offer it to me. This morning, actually. Right before all this shit happened."

"And..." Alex asked, looking like she was on pins and needles waiting for the answer.

"I said no. It was hard, but in the end, there's too much going on around here. Plus, I don't know what's going to happen with my dad."

"Do you like what you did at the bureau?" Alex asked her, and Arianna wondered where Alex was taking this.

Arianna didn't answer right away, because she wasn't sure how to explain how she felt about her job.

Alex continued, "Look, when I first met Ace and the others somewhere on the other side of the world, I was going through a rough patch. I was confused about where I wanted to take my future. It was Potter who finally asked me if I enjoyed what I was doing."

"And what did you tell him?"

"I told him that I enjoyed the aspect of helping others, but at the time, I wasn't enjoying how I was helping people. It took a lot out of me both mentally and physically."

Arianna thought about it for a moment and then answered. "I love working in forensics, but I don't think I want to continue doing it for the bureau. I have a disconnect with them because of everything that went down during and after my assignment."

Alex smiled. "Well, I can tell you there are multiple places here in Virginia Beach who could use a forensic expert."

"We may have to talk later," Arianna told her.

Arianna looked at Mia. She had meant to talk to her about Grace that worked at the clinic.

"Hey, Mia. What's the story with Grace?"

"Grace, from the shelter?" Mia responded, and Arianna nodded.

"Not much. She's pretty quiet for the most part and doesn't talk about her personal life. I know that she doesn't have any family around, though I have seen her have lunch with that attorney running for Senate. He and his wife are huge donors to the shelter. Why?"

"Dino and I ran into her on New Year's over at the air base. We were both concerned, considering how late it was and that she had ridden her bike there by herself. She mentioned that she goes there all of the time."

"Hmmm...That's not good. I know she doesn't have a car."

Arianna told the ladies how she invited Grace to come to the bar and hang out with them one night. Mia's eyes got wide.

"Her birthday is coming up in a few weeks. Why don't we plan a small party at the restaurant for her? Nothing too wild or extravagant." Mia glanced over at Alex and raised her eyebrows. Alex loved planning parties but had a habit of going a bit overboard at times. "Low key, like dinner and cake."

"And, maybe just a few balloons?" Alex said with a laugh and a slightly guilty look on her face.

Alex's idea of a few balloons would probably result in a balloon arch or something.

"Do you think she'll come?"

Mia smiled. "I'll convince her."

From there, the conversation turned to Mia and Stitch's upcoming wedding that was happening in just a couple of weeks.

Soon after, everyone left, and it was just her and Dino. They both stood in the living room.

"You good?" Dino asked her as he stood next to the couch with his hands in the front pockets of his jeans, looking mighty scrumptious if she said so herself.

"I am. Though it does feel a little weird."

"I don't want you to feel weird. I want you to feel comfortable here. Make yourself at home."

She took a deep breath and exhaled. She'd love to make herself at home in his house. Not only was his house gorgeous inside and outside, but *he* was what made up most of the home.

He stepped toward her, and her heart rate increased. Her palms felt sweaty, and she wiped them against her jeans.

Was he nervous? Giving him a little nudge, she squeezed his hand, letting him know it was okay to be nervous.

"I guess what I'm trying to say is that I want to make this work." She quirked her eyebrow. "I'm totally screwing this up." He went to walk away, but she wasn't letting him off the hook that fast. He was running, but she was done chasing.

"Dino, look at me." He turned and looked down toward her. God, she would love to be inside his head right now to know what battles he was fighting because she'd be the first on the front line to slay the demons holding him hostage.

"You are not screwing anything up." She smiled at him, and he pulled her close for a hug. She closed her eyes as she laid her head against his chest.

"I want to make us work." He admitted, his chin resting on the top of her head. She smiled.

"Me too." She whispered.

He released her and stepped back so he could look at her. "I need a little bit of time, though. There are some loose ends that I need to tie up before I can move on. I know that probably sounds ridiculous, but—"

She cut him off when she stood up on her tip toes and kissed him. It wasn't a sloppy kiss. It was a soft, gentle, lingering kiss that she melted into.

"I'm not going anywhere. When you're ready, you know where to find me." She smiled and kissed him one last time before calling Nigel and heading upstairs to get ready for bed. She just hoped he didn't take too long to sort out whatever it was he needed to.

Arianna rolled onto her back and looked at the clock on the table next to the bed. The large red numbers read 2:47 am. She stared at the ceiling fan above the bed, hoping that it would put her to sleep by watching the circular motion. She let out a big sigh when that didn't work. After climbing into bed, she hadn't been able to shut her mind off, which made it impossible to fall asleep. She tried reading one of her romance books until she had to put it down because it pissed her off. At least the character in the book got a happy ending and ended up with the love of her life. *Barf!*

Since then, she had been tossing and turning and not because she couldn't get comfortable. The mattress was freaking amazing, it molded to her body. With everything going on in her life right now, and her brain was overloaded.

She threw the covers back and got out of bed. Nigel was sound asleep. She tip-toed to the door so as not to wake the beast. She peeked out the door into the hallway, and it was quiet. All of the lights were off except for the little plug-in lights Dino had throughout the house. She quietly made it down the stairs and into the kitchen.

She knew Dino kept some over-the-counter meds in the cabinet next to the refrigerator because she saw him take a bottle of aspirin from there earlier. Hopefully, he had some nighttime meds. All she was looking for was something to help her fall asleep. She smiled when she opened the cabinet and saw the liquid bottle of potion specifically for sleeping.

She read the bottle and poured the dosage into the little plastic cup, then downed it. She coughed, hating the taste of the syrupy concoction.

After washing the cup and putting everything back in its spot, her stomach growled. She hadn't eaten much when everyone was over, and they had ordered pizza and sandwiches.

She opened a few cabinets looking for something to nibble on—something preferably sweet. After snooping in several of them, she struck out. Okay, the man was in shape and seemed to eat somewhat healthy, but he was a man. He had to have some snacks hidden somewhere. She padded over to the pantry, and her lips slowly curled into a smile as she opened the door. Apparently, Dino had a sweet tooth. Eyeing the package of double chocolate chip cookies, she snagged them off the shelf and tore into the package, not caring how loud the crinkling of the plastic was. She pulled one out and popped the whole thing in her mouth, and closed her eyes. They were the chewy ones she loved. She took a couple more and put the package back on the shelf.

She backed out of the pantry then turned to sit at the table when she was startled by the large, shirtless man standing a foot or two behind her. She screamed and threw her hands up in the air but doing that sent her cookies in her hand flying through the air.

Once she caught her breath and made sure she didn't need a change of underwear, she leveled her gaze on him.

"Jesus Christ! How about warning me next time you decide to sneak up on me." She sunk down in one of the chairs at the kitchen table. Her poor heart felt like a jackhammer inside her chest.

When she looked back up and saw the amusement in his eyes and the slight twitch in his lips, it lit a fire under her ass.

"You think this is funny? You could have given me a heart attack. Not to mention you ruined my snack, dammit." She looked at the cookies on the floor and stuck her lip out in a pout. "I really wanted those cookies."

Dino couldn't take it anymore and barked out a laugh which riled her up even more.

She stood up, but when she did, she got a really good look at him. He looked sizzling in the navy-blue silk pajama pants that hung low on his hips. Her tongue literally rolled out of her mouth and hit the floor, just like the cartoon characters. So Mr. Badass has a very, very sexy side to him.

"What?" Dino asked, standing in front of her with his hands on his hips. His muscles every so often would flex, and she found herself squeezing her thighs together. The hint of a smile playing on his lips made her realize he was instigating.

"What?" She asked, repeating his question. He was clearly distracting her. She couldn't take her eyes off of him. Her gaze lowered down his body to his stomach locking in on that sexy as sin V muscle that led below his waistband.

He chuckled and took a step toward her and swiped his thumb across her lower lip, then gave her a sexy grin that made her want to giggle like a little school girl and melt into the floor.

"You had a little bit of drool there."

She blinked her eyes then her mind registered what he said. "You ASS!" she yelled, stomping away as he doubled over in laughter. Oh, she'd make him pay for that. She had an entire arsenal of the sexiest lingerie in the world that she could choose from. Let's see who would be drooling once she slipped into one of her sexy numbers she wore on the runway.

She felt Dino on her heels as she climbed the stairs. When she got to her room, she turned around and came face-to-face with him. She could see the desire in his eyes. He wanted her. Well, guess what buddy? Not tonight.

She held her hand up as he went to take a step toward her, and he stopped.

She shook her head. "If I didn't get my snack, you don't get one either, and she slammed the door in his face."

She leaned back against the door and heard him mumble something under his breath as his footsteps could be heard, retreating back toward his room.

She put her hand over her mouth to keep from laughing out loud. She was going to have to make it up to him. But she'd let him suffer a little bit first.

With a smile on her face, she crawled back in bed and curled up on her side. The meds she took were starting to work, and she closed her eyes until she gave in to sleep.

CHAPTER TWENTY-TWO

Arianna putzed around behind the bar. It was a slower night than usual. The forecast of sleet and freezing rain didn't help as it kept folks from venturing out. But the ones who braved the weather and roads were happily eating and drinking. She had already restocked the entire bar and wiped down all of the bottles of liquor. Since business was slow, the downtime gave her mind plenty of time to wander, and boy, did she have a lot to think about.

The good news of the day was her dad was showing more signs of waking. At least that was what the doctors told her when she stopped by earlier to see him. They finally removed the ventilator, and he was breathing okay on his own and moving his hands and arms more. Dr. Rowtowski said he had observed his movements and that her dad appeared to be agitated. She didn't really care what kind of state he was in as long as he woke up.

"Now that is a look of someone who has a lot on their mind."

When she turned and looked up and saw Dino's sexy smile, she couldn't help but return the gesture. He just did that to her. During breakfast this morning, she apologized for leaving him hanging the night before. He said it was all good, but the devilish grin he gave her made her think he had some sort of payback in mind.

"Just got a lot on my mind."

"My ears are open if you want to talk it out."

"Thanks, but I prefer to dwell in my sorrows," she joked.

He looked across the room then said, "I'll be right back."

She tracked him with her eyes as he swaggered over to the old jukebox and dropped a few quarters into the machine. He pressed a couple of buttons, and then *John Michael Montgomery, I Swear* started to play through the speakers.

He strode back towards her, and his expression reminded her of a man on a mission. He didn't stop as he walked behind the bar and stood in front of her. The gleam in his eyes made her wonder what he was up to. She went to make a sarcastic remark about him not being allowed behind the bar, but he held his hand out.

"Dance with me." In most cases, it would be a question, but with Dino and his authoritative nature, it came out as an order.

This was a different side of him, so she decided to oblige and placed her hand in his much larger palm. He led them out to the small dance floor. She felt a little silly since only a handful of people were in the bar, but none of them were paying any attention to them. They took a relaxed, closed-hold dance position.

"Talk to me," he said. Her first thought was that it was the pot calling the kettle black. He had a lot that he needed to talk about, but it wasn't the time for that.

She laid her head against his shoulder, and they swayed to the beat of the music.

"My dad mainly. I feel that he is so close but still so far away."

"He's fighting to get back to you. Even the doctors said he is responding to the treatment."

"I know, but I miss him," her shaky voice was full of emotion.

Sensing her emotion, he pulled her close, and she burrowed in then closed her eyes, absorbing the connection she felt to him. Above her head, Dino sang along to the song, and she listened to each word, which made her heart soar. He had his odd ways of expressing his feelings without coming right out and saying it. And that was okay, because she truly believed they were headed in the right direction, and she'd take it.

Arianna set the clipboard down on the shelf next to her. She was in the basement going over the alcohol inventory. The distributor had delivered an order earlier in the day, but she hadn't had time to go over it until now. She looked down at her watch and sighed—three o'clock in the morning. She was still reeling from Dino's sweet gesture earlier when he pulled her onto the dance floor. It had been unexpected, but it was an opportunity to see another side of him.

Since it was a weekday and with the anticipation of bad weather, she decided to close early. She had sent both Bruno and Dino home a few hours ago against their wishes. They both tried to argue with her. Bruno said he wanted to stay and help her while Dino was just against her being by herself. She assured both that she'd be fine. It was the perfect opportunity to get the complete inventory done without getting interrupted.

She still had an entire wall full of cases of liquor to go through. However, she may have had it done by now if the previous bartenders had kept everything organized like they were supposed to. Disorganization was one of her dad's biggest pet peeves. He'd be pissed off right now if he saw the mess she had to sort through. Nothing was in its place like it should have been.

Dino had been texting her every thirty minutes, making sure she was okay. In her last message back to him, she told him to go to bed because he had work in the morning. She planned to work through the night and crash on the sofa in her dad's office and then head home later.

Just as she squatted down to lift two cases of Crown Royal, she heard a thump from above and immediately froze.

Other than her dad, Bruno, and herself, nobody else that she knew of had a key to the place, unless Victoria had a duplicate made before Arianna took her key from her.

Carefully, she set the cases back on the floor, pulled her phone from her back pocket, and called Bruno. It rang four times and went to voicemail. The footsteps got louder, signaling whoever was upstairs was making their way toward the office and closer to the door leading to the basement. Suddenly another set of footsteps followed, heading in the same direction and indicating that she was dealing with at least two people. Her heart began to race. As quietly as she could, she made her way across the room and flipped the light switch sending the entire basement into complete darkness. Using her phone as a light, she looked around for something to use as a weapon. Unfortunately, the gun her dad kept hidden was in the office locked in the desk drawer.

Not wanting to be heard, she texted nine-one-one instead of calling. She typed out that there was a break-in, the address, and where she was hiding. She had never texted the police before and wasn't sure how it worked, so for added insurance, she texted Dino.

"Someone broke in. I'm in the basement hiding. I texted 911 but not sure if it went through. Please send help."

Suddenly, she heard the door leading to the stairs creak open. It was the creepy sound she hated when watching a horror movie and knew something suspenseful was getting ready to happen. She felt like she was going to faint. She tried to control her breathing, but she was scared. She tip-toed over to the cases of whiskey and lowered herself behind a couple of the boxes. She felt her phone vibrate but didn't want to look because she didn't want the light from it to be seen.

"We don't need to be going down there. We were told the papers were in the office," a male voice said from the top of the stairs.

"I'm telling you, I heard something, and it came from down there," the other male voice said.

Arianna put her hand over her mouth to keep from making any noise as she stayed crouched behind the makeshift hiding spot. She wondered what papers they were talking about.

The light in the stairwell flicked on, illuminating the basement. Footsteps soon followed as one of them descended the stairs. Her heart was racing, and she prayed that the police were on the way. The shadows of the figures against the wall were throwing her off.

On her hands and knees and staying low enough behind liquor cases, she started to crawl toward the opposite side of the room. Suddenly a large hand latched onto her ankle, and her body was dragged across the rough cement floor. She screamed and tried to kick her way out when the other man appeared with a baseball bat in his hand. Both of them were wearing dark-colored ski masks.

She heard the clicking sound of a taser and turned back to the first guy. She saw him coming towards her with a taser. She scrambled to her feet as both men jumped toward her. She jumped to the right as the guy with the taser lunged at her. She swung her leg around like she was taught in the self-defense class and knocked the guy down with a roundhouse kick. The other guy came at her swinging the bat and just missed her head when she ducked at the last minute. She came up from behind him, and when he turned, she forearmed him in the throat. She heard a roar from across the room and saw the taser guy charging at her. There was nowhere for her to go, so she readied herself for the hit. He slammed into her and then fell into a stack of liquor bottle cases. The bottles crashed to the floor, shattering all around. As soon as they hit the cement floor, she rolled away from the glass, but the guy was right there with her. He swung his arm, his fist catching her in the eye, and she cried out.

In the distance, police sirens could be heard, and she prayed they were coming for her.

The one guy must have heard the same because he leaped up and pulled the other guy behind him.

"She ain't worth it. Let's get out of here before we get busted."

Arianna lay on the floor, holding her side that had taken the brunt of the fall. Minutes later, she was surrounded by chaos; police, paramedics, and one pissed off Navy SEAL.

Dino's heart was pounding as he flew down the side roads, racing to get to Arianna. Thankfully the weather hadn't been as bad as the forecasters had predicted as he made his trip to Bayside quicker and safer.

When Arianna's last text came through, he felt as if the world had stopped. When he texted her back but got no response, he called the police. They told him that they had already received a notification and that officers had been dispatched to the scene. He then called Ace to tell him what was going on, and Ace said he'd meet him there.

As he made the turn onto the road where Bayside was located, he saw the multiple cop cars with their lights flashing, along with an ambulance. Just as he pulled into the parking lot, Ace pulled up. He wasn't surprised to see Alex with him.

The three of them walked over to the cop that was standing outside. Ace knew the guy and told him that they were friends with Arianna.

The cop gave them a brief rundown on what he knew. There had been two suspects, but they escaped through the back door before the cops got there. They had units scouring the nearby streets and the beach.

Dino's only concern at the moment was Arianna.

"Where is Arianna?"

The cop looked like he was biting the inside of his cheek. "She's inside. A little banged up, but she'll be alright. She's a tough one and held her own against those two guys. You three can go in. They got her upstairs in the main room."

Dino yanked the door open. He didn't have to look far to seek her out. She was sitting at a table with two cops and a paramedic who had her shirt lifted and was checking her side. *Fuck!*

"Arianna!" He called out, and when she lifted her head, he saw her holding an ice pack against the left side of her face. He rushed over to the table, and she dropped the ice pack and fell into his arms, burying her face in his neck. He was careful, not knowing how bad she was hurt. Her body shook, and he felt the wet, hot tears against his skin. He kept whispering to her that he was there and that he'd take care of her. Jesus, he felt like ten years had been taken off of his life.

After a while, she started to pull back from him, but she kept her hands against his chest. Her eye was starting to swell and turn purplish. He brushed her hair off her face and placed his palms against her cheeks. "Are you hurt anywhere else?"

"Just my side is a little banged up," she told him, her voice sounding scratchy and rough.

"I don't think she broke anything, but she's going to be sore." The paramedic said as she started to gather her medic bag. She glanced at Arianna. "You may want to get an x-ray just to be sure."

"She will," Dino replied, and Arianna went to argue, but Dino just raised his eyebrows, telling her there was no point in arguing with him.

Ace and Alex joined them at the table. The police officer asked Arianna to go over everything one more time to make sure they had everything.

"You heard them say that someone told them that the papers were in the office?" The cop asked Arianna and she nodded.

"Yes. At least, I think that's what I heard."

Arianna rested her head in her hands, and Dino could tell that she was running on fumes. She'd been through enough for the night. He looked at the cop.

"Do you have everything you need?" Dino asked the cop.

"I think so. Bruno said that he would pull the video footage when he gets in and send it over to us. If we think of anything else, we'll reach out." He looked at Arianna. "If you remember anything else, give me a call. I wrote your case number down. If I'm not available, another officer can assist." He handed her a business card. "Forensics should be done shortly. They just have a few more areas to dust for prints, and then they'll be out of your hair."

Dino shook the guy's hand. "Thanks."

Dino sat down next to Arianna, and she leaned into him. She was barely able to keep her eyes open. Ace must have noticed, too, because he told Dino to take Arianna and go home, and that he and Alex would stay and lock up after the forensics team left. Moments like this were why Dino was proud to serve with the guys on his team. They all had each other's back, especially in a time of need.

Dino carried Arianna into the house and upstairs to her room. She was half asleep, cradled against his chest. Now that his mind had time to process everything that happened, he realized that he could've lost her. It bothered him that the cops didn't have a lot to go on. Hopefully, forensics came back with something, or the video footage produced a lead.

It appeared the guys who broke in were after something specific, but what that was, was the critical question. When the cops asked Arianna if she could think of anything that could be of importance in the office at the restaurant, she said no. All that she was aware of was just paperwork that pertained to the restaurant and bar.

He carried her into the bathroom and made her sit on the toilet lid while he started the shower for her. Her clothes were soaked with liquor. That must've happened when she fell and fought the guy on the floor. He was still upset that she was injured and pissed at himself for not being there. He should've followed his gut and told her she didn't have a choice and that he was staying with her. But that wasn't fair either. She wasn't his girlfriend. *Fuck!* His head was so messed up.

She didn't say anything as he helped her out of her clothes and into the shower. She leaned against the wall, letting the warm spray of water beat against her sore body. He removed his clothes and moved in behind her. He took her shower puff and squirted a little bit of her candy apple scented body wash on it. Starting with her feet, he gently scrubbed her skin, working his way up her legs to her arms. He made sure every inch of her flesh was covered in white bubbles. Once he was satisfied, he guided her under the spray and washed away the suds.

She surprised him when she turned around and slid her arms around his waist.

"Thank you," she murmured against his chest.

"What are you thanking me for?" He asked, running his hands down her bare back.

"Tonight, now, everything."

He placed his fingers under her chin and nudged her head up. She stared up at him, and he leaned down and kissed her lips. It was quick. "You should know by now that I'd do anything for you."

"I do. But I wanted you to know how much I appreciate you. If it weren't for you and our friends, I honestly don't know what I'd do."

He smiled. "Well, you don't have to worry about that," he said as he hugged her tight against him. He didn't want to let her go.

"Let's get you out of here and dried off. I think Nigel's waiting in bed already." That ignited a smile from her.

He turned the water off, grabbed the extra-large bath sheet, and wrapped her up in it before he grabbed the other and wrapped it around his waist.

He lifted her without any objections from her and carried her to the bed. She was almost asleep when he laid her down.

In a whisper, he asked, "Arianna, babe, what do you normally wear to bed?"

His dick became instantly hard when she responded. "Nothing, normally I sleep in nothing," she murmured in a sleepy voice before turning onto her side and burrowing into the pillow. Her towel came undone, revealing her beautiful breasts, and his mouth watered. He yearned to taste her.

Everything about her turned him on. Her beauty, enthusiastic personality, kindness, strength, and so much more were what he had always wanted in a woman.

Once he had the covers over her, he pulled the towel from her body. The sounds of her deep, even breaths became a relaxing rhythm. He couldn't hold back the small grin when a couple of soft snores escaped her lips.

She was perfect.

As he turned the light out and left her room to go to his bedroom, he started to think about all of the incidents throughout the last few weeks involving Arianna and her dad, and he began to wonder if they were all connected. There was one thing for sure; he would protect her at all costs. But first, there was one thing he needed to do.

CHAPTER TWENTY-THREE

The following day Dino slipped out of bed and pulled on a pair of sweats. He headed toward Arianna's room. He took a peek into her room and saw that she was still sound asleep. Nigel raised his head, and when he saw him, his tail started to wag, and he jumped down and followed him downstairs.

Derek had called him this morning and told him he didn't need to be at the base until their meeting at eleven. While he had Derek on the phone, he talked to him about the thought he had last night, and Derek agreed and said it was a possibility that things were connected somehow. He also suggested that when Bruno pulled the video from last night to give a copy to Tink to see if his team could pick out anything that the police may have missed.

Tink was a former SEAL and teammate of Derek's. When he retired from the SEALs, he formed his own elite security company in Virginia Beach. They did a variety of work ranging from personal security to classified black ops for the government. His staff was skilled and deadly.

He prepared the coffee pot, and while that was brewing, he got the box of pancake mix from the pantry. He'd make pancakes and sausage. He found it amusing that the last few times he had cooked had been for Arianna.

He was flipping the pancakes when he sensed movement behind him. He looked over his shoulder and saw Arianna. Nigel greeted her, and she bent down and gave him some loving.

He didn't move from where he stood by the stove. She walked up to him and kissed his cheek. "Morning."

"Morning," Dino said, trying to hide his anger, seeing the dark bruise under her left eye.

He gently rubbed his thumb down her cheek. "How do you feel this morning?"

"Surprisingly, not as sore as I thought I'd be."

Dino watched her closely as she walked to the coffee pot and poured a cup of coffee before she took a seat at the table. She seemed to be moving around okay.

"Aren't you supposed to be at work?" She asked him.

He scooped the four pancakes off the griddle and put two on each plate. Then added four sausage links. He tossed an extra link to Nigel, who didn't even chew it on his way over to the table—he just swallowed it.

He set a plate down in front of her.

"Thank you."

"You're welcome."

"So, you didn't answer my question. Why aren't you at work?"

He took a bite of food. "I'm going in at eleven. If you talk to Bruno today, can you ask him to make another copy of the footage from last night?"

"Sure. Why?"

"Derek wants to give it to Tink to have his team take a look at it."

"Yeah. I'll call him this morning."

"What do you have planned for today?" He asked her.

"Probably just go to the hospital for a while. Then probably come home. Right now, I'm not feeling up to hanging at Bayside."

Dino couldn't blame her.

She smiled at him. "Maybe I'll cook you dinner."

"Deal!" He told her, and she laughed.

They ate their breakfast, then cleaned up and got ready to start the day.

Arianna was kicked back in the recliner next to her dad's bed. It was getting close to dinner time.

Brianna, her dad's nurse, had just left after drawing more blood for testing. Both she and the doctors said her dad had another good night. She just wished he'd do something while she was there, so she saw it with her own two eyes.

She had been surprised when Brianna told her that Victoria had stopped by earlier in the day before Arianna got there. And that she had been extra nice to all of the staff. A complete one-eighty of how she acted the last time she was there.

She looked down at the notebook she had lying in her lap. She had started compiling a list of names that could have a motive to want to hurt her dad. She talked with Bruno, and he offered a couple of names. Some were guys who had served with her dad in the Marines but weren't good or ethical people. Others were customers who've been banned from Bayside because of their behavior. The police still didn't have any leads on the cyanide incident or the break-in. She also had a call into Chris back at the FBI to see if he had any updates on the Gabbert guy. Going by the picture he had sent her of him, she hasn't run into anyone that looked anything remotely like him.

She looked at her dad, watching his chest rise and fall with every breath he took. "Who did this to you?" She asked him, knowing she wasn't going to get a response, but hey, it was worth a shot.

She had just closed her eyes when she heard what sounded like a grunt coming from her dad. Her eyes popped open and zeroed in on her dad in the bed. She waited a minute or two, and then it happened again. This time his eyes opened.

She leaped up from the chair and took his hand in hers while her other hand fiddled with the call button to alert the hospital staff.

"Dad? Can you hear me?" She spoke softly to him.

Suddenly, his eyes blinked open, looked right at her, and spoke in a garbled whisper.

"The floor holds the answers."

Then just like that, his eyes closed, and he fell back into a deep sleep. She tried talking to him to get him to wake up, but she got nothing but light snores and the sound of his heart monitor. Moments later, nurses and doctors began to fill the room, and she explained what had happened. They tried a variety of ways to get him to wake again, but he wasn't responding.

She stood off to the side while they took vitals and checked him over. While the hospital staff did their job, she took a few minutes to think about her dad's words. *"The floor holds the answers."*

Jesus that made no sense.

"Ms. Roland"

Arianna looked up to see Dr. Rowtowski standing in front of her.

"What happened? Why did he wake up and then fall back under again?" She asked.

"Sometimes we experience this type of behavior with coma patients. Were you talking to him when he came to?"

"All I said was who did this to you."

"And what was his response again?"

"The floor holds the answers." She shook her head. "I have no idea what that means."

The doctor smiled. "What matters, Arianna, is that he responded to a direct question."

She hadn't even thought about that. All that she was concerned about was the fact he had opened his eyes.

"That never crossed my mind."

"Of course not, considering it's been days since he was brought in."

"So, does this mean he's turned the corner?"

"It's a step in the right direction."

She walked over to the bed. She was still trying to understand the meaning of his words.

"Arianna, why don't you head home for the night. I'm here all night, and if anything changes with his condition, I promise to call you right away."

When she nodded, he gave her a shoulder a reassuring squeeze then left the room so she could have a few minutes with her dad before she left.

She leaned over the bed railing and kissed his cheek.

"I love you, daddy."

As the sun started to set and darkness began to fall over the hospital parking lot, Arianna walked quickly to her car. By the time she had arrived near noon, all of the spots near the entrance had been taken, and she'd been forced to park in the back lot, which she realized was lacking sufficient lighting. Coming off of the ordeal from last night, her nerves and anxiousness was at an all-time high. She chuckled to herself, thinking how Dino would be proud of her for being aware of her surroundings.

She heard heavy footsteps behind her as she dug in her purse to find her keys—something she should've done before leaving the hospital. She was reluctant to turn around. Whoever the individual was must've had a limp because one foot sounded heavier. It was more of a stomp than a natural step. She could see her car, and she clicked the button to unlock it on her key fob. The steps got louder, indicating the person was closer. She couldn't take it any longer, and she spun around. She had expected to see a large man close by, but the closest person she could see was clear on the other side of the parking lot.

She scanned the area all around her; there was nothing. But there had been. She hadn't imagined it. The quietness around her made her hair stand on end. Something or someone was out there. She quickly got into her car and locked the door.

She wasn't in the mood to be alone, so instead of going back to Dino's house, she decided to head to Bayside. Plus, she could make sure things were running smoothly even though Bruno had assured her that everything was fine. As she made the turn out of the hospital's parking lot, she called Dino.

"Hello?" His deep voice came through the speaker in the car.

She pushed the hair-raising incident in the parking lot aside for the time being.

"You are not going to believe what happened today."

"What?"

"My dad woke up!"

"Seriously?"

"Yes! It was brief, but the doctors were thrilled."

"That is great news. I'll be sure to let the guys know."

"Listen, I know I said I'd cook tonight, but would you mind if we went up to Bayside instead?"

She heard him chuckle.

"I had a feeling you'd change your mind. Actually, I was going to give you a call anyway. We're finishing up a few things here at the base, and then the guys and I were going to head to Bayside for a beer."

"Perfect then. I'll meet you there."

"Are you still at the hospital?"

"No, I just left."

Out of the blue, her dad's words registered in her head. "*The answers lay in the floor.*" That was it! Her dad had to have been talking about the wood floor in the office at Bayside. She remembered a few years ago she had been sitting in his office talking, and her dad pointed to a spot on the floor covered by a throw rug. His words to her were that the floor holds all the secrets.

"Arianna? Are you still there?"

She shook her head. "Yeah, sorry." She pulled into her parking spot next to the rear door at Bayside. "Listen, I gotta go. I'll see you when you get here." She told him and hung up on him as he was telling her something. She jumped out of the car quickly and made her way inside.

On her way in, she noticed Alex was there and gave her a quick wave. Everyone was surprised to see her and tried to talk to her about the break-in, but she politely told them that she couldn't talk right now. As she passed by the bar, she told Selina, another waitress, she would be in the office and didn't want to be disturbed.

Inside the office, she threw her purse and coat on the chair and looked around. Her dad was good at hiding things. Her eyes zeroed in on the rug that ran under the heavy wood desk. Shit, that old desk weighed a ton, but if she had to move it, she would. Inch by inch, she pushed with all her might and slid the desk across the room until it was up against the wall and door. She'd pay for that tomorrow because her side was still sore from the night before.

Once the floor was exposed, she spotted two planks where the grain of the wood went in the opposite direction from the rest.

She went to the tool chest her dad kept in the office and pulled out a flathead screwdriver and hammer. She pulled her AirPods out of her purse and hit one of her playlists before she got down on her hands and knees and got to work, prying and pulling up the planks.

Twenty minutes later, she sat on the floor in a state of shock as she skimmed over pages of notes and bank receipts; some were from her dad's personal account, and there were a few from business accounts. The notes were all in her dad's handwriting. It was as if her dad had been documenting someone's life. There were dates and times noted in the margins next to detailed notes of locations and descriptions of people, but no names, which was odd. Why would her dad suddenly wake from a coma and lead her to this?

She looked into the small space below the floor. There were a few manila envelopes, file folders filled with papers, along with a small chest that had a lock on it.

She reached in and pulled one of the envelopes out and opened it. Several photographs fell out, and she studied them. They reminded her of surveillance photos. The picture on top was a guy who she had no clue who he was. When she flipped to the next set of images, she was shocked to see Victoria. Some of the shots were a little grainy like they were pulled from video footage and converted into still shots. One was of her standing at the cash register at the bar with her hand in the drawer; another where she was at the bank with a stack of cash on the bank tellers counter. The most interesting was a shot of her in a park with another guy. She flipped to the next picture. It was her and the same guy, except for this time it showed her passing a bundle of cash off to him.

She set the pictures down and began sorting through another stack of pages upon pages of notes.

The documents had validated what she had long suspected. Victoria was a no-good cunt who didn't deserve a man like her father. Hell, no man deserved a conniving and manipulative woman like her. From the papers she held in her hand, Victoria had been stealing money from her dad for over a year. He had been documenting everything.

She set the papers down next to her. Holy shit! Had she just busted open the case? Had Victoria tried to kill her dad?

With her AirPods in and the music blaring in her ears, she didn't hear Dino enter the room, and when he put his hands on her shoulders, she screamed.

❧

When Dino arrived at Bayside, Arianna was nowhere to be found. He spotted Alex at a table and asked her, "Did Arianna come in?"

"Yeah, she blew in here like a tornado, waved, then headed down the hall toward the office. She looked like she was on a mission."

"Thanks. She didn't sound right on the phone earlier. I'm going to go check on her."

He reached the far door down the hall, and he knocked but didn't get an answer. He checked the doorknob, and when it turned, he pushed on the door, but it barely budged. Something was blocking it.

"What the hell." He mumbled before calling out, "Arianna?"

He got no response. He tried to push the door again, but whatever was in the way was heavy. He could just see a glimpse into the room through the small gap in the door and could see the room was in shambles with part of the wood flooring peeled away.

"Damn it, Arianna, answer me." He shouted through the opening of the door.

Just then, Diego came walking down the hall.

"Hey man, everything okay?"

"No, can you help me push this door open?" Diego gave him a questionable look. "Arianna barricaded herself in the office. Something's going on. From what I can see, the room looks torn apart, and I can't get a response from her." He tried to stay calm but knowing Arianna could be hurt or in danger had him off-kilter.

The two of them put all their weight behind the door, and together they were able to open it enough to where Dino could slip in. He was stopped in his tracks as he looked at the disarray in the room. He had to wonder how in the hell she managed to move that desk all by herself. His eyes shifted to the hole in the floor where the desk once sat. Arianna sat next to it with papers surrounding her. He looked over at Diego, who just lifted his eyebrows and told him that he'd meet them out at the table.

He walked up behind her, and that was when he noticed the AirPods in her ears. *No wonder she couldn't hear me.* He mumbled to himself. He placed his hands on her shoulders and squeezed.

"For the love of freaking god, can you please stop sneaking up on me?" She reprimanded him as she straightened up the papers that were next to her on the floor.

He chuckled. "I didn't sneak up on you. In fact, I called your name several times, not to mention Diego had to help me push that damn door open because you blocked it with the desk." He looked around the room. "What the hell are you doing in here?"

She leaned back so she could look up at him, and as serious as she could be, she said, "I'm going to kill that bitch when I get my hands on her."

Her teeth were clenched, and Dino could see the rage consuming her. As mad as she looked, Dino didn't doubt she would follow through on that threat. However, he was curious as to whom the threat was directed toward.

"Whoa...slow down there, tiger. You aren't going to kill anyone. Settle down and tell me what's going on."

He took a seat next to her on the floor and put his arm around her as Arianna proceeded to show him everything she had found.

The more Dino read, the more his temper rose, showing his anger. "This is unbelievable." He ran his hand through his hair. "Why didn't Paul say anything or go to the cops. I mean, in my opinion, this is enough evidence for the police to bring her in for questioning."

Arianna shook her head. "I don't know. I know my dad, so there had to be a reason why he didn't." She shifted her body towards him and clutched his hands. "Dino, this makes me sick to even think about, but Victoria could've been the one to poison my dad because she knew he had evidence of her habit. But her plan backfired when he survived. Last night when the two guys came in here, they said they were looking for something. Do you think Victoria sent them? And, remember, I caught her in here a couple of days ago going through papers."

"It's very possible. You need to contact the detective and hand all this over to him. Let's do that now." He went to stand up, but she grabbed his arm, stopping him. He looked at her.

"I need to call the hospital and have her name removed from his authorized visitor's list. If she is the one behind this, I don't want her near my dad."

"Good call. Come on." He helped her to her feet and then looked around the room again.

"What are you going to do about this place?"

She shrugged her shoulders. "It needed a makeover anyway. I'll deal with it later."

CHAPTER TWENTY-FOUR

Demitri used his arm to wipe the sweat rolling down his forehead, but his eyes never left his opponent on the far side of the ring. He took a few deep breaths waiting for the opportune time to strike. Every now and then, he enjoyed jumping in the boxing ring and beating on some poor young soul who thought, just because they were ten to twenty years younger than him, that it would be a walk in the park. In his prime, when he used to fight, there was big money involved. Now, he did it to let off steam.

The last few weeks had been hectic and stressful. However, he couldn't bitch too much, considering he had secured two new clients, who together were guaranteed to deliver him a hefty payday. What was annoying was that his lawyers had instructed him to lay low for a few more weeks until the investigation involving the incident with Petro back in December had concluded. He knew the Feds were still trying to pin the attack on him, but they had nothing to back up their claims.

His opponent charged at him from across the ring. Demitri held his ground and ducked when the guy swung. He then spun around and drilled him in the throat. The guy dropped to the ground and didn't move. He shook his head in disgust—*Amateur,* he thought to himself.

He looked at one of his men standing near the ring. "Get him out of here, and next time find an opponent who will actually challenge me." The guy stepped up into the ring and rolled Demitri's opponent under the bottom rope and off the mat. He hit the ground with a thud.

Demitri climbed down off the ropes and found Carmine waiting for him. Carmine handed him a towel, and he wiped his face off before he pulled his gloves off.

"I take it Tristan wasn't what you were hoping for?"

Demitri shook his head and gave Carmine a dirty look. "No. I told Joran to find me a real opponent next time. I want one that will last more than two rounds."

"Well, I came to inform you that your request has been posted."

Demitri grinned. “That is outstanding news.”

Carmine nodded his head. “We already have several hits.”

“You’re joking?”

“No. No joke. It seems that Ms. Humphrey has many followers.”

Demitri couldn’t help to feel a little giddy. Anna Humphrey had been a hard woman to track down. Every lead they got, they would hit a brick wall and had to start over. He was growing impatient, so he decided to step up his game. He turned to the dark web to ask for help in locating her. All it took was to offer an incentive, and people talked.

Demitri loved the dark web for many reasons. One is because a few of his businesses were run on many sites in there. Because of the high level of encryption, websites weren’t able to track the users' IP addresses, which meant users couldn’t gain information about the host. Since the communication between the dark web users is highly encrypted, users can blog, share files, and talk confidentially.

“I’m starting to think she knows, and she’s playing a game of hide and seek,” Demitri said, grabbing his water bottle and taking a drink.

“If she is, then kudos to her because she is very good.”

“Or she had good help hiding,” Demitri replied, looking at Carmine.

“The reports did state that she retired and was taking time for herself.”

“And that sounded like a complete line of standard public relations bullshit. I think she’s scared. But the question is, who is protecting her?”

“Enzo?”

Demitri shook his head. “No. He’s been out and about, traveling all over.”

“Exactly. When he travels he often has multiple stops on his trips, which makes it difficult to track his movements. Maybe he stashed her somewhere, and that is his cover in checking up on her.”

Demitri thought about it. Enzo is a conniving and sneaky bastard who had always made it known he wanted Anna for himself. Who wouldn’t, though? The woman was a money-making machine. Throw on any piece of lingerie, and bam! It becomes the next big seller.

Demitri gave Carmine the nod. "Put someone on him, and let's find out. I'm guessing there hasn't been any word on what happened to that agent of hers. What was his name?"

Carmine rolled his eyes. "Miles. The cocaine addict. Actually, that guy would take anything he could get his hands on. I don't know how in the hell she ended up with him as her agent. He's still in the wind as well. Though Marcel from S.L.S. Magazine said he spotted him the other day downtown. Said he looked messed up."

Demitri grabbed his gear and started walking toward the showers. "He may not know where she is, but I bet you he could provide some information that could lead us to her."

"I can have Joran and Connor look for him."

"Do that. I'd be interested in hearing what he has to say."

"You got it. I'm going to do that now. Do you need anything else?"

"No. I think I'm going to go for a walk on the beach."

"Very well. I'll call you should I hear anything about your girl."

Demitri grinned and walked toward the showers. Anna Humphreys will most definitely become his girl. He inhaled, remembering how sweet her perfume smelled as he kissed her neck. He was growing hard, just imagining how great of a lover she will be once he has her in his bed. His mind was going crazy with all of the possibilities the future held for them. He smirked as he stripped out of his clothes and moved under the hot water. She wouldn't be able to hide from him for long.

CHAPTER TWENTY-FIVE

Arianna entered the walk-in cooler where all the beer was kept for the bar. She didn't need to grab anything out of it; she just needed a minute to herself to breathe. She sat down on a stack of cases and leaned against the wall behind her. The cold air blew out of the vent above her, sending a welcome relief to her overheated body. Both the restaurant and bar had been slammed all week long.

Her time management skills had definitely been put to the test the past week, not to mention her nerves were at an all-time high. There had been a lot of news over the past few days—the best was three days ago when her dad had finally come back to the land of the living and was able to carry on a coherent conversation with her and the hospital staff.

She had just left the police station when she had gotten the call from Brianna, her dad's nurse, telling her the wonderful news. When she walked into his room, and he said, "There's my little girl." she had completely lost it and broke down.

He still slept a lot throughout the day, but the doctors told her that was to be expected. She knew he felt better because his stubbornness had started to appear at times, especially when the nurses fussed over him. There were a few times when she had to bite back her laugh when he'd become ornery, and Brianna would set him straight. She wondered if her dad did it on purpose to get a rise out of her because a few times, she had caught him grinning while Brianna read him the riot act. Then the next minute, she was sweet as pie to him. Could there be something under the surface brewing between the two? Now that Victoria was out of the picture for good, there was a possibility. Now that would make a great story.

Victoria was in police custody facing a slew of charges—the most severe, attempted murder. Arianna turned over to the police all the evidence she had found hidden in the floor in her dad's office. They were quick to piece together all the facts and were able to have a judge sign off on a search warrant for any property belonging to Victoria or any residence she resided in. Investigators had hit the jackpot when they were combing through her dad's house and found that the protein powder, he made his breakfast shakes with had traces of cyanide in it. With her dad's statement confirming that Victoria had been the one who prepared the last few shakes for him along with everything else she had done—stealing, forgery, and several other lesser crimes, a warrant was issued for her arrest.

When they showed up at the house to arrest her, she wasn't there. Thankfully, with all the new technology, they tracked her phone to a residence in Hampton, Virginia. When they arrived, they found her with another man. It was the same man who appeared in some of the pictures found in her dad's things. According to the detective, as soon as they read the charges against her, she started singing like a canary—telling them that she was the victim and that the guy she was with had threatened her if she didn't do it.

Come to find out, the guy was actually her husband, and together they had a rap sheet a mile long and were well known up and down the east coast for being con artists. When they searched the house, they found several fake IDs and other documents to go along with bundles of cash and drugs. The guy had admitted that he was one of the two men who had broken into Bayside that night and attacked her. They had been looking for the papers that her dad had hidden. Arianna would make sure that all parties involved were prosecuted to the fullest extent of the law.

Arianna took a deep breath and exhaled. She had seen Dino and a few others come in a little while ago and take their usual table by the doors leading to the patio deck. She was happy to see him, they've rarely seen each other the last few days. They had talked a bit on the phone, but that was the extent of any communication. She'd barely been home because she'd been so busy trying to keep everything running, and he had some stuff going on at work that kept him late most evenings. By the time she got home, he was already asleep. The problem was that she felt she and Dino were drifting apart rather than closer. Not being around him for a few days made her realize how much she cared for and missed him. Maybe now that things had calmed down, they'd be able to spend some time together.

She looked at her watch and groaned. She still had four hours to go. Knowing that Selina was probably being mobbed at the bar, she stood up and went back out. When she walked back into the main room, she swore that the crowd had grown even larger. *What the hell?*

Arianna joined Selina, and the two of them tackled the bar, each taking an end. She rushed around, taking orders and re-filling drinks. Just when she thought she had a break to catch her breath, another customer filled the seat at the far end. She grabbed a coaster and made her way down there, but as she got closer, a smile appeared on her face when she saw who it was.

"Chris!" She greeted her former boss, and he gave her a chin lift and a slight finger wave.

"What brings you here?" She asked as she set the coaster down and rested her elbows on the bar.

"Well, I was hoping that if I came down and talked to you in person, you'd reconsider the job offer at the bureau." He raised his one eyebrow as if he wanted her to rethink her decision, but her decision had already been made. She was staying put in her hometown.

"Chris—"

He held up his hand. "I know. Your answer is still no. I had to try. Everyone misses you. Hell, Sam misses you most."

She smiled, thinking about her former colleagues. "Well, tell Sam hi for me."

"I will."

Arianna eyed him. It was obvious that there was another reason for Chris's impromptu visit.

"So, are you going to tell me why you're really here?" She asked with a slight tilt to her head.

He looked around the bustling bar. Nobody was paying any attention to them. Well, except for the three guys a few seats down. But they've been eyeing her all night and making comments to her. Selina knew them. They were all members of another SEAL team in town. They appeared young—probably their initial operational assignment. Meaning they were fairly new to town.

"Do you have a few minutes to talk?" He asked her, and she sensed it was important. Then again, why would he make an almost four-hour drive to talk to her in person?

"Sure." She called over to Selina and told her she'd be back in a little bit. Selina waved her off. That woman knew how to work a bar. Arianna had been thinking about promoting her to the new bar manager position she was creating.

Arianna told Chris to move down to the last seat. There were a few empty seats in between him and the next person. She poured him a beer and set it down in front of him.

"I didn't order that." He said.

"Yeah, but from the expression on your face, you looked like you needed it."

"You're right." He admitted and picked up the mug. He took a big gulp and set it down before he held her gaze. The fury in his eyes told her that this conversation wasn't going to be good.

"We've issued a warrant for Gabbert's arrest." He told her in a low voice, and she leaned further towards him, not wanting to miss any details. "We searched his house, and there were some *things* there that confirmed our suspicions."

"Things?" She questioned, wondering what he meant by *things*. There could be many different *things*.

"Because it's an active investigation, I can't disclose what was recovered; however, I can confirm with you that your dad is a target, and possibly you."

Her eyes widened in surprise. Great! Just when things looked like they were getting back to normal, along comes something else to throw it all back out of sorts. She almost lost her dad once to one psycho now she had to worry about another one. She couldn't deal with this.

She ran a hand down her face. "I'm thinking that since you're here, you believe he could be coming this way."

He stared blankly at her. "We don't think; we know he's here in the area somewhere. We used several items recovered from his home to track his location. One was a map that had routes drawn on it with coordinating numbers in various cities. The number that was marked near the Virginia Beach area is the same number found next to your dad's name on another document found within his belongings."

Arianna suddenly felt cold; the heat that had earlier consumed her body was long gone. She licked her lips and swallowed hard. She couldn't help to glance around the restaurant and bar seeking out any unfamiliar faces. She couldn't think even to form a sentence. Her main concern was her dad's safety, especially since he was still in a fragile state.

"We're working with the local field office in Chesapeake. They've already assigned around-the-clock protection for your dad at the hospital. There will be two agents at all times assigned to his floor."

She nodded her head. "When will they get there?"

"They've already been placed. We're not taking any chances, Arianna. This guy already killed two people from his list. Not to mention the numerous killings of suspects he was supposed to be investigating."

"What?"

"Yeah, this guy has a major screw loose. Many of Gabbert's former cases had been closed due to the death of the main suspect. And, I'm not talking about some guy having a heart attack or dying of natural causes. These people were all killed violently."

Arianna covered her mouth, leaned closer, and whispered, "He killed them?"

"He kept notes, Arianna. This guy is sick. My priority is making sure you and your dad are protected."

"I'm not so much worried about me. It's my dad who needs to be the priority."

At first, he looked as if he would try and argue with her, but his gaze traveled to something over her shoulder, and he gestured with his head toward the patio deck.

"It looks to me you already have some protection in place."

Not understanding what he was getting at, she followed his line of sight and met four sets of eyes staring back at her. Ace, Diego, and Irish all appeared concerned while the lone set was full of intensity and apprehension—Dino. Alex and Bailey were there too, but they looked to be more interested in who Chris was.

She turned back toward Chris. "They're my friends. And, yes, I think I'm covered as far as protection goes." How much safer could she be living with a Navy SEAL?

Chris's lips twitched, giving away his amusement. "Which of the two over there sitting alone are you seeing?"

Her mouth opened to say something, but then she snapped it shut. He chuckled and downed the rest of his beer. "You don't have to tell me. Judging from the one who looks like he wants to rip my head off, I think I know."

He got up to leave. "I'll be staying in town and working out of the Chesapeake office until further notice. If you see or hear anything unusual, call me."

"Will do."

He turned to leave but then spun back around and smiled. "Enzo told me to tell you hello."

That brought a smile to her face. She always thought about him and how he was doing. "Tell him hello the next time you talk to him."

With a slight nod, he turned and walked away.

She stood there for a few moments running everything through her mind. Her first thought was to call her dad, but it was too late, and he most likely was asleep anyway. She trusted Chris to protect her dad. Now she had to break the news to Dino. Being that she was living under his roof, he had a right to know if danger could be coming his way.

She started to head over to their table, but Selina stopped her and asked if she could take a quick ten-minute break. Knowing that Dino wasn't going anywhere, she knew ten minutes wasn't going to hurt, so she put herself back to work, starting with the three SEALs who were waving her over.

ஐ

Dino could tell from the moment he walked into Bayside that something was off with Arianna. He'd felt a little guilty the last couple of days because he hadn't been able to spend much time with her. It hadn't been because he didn't want to because he wanted to spend as much time as he could with her. It was just their schedules were conflicting. He hadn't even been home in three days.

He and the team had been moved up to stand-by as the U.S. government monitored a new development on a situation near the tripoint area where China, Russia, and North Korean borders met. Just last night, they had been loaded into a C-17 cargo plane, ready to depart to that region. However, a last-minute hiccup put the operation on hold. Hiccup might sound like a small problem, but a small hiccup could spell big trouble for someone in special forces.

He knew she saw him come in because she gave him one of her smiles though it wasn't the bright, infectious one he was used to seeing. That had been his first clue knowing she had something on her mind. But for all he knew, she could just be worn out, and it wouldn't surprise him considering everything she'd been juggling the last few weeks. Not to mention the toll all of it could take on someone's mental health as well.

He had watched her all night; he couldn't tear his eyes away from her as she strode up and down the bar waiting on customers. She was great with the customers, and they all loved her in return. Even when someone got upset about the food or the service, Arianna knew how to smooth the situation over and turn it into a positive for the customer. She'd seen her cover the entire check or give someone dessert on the house. That was just who she was.

At the moment, his focus was on the guy who came in a few minutes ago and had Arianna's full attention. It even caught the attention of the others at the table.

"Do you know who that is?" Irish asked him, and Dino shook his head no.

"Whatever they're discussing, it seems intense." Ace said, keeping an eye on the situation as well.

Dino was about to go over and make sure everything was alright when the guy Arianna was talking to looked directly at their table and nodded his head. His mouth was still moving, so he was still talking to her. Suddenly Arianna turned, her long hair swinging over her shoulder. She met his gaze briefly before she turned back to the guy and continued their conversation.

He fought himself to stay in his seat and not go over there. It could be a conversation that he shouldn't be a part of, but on the other hand, it drove him insane.

Finally, after a few more minutes, the guy got up and left. He had hoped that Arianna would come over to the table, but that idea was blown out of the water when he saw Selina, the bartender, grab her phone and go into the back.

Somebody at the bar whistled, and he looked around and spotted who it was. It didn't make him feel any better. It was those same three guys who had been flirting with Arianna earlier. Diego said they were newbies from Team 4.

Alex, who was sitting next to him, leaned over. "Those guys don't look like they have good intentions."

Dino tuned out the noise and focused on the group of three. Every time Arianna would bend over, all three would look at her ass. He knew those looks as they smirked and gave fist bumps to each other. They were scheming on how to get her into one of their beds. Or maybe all three.

Oh hell no! He had news for them. Arianna was off-limits.

Dino set his drink down and stood, ignoring Diego when he asked where he was going. He could feel their eyes on him; they would all know in a minute just what he had planned.

Dino didn't pay a bit of attention to the strange looks he received from other customers as he walked behind the bar. Bruno was sitting on the end, and he just laughed as if knowing what was about to happen.

He walked right up behind Arianna just as she bent over to pick up a box of liquor. The sight of her ass stuffed in the tight jeans she wore was enough to make his dick come alive. He smiled to himself as he could see the three dudes out of his peripheral vision watching every move he made.

He latched his hands onto her hips, the same time he pressed his lower half against her backside. She screeched and jumped up and tried to turn, but he held her still.

"It's only me." He whispered against her ear and saw the effect it had as goosebumps popped up along her arms. The beat of her pulse at the base of her neck caught his eye. He loved knowing he could make her body react like that.

She looked up and over her shoulder, her eyes meeting his. At that moment, he felt how strong the attraction was between them, and he questioned himself how he could not want to give his heart to this woman. She was everything he wanted in a wife. *Whoa! Don't put the cart before the horse.*

"Dino." She said. He could feel her warm breath against his jaw as she spoke.

Slowly he turned her in his arms, never breaking eye contact. Hell, the bar was packed full of patrons, music was playing, but it felt like it was just the two of them inside their own little bubble.

"Dino." She said again. "What are you doing?"

He squinted his eyes at her as his hands moved lower until they rested just above her lovely round ass. "I don't like men gawking at what is mine." He said to her in a serious tone.

He wanted to laugh at the way she wrinkled her forehead. "What is yours?" She asked.

He lowered his head. "You." That was all he said before taking her wet lips in a slow and passionate kiss that was going to leave his head buzzing. He thought he heard their friends cheering, but he tuned the noise out, only wanting to focus on the woman in his arms. She tasted so good he didn't want to release her, but he needed to breathe. Slowly he broke the kiss, so they could both catch their breath.

With her head still tilted upward, she opened her eyes. Her cheeks were flushed, her lips swollen and wet. He couldn't hold back his smile, knowing he did that to her.

Her tongue poked out, swiping her bottom lip. He wanted to feel and taste those lips again. She was an addiction.

"Dino, there is something I need to tell you." She whispered again, but he stopped her from saying anything else. This was a significant milestone between the two of them. Sure their friends knew they had fooled around, but never had they been intimate in public. He wasn't going to have this conversation with her here in the bar.

"We'll talk later."

He could tell she didn't want to wait for later. He gave her one last peck on the lips before turning away from her. As his eyes met the three guys, he grinned and winked. He wanted to laugh at their dejected expressions. *Sorry fellas, she's all mine.*

Moments later, his bubble was burst when the teams' phones started ringing in that familiar tone, meaning they were being summoned to base. Damn his job at times!

CHAPTER TWENTY-SIX

The following day Arianna did her usual when she got up. She had breakfast, then played with Nigel for a bit. He'd been feeling left out the last few days with her on the go so much and Dino working. After she jumped in the shower and got dressed, she headed to the hospital to visit her dad.

Last night she had been disappointed when Dino didn't return home, but she understood. The house had felt extra lonely without him there. After he had kissed her and left her standing there behind the bar, she hadn't been able to concentrate the rest of the night. After screwing up several orders, she finally conceded and called it quits. She spent the rest of the night locked in her office doing anything to keep her mind off the one man who had the potential to destroy her sanity.

When she arrived at the hospital, she navigated the halls making her way to the elevator, when she stepped off the elevator on the second floor, she felt relieved seeing an agent sitting at the nurses' station in clear view of the elevators and the stairwell. She said good morning to Brianna and handed her a French vanilla latte she had picked up for her on the way. Brianna warned her that her dad was a little stubborn, so she got her game face on as she walked down to his room. Sitting outside his room was another agent, and she introduced herself. As it was her first time there since the agents were put on watch, she showed him her ID, which made her happy that he took his job seriously.

As soon as she entered the room and took one look at her dad's face, she wasn't sure if she should be frightened or laugh. He was sitting up, arms crossed in front of his chest, with a frown on his face. She recognized that expression and body language—the Marine in him was forefront and ready for battle.

She dropped her purse and coat into the chair and walked over to his bed. "What has you wound up this bright and early? I thought you'd be happy hearing that you could get to go home in a few days."

"I have to take a shit." He said with a deadpan look, and she froze and just stared at him for a moment. At first, she thought he was joking, but the frown on his face grew.

"O-okay. So, what's the problem then?" She asked, trying not to laugh because there could've been a legitimate medical reason he couldn't have a bowel movement, in all honesty.

"They want to me shit in a pan."

A small snort of laughter came out, and she bit down on her lip to not laugh harder.

"Did they tell you why?"

"Because they don't want me to get up yet. The doctor is supposed to be in later this afternoon, and if everything looks okay, they said he'd let me get up and start walking around a little."

"Well, then you should listen to the medical professionals."

He furrowed his eyebrows at her. "I'm not shitting in a pan."

God forbid the man used the word bowel movement or at least poop.

"Why not? I mean, you've been peeing in a bottle since they removed your catheter."

"That's different."

She started to laugh, which only made him more frustrated.

"It isn't funny. They give you liquids because they tell you they want you to shit, but then they conveniently forget to tell you that you have to shit in a pan."

She held her stomach because she was full out laughing. All she could think of was the movie *Van Wilder* when the girlfriend puts the *Colon Blast* into her soon-to-be ex-boyfriend's smoothie.

Brianna chose that moment to walk into the room, and as upset as her dad was, she didn't miss the way his eyes lit up when he laid eyes on the pretty nurse. Brianna walked over to the side of the bed and checked his IV line, and then she looked at Paul.

"Are you still being stubborn?" She asked him, and Arianna almost laughed again when her dad's cheeks turned pinkish.

Her dad looked at Brianna and covered her hand with his as her hand was resting on the bed rail, which shocked Arianna. This was like watching a soap opera play out.

"I'm sorry for being cranky. It's just I can't and won't sh—"

"Dad!" Arianna shouted at him and gave him the stink eye for his language.

He rolled his eyes. "Sorry. I'm not going to the bathroom in a pan." He stated and then looked at Arianna. "Better?"

She grinned. "Much."

Brianna's eyes were sparkling, and Arianna couldn't believe she was witnessing her dad acting this way. Brianna used her other hand and covered his.

"Well, since you did apologize and the doctor said it was okay to allow you up for short walks, I guess I can help you up and assist you to the bathroom."

"Really?!" Her dad exclaimed, but then he turned serious. "You're not going to stay in there with me, are you?"

Brianna started laughing as she lowered the bed rail. When Paul wasn't looking, she winked at Arianna. "With the amount of liquid magnesium citrate, we gave you? No way am I staying in there with you."

Arianna covered her mouth to keep from laughing at how her dad's mouth hung open, but no words came out.

Finally, Brianna snickered and patted his leg. "I'm only joking. Now come on, let's get you to the bathroom so you'll cheer up."

Arianna offered to help, but Brianna told her that she had it under control. She watched in awe as this tiny spitfire of a woman handled her dad like a pro. Once she had him standing, she slid her arm around his waist while Paul held on to her shoulders. Together as a team, they slowly—very slowly walked across the room while Brianna encouraged him.

Arianna couldn't help but smile. They were perfect for each other.

Later that afternoon, Arianna met Alex at the mall. She needed to find a dress for Stitch and Mia's wedding that was supposed to happen tomorrow.

According to Alex, the team was still at the base and running through preparations, and that as of right now, the wedding was still a go.

"So, what exactly is up between you and Dino?" Alex asked as they both browsed through racks of dresses.

Arianna shook her head. How could she answer that honestly when she didn't even know?

"Honestly, I really don't know. Something is holding him back from taking that final step. I'll admit that his public show of affection last night at Bayside caught me off guard. He said we would talk, but then he got the call."

Alex stopped and looked at Arianna. "You really like him, don't you?"

Arianna sighed. "I do. I tried not to let my feelings for him go any further than the arrangement he and I had made, but the more I got to know him and see what kind of a person he is, he just sucked me right in."

Alex chuckled. "You guys sort of remind me of Ace and I."

"You seem like you're speaking from experience."

"When I met Ace overseas on a mission, I tried everything not to fall for his charm. He was adamant, but I kept blowing him off even though I wanted to get close to him."

"What was the turning point for you?"

"A near-death experience."

"Alex."

Alex waved her off. "It all worked out, but during a very intense mission, I had a come-to-Jesus' moment with myself. I realized everything I could've lost, including my future."

Arianna didn't want to have any regrets, but she didn't know how to get Dino to open up about his fears.

"If you're worried what kind of guy Dino is, I can vouch for him. He's quiet and can come across as abrupt, but he'd do anything for those he cares about, including letting someone move into his home." Alex said the last part of the sentence with a grin on her face.

"I'm not worried about him as a person. My problem is getting him to open up. He's got something deep down that has a hold of his heart. I've told him more than once that when he was ready to talk, I'd be there to listen."

Alex gave her a sympathetic smile. "That's all you can do. I just like to see people get their happily ever after. You and Dino are definitely a match. Who knows, maybe one day, I'll be planning your wedding in my backyard."

Arianna laughed. "Yeah, I heard that Stitch and Mia's wedding was the fourth wedding you hosted."

"Yeah, it's kinda become a tradition, I guess. I'm so happy for them. I just hope that whatever is brewing out in the world holds off long enough for them to say, 'I do.'"

"When is the big day for you and Ace?"

Alex got quiet for a moment, then shrugged her shoulder. "I honestly couldn't tell you. We've tried a couple of times, but life got in the way." She smiled. "The most important thing is that Ace and I love each other."

"Well, seeing what you've done for Stitch and Mia, I can't wait to see what you have in store for your own wedding."

Not finding any dresses that appealed to them, they went next door. As soon as Alex walked into *Victoria's Secret,* she started laughing.

"Oh my, god. Ace wouldn't be happy with me right now."

Arianna gave her a questionable look. "Why?"

Alex told her the story of that time she and Tenley were in Victoria's Secret trying on bras and had tortured poor Ace and Potter, who could hear every word they were saying in the dressing rooms.

Arianna laughed. "That is a good one."

Arianna then spotted an emerald green satin and lace teddy. She plucked it from the rack and held it up for Alex to see.

"Oh my gosh, Alex, this sexy number would look fantastic on you."

"Yeah, right," Alex said with an eye roll.

"Seriously, with your complexion, and curves not to mention your eye color. I think Ace would agree with me."

Alex went to argue, but someone behind them spoke.

"Excuse me."

Arianna turned toward the female voice and found two young ladies, probably in their early twenties, if she had to guess, standing there.

The girl on the left covered her mouth. "Oh my gosh! Are you Anna Humphreys the model?"

Arianna was startled at being recognized but tried to cover it with a smile. "I am."

The girl turned to her friend. "I told you it was her." She turned back toward Arianna. "I did an internship in Paris last year, and my boss at the time gave me tickets to one of the shows you were in." The girl was overly excited, and Arianna couldn't help but smile.

"Aren't you glad you listened to the guy in the food court?" The friend said to the girl who was totally fan Girling.

That statement made Arianna's alarm bells start ringing, and she immediately thought about Gabbert. She looked at the other girl. "What guy?"

"Oh, a guy was sitting at the table next to us. He overheard Bridget," she pointed to her friend, "mention your name. He said that his wife noticed you too and that you were really nice and that we should come over and say hi."

Arianna was standing near the entrance to the store, which was directly across from the food court. She scanned the area. There weren't too many people out there, but nobody appeared to be looking in their direction or seemed out of place. But it also didn't make her comfortable.

She eyed the phone in the girl, Bridget's hand. "Would you like a picture?" She asked her wanting to get this over with.

"Really? I mean, if it isn't too much to ask." Arianna wanted to laugh at the star-struck look on her face.

"Not at all. If you'd like, I can have my friend," she pointed to Alex, "take the picture."

"That would be awesome." The girl handed her phone to Alex. She put her arm around the girl, and Alex snapped the picture. Both girls thanked her and went on their merry way, chatting up a storm.

As soon as the girls were far enough away, Arianna turned toward Alex. "We need to leave now."

Alex raised her eyebrows but didn't say a word. She just nodded her head, and they both left the store and headed toward the exit where they were parked. Once they were out in the parking lot, Alex asked.

"What's going on? You look totally spooked out right now."

Arianna leaned against her car. "The guy last night that came into Bayside. The one you guys were looking at."

"Oh yeah. The guy at the bar with the real short dirty blonde hair."

"Yeah him. He is my former boss at the FBI. The one I worked for when I was undercover."

Arianna explained everything that Chris had told her, and Alex came across as concerned as well.

"Shit. Do you think it was him inside that confirmed your identity?"

"I don't know, but what are the odds of something like that happening?"

"I don't think you should be staying alone. Not until Dino gets back. Wait, does Dino know about this guy?"

"No. I tried to tell him last night after he kissed me, and that was when he said that we would talk, but then you know the rest."

"Okay. I'll follow you back to Dino's, and you can pack an overnight bag and grab Nigel. You can stay with me tonight unless the guys come home."

Arianna didn't argue. She didn't want to stay by herself, not after that. She got into her car, and the first thing she did was call Chris. He told her that he'd look into it. When she asked if they had any leads, he told her no. He agreed that she shouldn't stay by herself. He also said he was sending officers to Alex's house just for precaution.

Later that night, Arianna sat in the kitchen going over some of her dad's hospital bills while Alex did some last-minute preparations for the wedding tomorrow.

Tink, Alex's uncle who owned the security business, sat with them. Alex had called him and told him everything that was going on, and he agreed to come and stay with them just to be on the safe side. Chris had followed through on his promise as two police cruisers were sitting out in front of the house.

Tink set his book down on the table, then took a drink from his glass of water. He was a massive man with muscles all over.

"So, Arianna, Alex tells me that you worked in the Forensics Division at the FBI."

"I did. I was a Forensics Accountant. I like numbers."

He rubbed his chin like he was thinking. Then he said, "My company's looking for someone in that field. Is that something that you're still interested in doing?"

Arianna perked up a little, and she took a quick look at Alex, who was standing by the breakfast bar. Alex winked.

"I am. I enjoyed it, but like I told Alex, the FBI isn't for me anymore. It's hard to work for someone when you can't trust them."

Tink smirked. "I can relate. I've had many contracts over the years where I've had to work with teams from the bureau. Some I have the utmost respect for, while others not so much."

"You couldn't have said it any better," Arianna said with a slight smile.

"What do you say about coming in next week and interviewing with a few people?"

"Seriously?" She asked, and he nodded his head and grinned.

"You already got past the pre-interview phase."

"I did?" She wondered how that was because this was the first time, she even heard about this.

Tink gestured with his hand to Alex, and Alex stood there grinning like a fool. "I may have put in a good word for you." She told her.

"Thank you."

"You don't have to thank me. Tink would've figured it out sooner or later. I just sped up the process."

Arianna looked between the two and then settled her eyes on the large hulking of a man. "I'd like that very much. Thank you for the opportunity."

He smiled. "Great. I'll have my assistant give you a call next week, and the two of you can coordinate it."

His phone rang, and he excused himself.

Arianna still sat there dazed at what just happened. It was a win-win for her. If she aced the interviews and got hired, she'd get her two wishes—to stay in her hometown and do what she loved.

Alex joined her at the table. "You'll do great. Tink's a great guy to work for."

"I'm sure he is. Thanks again."

"Don't mention it." Alex looked at all of the papers strewn across the table. "What's all this?" She asked.

"Just going through some things."

"Like what? Can I help?"

Arianna laughed.

"I wish. It's just the tip of the iceberg of the many hospital bills for my dad starting to come in. His insurance pays a portion of it, but there is still a good chunk he is responsible for.

Alex picked up one of the insurance claims and grimaced, "Damn."

"Yeah, now you see my dilemma. I mean, I know he has money, but one, I don't have access to his accounts, and two, I don't want him to have to drain his life savings because his psycho ex-girlfriend tried to off him."

"Arianna, Paul is a veteran. My foundation can help him with his bills. This is why I created it."

Arianna shook her head. "No."

"Why not?" Alex shot back.

"Because, unlike my dad, there are veterans and families who have nothing. My dad is getting care, and the hospital is getting some money from the insurance company. I don't want to take money and assistance away from someone who needs it more than we do. I can set up payment plans."

"You always thought with your heart. Well, if you change your mind, I'm here to help."

"I appreciate it, Alex. Thank you."

Alex sat there tapping her finger on the table when she suddenly looked up, "What about a fundraiser of some sort?"

"Like what?"

"I don't know. There are so many different kinds. It wouldn't matter because whatever you decide would draw the entire community. Paul is a well-respected man and has done so much for others that I'm positive you would have a good showing and could put a nice dent in those medical bills."

"Like a 50/50 raffle or a dinner?"

"That or..."

"Or what?" Arianna was suspicious of the gleam in Alex's eyes.

"A fashion show."

"A fashion show?" She questioned.

"Not just any fashion show, but a fashion show featuring one of Europe's sexiest lingerie models."

Arianna's head was shaking before Alex even finished her sentence.

"No way! That part of my life is behind me."

"Come on, Arianna. You could make a killing with something like that. Do you know how many men frequent Bayside? They would go nuts. You'd sell tickets to it. Can you imagine what you could bring in between tickets coupled with all the food and beverage sold for the night? You don't even have to offer a full menu, just offer a limited menu with drink specials. It's a no-brainer."

Arianna thought about it. Posing for photo shoots and walking the runway in Europe was one thing but being back here and getting up in front of people she knew was a different story. But Alex was right. Something like that would surely draw a crowd.

"God help me. I can't believe I'm agreeing to something like this."

"Yes!" Alex shouted as she pumped her fist in the air. "It is going to be great. Oh crap..."

"What?"

"Where do we get the merchandise from? I mean, who will you be promoting?"

Arianna closed her eyes. She knew the one person she could call who would be more than happy to assist.

"Let me make a phone call."

"This is going to be so exciting."

“Well, you better start practicing because your ass is going to be up on that runway.”

“Me?” Alex pointed to herself. “Uh, no way.”

Arianna chuckled. “Oh yes, way. This was your big idea, and I need models, so you are my first volunteer.” Alex went to argue, but Arianna cut her off, “Write down your sizes, so I will know what I need.”

CHAPTER TWENTY-SEVEN

Demitri was at his desk making another pass of a new contract when Carmine burst through his office door. He looked up at his lead guy with a frown and raised his eyebrows. Everyone, including Carmine, knew that when he was reviewing contracts that there were to be no interruptions. Contracts as such had to be precise, detailed, and free of any mistake. Even if just minor, just one gaffe could lead to the loss of tens of thousands of dollars.

Demitri stared at Carmine. "What is so important that you had to barge in here and disrupt my train of thought? You of all people know how important these contracts are." He scolded Carmine.

His berating didn't even make Carmine flinch.

Carmine approached the desk and laid his phone on the desk in front of Demitri. Demitri just looked at him, but Carmine nodded his head as if telling him to look. Frustrated, to say the least, he looked down. When his eyes saw the woman staring back at him, he became immobilized, except for his dick that began to harden. His body knew what it wanted.

His head snapped up, and his eyes centered on Carmine. He spoke only one word. "Where?"

Carmine arrogantly smirked, which any other man would be killed on the spot. "She is back in the states. Virginia Beach, Virginia, if that post is correct."

Demitri knew the area well. In fact, there was an incident not too long ago that occurred between a good friend of his and the woman, a former employee of his, that he was seeking. Unfortunately, his friend Dr. Walters was killed trying to kidnap her in the mountains. The last time Demitri checked, the woman, Dr. Mia Chambers, was living in Virginia Beach. He laughed to himself, wondering what she would do if he showed up at her clinic. He had an excellent memory of Dr. Chambers—another beautiful woman and one time a woman he would've allowed into his bed. However, a new leading lady has taken that spot.

He picked up the phone and looked at the picture again. It was his Black Swan. Her black hair hung loosely below her shoulders, and that gorgeous smile of hers is what made the picture. Some college girl had met her at a mall and posted it on social media.

He looked back at Carmine. “How did you find this?”

Carmine’s face grew grim, and Demitri knew that look. What Carmine had to tell him most likely was going to anger him. He looked toward the door and shouted to someone outside.

“Bring him in.”

It was a good thing that Demitri had been sitting down because two surprises in one day were a lot to take in.

Joran, another employee of his, ushered in the man that they’ve all been searching for—Miles Thackenburg—Anna’s agent.

Demitri sat back in his chair and leveled his stare at the man who looked like he had seen better days.

“Mr. Thackenburg, what brings you here today?”

Miles wiped his nose. A tell-tale sign of a cocaine addict, which everyone already knew he was.

“I heard you were offering a reward for information on Anna Humphreys.”

Demitri nonchalantly shrugged his one shoulder. “Possibly. It depends on how enlightening the information is that is given.” Demitri eyed him over. “Did you come forward with this?” He asked as he held up the phone containing the picture of the Black Swan.

“Yes, Sir. When this man here,” he pointed to Joran, “confronted me and asked if I knew anything about her whereabouts. When I told him that it was possible, he threatened me and told me that if I wanted to live, then I should comply.”

Dimitri glanced at Joran and nodded his head. His employees knew how to get answers and get a job done.

“I’m assuming that since you are standing here in front of me that you have other information than just this picture.”

He snorted sarcastically and wiped his nose again. "I have details about the real Anna Humphreys that will knock your socks off."

Demitri rolled his eyes and motioned with his hand for the guy to continue. He just wanted to get this over with.

"The first detail you need to know is that her real name is Arianna Roland."

Demitri leaned forward in his chair and rested his elbows on his desk. "Anna Humphreys is not her real name?" He glanced at Carmine, who shrugged his shoulders. The background check they had done on Anna or Arianna as this coke head in front of him claims had come back clean and with no mention of an alternate name.

"No, sir."

"And how do you know this—or should I say why should I believe you.?"

The guy gave him a cheesy smile, revealing his yellowed teeth—disgusting.

"Because she and I worked together. I know everything there is about her."

Okay, the guy did have a point. Most agents know a lot about their clients. As if knowing what Demitri was thinking, the guy followed up, "It's not what you're thinking. You see, I'm not really an agent, and Anna, err, Arianna is not a real model. Well, at least she didn't use to be. The FBI hired her and me to infiltrate your organization."

The amusement on Demitri's face vanished in an instant. Carmine also took up more of a defensive stance.

"What do you mean the FBI hired you two?" Demitri questioned.

Miles threw his hands up in the air like he was surrendering. "Hey, man. Look, I don't work for them anymore. And I especially don't have much respect for that bitch. She threw me under the bus, and now I'm a wanted man as well. When I heard that you were trying to find her and offered a reward, I decided why not come forward. You get what you want, and I get revenge along with a nice payment."

Demitri had no intentions of paying this guy, but he would play along for now— especially if it meant finding Anna or Arianna as this man claims.

"I'll make you a deal." Miles's eyes lit up like a Christmas tree. "If you say you know everything about her, then you clean yourself up and help bring her to me, and then you and I will discuss your payday. But only if you get her to me." He warned.

"Deal."

Demitri nodded to Joran to remove Miles from his office. He'd know what to do with him to get him cleaned up.

Once they were gone and it was just, he and Carmine left in the room, Carmine stepped forward and took the seat directly in front of Demitri's desk.

"We were wrong," Carmine said.

Demitri was so furious that he wasn't sure he could even speak. This news changed everything. Well, except for one thing—he still wanted her. But he'd make her pay for her mistake in deceiving him.

He looked at Carmine. You will go with him because I can't. If I step one foot on American soil, I know I'll have the FBI and every other law enforcement agency up my ass in no time. Once he gets the girl, you know what to do with him.

Carmine nodded. "I'll start making the arrangements.

CHAPTER TWENTY-EIGHT

It was wedding day, and it was complete chaos as Alex and Arianna flew around the house, getting things prepared for the bride and groom's arrival. Derek had called Alex at four in the morning and told her that he could guarantee that Stitch would be there for the wedding ceremony at two o'clock but that there was a strong chance that the guys would be leaving in the evening. After talks between Mia and Stitch, they both decided that they didn't want to wait and if they had the time to at least get the ceremony in, they were all for it.

It had been a team effort between all the women to pull off the blissful event. Even though Alex had done most of the prep work, there were still some last-minute tasks that needed to be done.

Mia was due to arrive momentarily with her mom and sisters. They would be getting ready upstairs. Tenley had all of the kids next door at her house and would bring them over right before the ceremony started. Autumn ran to the party store to pick up the balloons and a few other small items while Bailey was at her friend's house picking up the cake. Juliette went to the base to deliver to the guys their dress uniforms to wear for the ceremony.

Arianna stood on Alex's back patio and looked around her. She felt like she had just stepped into a wedding magazine. It was absolutely breathtaking. Alex was a genius and very creative when it came to party planning.

While Arianna was helping Alex set up last night, Alex had told her about the ordeal that Mia had gotten caught up in not too long ago that involved her former boss. But she also explained how that incident had finally brought Stitch and Mia together.

Both Stitch and Mia chose a rustic woodland theme for their wedding because of their connection with his cabin in the mountains. They couldn't have asked for better weather. Though it was chilly out, the sky was free of clouds and bright. The portable heaters staged around the patio would keep everyone cozy.

The lower level of the patio near the pool was the setting for the ceremony. Chairs were lined up to create an aisle for Mia to walk down to meet Stitch under the arbor. At the same time, the upper level of the deck would serve as the space for the reception.

Alex walked out with the final log candle centerpiece and placed it on the table. "I cannot believe we pulled this off." She said to Arianna, and she too, took a step back to look over her masterpiece.

Arianna looked around again, still amazed at Alex's creativity. "This is gorgeous, Alex."

Alex smiled. "Thanks. I call it my hobby."

Arianna gave her a skeptical look. "Your hobby? Hell, woman, do you realize how much money you could make planning parties?"

"I barely have a life right now with my charity foundation. There would be no way I could take on an additional business. I enjoy doing this for friends and family."

Arianna then remembered she wanted to talk to Alex about something regarding her foundation.

"Speaking of your foundation, do you have any need for a therapy dog?"

"Yes! I'd love to get a therapy dog for the location, maybe even more than one. Why do you ask?"

"Well, I was thinking about getting Nigel certified. He's sweet, gentle, and well-behaved."

"That's a great idea. And, yes, once he gets his certification, we'd love to have Nigel come to visit."

"I think he'd love it too."

Alex looked at her watch. "Well, I think we've got everything done that we can. Once Autumn gets back with the balloon bouquets, we can place those on the gift and buffet tables. The cake table is all set for Bailey." She gave Arianna a high five. "Let's go get ready."

Arianna stood at the back door. She wasn't sure if she should go and take a seat or wait for Dino. All of the guests had arrived, and all they were waiting on were for the guys to get there. Derek had texted Alex and told her they were on their way.

She smoothed her hands down her one-shoulder floor-length chiffon dress. It was light, airy, and one of her favorite dresses she owned. Just as she turned to head outside, she heard the front door open, followed by a deep laugh from one of the guys.

She waited with anticipation to see Dino in his dress uniform. She'd admit she was a sucker for a man in uniform. Dino didn't disappoint as he came around the corner and came to a halt as his eyes met hers. She looked him over. He wore the uniform well.

She smiled, and he gave her that sexy signature smirk. As he walked towards her, she tuned everyone else out. He stopped in front of her, leaned down, and kissed her cheek. "You look amazing."

She blushed a tad bit but reciprocated the compliment. "You do too."

He held out his arm. "Shall we?"

They found their seats and Skittles took the seat on the other side of her. She found his nickname funny. As they sat there and waited for the ceremony to begin, she looked at him. "Why do they call you Skittles?"

She heard Dino snort a laugh from her other side, but Skittles shook his head.

"That is a story that I'm not getting into right now."

With an answer like that, she knew she had to know. She looked at Dino, but all he did was a wink. She went to turn back to Skittles when the music started to play. Mia appeared in the doorway, looking as beautiful as Arianna had imagined she'd be. She had chosen to wear her mom's wedding dress with a few modifications and alterations. Watching Ace walk Mia down the small aisle caused Arianna to get a little choked up. Ever since she was a little girl, she dreamed of meeting her Prince Charming and having her dad escort her down the aisle on her wedding day. Thinking now how she almost lost that opportunity played with her emotions. She tried to sniffle quietly and blink back her tears. She pulled a tissue from her small clutch and dabbed her eyes, hoping nobody noticed, but it was too late. Dino glanced her way, and as if knowing what crazy thoughts, she had been having, he put his arm around her shoulders and pulled her close. She accepted his thoughtfulness and leaned against him. They stayed that way through the entire ceremony. He was her rock, her protector, and her man.

After the ceremony and dinner, everyone mingled and danced. The guys were pouting because they were only allowed to have one drink. At first, Arianna didn't understand, but then Dino explained that they had to watch their alcohol intake because there was a strong possibility that they would be deployed later that night.

Derek and Dino had pulled Arianna aside after dinner and spoke with her about the situation involving Gabbert. They were both thrilled that she hadn't tried to argue with them about not staying at the house by herself. If the team was called out, she assured them both that she'd stay put at Alex's.

She was standing next to Autumn, talking to her about doing a presentation on forensics to Cody's Sea Cadet Unit when Dino approached. They really hadn't had any one-on-one time since he arrived, and it was getting late. Everyone was on pins and needles waiting for that call to come through to the guys.

She looked up at Dino, and he held his hand out just like he had done at Bayside.

"Dance with me?" He said, staring into her eyes.

She set her drink down, took his hand, and he led them to the dance floor, joining a few other couples.

When *Luke Combs, Beautiful Crazy,* started to play, she melted into him as he pulled her close and wrapped his arms around her waist. She slid her arms under his and placed them against his upper back. They made eye contact, and slowly they started to move with the beat of the music.

After the song's first verse, Dino cupped her cheek, and she leaned into his hand and closed her eyes. She wondered what was happening. She was strung high with excitement, yet her nerves were on edge a little.

"I'm sorry." She heard him say, and her eyes popped open.

She stared into his dark blue eyes. "What are you sorry for?"

He took a deep breath, and Arianna held her breath, waiting for him to answer. She searched his eyes and face. He looked conflicted. She saw the sadness, but there was also love in there. She knew this man had so much love to give if he'd just confront his fears.

"Dino?" She pressed but not aggressively.

"There is so much I want to say to you right now, but I'm afraid I'm going to screw it up by not making any sense." He took another deep breath. "My issue is that I'm conflicted on where to start."

She gave him a soft smile and placed her hands on his cheeks. "You start where you feel the most comfortable."

Suddenly, before he could utter another word, his phone began ringing, and he swore. "You've got to be fucking kidding me."

She looked up at him. "What is it?" But as the phone's belonging to the team started to ring, she knew what that meant.

"I gotta go." He said to her, and her heart began to ache for the both of them. But she wasn't going to let him go until he answered the one question, she had for him.

She stood up on her tiptoes, secured her arms around his neck, and looked deep into his eyes. "Answer one question for me before you go."

"Okay."

"Do you love me?"

He stared down at her and she waited for him to answer. He started to speak but stopped, and she could see the struggle was real as he tried to fight off those demons that have held his happiness and future hostage. Just when she thought he would give in to the monsters, he pulled her closer against him and whispered "I do" against her lips before he kissed her like he never had before. He took his time and was gentle yet sensual. When he released her lips, he smiled.

"Be safe." He told her.

"You too and remember you have me waiting here for you."

He didn't say anything. Instead, he gave her another kiss that left her breathless and counting down the time until she saw him again.

ര

The team sat in the briefing room at the hangar as they awaited word from the flight deck to board their ride to the Tripoint area. Their mission was to rescue an American scientist who had been abducted while in North Korea visiting family, but he was now being used as a pawn in an exchange with Iranian forces. According to Intel, in exchange for oil, North Korea agreed to hand over the American hostage to the Iranians to help further their ballistic missile program.

Derek entered the room, and Ace sounded off, "Attention on deck," and everyone jumped to their feet and stood at attention.

Derek hadn't made it five steps into the room before the coffee he had just taken a drink of spewed from his mouth. Luckily, he avoided spraying anyone.

"For fucks sake, Dino."

Dino looked around, wondering what he had done to get a reaction like that from the commander. Hell, all he did was stand up. He noticed some of the guys in the chairs behind him looked like they were about to bust a gasket. *What the hell was the joke on him?*

"Sir?" Dino questioned.

Derek set his coffee cup down along with some papers on the table at the front of the room. He turned and looked at him.

"Did the Navy change uniform regulations in the last twenty-four hours?"

"No, Sir. At least not that I'm aware of."

"Huh...well, then you may want to remove the extra accessory there on the back of your trousers."

"Sir?" He still wasn't understanding.

Derek waved his hand in the air, "For the love of God, would someone help their teammate out."

Diego leaned forward and pulled something that was stuck to Dino's ass.

"Next time you do your laundry, make sure your roommate's clothes aren't in the dryer." Diego teased as he threw a pair of leopard print panties at him. Dino caught them and just stared at them. *Son of a bitch!*

Everyone laughed, hell even Potter managed to crack a small smile. Seconds later, he found himself chuckling at his own misfortune, although at least he had something now to remind him of what he had waiting back home.

The next few minutes were spent going over their orders. If everything flowed like they've practiced, the operation should be simple in and out. However, in their line of work, simple was overrated.

CHAPTER TWENTY-NINE

Dino dove for cover just as the bullet whizzed by his head and ricocheted off the rock next to him.

"Motherfucker!"

He and the team had stirred up a hornet's nest. What was supposed to be a routine grab and go turned into a complete shit show.

As soon as the mission was green-lighted, everything had fallen into place, just like they'd rehearsed. An hour before sunset, the team was dropped into the middle of the Sea of Japan along with their Zodiac Combat Rubber Raiding Craft. They traveled the two-hundred-seventy-six miles to their beach landing point—a deserted beach at the mouth of the Tumen River, separating North Korea and Russia. From that point, it was a six-mile trek on foot up the river using the cliffs and darkness as cover. Just as they were about a mile from where the trade-off was to occur, the team split up into two-man teams. Doing this would allow the team to set up a perimeter around the spot where the exchange was supposed to happen.

Dino was paired up with Skittles. The two of them made their way up the riverbed when suddenly they were ambushed from the cliff areas. As gunfire rained down on them, they took cover behind a cluster of large rocks near the waterline. They were pinned down, and their only hope of getting out alive fell onto the shoulders of their other team members.

"Where in the hell is that distraction that Potter promised?" Dino barked out as he and Skittles took up positions and returned fire.

They were running out of time, and the longer they sat there like sitting ducks, the more the insurgents moved toward them.

"Alpha six and Alpha seven—suppressed by enemy fire. Repeat Alpha six and Alpha seven—suppressed by enemy fire." Skittles communicated to the command.

"Copy Alpha seven. Alpha eight and Alpha two, what is your position?"

Potter's voice echoed through the comms unit. "Diversions set and retreating to Alpha one's location."

Those diversions better come soon, Dino thought to himself as he held his ground and kept firing at the approaching forces. Another ten or fifteen minutes, and he and Skittles would be overtaken.

"Alpha four, what is your status?" Dino barked.

"Alpha four and Alpha three in place," Irish replied. Irish and Frost were supposed to be in an overwatch position; however, with the surprise attack from the enemy, Dino knew they hadn't made it to where they should've been.

Irish's voice sounded again through the comms. "Alpha six and Alpha seven, sit tight."

"Sit tight? Is he fucking kidding?" He said to Skittles sarcastically.

Derek's voice came over the comms.

"Alpha team, you've got two vehicles approaching Alpha six and Alpha seven's location. They are approximately two-hundred-twenty-five yards north and closing. You all need to get the hell out of there."

"You do remember how to fire your weapon?" Dino asked Irish with some amusement, but he was also serious. Things were getting sketchy down on the beach.

"Don't get your panties in a twist," Irish spoke back. Dino would give the man credit. Nothing got under the sniper's skin. Always while in action, he was calm, relaxed, and collected.

Suddenly, three sets of explosives went off simultaneously above the cliffs sending debris into the air and down onto the beach.

Enemy forces started running towards the water, directly in the path of where Skittles and Dino were. The gunfire doubled as the team joined in on the battle. Dino watched as enemy forces were picked off one by one.

Dino felt some relief knowing his team were engaging. Suddenly an object fell from the sky and landed right in between Dino and Skittles. Dino knew immediately what it was, and there was nothing he could do. It was as if time had stood still and all the commotion had ceased. He closed his eyes as his life flashed before his eyes—his troubled past, his future, and the woman he loved. When he opened his eyes and found Skittles still standing across from him staring at the same object, he realized that angels were watching over them.

That grenade should've detonated. Skittles must have had the same thought as they both continued to stare at the device. They both had long forgotten the gunfire directed toward them. Dino studied the object and noticed that the pin was pulled, but the spring lever didn't deploy. He pointed to it, letting Skittles know what he saw. The percentage of a grenade malfunctioning was only two to three percent.

Skittles started to reach for it, and Dino's eyes widened. "What the fuck are you doing?"

"I am not going to fucking sit here and wait for it to pop like a jack in the box."

"Dino held his breath as Skittles skillfully placed the live grenade into his hand. The next couple of seconds felt like a lifetime. Skittles then lobbed the explosive back over to the "other" team. This time as soon as it landed, it detonated, sending people, debris, and smoke into the air. Another huge fireball erupted just down the beach. Moments later, it was followed by Potter's voice. "Enemy vehicles have been eliminated. What do you say we all get the fuck out of here?"

Dino wasn't one to argue. There were some lone enemies who had retreated that were still engaging in the firefight, but he and Skittles used the elements along the beach to take cover as they moved back down the coast to the rendezvous point.

It wasn't until Dino was back in the belly of the C-17 headed home when he came to terms with what he could've lost today. That had been the closest he had ever come to losing his life, and it put a lot in perspective.

He had been so stupid to let his past dictate his life up to now. What happened to him had destroyed his trust in people. He believed that the saying was, *"If you can't trust family, then who can you trust?"* That was the way he had always looked at it. It took the Navy and his current team to instill a lot of that trust back into him. But the one thing he never thought he'd be able to do again was trust with his heart. That was until he came across one woman who managed to find a way to infiltrate the solid wall guarding his heart and bring it back to life. She had been so patient and understanding while he dealt with his feelings. She made him whole. She was perfect. She was his.

Ace sat down in the seat beside him. He was quiet at first, but he asked, "You doing okay?"

Dino leaned his head back against the metal of the fuselage and took a deep breath. "I've never been that scared in my entire life."

Ace nodded. "I can imagine. Focus on the positive, you're still alive."

Dino turned his head in Ace's direction. "That's all that I can focus on. That, and how much of my life that I let slip by all because I held onto something from the past." He let out a dry laugh. "Jesus, what the fuck is wrong with me?" He stated, running both of his hands through his hair.

"Whatever it was must've been tragic for you to keep it bottled up this long."

"I don't want to anymore. Meeting Arianna made me open my eyes and really look around me and see everything I was letting slip by. I'll admit it, I envy you, Potter, Frost, Irish, and Stitch. You each found an amazing woman who loves and respects you for who you are. One that doesn't complain when you get called out, but instead supports you."

"If you'd open your eyes wide enough, you'd realize you have one amazing woman waiting for you at home who shares those same qualities."

Dino grinned. "I know. And, damn this mission, because I was in the right frame of mind while she and I were on that dance floor, and I wanted to pour my heart out. But then the fucking phone rang."

Ace laughed. "Hey, I didn't say it was easy." Ace gripped Dino's shoulder. "All I can say is that if it feels right, then act on it. That's what happened in Afghanistan with Alex. And, I'm sure as shit glad that I acted instead of pushing my feelings to the side."

They both sat there staring at the other side of the plane. They could hear some of the other guys talking at the other end, mixed with the deep humming sound of the plane's engines.

After a while, Dino spoke, "I'm sure you've realized now that I don't talk about my family. I don't speak about them to anyone. In my mind, they don't even exist anymore. But as I sit here and talk about my trust issues, I realize that I need to turn the mirror around because I haven't been honest with you guys. You are my family, and you deserve to know the truth."

Ace didn't say a word, but Dino knew he had his full attention.

"Have you ever heard of the Michetti family?"

"Can't say I have." Ace answered.

"The Michetti family was run by my grandfather."

Ace's eyes widened in surprise. "Dude, are you saying that—"

Dino nodded. "Yes, unfortunately by blood, I'm connected to a crime family. After my grandfather passed away, my dad and two uncles spent years trying to keep the business going. Once I was old enough to understand what activities were taking place, I knew I didn't want to be a part of it. Surprisingly my parents were okay with it. I kept myself busy by playing sports. I joined other clubs after school and even got a job." He took a deep breath. "When I was seventeen and a senior in high school, I met a girl, and we fell in love. Her family also had a reputation, but they were allies of our family."

"She and I were so in love that we were already talking about getting married right after we graduated. We spent every waking hour we could together. But I should've known something was wrong when she started to spend more time with her friends—at least that was what she told me she was doing. I also noticed around that time my older brother Dexter had been hanging around the house more. Unlike me, Dexter, who was four years older than me, chose the family business. He and I were never close, even when we were kids."

Dino closed his eyes, remembering the day that turned his world upside down.

"It was a Friday—Valentine's Day, and she and I had planned to go to dinner and then spend the rest of the evening together. She told me at lunch during school that she had to cancel our plans because her grandmother was very sick, and the family wanted her to be with them. I didn't argue because I knew how much family meant to her. Instead, I spent the night at my friend's house. When I arrived home early the next morning, our driveway was flooded with police cars and ambulances. I had no clue what was going on. I found my mom, and she was in such a state of shock that she couldn't even put a complete sentence together as the paramedics were trying to calm her down. It was chaos. I couldn't find my dad. I finally found one of my uncles. His face was white as a ghost. He told me that the police were questioning my dad. I asked him what was going on, and first, he was reluctant to tell me. But then my aunt showed up, and she made him tell me."

Dino felt his chest start to tighten, recalling the news his uncle delivered to him.

"My brother and my girlfriend had been seeing each other behind my back. All those days and nights when she said she was spending time with friends, she had been secretly meeting with him." He shook his head. "I can't really say they were secretly meeting because I found out later on that my parents knew about it. Anyway, my brother apparently was involved in a big deal, and the deal had gone south, costing another family a lot of money and territory. They found out that it was my brother's doing, and they wanted to show the world that nobody crossed them and got away with it."

"Sometime in the early hours of the morning, a hitman entered my brother's apartment over the garage and started shooting. I guess he hadn't realized that my brother had company the previous night and was in bed with him."

Ace cursed under his breath. "Shit. It was your girlfriend."

Dino nodded his head somberly. "At first, I didn't want to believe it but then reality set in." He shook his head. "I don't know which hurt worse—the fact that my own brother was sleeping with my girlfriend or the fact that my parents knew and condoned it. Not to mention that I lost both of them—cold-blooded murder."

"What happened after that?"

"My mom sent me to live with a distant cousin. We had my birth certificate altered to make it look like she was my mother. I just wanted to get away from everything and everyone. One day about a month before graduation, a Navy Recruiter was at my school. I went up and started talking to him. He said a lot of things that I had needed to hear. Right after I graduated, I enlisted, and here I am."

"Damn, man. I don't even know what to say. The first thing that comes to mind is fucked up. I just hate that you've had to carry that grief with you for all these years. Are your parents still alive?"

"They are. They live up near Boston."

"Do you ever speak to them?"

"No."

"Well, you'll always have us. And don't ever think you can't come and talk to one of us. We've all been through something tragic, but we've also overcome it."

Dino smiled. "Thanks, man. For listening and just being a great friend."

Just then, a couple of the guys came over and started telling him and Ace that Derek had gotten a message about some sort of show that the women were hosting as a fundraiser for Paul's medical expenses.

As Dino sat there and conversed with his brothers in arms, he felt at peace and as if an entire world had been lifted off of his shoulders. But most importantly, he felt free of his past.

CHAPTER THIRTY

Arianna bounced her leg up and down nervously. The charity lingerie show that she and other ladies put together was due to start in ten minutes. Enzo had come through huge and had over fifty pieces of his collection delivered to her. When she called him a few days ago and explained what she was planning, he hadn't batted an eye and told her that he'd be more than happy to accommodate her though he would be sad that he wouldn't be able to see her in them. She hadn't told him, but she asked a friend who was a photographer if she could take some pictures during the show. Once she got the prints, she'd pick out a few and send them to him.

"Will you stop." Alex scolded her.

"I can't help it. I'm a nervous wreck right now."

"You're nervous? How do you think Tenley, Autumn, Bailey, Mia, and I feel? We've never done anything like this before."

Arianna waved her off. "You'll be fine. Like I said, with all of the bright lights shining in your face, you won't even be able to see anyone looking at you."

Arianna looked around. It was a packed house. They had made thousands from ticket sales alone. She hadn't even begun to count the numerous donations that came in, but she suspected they were in the thousands as well.

She smiled as she recalled the other day when she told her dad what she had planned. At first, he thought it was going to be a fashion show with actual clothing. When she explained that it was lingerie, he had told her that he was glad he was in the hospital and couldn't attend because there was no way in hell, he would watch her parade around in underwear. She had laughed at him, and that only riled him up more.

All the logistics were handled, and everything seemed to be a go. All that was missing were the guys. Alex said she heard from

Ace and that they had arrived home a few hours ago. They said they would get there as soon as they could. She chuckled to herself. They had no clue what type of show this was. Boy, were they in for a big surprise!

She was anxious and excited to see Dino. She hoped they could continue where they had left off on the dance floor. Even though he hadn't come right out and said that he loved her, he still acknowledged it when she asked him if he loved her. That was enough for her to know there was hope for them. It was a moment that she would never forget.

Alex nudged Arianna's arm. "I think Nick is trying to get your attention."

She looked up towards the stage area, and there he was, waving to her. Nick was one of the bouncers they used on the weekends when it is more crowded. He was going to be serving as the MC for the evening. She got up from her chair.

"I guess I better go check and see what he needs. I'll meet you and the others backstage in just a minute."

After she got Nick all set, she headed backstage to get ready.

"Why are we here again?" Frost asked Ace as everyone from the team walked into Bayside.

Dino looked around and was shocked at how many people were there. Every chair was filled, and there was barely any standing room left.

"Because Alex said so. All the proceeds from the event are going towards Paul's medical bills," replied Ace.

"Okay, but a fashion show?" asked Frost

Diego grinned. "I'm all for it."

Dino noticed Skittles seemed preoccupied with someone or something across the room.

"Hey man, everything okay?"

"Yeah, sorry, I just thought I recognized someone."

"Who?" Dino asked as he glanced in the direction Skittles was looking, but there were so many people he couldn't tell who the kid was looking at.

"There was a blonde over there." But then Skittles shook his head. "You know what, never mind. It wasn't her." He went and took one of the empty seats the ladies had reserved for them. Dino sympathized with the guy. He wished Skittles could get closure on his missing friend.

The lights in the room started to dim, and Dino figured that meant the show was getting ready to start. He took the open seat next to Ace.

Stitch leaned forward. "Hey, have any of you seen any of the ladies?"

Before anyone could respond, a gentleman dressed in a tuxedo appeared on the stage.

"Good evening and welcome! Tonight, we've got a line-up full of beautiful models that will be showcasing some of Europe's finest lingerie."

Everyone started clapping, and many of the men in the room began to whistle and make catcalls.

"Lingerie?" Potter and Ace both said at the same time.

"Now we're talking," Diego said, rubbing his hands together with a massive smile on his face.

The lights went lower, and spotlights were directed at the stage. Moments later, music began pumping through the speakers, and the spotlights changed colors.

The silver curtain at the far end of the stage peeled back, and one by one, a parade of women started down the makeshift runway. The crowd went crazy.

"What the fuck?" Ace blurted out when his eyes landed on Alex wearing a royal blue sheer chemise with what appeared to be matching panties underneath. Thank goodness her breasts weren't showing.

"Oh, hell no," Potter said next, followed by gumbles and growls of displeasure from Stitch and Frost as Tenley, Mia, and Autumn appeared on stage.

Tenley wore a lavender lace cutout bodysuit. Mia donned a black bra and panty set, overlayed with a black short, sheer robe, while Autumn modeled a silk, emerald green, flowy babydoll nightie.

Irish was the only one sitting there was a smile on his face as he watched his wife show off the baby blue, long lace maxi gown she donned.

When Dino looked up, he was so focused on the woman leading the pack toward him and the guys down the runway. He wasn't paying a bit of attention to his friends' moaning and groaning at seeing their women strutting their stuff.

He couldn't pull his eyes away from Arianna's beauty and grace. Her movements were fluid and natural as she turned on the stilettos she wore. She was in her element, and he could see why she was sought after in Europe. Her focus never wavered, even with all of the guys whistling and making comments. Not to mention all of the camera flashes directed her way. The red, strappy one-piece she wore was classy yet sexy and left little to the imagination. However, he didn't have to imagine. He knew first-hand what was beneath the silk and lace garment. He reached down and had to adjust himself to make room for his growing cock.

As he looked down the row of chairs at his friends, he knew exactly how they felt. What a great feeling it was to say that one of those women up there was his!

After the show concluded, the majority of the people had stuck around for the party afterward. He had waited a few minutes for Arianna to appear from backstage, but one of the other models told him that she was getting dressed and then packing up some of the props and equipment.

He didn't want to bother her while she was doing all that, plus he didn't want to barge backstage knowing there were still some of the other models back there changing. Since the room was crowded, he decided to head out to the patio and get some fresh air.

He hadn't been out there for five minutes when Alex came walking out.

She offered him that bright and cheerful smile she was known for. "Hey. What are you doing out here?"

He turned around and leaned his backside against the railing. "Just came out for some fresh air. How about you?"

"Same." She walked over and stood next to him.

"You and the rest of the ladies looked beautiful tonight. It looked like it was a great turnout for Paul."

"Thank you." She laughed. "I've done a lot during my career in the operative world, but modeling was never one of them. As for the event itself—that was all Arianna's doing. She pulled this off. Speaking of Arianna, you want to talk about why you're out here while she's inside being swooned over by single men?"

He saw the twinkle, coupled with the mischievous look in her eyes, and knew she was trying to rile him up.

"Last I checked, she was still backstage." He replied. "I just needed a minute."

"Everything okay?" She asked.

"Let's just say a bad mission managed to turn my life around, and it has my head all screwed up."

"That's understandable. Been there before."

Alex was a blessing. He loved her and was so fortunate she had dropped in the team's lives during the mission in Afghanistan a year and a half ago. She understood the sensitivity of their jobs and knew not to ask questions but, at the same time, was supportive. Ace was a lucky man to have a woman with as much love and devotion that Alex had, which brought him full circle around to his current dilemma with Arianna.

"You know when I was kidnapped in Afghanistan, there was a moment that I just wanted to die." She told him.

His head snapped up, and he looked at her. She was staring out at the ocean, but then her eyes found his.

"Alex..."

"No, I'm okay talking about it. I'm glad you guys were there. There is no one else I can talk to because of its classified nature."

He nodded.

"Anyway, I wanted to give up. And I almost did, but I didn't want to have regrets. I knew I was stronger than what my mind was starting to believe. I held on. But doing so gave me the strength to fight. I wanted to live."

"I don't want to get into it again, but I talked with Ace on the way home. He knows what happened and why I've chosen to keep my heart guarded for the last fifteen years. Until now."

"How do you feel now that you've told someone?"

He half-smiled. "It feels really good. It feels freeing, especially knowing what I have in front of me. I was so afraid of history repeating itself, but over the last twenty-four hours, I've realized that I can't dwell on something that can't be reversed. And that there is so much the world has to offer me."

She placed her hand on his forearm. "I can assure you that Arianna would never hurt you, at least, not intentionally."

He smiled. "I know that."

Before they could continue, Ace appeared and walked over. He stood behind Alex and rested his hands on her shoulders. She looked up at Ace, and it suddenly hit Dino. He wanted that connection. The way Ace and Alex expressed their love for each other was a prime example of what he was missing out on.

"I'm going to head back inside," Alex said before looking at Dino. "Follow your heart."

Dino smiled. "I will."

Both Ace and Dino watched Alex go back inside.

Dino glanced at Ace. "You hold on to her tight, man. She is one in a million."

"You don't have to tell me that. Sometimes though, I'm worried about her running herself down. I mean, I'm so fucking proud of her and what all she has accomplished, but she has to slow down sometime and take a breather." He paused and stared out at the water. "There is speculation that a group out in San Diego may be calling to talk to Alex about expanding."

"Holy shit!" Dino exclaimed.

"Yeah. It's great. Her organization is helping so many veterans and military personnel and their families, but I'm afraid that one day she is going to crash."

"Her dad was her life, Ace. Alex cannot just sit around and do nothing. She always has to have her hands in something. Is there someone at the foundation—like another volunteer who she could delegate some of her workload to?"

"She was interviewing a few candidates for a management position."

"Any leads?"

"There is one that she said she really liked and could see herself working with. The woman's brother was a Marine, and he went through a rough patch when he was medically discharged. He ended up taking his life."

"That sucks."

"It does. But this girl became an advocate for suicide prevention. Alex thinks she'd be a really good fit."

"That's awesome."

"Yeah, it is. I just hope it works out." Ace lifted his beer to his lips and took a swig.

The door behind them opened, and when Dino turned, he felt his body come alive at the sight of Arianna standing there. She had changed into a pair of jeans and a green sweater. She had washed all of the makeup off her face, and her skin looked radiant.

Ace told him he'd talk to him later, and he went back inside.

Arianna walked toward him and stopped directly in front of him. "Welcome home." She said.

"It's good to be back."

"Why is that?" She asked with her head slightly tilted to one side.

He snagged her around the waist and pulled her closer. The wind picked up and blew her hair into her face, and he brushed it back. He knew she was waiting for him to make the first move.

He lowered his head and positioned his lips over hers but not touching them. The warmth of her breath could be felt against his lips.

"Because I missed you." He told her before his lips lightly brushed against hers. She tasted like vanilla as he deepened the kiss, slipping his tongue inside her warm cavern and exploring. He moved his hand to the back of her neck, cupping it to pull her in closer. He couldn't get enough of her. Her hands found their way under his t-shirt and swept along his rib cage, sending an electric current racing through his body. He had to pull away; otherwise, he'd end up taking her right on the deck.

They both panted for breath while still embracing each other. He kissed the top of her head, and she leaned back so she could look up at him. Her eyes were bright and full of desire. He smiled.

"What do you say we get out of here?"

"Where do you propose we go?"

"Home," he told her. "Because I believe that there is a long-overdue conversation that you and I need to have."

CHAPTER THIRTY-ONE

They each drove their own cars back to Dino's house. The closer Arianna got to the house, the more her anxiety level rose. She gripped the steering wheel tighter and took a deep breath as she tried to concentrate on the road in front of her, but it wasn't easy to do when her mind was racing with several thoughts.

Something had changed in Dino while he was gone, and not in a bad way. He seemed more relaxed and content with himself and not as nervous or guarded like he'd been before he left on this last deployment. His kiss earlier had meaning behind it. From the way, he held her in his arms to the tenderness of his kiss. It was deep but slow and gentle.

She knew without a doubt that tonight would reshape their lives and their future. She also understood that this would be a monumental night for Dino, and she was prepared for the onslaught of emotions that she expected to come with it.

As soon as she pulled into the driveway Dino was there to open her door. He extended his hand to her and helped her from the car. Together, hand-in-hand they walked up the steps of the porch, and Dino opened the front door and ushered her inside.

It felt strange and quiet without Nigel around since he was still at Alex's house.

Dino led her into the living room, and she placed her purse down on the coffee table. He was still holding her hand when he started to laugh, breaking the thick silence between them. His deep laugh made her chuckle.

"I'm sorry." He told her once he got himself under control.

She thought it was cute. Again, a completely different side of him. Maybe what they both needed before they sat was a drink.

"Do you want a drink? Because I think we both need one right now." She offered, and he nodded.

"Please."

She went into the kitchen and grabbed two beers out of the refrigerator, along with a couple of bottles of water. She made a detour to the pantry and snagged the package of chocolate chip cookies. Once she had everything gathered in her arms, she made her way back to the living room.

Dino was building a fire in the fireplace, and she noticed he had laid a big fluffy blanket down in front of it along with a few pillows from the couch. He glanced over his shoulder at her then patted the spot next to him. She set the drinks down on the fireplace hearth then took a seat next to him. While he finished messing with the fire, she took her shoes off, stretched out on her side, and made herself more comfortable.

Once he finished, he turned and removed his shoes, then took up the same position next to her with inches between them, face to face. It was silent except for the crackling of the fire. Arianna felt how the energy in the atmosphere had shifted. She felt the energy pulling between them.

He stared into her eyes before he leaned forward and pressed his forehead against hers. Using her free hand, she placed it on his cheek. It felt warm from being in front of the fire. He pulled back slightly, then kissed her nose and then her cheeks before kissing her lips. It was more of a peck but a lingering peck. It was sweet.

When he released her lips, he smiled, and she loved seeing the sparkle in his eyes. He rolled over onto his back and rested his head on one of the throw pillows. He gazed up at her.

"Come here." He said, opening his arm for her to lay with him.

She laid down and got comfortable with her head resting on his shoulder. She pressed her nose closer to his neck and inhaled as she closed her eyes. She loved the smell of his soap and aftershave. Her hand was splayed over his chest, and she could feel his strong and steady heartbeat beneath her fingertips. He folded his arm around her shoulder and lightly caressed her arm.

"I missed you so much. I love having you in my arms." He admitted, causing her to smile and lift her head so she could see him.

"I missed you too."

He winked at her then lightly pressed her head back down against his chest.

He took a deep breath, and she closed her eyes and squeezed his body for good measure as she patiently waited for him to begin.

"Fifteen years ago, I learned the hard way that love and family could both be ripped from you in a blink of an eye."

Arianna stayed quiet and listened intently to every word as Dino fought through his emotions as he told her his story of love, betrayal, and heartbreak. She could never understand how a person could be unfaithful to someone that they say they love. Love is supposed to be built on respect, integrity, honesty, trust, intimacy, and partnership. In Dino's situation, he was dealt with not one betrayal but four; his girlfriend, his brother, his mom, and his dad. Her heart broke for him. For fifteen years, he carried that fear and sadness alone. The tears built in her eyes, and eventually, they spilled over, and she silently wept for him.

Dino felt the wetness through the material of his t-shirt and knew that Arianna was crying. He didn't tell her his story to upset her. He had already shed enough tears over the years that nobody else needed to. After tonight, his past was just that—the past. Tonight, was the beginning of a new era for him. It was about moving on and living in the present. It meant taking the leap and opening his heart to the woman he has fallen in love with.

"Arianna." He called to her in a whispered voice.

She got up on her knees, and tears were still streaming down her face. "I'm so sorry." She told him, and then she pressed her hands against her chest over her where her heart was. "My heart aches for you."

He sat up and used his thumbs to wipe away the tears from her cheeks.

"I didn't tell you all of that to upset you. I wanted you to know so that you understood that it was my fear and insecurity that held me back from making that commitment." He took her face between his hands. "I was stupid to think I could ward off the feelings I had toward you. You are everything I want, Arianna. I don't know how you did it. But you have managed to mend a heart that I thought would be broken forever."

She sniffled then covered his hands that were still on her cheeks with hers. Her eyes glistened like diamonds with unshed tears.

"I've never felt a connection with anyone else like what you and I have. When you're around, I get weak in the knees. I get butterflies in my belly. You make me feel special, beautiful, and sexy. You complete me. I love you, Dino."

He released her face and stood up. He held his hand out.

She looked from his hand to his eyes, and he held his breath.

"Take it." He told her.

Slowly she reached for his hand and the feeling of her fingers clasping with his sent a sensation through his body.

He walked her out of the living room then led her up the stairs. Instead of making a right to take her to her bedroom, he turned left. He was taking her to his bedroom, where she belonged.

He stopped in the doorway and looked down at her. She stared at him, and her large hazel eyes watched him carefully.

"Once you cross this threshold, you are mine forever."

She looked down at her feet that were just outside of the room. She glanced back up at him, took one, then two steps crossing into his bedroom.

He followed her in and closed the door behind him. Slowly, he turned her around to face him and stared deep into her eyes.

"I love you, Arianna Roland."

She gave him a sappy smile. "I love you too."

He closed his eyes and claimed her lips in a passionate yet scorching kiss. One hand slid into her hair, and his fingers latched onto her silky locks while his other hand slid down to her ass.

She broke from the kiss. "I need you." She told him and started to pull her sweater off.

He placed his hand over hers and stopped her. She gave him a questioning look. He wasn't going to blow this opportunity.

"I want and need you too, but tonight isn't going to be like the times we've fucked in the past."

"Let me." He told her and gently moved aside her hands. While staring into her eyes, he slowly lifted her sweater, exposing her skin inch by inch. His eyes widened in surprise when he saw she had no bra on. His mouth watered at the sight of her.

"We are going to do this right. Tonight, I'm making love to you. I'm going to give every inch of this body the attention it deserves, starting with these pretty little things."

He leaned forward and took one of her nipples into his mouth, sucking gently. He twirled his tongue around it before he gently nipped it. Her knees buckled, and he caught her. Once she was steady, he walked her backward toward the bed. When the back of her knees hit the mattress, she sat down.

He reached back and pulled his shirt over his head and threw it to the side. Not wanting to wait any longer, he shoved his jeans down, and his cock sprang free. He smirked when she licked her lips. She went to reach for it when he stopped her. She tilted her head sideways and looked at him.

"Babe, as much as I would love to feel your lips around my cock, I'm already there and will explode before I can get inside your warm, sweet pussy."

Dino thought that he would explode? Hell, she was already soaked with excitement.

He stepped toward her as his impressive cock continued to bob in front of her. She couldn't tear her eyes away from it.

When his hands landed on her shoulders, she looked up, and damn did he look hungry.

Slowly and gently, he laid her back onto the bed and raked his fingers down her body. He kissed her neck then down to her collarbone, leaving behind a trail of wetness. The further he went, the stronger the butterflies felt in her stomach. She was so wound up that it wasn't going to take much to cause that string to snap, and she would go flying.

He licked down her chest to her belly, and his tongue dipped into her belly button. She didn't want him to stop; she wanted to feel that tongue lower. He took his time, and it was killing her. His lips trailed along her hip bone, and he used his hand to flick the button to her jeans and lowered the zipper. As he started to pull her jeans down, she heard his sharp intake of breath and smiled to herself. She hadn't bothered to put any panties on when she changed after the show.

He lifted his head and locked gazes with her. There was a storm brewing in his dark eyes.

"You aren't the only one who likes to go commando." She told him.

He got onto the bed and crawled up her body until he was settled between her thighs and hovering over her.

"You know, I always used to rag the guys about being pussy whipped, but I understand now what they go through. I'm just as pussy whipped as they are."

She laughed. "I wouldn't go that far. You just like my pus—" He cut her off with a scorching kiss as he pressed the tip of his cock against her entrance. He reached for her hands and pulled them up and over her head, holding them there. He slowly pushed inside of her. It was too much for her, and she thrust upward, causing him to penetrate deeper, and she moaned when his cock hit her sweet spot.

He let go of her hands and flexed his hips as he raised her thighs as he made love to her. She moved her hands to his shoulders and held on as he pumped his hips faster. She felt like she would lose control and explode when Dino shifted his hips and penetrated deeper as he ground into her.

As his speed increased, she felt his body start to tighten. She closed her eyes and arched her back as the pressure inside of her started to build. Suddenly, it was like fireworks went off as she went over the edge. Dino buried his face in the crook of her neck and moaned as he released his seed into her.

Dino rolled them to the side and slid out of her, but they stayed in each other's arms. Dino kissed her temple, and she smiled.

"That was amazing."

He was still breathing hard, but he smiled and pulled her closer. "I love you."

She would never get tired of hearing that. She snuggled against him and kissed his chest. "I love you too." She yawned, and before she knew it, she was fast asleep.

CHAPTER THIRTY-TWO

Dino's eyes popped open. His training told him that something didn't feel right. His eyes focused, and he looked around the room. It was dark still, but the house seemed quiet—too quiet. He glanced over next to him and found Arianna sound asleep. He laid there for a minute. All of his senses were in overdrive. He turned to look at the clock on the table next to the bed and saw it wasn't lit up. He lifted up so he could see the shelf that held all of the TV electronics. None of the normal green lights signaling that there was power were lit either. Something caused the power to go out. But there was something else. He sensed it in his gut.

He listened, trying to pick up on any sounds. Then suddenly, there was a clicking noise. It wasn't loud, but he'd heard it. It stopped, and he waited to see if he heard it again. Seconds later, there was a different sound, like a doorknob jiggling.

Somebody was in the house. He quietly reached over to the table beside him and pulled his Glock out of the top drawer. He needed to wake up Arianna and get her into the bathroom. It wasn't ideal, but at least she'd have a locked door between her and the imminent danger they were facing.

Just as he reached over to nudge her, the sound of glass breaking downstairs echoed in the quiet house. His heart rate increase as the adrenaline began to flow.

"Arianna?" He whispered close to her ear as she gave her a little shake.

Thankfully she wasn't that heavy of a sleeper and woke right up. She went to say something, but he covered her mouth with his hand. He raised his finger to his lips as if telling her to be quiet. When she saw the gun in his other hand, he knew she understood what was going on and nodded.

He pushed the blanket off of them. They were both still naked from last night. He found his t-shirt next to the bed and threw it at her, and she quickly pulled it over her head. He slipped into a pair of shorts then quickly pulled her towards the bathroom. He handed her his phone.

"Lock yourself in the bathroom and call the police. And stay away from the door. If it comes to it, you go out the window. You won't be able to climb down, but there is a small ledge where you can go up further on the roof. Do you understand?"

"Yes, go." She told him, and he gave her a quick kiss before closing her in. He didn't move away from the door until he heard her engage the lock.

When he heard the click, he then slowly and silently walked towards the door leading to the hallway. He had his weapon armed and ready to fire. As he reached for the doorknob, he heard the floor creak from the other side of the door. Before he could move out of the way, the door was shoved open with a lot of force behind it. He tried to jump out of the way, but the edge of it slammed into his hand, causing him to lose the grip on his gun. It fell to the floor somewhere near his feet. He didn't have time to look for it because a large person dressed all in black appeared in front of him and took a swing at him. Dino ducked under the guy's arm, then came back up and delivered a blow to the guy's upper back. As the guy was bent over, Dino grabbed him from behind and put him in a chokehold, but the guy fought back and rammed his elbow into Dino's rib cage. Dino let go but not before he shoved the guy to the floor.

The guy got to his feet. Dino could only see his eyes and mouth as everything else was concealed by the mask he wore. The wild look in his eyes told Dino a lot. This guy wasn't your everyday burglar. This guy was here to harm. But Dino wasn't going to let that happen—not on his watch.

Dino was in the position where he blocked the only way out. So, if this person wanted to leave; he'd have to go through him. They were too high up off the ground for him to jump out the window. He'd break his legs. There was no escape.

Dino was known as one of the best hand-to-hand combat fighters in the teams. He was trained in several forms of martial arts and had earned numerous awards for his skills.

The guy grabbed the lamp off the nightstand and threw it at Dino. Dino ducked out of the way, and it smashed into the wall behind him. Dino went to engage when the guy pulled out a knife, and it was a pretty decent size. It was large enough to do severe damage if you knew where to hit.

"Where are you hiding the little bitch at? I know she's here." he snarled in a raspy smoker's voice, and Dino could hear how labored his breathing was.

Dino didn't respond, though it made him wonder who this guy was and how it connected to Arianna. Suddenly, a loud crashing sound came from the bathroom, and the guy's head whipped around toward the door. That tiny split second was all the time that Dino needed to make his move. He leaped into the air, and his leg extended out, delivering a crushing blow to the side of the guys' head. The guy instantly dropped to the floor and didn't move. Dino kicked the knife away from the intruder's body and then pulled the wire from the demolished lamp and used it to tie the guy's hands behind his back. He used a rope he found on the floor to tie his ankles together. He patted him down and found he was carrying a small pistol in a holster strapped to his ankle.

He heard the sirens of the approaching police vehicles. He went to the bathroom door and knocked.

"Arianna. Open up." He didn't mean for his tone to sound so rough and abrupt, but he was still jacked up from the altercation. He looked around the bedroom that was in disarray and closed his eyes.

If it weren't for his trained instincts, this situation may have had a completely different outcome.

He heard the lock disengage, and then the door flew open. Before he could utter a word, Arianna slammed into him and buried herself in his arms. Her body trembled, and he squeezed her tight.

"It's over." He whispered above her head.

She sniffled a few times before she leaned back and tilted her head back to look up at him. She placed her shaky hand against his cheek. He closed his eyes and leaned into her comforting palm. "Are you okay?" she asked, and he couldn't find the words he wanted to say, so he just nodded instead. He was alive, and she was safe. That was all that mattered. He turned his head and kissed her palm.

"We need to go downstairs because the police are here."

"Do we know who he is?" She asked as he led her around the guy who was unconscious and tied up at the moment. Dino did check to make sure he was still breathing.

"I don't know. Let's see." He bent down and pulled the mask off and Arianna gasped.

Dino looked at her. "Do you know him?"

"Yes. That's Travis Gabbert, the guy that I told you about. He was the one the FBI was looking for. They thought he was going to go after my dad."

Dino stood up. "Well, he won't be going after anyone again."

He found her jeans on the floor and handed them to her. While she slipped into them, he pulled on a shirt. Taking her hand, he led her around all of the broken glass in the bedroom then down the stairs. They could see all of the flashing lights out in front of the house. He opened the door as the first set of officers approached the house. He explained who they were and what had taken place. Then directed them upstairs where Gabbert was.

It was nearly ten in the morning when the police and FBI investigators left the house. All their friends were there, including Chris from the FBI.

Everyone was gathered in the kitchen area. Arianna sat at the kitchen table. She was still in shock that Gabbert had broken into the house with all intentions to kill her.

She looked at Chris and shook her head. She felt numb. "I don't understand. Why come after me? What did I ever do to him? If anyone should be mad, it should be me, considering he's the one who threw me under the bus with that bogus complaint."

Chris gave her a sympathetic look. "My guess is that he realized he wasn't going to be able to get close enough to your dad, and he knew his time was running out here. So, he went after you instead. Killing you would've made your dad suffer in other ways."

"So now that Gabbert has been found, I guess that means you're headed back to D.C.?"

"In a few days. I need to process a lot of paperwork, so I'll be sticking around for a little bit longer."

Dino got up and shook Chris's hand. "We appreciate everything you've done."

Chris furrowed his eyebrows. "I'm just sorry we couldn't have caught him sooner."

"It is what it is," Dino replied, and Chris agreed.

After Chris left, the entire team stayed and helped clean up the mess from the altercation.

Arianna went into the garage to get the dustpan. She heard the door close behind her, and it startled her, making her jump.

When she turned, she saw Dino standing there. His hands were on his hips, and his expression was blank. She wondered if something was wrong.

"Is everything okay?" she asked as he began to stalk towards her.

When he got to her, he surprised her when he lifted her into the air and sat her down on a stack of nearby boxes. Her legs were wrapped around his waist and her arms looped around his neck. They were eye level. He didn't say anything—he just stared into her eyes.

"Dino?"

"I want to say thank you."

She pulled back a little and cocked her head. "Thank me?"

"For listening to me and not putting yourself in danger."

She grinned. "I think I'm smart enough to know when to listen to someone who knows what is best for me, especially when it comes to my safety."

"I love you." He said, then closed the distance between them and kissed her.

He released her lips and pulled her into a hug. She held on tight. In fact, she was never letting him go.

"I love you, too." She whispered.

CHAPTER THIRTY-THREE

Arianna was in the garage going through a couple of boxes when she came across a bag of items that was from her final night in Rome. It was her torn dress that had bloodstains on it. She had no plans on keeping that as a souvenir. She threw it into the trashcan, but when it landed, she heard a thump. Like something heavier was inside. She walked over and fished the bag out, and opened it. She pulled out the dress, a pair of panties, and a towel. At the bottom of the bag, she found the clutch she had used. She had forgotten that Enzo had picked it up. She opened it, and all of her usual stuff was in there; lip gloss, mint breath strips, a little bit of cash, but what caught her eye was the object at the bottom. She reached in and pulled out a black flash drive. She had no clue whom it belonged to or how it got there.

She pulled her phone from her back pocket and called the one person who may know.

"Arianna!" The Greek's loud voice boomed over the phone.

"Hi, Enzo. How are you?"

"I'm great now that you called." He teased. "What can I do for you, beautiful?"

"Well, I'm calling because I found something today, and I'm not sure where it came from."

"Okay."

"I was going through some of my things from Italy, and I found my black clutch that you found during the mess with Demitri. And inside, there was a black flash drive. It doesn't have any markings on it."

"I remember that. It was inside one of the pockets in the jacket you were wearing. When you passed out, I took the jacket off of you, and when I did, the flash drive fell out. I thought it belonged to you."

"No." She told him. But then suddenly realized what jacket she had been wearing.

"Oh shit!"

"What?"

"That was Demitri's jacket."

Enzo whistled low. "If you open it, be sure you have someone who knows how to hack passwords. Demitri is known to program files that will wipe everything clean from the file if a wrong password is used."

"And how do you know this?"

"Eh…I have my ways."

"Okay. Well, let me go so I can figure out what to do with this."

"Good luck." He told her before he disconnected.

She held the drive in her hand. She was curious and wanted to know what was on there. She was good on the computer, but without the proper equipment, she wasn't taking a chance. She didn't want to lose the data on it or have someone be able to trace the drive if there was a code attached to it.

She hit Dino's number and waited for him to answer. He was over at Diego's, helping him paint.

"Hey."

"Hi."

"You okay?"

"Yeah. Does your friend Skittles have access to a computer that's secure?"

"Maybe. If not, he can probably get his hands on one. Why? What's up?"

"I have a flash drive that I need to gain access to, however, because of where it came from, I'm a little leery of opening it on a general computer."

"Let me give him a call."

"That would be great. I'm heading to the bar right now. Just give me a call and let me know."

"Will do."

"Love you." She told him.

"Love you back."

A little over an hour later, Skittles walked into the bar and Arianna waved to him.

"Hey. Dino said you needed help accessing a flash drive?"

"Yeah. I think it's probably encrypted too. Do you think you can crack it?"

"Probably. I'll have to take a look at it first. It might take some time depending on what type of program was used."

She pulled the drive from her pocket.

"Can I take it?"

She bit her lip nervously. Not that she didn't trust Skittles, but if something were to happen, that was her only copy.

Skittles chuckled.

"I can tell by your expression that you'd rather me not. Give me the drive, and I'll work on it here."

"I'm sorry. It's not that I don't—"

He held up his hand. "Say no more, I get it, and no offense taken."

He slid off the stool. "Let me run to my car and grab my laptop and bag."

"Thank you. You can use the office if you want."

He nodded. "That'll work."

Arianna hoped Skittles could access the information because she was eager to see what Demitri had hidden on there. Her thoughts were interrupted by a customer.

"Hey sweet cheeks, how about another round down here?"

She turned toward the big burly fisherman and rolled her eyes. He was a harmless guy who knew how to put away his alcohol and sometimes make inappropriate comments to women. He thought they were pick-up lines, or so he said. When the alcohol was flowing, he had no filter on his mouth.

She pulled four mugs from the cooler and poured them from the tap. She walked them down to Captain Rusty and the three other men sitting with him.

"Here you guys go. Enjoy!" She smiled.

Rusty grinned and winked.

"Arianna, have you met my oldest son, Spencer?"

He slapped the youngest looking of the four on the back, and Arianna wanted to laugh when Spencer rolled his eyes.

"Jesus, dad, Arianna, and I went to high school together."

Arianna chuckled when Rusty looked between her and Spencer.

"Hell, son, this here is a fine woman. You should ask her out."

He looked at Arianna. "You aren't seeing anyone, right sweet cheeks?"

She squinted her eyes. "How would you know? Maybe I have a sugar daddy waiting for me back at home."

Rusty's eyes widened before he barked out a loud, boisterous laugh. He looked at Spencer. "And she has a sense of humor."

Thank god Skittles was coming back in. His timing couldn't be any more perfect.

She pointed at Rusty. "You behave."

"Awe, now what fun would that be?" he teased, and she smiled and shook her head.

Captain Rusty suddenly sobered. "Honey, whoever manages to steal your heart is going to be one lucky guy."

She smiled. "Holler if y'all need anything."

She met Skittles by the end of the bar, and they walked down the hallway that led to the office.

"What was that about?" Skittles asked.

"Just some customers having a good time."

"Huh…"

"What?" She asked, looking up at him.

She followed Skittles into the office. He took the seat at the desk, and Arianna watched him connect several cables to his laptop. Then he took one of the cables and connected it to a small black box.

He fired up the computer and went through his normal process of logging in. When he told her he was ready, she took a big breath and handed the drive over to him.

He slid it into the port and went to work on it. It took a good twenty minutes and one wrong log-in attempt, but he finally accessed it.

Suddenly, numbers started scrolling up the screen.

"What in the hell is this? It looks like just a bunch of numbers." Skittles asked, and she studied it.

Arianna couldn't believe it. It was a list of numbers, but it's code.

She pulled another chair over and sat down next to Skittles. There were hundreds if not thousands of sets of numbers listed.

"ASCII. I've seen it before." She looked at Skittles and seemed to know then what she was talking about. He just had never seen it before—American Standard Code for Information.

"How did you end up with this?"

Arianna sat back in her chair. "It was a little luck and a very good friend." She looked at Skittles and smiled. "Someone who wants to put away Demitri Barros just as bad as I do."

She glanced back at the screen and still couldn't believe it. "This is the motherload of evidence to nail the bastard."

Skittles eyes widened, and his jaw dropped. "Wait! Is this the guy that you were working undercover to get information on?"

She nodded and then explained how they could've arrested him on some lower-level crimes that may not even stick, but they want to nail him on the trafficking charge that carries a larger sentence.

Skittles rubbed his jaw. "Damn. Who do you need to call about this?"

She reached for the phone on the desk. "Chris." She answered, and Skittles nodded, knowing who Chris was since he had met him the other morning at the house when the whole Gabbert ordeal went down.

"I'm going to give him call while I drive over to the hospital," she told Skittles and left for her car.

As she pulled out of the parking lot and headed toward the main road, she dialed Chris' number.

"Unless you're calling to tell me that you've reconsidered our offer, I don't want to talk to you," Chris joked as he answered the phone.

"Well, considering what I have to tell you, I would hope that the FBI would consider throwing in a little more from their previous offer. Although, my intentions are still the same. I'm happy where I'm at." She didn't mention that she had interviews with Tink and some of his staff yesterday and that she would be their new Forensics Accountant.

"Okay, you've got my attention."

She started telling him what she found and what all it included. By the time she was finished, she had thought that he hung up because he was so quiet.

"Arianna, I hope this isn't one of your jokes."

"No joke, Chris. This is what we've been looking for."

"Jesus Christ. And you have it with you?"

"Yep."

"Where are you now?"

She looked at the street sign. "I'm at Douglas and 8th Street."

"Where are you headed?"

"The hospital. My dad's supposed to be discharged tomorrow."

"That's great to hear about your dad. Listen, do you mind if I meet you there to get the drive?"

"No, not at all. I should be there in about fifteen minutes or so."

"Okay. I need to finish up a few things here at the office, but I'll meet you there. Give me about an hour?"

"Yeah. No problem. I'll see you then."

"Arianna?"

"Yeah?"

"Great work."

She smiled. "Thanks. But I'm still not coming back," she teased, and he snickered.

"I'll see ya soon," he told her and then disconnected.

Funny how things turn out, she thought to herself.

CHAPTER THIRTY-FOUR

"For the love of God, Arianna, will you please stop fussing over me?" Paul scolded his daughter, even though Arianna knew he wasn't serious.

She raised her eyebrow at him. "Someone seems a little cranky today."

"You'd be cranky too if you were in my place."

Arianna wasn't sure why suddenly she felt emotional. She stared at her dad. Yes, he was alive and awake but knowing how close she came to losing him, it hit her hard right at this very moment. She wiped her eye before the tear could fall, and her dad's face softened.

"What's wrong?" He asked her.

She shook her head. She had a huge lump in her throat that prevented her from speaking. A tear slipped out, and she wiped it, but then another fell. Soon it was too many to keep up with.

"I'm sorry." She told him, and his expression softened, and he spread his arms.

"Come here, Arianna."

She went, and he hugged her. Maybe that was what she needed—just a simple hug from her dad. She soon felt better, stepped back, slid the chair closer to his bed, and then sat down. She noticed her dad's eyelids got droopy, so she sat back and pulled out her e-reader. She would get lost in a book while he took a nap.

Arianna was so engrossed in the book she was reading that she almost didn't hear the light tap on the door. She was surprised when Dino stuck his head in, but she couldn't stop the smile on her face.

"Hey." She whispered, being careful not to wake her dad.

He smiled as he entered the room. Just the sight of him gave her instant butterflies in the stomach. He looked scrumptious in his jeans and long sleeve t-shirt. He leaned down and kissed her cheek.

"How's he doing?"

She smiled up at him. "Great. He just gets tired easily, but the doctors said that was okay. He's scheduled to be discharged tomorrow."

"That's really great news."

He sat down in the chair next to her and draped his arm over her shoulder. She rested her head against his shoulder.

She looked up at him. "What made you stop by?"

"I had some errands to run and wanted to see how he was doing."

"Thank you for coming." She told him and leaned in and kissed him.

They were interrupted by someone clearing their throat. When Arianna looked over, she found her dad staring at both of them. He had a slightly lopsided grin.

"When did this happen?" He asked.

She glanced up at Dino, who stood there with his hands in his pocket, looking like he wasn't sure what to say.

She shrugged her shoulders. "It's new."

Dino walked over and shook Paul's hand. "It's nice to see you awake."

"It's nice to be awake and coherent. Hey, do you mind handing me that Styrofoam cup over there?" He asked Dino and pointed to a food tray.

Dino handed it to him, and he took a bite of what looked to be some sort of rice. Paul made a sour face and spat it back into the cup. Arianna stared at him while he wiped his mouth with the napkin.

"The MRE's they fed us in the military tasted better than this shit."

Arianna snickered. It had to taste really bad for her dad not to eat it. Being that he had his own restaurant he was constantly comparing others' food to what he served. But again, this was hospital food he was critiquing. Hospital food was bland, to begin with.

"Dad…"

"I just want a bacon cheeseburger. The way Wade makes it."

Arianna's mouth started to water at the mention of Wade's bacon, cheeseburgers. They were the absolute bomb and voted by the local newspaper as the best cheeseburger in town for almost ten years. To this day, nobody knew what spices he added to the meat to get them to taste so delicious, and they were juicy.

Her dad chuckled. "You want one too, don't you?"

She laughed. "It does sound good right now."

"I'll make you a deal. As long as your doctor says you can have a burger, I'll bring you one when I come back later."

"There's my favorite patient," Brianna said, walking into the room with her caddy of supplies.

Her dad was beaming. "And there's my favorite nurse." He winked at Brianna, and Brianna's cheeks took on a pinkish color.

Arianna waited until Brianna took her dad's vitals.

"Everything looks good, Mr. Roland."

Her dad frowned. "Brianna, how many times have I told you to call me Paul."

Brianna smirked. "I've lost track, Mr. Roland."

Arianna laughed and then looked at Brianna. "So, Dad is insisting I bring him back a burger from his restaurant. Would that be okay?"

Brianna put her hands on her hips and looked at Paul. "What? Is the hospital food not up to your liking?"

Paul furrowed in eyebrows, and then Brianna laughed.

"I'm just messing with you. I don't see any issue but let me run it by the doctor just to make sure." She looked over at Arianna and winked.

Paul looked at Arianna. "She's nice. I like her."

Arianna snorted a laugh. "I think she likes you too."

"You do?" He asked with wide eyes. Arianna thought it was funny.

Arianna nodded her head. "I do. And do you know what I think?

"What?" He asked, looking almost afraid to ask.

Arianna grinned. "I think you should ask her out."

His cheeks turned a little shade of pink. "We'll see." He told her. But Arianna knew her dad well and felt that Brianna could become someone close to all of them.

After Brianna came back and said that the doctor gave the okay that Paul could have a burger, Dino volunteered to pick them up for everyone and bring them back.

Arianna stayed because she wanted to talk to her dad. They talked a lot about the bar. But then he focused on her career. She hadn't told him about her decision to stay in town.

"Have you made your decision yet?"

She played with the button on her shirt. "I think so."

"You think?"

She smiled. "I love doing forensics work, but I also forgot how much I enjoyed the bar and atmosphere there. I've also missed being with real friends."

"So, you're going to give up a good-paying job to be a bar owner?" He asked.

"Well, no, not exactly. I talked with Alex the other day, and she mentioned that she went through a similar dilemma when she got back from wherever she was." Paul nodded his head as if knowing where she was, and of course, he probably did know. Her dad had a way of knowing everyone's business. "Anyway, she asked me a question that someone once had asked her."

"And that was?"

"Did I enjoy my job?"

"Do you?"

"I enjoyed the forensics aspect. I liked being behind the computer and solving the numbers puzzle."

"Well, can't you go back to doing that for the agency?"

"I can, but I don't want to. I've always been loyal to those who I work for. But sadly, I can't say the same when you turn that around. I saw a whole other side of the agency while I was undercover and the aftermath. I don't want to be a pawn in their big web. Plus, being back here made me see how much I was missing everything and everyone, you, especially. I went a whole two years not seeing you."

"So, what are you going to do?"

"Well, with the help of some really great friends, I had an interview the other day with a very reputable security company."

"Where?"

"Here in Virginia Beach."

She knew her dad realized right away who it was with.

"No shit! Tink?"

She smiled and nodded her head. He's been looking to add a forensics expert to his team."

"Arianna, that is great! Tink is a great guy—a hardass and will demand one hundred percent every day, but if I ever had an opportunity to work for him, I'd do it in a heartbeat. Do you think the interview went well?"

She smiled again. "I think so, considering he offered me the job on the spot."

Her dad was beaming, and he took her hand and squeezed it. "I am so damn proud of you."

"Thanks. I'm pretty stoked about it."

"Well, if the bar becomes too much…."

"I'll be fine, dad. Especially once you get back on your feet."

"So, I guess this is good news for you and Dino as well?" He stated with a sly grin, and she just smiled.

"I love him, dad."

He gave her a heart-felt smile and covered her hand with his. "As long as he loves and respects you, then I'm happy for you. From what I know about him, he's a good man."

"Yeah, he is."

A few minutes later, Brianna poked her head into the room. "I'm sorry, Arianna, but there is an FBI Agent here to see you."

Arianna wrinkled her forehead and wondered who it could be. But then she remembered Chris said he would be by to pick up the drive. She smiled at Brianna. "Thanks. I'll be out in just a minute."

Her dad gave her a concerned look. "What's that all about?" He asked.

"Something that I can say I worked hard to get."

She stood up from the chair, leaned down, and kissed him on the cheek. "I'll be back in a few minutes. If Dino gets here before I'm back, make sure he doesn't eat my burger."

Her dad laughed, but she wasn't joking. She was craving that damn burger.

Arianna walked down the hall to the nurses' station, but all she saw was Brianna. Brianna looked up and pointed toward the stairs. "He got a call, and it seemed important. He went into the stairwell so he wouldn't bother anyone. He said you could meet him there."

She thanked her and slowly made her way toward the door with the picture of the stairs on it. She pressed the bar and pushed the door open. There was nobody there. She pulled her phone out and got ready to text Chris but then she heard a man's voice down below. She went down the flight of stairs to the ground level, figuring it was him. When she made it to the landing, she saw a guy in a suit, but it wasn't Chris. It was Miles Thakenburg; her former partner turned drug addict. *What in the hell was he doing here?*

"Miles." She said in a surprised tone.

He nodded his head and took a step towards her. "Arianna. It's nice to see you."

She completely ignored his pleasantry and cut to the chase. "What are you doing here? Last I heard, you were a wanted man."

He sneered at her then wiped his nose. No surprise there, she guessed he was still using. She began to feel a little uneasy.

"I'm here to collect my pay."

"Your pay?" She repeated. What in the hell was the guy even talking about?

He took another step closer. "Yes. My pay. You see, a fairly new friend of yours has been trying to track you down. But when he offered a generous reward leading to your whereabouts, I figured why not help the guy out." The grin he offered her was wicked and evil. Her panic level skyrocketed.

She moved back toward the stairs. She didn't trust Miles as far as she could throw.

"I'm curious to know what friend you're referring to since you and I don't have any mutual friends."

"Awe. I think Mr. Barros would find that insulting."

Arianna paused her movement, and her body went rigid. Miles was friends with Demitri?

"I think he would, be considering the evening you and he spent together." A voice behind her on the stairs said, and she spun around.

It was Carmine, Demitri's second in command. He started to move towards her down the stairs. She only had two choices. Either go through Carmine up the stairs or take on Miles and go out the emergency exit. The pick was easy, but before she could make her first move, Miles stabbed her in the neck with something. It felt like a bad bee sting, and she covered the spot with her hand before she fell to the floor. The concrete room began to spin, and she didn't feel right. She tried to speak, but her words came out slurred. She wasn't able to focus no matter how hard she tried.

"Help me get her up and to the car." One of them said. She was too out of it to focus on the voice. Her body was suddenly lifted off the ground, but she couldn't stand. She had no feeling in her legs. The person holding her cursed and then began to drag her out the door. She tried to look around to call for help, but nobody was there, just a black sedan with tinted windows. The front passenger side door opened, and another man stepped out. He looked at Miles.

"Nice work. Demitri said thank you." Then he pulled out a gun and shot Miles.

Carmine slid into the seat next to her and slammed the door. "Go!" He shouted to the driver, and the car lurched forward at a high rate of speed.

Tears ran down her face, though she couldn't feel anything.

"Don't cry. Once we arrive in Crete, Demitri will take good care of you." Carmine told her as her eyes closed and her mind shut off.

Special Agent Hurts was on his way to meet Arianna at the hospital when he got a call from headquarters. It wasn't the news he wanted to hear. The cybercrime division had come across a post on a website hosted on the dark web that was offering a reward for any information leading to the whereabouts of the Black Swan. It included a picture of Arianna.

As he pulled his car into the parking lot at the hospital, he saw Arianna's boyfriend walking toward the front entrance with bags in his hands. He grabbed his phone and exited the vehicle. He called out, "Dino!"

Dino turned and offered him a smile. "Hey, man. Arianna said you were going to come by."

"Yeah, there's also something else I need to talk to her about." When Dino questioned him, he told him everything about the posted reward for Arianna.

"Shit. That's not good." Dino stated and looked angry. Chris couldn't blame the guy. He was pissed as well, and Arianna wasn't his girlfriend.

"She's upstairs with her dad. Come on; I'll walk with you." Dino said to him as they made their way through the automatic sliding doors.

Just as they were approaching the elevator bank, his phone rang again, and he looked at it. It was headquarters again. He held his finger up for Dino to wait.

"Hurts." He answered.

"It's Scarborough. Are you at the hospital yet?" His director asked, and if Chris wasn't mistaken, his boss sounded a little on edge.

"Yeah, I just got here. I'm actually getting ready to get on the elevator. What's up?"

"I just got notified that Miles Thakenburg flew into Virginia Beach this morning."

That information surprised Chris considering a team of agents had been hunting him over in Europe.

"Do we know why or where he went?"

"Twenty minutes ago, he was seen entering the hospital."

"Are you saying he is here?"

"We think so. And Chris?"

"Yeah?"

"He's not alone. The private jet was reserved under the name Carmine Johnston."

"Oh shit!"

"Yeah. Go find Arianna. I'm making a call to the field office now and will have agents there in a few."

Chris put his phone away just as the elevator opened and jumped in with Dino. He relayed everything Scarborough told him to Dino, and now Dino looked worried. As soon as they got to the second floor, they took off running down the hall towards Paul's room. When they arrived, only Paul was in the room.

"Paul, where's Arianna?" Dino asked hurriedly.

"She went to go meet an agent. Some guy named Chris."

"Fuck!" Chris swore.

"What's going on?" Paul asked, but there was no time. They needed to find Arianna.

"Do you know where she was meeting this guy?"

"No. But Brianna, the nurse out front, may know. She's the one who came and told Arianna.

Dino's heart was racing as he sprinted down to the nurses' station. Seeing him coming, Brianna stood up.

"What's wrong?"

"Do you know which way Arianna went?"

"Yes. She went into the stairwell." And she pointed down the other side of the hallway.

Dino took off with Chris right behind him. He busted through the heavy metal door and looked around. When he leaned over the railing and looked down towards the first-floor landing, he spotted Arianna's phone on the ground. He called out to Chris, who was moving up the steps while talking to someone on the phone. When he landed at the bottom, he picked the phone up and saw the screen was cracked.

Then Chris called out. "Dino, over here."

When Dino turned, Chris had the exit door open. When he glanced out and saw the dead body sprawled out on the concrete, he knew they were too late. He heard Chris tell whoever was on the phone to call in back up and start looking for Arianna. But being that the FBI was a legit law enforcement agency, they had to play everything by the book. Well, fuck that shit. He had his own team with their own set of rules. He pulled his phone out and dialed his commander.

CHAPTER THIRTY-FIVE

Arianna held onto a shelf that was bolted to the wall, it was the only secured fixture in the tiny room that she could find. The boat she was on was a small fishing trawler. When she arrived in Crete, Greece, she was still a little loopy from the tranquilizers that Carmine had given her. She guessed he didn't want her to be a bother during the fifteen-hour flight.

As soon as the private jet she was on landed at the airport; she was shuffled into an awaiting car. It had been three or four hours since she, Carmine, and some other big dude whom she wasn't familiar with has gotten into the car. She'd lost track of time since Carmine took her watch.

A few minutes ago, she had felt and heard the boat's engines fire up. Judging from the world bobbing beneath her feet; she was pretty sure they were heading somewhere on the water. Once in a while, they'd hit a larger wave, and it would throw her off balance.

She couldn't stop thinking about Dino, her dad, and all her friends and what they must be going through. She wondered if they had any idea where she was. Most likely, they didn't, but she needed to stay positive and try to find a way out of the situation.

She still couldn't believe that Miles was part of the plan. But it also hadn't been a huge surprise considering Miles was always looking to score money any way he knew how. He got exactly what he deserved.

She kept chastising herself for letting her guard down around Miles. She gave him the opportunity, and he took it.

Now she needed to worry about what they had planned for her. Carmine and the other guy had barely spoken a word in front of her. She thought she would've seen Demitri by now, but she guessed he wasn't on the boat.

What really bothered her was the nasty fish smell. She had already thrown up once because of it.

She looked around the small room. There was a lot of junk. She walked over to a stack of boxes and started looking through them. She was hoping to find something she could use as a weapon. When she got to the third box, there were a couple of items that she could improvise with. When she lifted a fishing book, she saw what appeared to be a gun. At least she thought it was. After further examination, she determined it was a flare gun. That was something that could come in handy, she thought. It might not shoot bullets, but it would shoot fire, and you could still kill someone with it. *I think I'll be keeping that,* she said to herself. She removed the gun from the box and stuffed it in the waistband of her jeans, pulling her shirt over it.

She was putting everything back in the boxes when she heard the door to the room rattle. She hurried over to the other side, not wanting to get caught. She heard the snick of the lock then the door opened. Since she wasn't sure what time it was and the room didn't have windows she was surprised to see it was dark out. Carmine appeared in the doorway and motioned for her to come to him. It wasn't like she could run there was nowhere for her to go. Maybe if she got outside, she'd have a chance. At least out there, she could jump into the water.

She walked toward the door, and Carmine grabbed her upper arm. She guessed he had been reading her mind. Once they got out onto the deck, Arianna immediately began to scan her surroundings, looking for any exit points off the boat. Unfortunately, she didn't see any that stood out. Worst case scenario, if it came down to it, she'd climb over the railing and jump.

She wasn't paying attention and hadn't seen that another person had joined them on the deck. She was startled when the deep voice spoke from behind her.

"Hello, Arianna."

Arianna spun around, surprised to see someone standing there. She locked gazes with Demitri. The man was intimidating just standing there. She could feel herself shaking. Just by the coldness in his eyes, she knew this situation wasn't going to be good for her.

"Hello, Mr. Barros." She knew he hated it when she called him that. Apparently, that hadn't changed because he stomped toward her. Before she could flinch, he backhanded her across the face, and she fell to the deck.

He was on her quickly as he grabbed a handful of her hair and yanked her head up, so she was looking at him. His jaw was clenched and looked fierce. “Intentionally pissing me off isn’t going to work in your favor.” He knelt next to her and put his face right up against hers. “Tell me why I shouldn’t put a bullet in your head right now?”

She stared into his eyes because there was nowhere else to look. He was in control and too powerful of a man to fight. She was scared, and when she didn’t answer him, he stood up and pulled her by her hair across the deck to the other side. He shoved her against the railing and pushed her on her upper back, so she was dangling over the side. This was it, she thought. This was how her life was going to end.

But when nothing happened, she wondered if he had second thoughts. Suddenly she heard the sound of rotors. There was a helicopter nearby. She waited and listened as they grew louder. Could this be her one shot? She had the flare gun, and the pilots would have to see it considering they were out in the middle of nowhere and it was dark.

Out of the blue, the story Alex told her about her survival popped into her head. Alex had said to her that if you wanted to live that you had to fight. Yes, she told herself. She wanted to live. She didn’t want to die out in the middle of the ocean.

She started to see the lights from the helicopter. They were shining a spotlight into the water. Were they looking for her?

Done playing games, she reached for the flare gun under her shirt. Once she had, it secured she cocked it, and as difficult as it was to aim it into the air while she was upside down, she did it. Her finger pressed the trigger. It looked like a firework shooting up into the air. The light from it illuminated the area below it.

Her happiness was short-lived when Demitri yanked her back up to the deck and threw her to the ground.

“You bitch!” He screamed at her. He was seething.

Arianna crabbed walked herself backward until she hit something and couldn’t go any further. Suddenly Demitri faced her, and she knew that look. It was the look of a killer. He started stalking towards her and she did the only thing she could do. She protected herself. She raised the flare gun and fired. It hit him right in the stomach and he flew backward. Carmine ran to him. She couldn't move. She could only stare.

Carmine swung his head and directed an evil glare at her. She scrambled to her feet, and so did he. He fired his gun, and she dove behind a metal box container to take cover. When she landed, she cut her arm on the side of it, and she cried out. But she didn't stop. She looked around for a hiding spot. She heard Carmine fire his gun again, but it just made a clicking sound. He was out of bullets. She saw him go into the cockpit and knew this was her chance.

She stood up and started running across the deck. The helicopter was almost right over them. As she passed by the door to the cockpit, Carmine jumped out and grabbed her. He put her in a headlock, but she twisted out of his grasp and kicked him, causing him to stumble backward.

Something inside the cockpit caught her eye. It was a propane tank. She looked at the flare gun in hand and back at the propane tank and an idea formed in her head. She ran towards the back of the boat. She knew she only had one shot left in the flare gun, so she needed to make this one count. She lined up her shot and fired. She watched the bright streak of orange sail into the cockpit. She quickly climbed over the railing and was prepared to jump into the water when she heard her name. She looked up and couldn't believe her eyes. They came for her. But then suddenly, an object slammed into the back of her head, and she lost all focus and tumbled over the railing into the black sea.

As soon as the team's plane touched down at the Naval Base in Crete, they gathered their gear and headed to the vehicles waiting to take them to the other side of the base so they could board a couple of the boats to assist in the search for Arianna.

Dino wasn't upset, he was pissed off, and he had every intention to make every single person pay who was involved in Arianna's abduction.

Chris from the FBI actually blew off his superior's warning when he told them that he was going with the team to help. Again, the bureau wanted to play by the rules. Arianna didn't have time for that.

With the surveillance videos from the hospital, along with CCTV footage, they were able to track Arianna and the people who took her. They found out from the small airport that the private jet they believed Arianna to be on was bound for Crete, Greece. Derek, along with a few others with some pull, called in some favors and explained what was going on. They were able to get a ride to the Naval Base in Souda Bay.

Chris called many of his contacts in the area, including the local police, who then notified the Hellenic Coast Guard, equivalent to the US Coast Guard. They, too, were sending boats and helicopters to assist in the search.

The last update that came in about twenty minutes ago stated that there were witnesses who saw people matching Demitri and Arianna's description at a nearby marina. Calls had been made, and shortly afterward, it was confirmed that it was Demitri who rented a small fishing boat.

Derek was talking to the base commander, and when he was finished, he walked and gave them a brief update.

"Both the Naval Base and the local Coast Guard have boats and choppers already out looking. Another boat reported they saw a fishing boat matching the description of the one that Arianna is believed to be on."

"How long ago was that?" Ace asked.

"Around the same time as our update—approximately twenty minutes ago. We've radioed to all parties assisting in the search to head in that direction."

"What's the plan for us?" Dino asked, feeling jumpy.

He pointed toward the pier, and the two boats docked there. "We're getting on those and will meet up with the search party."

As they walked toward the boats, Ace caught up with Dino. "Listen, man, I'm speaking from experience. When we get out there, you need to keep your cool. No rogue shit, no attitude."

Dino stopped mid-stride and turned toward Ace. "I know better. I've been through shit like this five times now, and I'm fucking sick and tired of having a member of our family targeted."

Irish, who usually was the calm comedian of the team gripped Dino's shoulder.

"Dino, a lot of us know what you're going through right now. Believe me, we do. But the best thing you can do is to keep a positive attitude. She's out there, and we've got a lot of people looking for her. We'll find her."

Dino knew they were right. It wasn't worth it to have a negative attitude. He looked at everyone standing there with him.

"Let's do this. Let's find her and bring her home."

The guys gave a big Hooyah and then boarded the boats.

They barely had made it out of the port when one of the choppers from the Coast Guard radioed in.

"We've got some boating activity in the shallow waters just off the southeast coast of Skopelos Glaronisi Island and it appears to be the boat in question. Sending coordinates through."

Chris looked at the team. "That has to be them. That is one of the worst fishing spots in the area. No fisherman in their right mind would waste their time there."

"How far is that from us?" Derek asked the skipper of the boat.

"About nine miles, sir."

"Then let's head there."

Suddenly, someone shouted from the starboard side. "Flare!"

Everyone looked in the direction the guy was pointing, and he was correct. It was a distress signal, and additional reports started being relayed from the other parties involved in the search.

As their boat was closing in on the suspected fishing boat, Dino saw Arianna appear on the port side. She was holding her arm. A guy came out of the cockpit and lunged at her. He had her in a headlock, but then she twisted out of his grasp and kicked him, causing him to stumble backward.

They watched as she turned and fired the flare gun inside the cockpit.

"What in the hell is she doing?" Ace muttered out loud, and Dino could only shake his head and wonder the same. She then ran toward the aft of the boat and prepared to jump into the water when the guy ran up behind her with a long pole in his hand. Dino and some of the others were shouting at her trying to get her attention as they sped towards her. She must've heard them because she looked up and right at them, but it was too late. The guy swung the pole and slammed it against the back of her head. Everyone watched in horror as her body tumbled into the dark open water.

Not five seconds after Arianna hit the water and the boat exploded, creating a huge fireball.

"Nooo!" Dino shouted.

"Get over there now!" Derek yelled to the driver of the boat.

As the boat approached the area where Arianna fell in, Dino, Frost, Ace, and Skittles jumped in the water while the others shined spotlights in the water.

Another boat pulled up, and a few from their crew jumped in to help look.

Dino started to panic when they couldn't find her. It was as if the black water had swallowed her up. Suddenly, he heard Frost. "I got her!" Dino swam over and she looked like she was out cold. He checked for a pulse and felt some relief when he felt the steady beat.

They got her to the side of the boat and handed her up to the others on board. Dino climbed up and went to her side. Stitch was there looking her over along with another medic.

She wasn't waking up, and Dino feared she might have head trauma from when the guy hit her. He held her hand and leaned down next to her ear. "I love you." He whispered as tears formed in his eyes.

Stitch took a packet of smelling salts and held it under her nose. Dino and everyone else held their breath and waited to see if that would stimulate her. When her head started to move from side to side, Dino thought he was going to lose his shit. He couldn't speak at first and had to swallow down all the emotion caught in his throat.

He laid down with her, and some of the other guys covered them with blankets. When they reached the base, an ambulance was waiting to take Arianna to the hospital. He went with her and continued to hold her hand. It was in the ambulance when she opened her eyes for the first time since they pulled her out of the water. She looked directly at him; those big hazel-colored eyes were a sight to see.

"I love you, too." She rasped out, and Dino couldn't stop smiling. She had heard him back on the boat when he had told her that he loved her.

He leaned down and gently pressed his lips against hers. She fought, and she survived.

EPILOGUE

Arianna smiled as the sand squished between her toes and the cool breeze blew across her face. She tilted her face up towards the sky and closed her eyes. She loved the beach and was glad she had decided to come home for good where she was surrounded by her family, friends, and most of all, the love of her life.

A couple of weeks had gone by since her kidnapping ordeal. Luckily, she had only suffered a concussion from the hit she sustained while trying to escape. The good news was that with the flash drive she had found, the FBI could decode all of the transactions in the file and were working with law enforcement all over the world to help bring home all of the missing women who Demitri had taken.

Paul was released from the hospital while Arianna was in Greece. He was starting to get back into his usual routine, but he did make room for one more person in his life. He and Brianna had started dating. So far, the doctors hadn't seen any signs of any long-term effects from the cyanide. She herself had started her new job for Tink's company, and she loved it. As for her and Dino, things were perfect. They were happy, content, and in love.

A deep, loud bark in the distance caught her attention, and when she turned, she saw Nigel galloping down the beach, kicking up the sand in his wake. As he got closer, she knelt, and he ran right into her, almost knocking her over. She chuckled, seeing how excited he was to see her. His tail swished back and forth a mile a minute, and he wouldn't stop licking her. She hugged him and scratched his favorite spot—behind his ears.

She went to adjust his collar when her fingers felt something soft. She spun the collar around so she could see the fastener clip. There was a tiny purple bag attached to it. It had no markings on it. She got Nigel to sit while she untied the string. As she opened the bag and peered into it, she lost her breath when the diamond ring came into view. Her eyes welled with tears as she looked down the beach in the direction that Nigel had come from, but nobody was there.

She turned around to look in the other direction and gasped when she saw Dino standing there. He looked calm and relaxed, and of course, he was wearing that signature, sexy smirk of his.

With the ring in her trembling hand, she took the two steps forward and stood in front of him. His eyes shined with love and happiness.

He reached out and took her left hand, and it was only then she could tell by the slight tremble of his hand that he was nervous.

"I never thought I would ever be able to open my heart up to love someone again until the day I met you. You changed me in ways that I never thought were possible. You showed me what love is. That when you truly love your partner, you see them as part of your life and your future." He paused, then lifted her hand to his lips and kissed it. His eyes never left hers as he lowered himself to one knee. "I want you as a part of my life forever. Arianna Roland, will you marry me?"

Arianna was filled with so much joy and happiness that she thought she was going to burst. She cried silent tears as her emotions had stolen her voice.

"Yes." She managed to whisper out. "Yes, I'll marry you."

Dino's smile couldn't have gotten any bigger as he stood and pulled her into his arms and lifted her into the air. He spun her around as he held her tight. She laughed, and Nigel barked playfully. Still holding her, he looked deep into her eyes.

"I love you." He told her.

"I love you, too."

He set her down on her feet, took the ring that she was holding, and slowly slid it on her left hand. He then leaned forward and sealed it with a heart-stopping kiss. As they embraced each other, in the distance, they could hear the cheers from their family and friends as they all had gathered on the patio deck of Bayside to watch as two hearts became one.

Arianna helped Alex tie balloons to the chairs while Tenley brought the cake out from the back and placed it on the table.

It had taken a lot of convincing, but Mia and Arianna finally got Grace to agree to come to Bayside and celebrate her birthday with them.

The only person that Arianna could see who was missing was Skittles. She walked over to where Dino was standing, talking to her dad. He smiled and placed his arm around her shoulder. She looked at her dad, and he smiled.

"The place looks nice," Dino told her.

"Thanks. I haven't seen Skittles yet. Is everything okay with him?" She asked. She was a little concerned since he had told her that he'd be there.

"I think it has to do with that friend of his who went missing. Skittles is good for his word, though. If he said he'd be here, then he'll show up."

"Hmmm…I wish there was something we could do to help him."

Dino gave a somber expression. "Closure is the only thing that is going to help him."

Movement outside of one of the windows caught Arianna's attention. It was Grace riding her bike up the sidewalk. She looked up at Dino and could tell that Dino was upset that Grace was still riding her bike around town at night. And especially the distance that she travels.

"I'll talk to her later about it." She assured Dino, and together they went to greet her.

Skittles pulled his pick-up truck into the parking lot and found a spot right near the front door. He exhaled and closed his eyes. He wasn't up for company tonight. All he wanted to do was sit in his apartment and sulk.

Over the last few days, he'd been beating himself up over whether he should continue to seek answers in A.G.'s disappearance or just leave it be. He had pretty much exhausted all of his leads, and any new information was few and far between.

But giving up made him feel as if he was giving up on her. What would happen if she was still out there somewhere and in need of help. Sure, it's been ten years since she vanished without a trace, but there have been cases of people in the same situation, and gone even longer, who were eventually found.

He ran his hand down his face. What made matters worse was that today would've been her twenty-fifth birthday.

He made a decision the day he was told about A.G.'s disappearance, and he was going to stick to it. She was out there somewhere, and he was determined to find her and bring her home.

As he got out of the truck and walked towards the door, he saw a girl riding her bicycle through the parking lot. He watched her park it at the bike rack that Paul had installed last summer.

Realization hit him that she must be Grace, the person's birthday they were all there to celebrate. He remembered that Arianna mentioned she rode a bike. That made him wonder where she lived, considering Arianna and Dino had seen her near the airbase watching the jets. If she lived over that way, she had to have ridden miles along some pretty dark roads. That didn't sit right with him. Not that the town was bustling with crime, but certain areas, as with any other town, had their problems. She didn't need to be around those places, especially when darkness fell.

He walked behind her; her platinum blonde hair was visible under the ballcap she wore. She reached for the door handle but being the gentleman, he was taught to be, he reached around her and grabbed hold of the door.

"Here, let me get that for you." He offered.

She turned her head and looked up into his eyes, and Skittles thought he felt the earth shake. There was no mistaking those violet-colored eyes that haunted his dreams almost every night he fell asleep.

"A.G.?" He whispered and tried to touch her face. She recoiled and slowly started to back away from him.

Her gasp and wide eyes told him all he needed to know. Then without any word or warning, she spun around and took off through the parking lot.

Skittles couldn't move. His feet felt like cement blocks, and his body was numb.

The front door flew open, and Arianna and Dino were there.

"Was that Grace that just took off running? We saw her through the window." Arianna asked, looking concerned.

Dino stood in front of him. “Skittles, what the fuck happened? You look like you just saw a ghost.”

He looked Dino in the eye. “I think I just did.”

Skittles and Anna Grace’s story is now available!

BOOK LIST

The Trident Series

ACE

POTTER

FROST

IRISH

STITCH

DINO

SKITTLES

DIEGO

A TRIDENT WEDDING

The Trident Series II - BRAVO Team

JOKER

BEAR

DUKE *(2023)*

PLAYBOY *(2023)*

AUSSIE *(2023)*

NAILS *(TBD)*

SNOW *(TBD)*

JAY BIRD *(TBD)*

ABOUT THE AUTHOR

Jaime Lewis entered the indie author world in June 2020 with ACE, the first book in the Trident Series.

With a barrage of positive reviews and a series embraced by readers, Jaime is a rising star in the romantic suspense genre.

Coming from a military family, she describes as very patriotic; it's no surprise that her books are known for their accurate portrayal of life in the service.

Passionate in her support of the military, veterans, and first responders, Jaime volunteers with the Daytona Division of the US Naval Sea Cadet Corps, a non-profit youth leadership development program sponsored by the U.S. Navy. Together with her son, she also manages a charity organization that supports military personnel and their families, along with veterans and first responders.

Born and raised in Edgewater, Maryland, Jaime now resides in Ormond Beach, Florida with her husband and two very active boys.

Between her day job, her two boys, and writing, she doesn't have a heap of spare time, but if she does, you'll find her somewhere in the outdoors. Jaime is also an avid sports fan.

Follow Jaime:

Facebook: https://www.facebook.com/jaime.lewis.58152
Jaime's Convoy: https://www.facebook.com/groups/jaimesconvoy
Bookbub: https://www.bookbub.com/profile/jaime-lewis
Goodreads: https://www.goodreads.com/author/show/17048191.Jaime_Lewis
Instagram: authorjaimelewis